"Compulsively readable . . .
a fitting successor to *Cold Mountain.*"
—*St. Louis Post-Dispatch*

"Magical . . . fascinating and moving . . . You will find much to admire and savor in *Thirteen Moons.*"
—*USA Today*

"Frazier uses his sense of time and place and his lyrical, pointillist prose to give the reader an aching appreciation of the Indians' plight in the late nineteenth century."
—*The New York Times*

"Brimming with vivid, adventurous incident."
—Raleigh *News & Observer*

"Reading a Frazier novel is like listening to a fine symphony. . . . Take the time to savor Frazier's work, to take in each thought, to relish the turn of phrase or the imagery of a craftsman."
—*The Denver Post*

"Commanding . . .
Frazier's faithful will not be disappointed."
—*People* (four stars)

"Superbly entertaining."
—*Richmond Times-Dispatch*

"Fascinating . . . vivid and alive."
—*Newsweek*

M60
1-

Praise for *Thirteen Moons*

"Gorgeous . . . *Thirteen Moons* calls *Cold Mountain* to mind in its wonder at the natural world; its pacifist undercurrents; its dismay at the dismantling of what matters; and its conviction that one love, no matter how tortured and inexplicable, can be life-defining." —*Newsweek*

"Reading *Thirteen Moons* is an intoxicating experience. . . . This is twenty-first-century literary fiction at its very best." —*BookPage*

"*Thirteen Moons* brings this vanished world thrillingly to life. . . . One of the great Native American—and American—stories, and a great gift to all of us, from one of our very best writers." —*Kirkus Reviews*

"What a story! . . . Frazier's creation, Will Cooper, is utterly charismatic. . . . Frazier's genius lies in his ability to convey emotions that feel pure and genuine. . . . It was worth the wait." —*Dayton Daily News*

"Splendidly written." —New York *Daily News*

"Mesmerizing . . . a bountiful literary panorama . . . The history that Frazier hauntingly unwinds through Will is as melodic as it is melancholy, but the sublime love story is the narrative's true heart."

—*Publishers Weekly* (starred review)

"Verdict: A powerhouse second act . . . a brilliant success. . . . Frazier's second act should convince everyone that he's here to stay. It is a powerful, dramatic, often surprising and memorable novel."

—*The Atlanta Journal-Constitution*

"There are things so masterful that words can't do them justice. Frazier's writing falls in that category. . . . With *Thirteen Moons*, he's doing important work filling in the gaps, helping restore the roots, of our knowledge of our own history." —*Asheville Citizen-Times*

Also by

CHARLES FRAZIER

cold mountain

THIRTEEN MOONS

RANDOM HOUSE TRADE PAPERBACKS

NEW YORK

thirteen moons

A NOVEL

CHARLES FRAZIER

This is a work of fiction. Names, characters, places, and incidents are the products of the author's imagination or are used fictitiously. Any resemblance to actual events, locales, or persons, living or dead, is entirely coincidental.

2007 Random House Trade Paperback Edition

Published in the United States by Random House Trade Paperbacks, an imprint of The Random House Publishing Group, a division of Random House, Inc., New York.

RANDOM HOUSE TRADE PAPERBACKS and colophon are trademarks of Random House, Inc.

Originally published in hardcover in the United States by Random House, an imprint of The Random House Publishing Group, a division of Random House, Inc., in 2006.

ISBN-13 978-0-8129-6758-6

Printed in the United States of America

www.atrandom.com

2 4 6 8 9 7 5 3 1

Book design by Barbara M. Bachman

For Charles O. Frazier and William F. Beal, Jr.

PART ONE

. . .

bone moon

1

THERE IS NO SCATHELESS RAPTURE. LOVE AND TIME PUT ME IN this condition. I am leaving soon for the Nightland, where all the ghosts of men and animals yearn to travel. We're called to it. I feel it pulling at me, same as everyone else. It is the last unmapped country, and a dark way getting there. A sorrowful path. And maybe not exactly Paradise at the end. The belief I've acquired over a generous and nevertheless inadequate time on earth is that we arrive in the afterlife as broken as when we departed from the world. But, on the other hand, I've always enjoyed a journey.

Cloudy days, I sit by the fire and talk nothing but Cherokee. Or else I sit silent with pen and paper, rendering the language into Sequoyah's syllabary, the characters forming under my hand like hen-scratch hieroglyphs. On sunny days, I usually rock on the porch wrapped in a blanket and read and admire the vista. Many decades ago, when I built my farm out of raw land, I oriented the front of the house to aim west toward the highest range of mountains. It is a grand long view. The river and valley, and then the coves and blue ridges heaved up and ragged to the limits of eyesight.

Bear and I once owned all the landscape visible from my porch and a great deal more. People claimed that in Old Europe our holdings would have been enough land to make a minor country. Now I have just the one little cove opening onto the river. The hideous new railroad, of which I own quite a few shares, runs through my front yard. The black trains come smoking along twice a day, and in the summer when the house windows are open, the help wipes the soot off the horizontal faces of furniture at least three times a week. On the other side of the river is a road that has been there as some form of passway since the time of elk and buffalo, both long since extinguished. Now, mules drawing wagons flare sideways in the traces when automobiles pass. I saw a pretty one go by the other day. Yellow as a canary and trimmed with polished brass. It had a windshield like an oversized monocle, and it went ripping by at a speed that must have been close to a mile a minute. The end of the driver's red scarf flagged straight out behind him, three feet long. I hated the racket and the dust that hung in the air long after the automobile was gone. But if I was twenty, I'd probably be trying to find out where you buy one of those fast bastards.

THE NIGHT HAS become electrified. Midevening, May comes to my room. The turn of doorknob, click of bolt in hasp. The opening door casts a wedge of yellow hall light against the wall. Her slender dark hand twists the switch and closes the door. Not a word spoken. The brutal light is message enough. A clear glass bulb hangs in the center of the room from a cord of brown woven cloth. New wires run down the wall in an ugly metal conduit. The bare bulb's little blazing filament burns an angry cloverleaf shape onto my eyeballs that will last until dawn. It's either get up and shut off the electricity and light a candle to read by, or else be blinded.

I get up and turn off the light.

May is foolish enough to trust me with matches. I set fire to two tapers and prop a polished tin pie plate to reflect yellow light. The same way I lit book pages and notebook pages at a thousand campfires in the last century.

I'm reading *The Knight of the Cart*, a story I've known since youth.

Lancelot is waiting where I left him the last time. Still every bit as anguished and torn about whether to protect his precious honor or to climb onto the shameful cart with the malefic dwarf driver, and perhaps by doing so to save Guinevere, perhaps *have* Guinevere for his own true love. Choosing incorrectly means losing all. I turn the pages and read on, hoping Lancelot will choose better if given one more chance. I want him to claim love over everything, but so far he has failed. How many more chances will I be able to give him?

The gist of the story is that even when all else is lost and gone forever, there is yearning. One of the few welcome lessons age teaches is that only desire trumps time.

A bedtime drink would be helpful. At some point in life, everybody needs medication to get by. A little something to ease the pain, smooth the path forward. But my doctor prohibits liquor, and so my own home has become as strict as if it were run by hard-shell Baptists. Memory is about the only intoxicant left.

I read on into the night until the house falls quiet. Lancelot is hopeless. I am dream-stricken to think he will ever choose better.

At some point, I put the book down and hold my right palm to the light. The silver scar running diagonal across all the deep lines seems to itch, but scratching does not help.

Late in the night, the door opens again. Scalding metallic light pours in from the hallway. May enters and walks to my bed. Her skin is the color of tanned deerhide, a mixture of several bloods—white and red and black—complex enough to confound those legislators who insist on naming every shade down to the thirty-second fraction. Whatever the precise formula is for May, it worked out beautifully. She's too pretty to be real.

I knew her grandfather back in slavery days. Knew him and also owned him, if I'm to tell the truth. I still wonder why he didn't cut my throat some night while I was asleep. I'd have had it coming. All us big men would have. But through some unaccountable generosity, May is as kind and protective as her grandfather was.

May takes the book as from a sleepy child, flaps it face down on the nightstand, blows out the candle with a moist breath, full lips pursed and shaped like a bow. I hear a hint of rattle in the lungs as the breath expires. I worry for her, though my doctor says she is fine. Consumption, though, is a long way to die. I've seen it happen more than once. May steps back to the door and is a black spirit shape against the light, like a messenger in a significant dream.

—Sleep, Colonel. You've read late.

Funny thing is, I actually try. I lie flat on my back in the dark with my arms on my chest. But I can't sleep. It is a bitter-cold night and the fire has burnt down to hissing coals. I don't ever sleep well anymore. I lie in bed in the dark and let the past sweep over me like stinging sheets of windblown rain. My future is behind me. I let gravity take me into the bed and before long I'm barely breathing. Practicing for the Nightland.

SURVIVE LONG ENOUGH and you get to a far point in life where nothing else of particular interest is going to happen. After that, if you don't watch out, you can spend all your time tallying your losses and gains in endless narrative. All you love has fled or been taken away. Everything fallen from you except the possibility of jolting and unforewarned memory springing out of the dark, rushing over you with the velocity of heartbreak. May walking down the hall humming an old song—"The Girl I Left Behind Me"—or the mere fragrance of clove in spiced tea can set you weeping and howling when all you've been for weeks on end is numb.

At least that last one is explainable. Back in green youth, Claire became an advocate for flavored kisses. She would break off new spring growth at the end of a birch twig, peel the dark bark to the wet green pulp, and fray the fibers with her thumbnail—then put the twig in her mouth and hold it there like a cheroot. After a minute she'd toss it away and say, Now kiss me. And her mouth had the sweet sharp taste of birch. In summer, she did the same with the clear drop of liquid at the tip of honeysuckle blossoms, and in the fall with the white pulp of honey-locust pods. And in winter with a dried clove and a broken stick of cinnamon. Now kiss me.

AT MAY'S URGING, I recently agreed to buy an Edison music machine. The Fireside model. It cost an unimaginable twenty-two dollars. She tells me the way it works is that singers up North holler songs into an enormous metal cone, whereupon their voices are scarified in a thin gyre on a wax cylinder the size of a bean can. I imagine the singers looking as if they are being swallowed by a bear. After digestion, they come out of my corresponding little cone sounding tiny and earnest and far, far away.

May is relentlessly modern, which makes me wonder why she takes care of me, for I am resolutely antique. Her enthusiasm for the movies is beyond measure, though the nearest nickelodeon is half a day's train ride away. Sometimes I give her a few dollars for the train ticket and the movie ticket, with some money left over for dinner along the way. She comes back all excited and full of talk about the thrill of the compact narratives, the inhuman beauty of certain actresses and actors, the magnitude of the images. I have never witnessed a movie other than once in Charleston, when I dropped a nickel into the slot of a kinetoscope viewer and wound the crank until the bell rang and put the sound tubes like a stethoscope to my ears and then bent to the eyepieces. All I perceived were senseless blurs moving tiny across my mind. I could not adjust my eyes to the pictures. Something looked a little like a man, but he seemed to have a dozen arms and legs and seemed not to occupy any specific world at all but just a grey fog broken by looming vague shapes. For all I could determine of his surroundings, the man might have been playing baseball or plowing a cornfield, or maybe boxing in a ring. I lost interest in the movies at that point.

But I understand that a movie has been made about my earlier life, and May described it to me in enthusiastic detail after it played in the nearest town. The title of it is *The White Chief*. I didn't care to see it. Who wants every bit of life you've ever known boiled down to a few short minutes? I don't need prompting. Memories from those way-back times flash up with great particularity—even individual trees, dead since long before the War, remain standing in my mind with every leaf etched distinct down to the pale palmate veins, their whole beings meaningful and bright with color. So why choose to enter that distressing grey cinema fog only to find some lost unrecognizable phantom of yourself moving through a vague and uncertain world?

IN SUMMER I STILL rally myself to go to the Warm Springs Hotel, a place I have frequented for more than half a century. Sometimes at the Springs I'm introduced to people who recognize my name, and I can see the incredulity on their faces. This example I'm about to tell happened last summer and will have to stand as representative for a number of similar occurrences.

A prominent family from down in the smothering part of the state had come up to the mountains to enjoy our cool climate. The father was a slight acquaintance of mine, and the son was a recently elected member of the state house. The father was young enough to be my child. They found me sitting on the gallery, reading the most recent number of a periodical—*The North American Review* to be specific, for I have been a subscriber over a span of time encompassing parts of eight decades.

The father shook my hand and turned to his boy. He said, Son, I want you to meet someone. I'm sure you will find him interesting. He was a senator and a colonel in the War. And, most romantically, white chief of the Indians. He made and lost and made again several fortunes in business and land and railroad speculation. When I was a boy, he was a hero. I dreamed of being half the man he was.

Something about the edge to his tone when he said the words *chief*, *colonel*, and *senator* rubbed me the wrong way. It suggested something ironic in those honorifics, which, beyond the general irony of everything, there is not. I nearly said, Hell, I'm twice the man you are now, despite our difference in age, so things didn't work out so bright for your condescending hopes. And, by the way, what other than our disparity of age confers upon you the right to talk about me as if I'm not present? But I held my tongue. I don't care. People can say whatever they want to about me when I've passed. And they can inflect whatever tone they care to use in the telling.

The son said, He's not Cooper, is he? He blurted it out and was immediately sorry to sound completely ridiculous.

Even to me it sounded ridiculous. Almost as if the boy had asserted that Daniel Boone or Crockett yet lived. Perhaps Natty Bumppo. Some mythic relic of the time when the frontier ran down the crest of the Blue Ridge and most of the country was a sea of forest and savanna and mountains prowled by savage Indians. A time of long rifles and bears as big as railcars. Bloodthirsty wolves and mountain lions. Days of yore when America was no more than a strip of land stretching a couple of hundred miles west of the Atlantic and the rest was just a very compelling idea. I represented an old America of coonskin hats erupting into the now of telephones and mile-a-minute automobiles and electric lights and moving pictures and trains.

Maybe there is an odor of must and camphor about me. But I live on. My eyes are quick and blue behind the folded grey lids. I am amazed by their brightness every time I gather courage to look in the mirror, which is seldom. How possible that any living thing from that distant time yet survives?

I could see in the son's expression that he was doing the arithmetic in his head, working the numbers. And then his face lit up when he realized that it summed.

I am not impossible, just very old.

I reached out my hand to shake and said, Will Cooper, live and in person.

He shook my hand and said something respectful about my awfully long and varied life.

That was the point where I might have reared back, as elderly men of means so often feel compelled to do, and pitched into a monologue about how I went out into a harsh world bereft of anything but a stout spirit, a sharp mind, and a willingness for hard work. The way such blowhards tell it, luck means nothing. Their innate superiority alone makes their rise a happy proof of natural law. But I'd rather think I made my way more like a highwayman, by being willing to pull a pistol—or something metaphorically like it—on the world when I needed to.

HAVING A TELEPHONE installed was May's idea. My argument was simple. What does a telephone mean to me? When the few survivors among my acquaintances wish to communicate, they use the post.

May said, Do you even know how telephones work?

Of course I know. You listen and talk, and the discourse passes instantly across vast distances. Along that ugly mess of wires drooping from the crucifixes that have erupted along every roadway as suddenly as toadstools after rain. I asked May why we needed a telephone, and she said, What if you keeled over with a heart attack or a stroke? I said I reckoned in that case I might die. May said she didn't want to have to go for the doctor to make sure I was gone. It would be easier just to call. Shortly afterward, a man came and ran more ugly wires through the house.

The telephone rested silent on the wall for days. Then one afternoon when I was sitting on the porch reading, it rang. So urgent, like a watchman sounding a fire alarm, but surely false in the shrill report of the tiny hammer beating frantically against the two acorn-shaped bells. What message short of disaster could be so pressing as to require that horrible jangle? Use the post and learn the virtues of patience and silence.

I waited for someone else to deal with it, but no one did. It kept shrilling. I closed my book and went down the hall to the oak box. It looked somewhat like a coffee grinder. I turned the crank and put the cold circumference of the black earpiece to my head. I heard a tiny voice, more like the scraping of crickets than human speech. The same sound repeated over and over, and all I could tell was that its inflection seemed to suggest a question.

Then, after several more repetitions, I believed it was my name being spoken.

—Will? the voice said.

I leaned toward the mouthpiece projecting from the wooden box and put my mouth to the rim of it, which flanged like a nostril on a horse. What was the etiquette of this device? What salutation or acknowledgment of identity was called for when you were summoned to speak?

—Will? the little voice said again.

—Present, I said.

There was a pause filled only with a sound like ham frying faintly in the distance.

—Will?

—Yes, I said. Will Cooper. Right here now.

The earpiece hissed. A faint voice said two syllables. I believe it said, It's Claire.

Then nothing further. I said, Yes? Yes?

The only answer was sizzle and hum.

I said, Claire? Claire? Saying it loud enough to carry down the wires.

I held the earpiece pressed tight for a long time, but nothing else emerged except a hollow sound, a ghost moving away.

May came down the hall. I said, How does one bring this to an end?

She turned the crank on the side of the box and rested the earpiece in its fork. The brown woven cord hung in a deep droop almost to the floor and swayed in a small diminishing arc like the pendulum to a wound-down clock.

—Who is she, Colonel? Claire?

—Someone I lost a long time ago.

2

THE HISTORY OF INDIAN RESISTANCE ON THIS CONTINENT IS A grim record of failure, even though a few battles were won now and again. As prime examples, I'll use the somewhat recent Little Big Horn; also, much earlier, the nearby fight at Echoee against the English. Indians won those battles, along with some others. Wars, though, were inevitably lost. To take my point, see the widely published recent photographs of fierce Geronimo all swollen up like a brood sow riding in a Cadillac automobile.

So what Bear accomplished was remarkable. If he did not prevail against America, I think it is at least fair to say he fought to a draw. In his battle, Bear used all the weapons at hand, including me. But the only killing shots any of us fired were against our own. Charley and his boys.

Bear was not one of your mystic Indians. He was only interested in this one momentary world, not some hypothetical other. Bear loved all the tangible manifestations of Creation as fervently as Baptists do King Jesus. It was not the spirits of winds, rivers, mountains, trees that he worshiped, but the living things themselves.

Bear was the possessor of the deepest and sharpest mind to which I have ever been exposed, and I say this as one who has known presidents, though, to be fair, only vicious Jackson and dim Johnson. That's if you don't count President Davis, who was plenty smart, but whose mind was thin and brittle as a water cracker. Bear, though, could not read or write, neither English nor the syllabary. Still, he more than held his own. The way I look at it, we have all *been* illiterate. Only a few of us stay that way, usually for the worst of reasons. Poverty in some cases. Law in others, at least back in the day of slavery. Bear, though, remained illiterate out of personal philosophy. But he loved stories, even the ones written down in books. I remember, when I was a boy, reading him long episodes from the *Morte d'Arthur* and the *Quixote,* translating into Cherokee on the fly. Bear would listen for as long as I cared to read, late into cold endless January nights when the whole world contracted within the circle of light from the fire in the center of his winterhouse.

But Bear was not some isolate, living within a little narrow circumference of experience. He had seen a lot of what there was to America back then. As a young man, he had taken a blood grudge against a whiteman and sworn to kill him. He pursued the man for a year and a half, all up through Virginia and Kentucky and Tennessee and down into the wastes of Alabama and Georgia. Traveling rough and light, but happy knowing how hard he was pushing the man ahead of him across the land, like desperate game driven by beaters. When they'd finally made a great circle and come back nearly to home, the man quit running and holed up in a barn to make a final stand. Bear went in with nothing but a hawkbill knife.

—I'd a mind to gut him out, Bear said when he told me the tale.

But instead, after he had cornered the man in the hayloft, Bear just touched him with the crook of the blade and walked away. It was an exquisite point of honor.

In his middle years, Bear saw even more of America when he traveled all through the coastal plantation country chasing after a Cherokee girl of nine or ten who had been stolen by slavers passing through the mountains. The girl, named Blossom, wasn't even clan kin to Bear, but the whole business angered him. Slaver trash coming onto his land and hauling children off. He set out afoot and was gone for months tracking

Blossom from town to town, slave market to slave market. He went down to Hillsborough and Fayetteville and from there to the coast and then south right into the heart of Charleston to the big market and from there out into the countryside to find the people who had ultimately bought the girl.

Back then, years before I first met him, he would have been an even taller man than I remember, unstooped by age, broad-shouldered and full across the forehead, his long nose like a hatchet blade and his black hair long and loose except for the one little plait he liked to wear in the back. I can see him walking up the tree-lined drive of a great Charleston plantation, his linen hunting shirt and deerleather leggings dusty from the road. A look on his face of utter calm and disinterest, but intent on claiming the kidnapped girl. And back then, he probably had a drink or two in him, for he achieved temperance only occasionally, in old age.

He talked with the first whiteman he saw, a stout little music tutor, sitting on a horse watching two men making a wheel hoop in a blacksmith shed. The tutor passed Bear up the chain of command to the foreman and finally to the actual owner and his pale slim wife. They came out from the big house and talked to the dashing and handsome Indian just for the entertainment of it. They disagreed with Bear's assessment of the situation. And though Bear wanted to take out his knife and kill the man where he stood, he went back to town and found a lawyer. Not an honest lawyer but, better yet for his purposes, a smart mean little bastard with personal and political grudges against the plantation owner and eager to go against him in court.

For a month, Bear slept every night down by the water in a rope hammock strung in a stand of palmettos, and by day he and his lawyer fielded every argument they could muster, including expert microscopic evidence to show that the girl's hair bore no Negro characteristics. The long and short of it is, they won. Bear came walking back into the village with Blossom by his side and restored her to her home.

I asked him one time how he knew to use the law in his favor. He said that the law is an axe. It cuts whatever it falls on. The man that wins knows how to aim the sharp edge away from himself.

He didn't much care to talk about the court business, but as an old man he still remembered with great favor the enormous and tasty fish he caught from the sand beach at his campsite. The water, though, was the worst he had ever put in his mouth. When I asked him how he managed to conduct all this business not speaking the English language, he said maybe back then he knew a word or two but not anymore.

TO BE EVENHANDED, I should also tell a representative story about Featherstone, for he was fatherlike to me as well. But more the kind of father you want to kill. Or one who wants to kill you. When I think back on the single instance when we actually exchanged pistol fire, I sometimes still wish I had taken him down. Also I still miss him, and the world seems poorer for his absence. To be entirely fair, when I was a boy and young man, Featherstone provided another pattern of manhood entirely different from Bear's. I'm sure it is one of my greatest failures in life that, of my two flawed fathers, I more closely mirror Featherstone's example. I heard this account from a number of older men back when I was a boy, for if it was only on Featherstone's word, I wouldn't dignify the tale with repetition.

Until some years after the Revolution, the Cherokee system of justice remained very direct and without interference of judge and jury and lawyer. The penalty for murder was that the clan of the victim became entitled to kill the murderer. I think we could all accede to the fairness of that. But various complications sometimes arose, and as a boy Featherstone was caught up in one of them. His maternal uncle, Slow Water, a man of some considerable property and power within the community, happened to kill a man of the Wild Potato Clan as a result of bad whiskey and high feelings after losing a momentous wager at a ball game. Slow Water had bet several horses, many skipples of shell corn, a house. When the game ended with its final brutal skirmishes leading to a pair of goals scored in quick succession by the opposing team to win the match, the Wild Potato Clan fellow looked at Slow Water and smirked. He didn't say a word, but just that look, the twist of mouth, was enough. Come winter, he'd be eating Slow Water's cornbread in Slow Water's house.

Slow Water reached to his waist and pulled a long skinning knife from under his coat and ran it through the man's neck until the point came out the other side. And then he watched the man bleed out right on the bruised grass of the ball field.

Justice should have played along as normal, with Slow Water hunted down and killed by the men of Wild Potato Clan, and then life would be balanced and ordered again and could go on harmoniously. That was the way it ordinarily was. At worst, there might be one or two further bouts of justice before matters finally settled down. But Slow Water's clan, the Long Hairs, met and reckoned unanimously that Slow Water was too valuable to forfeit. They agreed to offer Featherstone in Slow Water's place, and even his mother would not break with the consensus of the clan. Featherstone was then a fatherless redheaded freckled Indian boy of sixteen. His natural daddy had been a Border Scot trader, and his mother's father was Highland Scot. But in those days identity still went through the women, and if your mother belonged to a clan, you did too. Blood degree didn't factor.

Featherstone had not even been in attendance at the ball game. He had been on a pony-club outing, and they had run a string of stolen horses from the piedmont of North Carolina across the Cherokee Nation and sold them outside of Nashville. All in all, it had been a jaunty and satisfactory month of desperate scrapes and high spirits. Hilarious rum camps and long ass-blistering days a-saddle. None of the six-member party was more than eighteen, and they returned to Valley River splendidly mounted, leather pistol buckets hanging paired before their saddles. All of them rode cocky with cash money in their pocketbooks, fine new suits of clothes on their backs, and well-constructed stories to tell.

Slow Water met Featherstone as he came into town, and the uncle's face was grim. They stepped aside and Slow Water laid it out. He detailed the sacrifice Featherstone was called to make for his clan. Featherstone was undoubtedly slightly drunk. He said, Well, shit on you.

And fuck them Wild Potato boys. Maybe they better watch out I don't kill them first. And then maybe come looking for you when I'm done.

Everyone in town knew how the matter stood, and they had come out of their houses to loiter around the squareground and watch Featherstone's progress. He rode past them, his back straight as if a fire poker had been driven up the circle of his spine. He spurred his mare and reined in at the same time so that she went compressed, with her neck arched and her legs bunched under her, trotting nearly sideways in response to Featherstone's contradictory suggestions.

Featherstone rode to his mother's house. She but confirmed Slow Water's report and offered no advice other than that maybe he ought to leave the Nation for good, maybe slope for Texas. She gave him several little bean-bread tamales, wrapped in their scalded fodder blades, and said that was about all she could do for him.

Featherstone went outside and stood with his head on his mare's damp shoulder and breathed in her sweet scent and thought awhile. He took out one of several pints of black Barbados rum from his saddlebag and drank and then looked to his weaponry, of which he had aplenty. The matched pair of pistols. A shotgun with an oiled walnut stock and a pair of great dark bores that seemed even larger because of the extreme shortness of the barrels, the paired hammers sporting big pointed thumbpieces so that when they were at full cock they were reminiscent of a horse with its ears pinned. At that time it was a fresh concept in firearms. Also a fighting hatchet with a bright honed edge to its head and blue-jay feathers dressing its hickory handle. And several knives, one of fine Damascus steel with a blade as wide as his hand and an ugly upcurve to the blade like a stubbed scimitar, a style of knife that would later be dubbed Bowie.

He mounted and rode back through town, and all the people were still there as audience. He announced in English and Cherokee, for all to hear, that anyone who came after him would have to die. Sad to say, but there was no way around it. Give me but a long willow switch, he shouted, and my pursuers will be no more than a wet heap of shreds when I'm done. Soup meat.

And he told them where to find him. A place where three roads met down by the river. Tomorrow morning. But after breakfast. I ain't missing a meal for you shit.

He went straight to the place he had named and waited through the night just inside a laurel thicket uphill from the specified field of combat. He expected to be set upon and killed at any moment. He sat fireless in the dark and drank from a succession of pint bottles, and when he had reached the small hours of morning, with dew beading on the glossy laurel leaves, he was inspired by the black rum to wish enthusiastically that his killers would hurry up and come on.

And they did come, at daybreak, with the fog still heavy along the river. Three boys his age and two grown men riding out of the fog into the crossroads, thinking they had arrived early enough to set an ambush. They were dressed in their greatest finery as for a special occasion. The men were full-bloods and wore traditional long hunting shirts, vests, blue and red turbans, deerskin leggings with silk garters. The boys were all mixed-bloods and wore such assortment of white and Indian clothing as to suggest divided allegiances. They sat in the road discussing how to array themselves for ambush and arguing over who had the right to strike the first blow and who had first claim to the kill.

Before they reached agreement, Featherstone erupted out of the laurels in a rain of flung dew and rode down among them with his hatchet in one hand, the great Damascus knife in the other, and the reins in his teeth like some berserk battleground Celt, which he more than three quarters was. He went into them slashing two-handed at anything that moved. His mare wheeled in the road two times and he cut a swath around him as she turned, and then she collected her hindquarters under her and burst off down the road at a gallop.

In that one instant, before they could even think toward defense, the ambushers had all taken wounds, some rather dire. One of the men was cut down to the white joint of his shoulder. Blood ran down his arm and dripped from his four fingers and painted the neck of his horse in red stripes. The other man had lost a divot of muscle from his upper thigh, and he looked at the raw gape as if it held a revelation. Both wounds were from the hatchet. The boys grabbed at themselves in various places and howled as high-pitched as coon dogs, and the blood welled out between their fingers from knife cuts in their arms and deep rakings along their ribs.

Featherstone was by then only a diminishing muffled sound of hooves beating on dirt, long lost in the river fog.

In the following weeks, men and boys from the Wild Potato Clan rode out like Percival and Gawain. They pursued Featherstone day and night, horseback and afoot. They used all the woodcraft and tracking skills they knew in order to find and kill him, and yet over and over they failed.

Featherstone rode days, letting mileage serve for security. Nights, he squatted sleepless in drizzly dark. The Wild Potato Clan pursued him through the Lower Towns, Middle Towns, Upper Towns. Across land planted in corn with bean vines growing up the cornstalks and pumpkins glowing orange on the ground beneath. They drove him deep into wilderness marked only by the passways of departed bison flowing along the hillsides like ancient watercourses gone dry. He hid from them, fled from them, fought them with deadly intent when he had to fight. Wild Potato Clan boys sat by wilderness fires using porcupine quills to dig out lead shot from where it lay like a spray of welted blue boils under the skin of their backs and chests and faces. They dressed knife wounds with poultices of yarrow. One man lay for days under the fever of an infected wound from a pistol ball until Sixkiller took the man to water and conjured out the heat from the wound and so enabled him to live.

In one encounter, a running battle that covered many miles of valley floor and ridgetop, Featherstone bloodied higher than a dozen men and boys, mostly with the shotgun. He reloaded as he rode and fired at the gallop with considerable accuracy, and they fell one by one behind him until he rode alone into dark. He bivouacked that night fireless. He ate cold potato and hated all men and wished to wipe them away with the swipe of a blade. He lived in fear, and as a result swore to spread blood in his wake, leave a trail of dead to mark his brief passage through the world.

The conclusion of the matter was somewhat anticlimactic, both for Featherstone and for those of the community needing a fatal showdown to satisfy their sense of an ending. What Featherstone did was to take his pony-club money and go down from the mountains into cotton country and buy a skinny mulatto girl of fourteen who had been brought recently from Jamaica and spoke an indecipherable brand of English. She was the only person he could afford, even driving the thriftiest bargain he could. He rode her behind him on the mare five days' journey back to Valley River with her thin arms circling his waist tightly the whole way, for she was terrified of horses, with their red-rimmed eyes and yellow teeth and flaring nostrils. They reminded her of the violent mounted foremen in the cane fields.

Featherstone offered her to the Wild Potato Clan as replacement for the man Slow Water had killed. A life for a life. She didn't look like much, but rather than continue to battle with Featherstone, the clan agreed that she would do. They took her unreservedly as one of them, and she became a member of the Wild Potato Clan. They renamed her Martha, though she already had the perfectly serviceable name of Dolly. But all her life, they mostly called her Bite because when she and Featherstone arrived in Valley River, he had the red crescent marks of her teeth, uppers and lowers both, scabbing on the sides of his neck just above the collar line. The clan speculated at length on the possible range of circumstances under which the wounds had been made, but mainly they honored her as the only member of Wild Potato Clan who had been able to draw blood from Featherstone.

And as far as I know, the only whiteman to do so was me.

3

I CANNOT DECIDE WHETHER IT IS AN ILLNESS OR A SIN, THE NEED TO write things down and fix the flowing world in one rigid form. Bear believed writing dulled the spirit, stilled some holy breath. Smothered it. Words, when they've been captured and imprisoned on paper, become a barrier against the world, one best left unerected. Everything that happens is fluid, changeable. After they've passed, events are only as your memory makes them, and they shift shapes over time. Writing a thing down fixes it in place as surely as a rattlesnake skin stripped from the meat and stretched and tacked to a barn wall. Every bit as stationary, and every bit as false to the original thing. Flat and still and harmless. Bear recognized that all writing memorializes a momentary line of thought as if it were final.

But I was always word-smitten. Always reading in a book or writing in a journal. When I was fifteen, Bear's people called me Turkey Wing because of the quills usually fanned in the breast pocket of my coat or tucked behind my ear, for turkey was the source of my favorite writing feather. And me being right-handed, the curve of quills from the right wing fit my hand best, so on hunts they knew to save those in particular.

Up in the attic, there are crates of my journals stacked to the rafters. They descend into the past as deep as the Monroe administration, telling exactly what happened to me all the way back to my boyhood. Every date and event remotely worth noting. Enough ink to fill a washtub. Scratched out with every manner of bird quill and steel nib into one long looping line of script that runs a lifetime. Several pages from the fall of 1838 were written with a sharpened stick and boiled huckleberry juice because I had lost my writing tackle back in the mountains. Another whole journal from a few years later is all bucked and stained and nearly unreadable from being soaked during a river crossing in spring floodtime. A few pages were written with a quill taken from an eagle's wing, which proved less inspirational than I would have thought. The first journals are little handmade coverless booklets of folded paper, a boy's crude handiwork. From there they make progressions of refinement in craft until, at some point, the journals become uniform right through to now, fine leather-bound books with ruled watermarked cotton paper made by stationers in Washington. I've had a standing order for decades. Six a year. They still come every April, a tidy parcel wrapped in brown paper with the ends all neatly folded and tucked, tied with jute twine. And always a nice note from the proprietor, the grandson of the man with whom I first did business. Out of habit, I still fill the volumes, though nothing new happens to me. I go back to the previous century, re-plowing the same old clearings, emending, adding, summarizing, inventing.

I have periods where everything I ever encountered—grass and trees, music, the taste of food, the way people move, the miracle of colors, even my own worn thoughts—seems luminous and razor-cut in clarity, exactly like the whole world seemed to me at seventeen. What a gift at this late date. Memories from deep into the last century come blowing through me and I can hardly stand against their force. We all reach a point where we would like to draw a line across time and declare everything on the far side null. Shed our past life like a pair of wet and muddy trousers, just roll their heavy clinging fabric down our legs and step away. We also reach a point where we would give the rest of our withering days for the month of July in our seventeenth year. But no thread of Ariadne exists to lead us back there.

Nevertheless, let us begin. But not with senator, colonel, or chief. With a bound boy.

PART TWO

. . .

arrival

1

One afternoon in the early spring, an orphan, twelve years old, rode up a narrow trail through mountain wilderness. He was alone, and rain blew nearly sideways. He carried a long knife at his belt and went with his trousers tucked into his boot tops, affecting the look of a seasoned traveler set out on the open road for a far and uncertain destination. This orphan knew stories, tales of a like-abandoned boy named Jack. As a little child he'd many times heard an old teller, a folk-sayer, some greybeard grandfather on a farm down the road, recount Jack's Tales with laconic expressiveness to bunches of little fireside children. The boy still remembered some of the lines, and he declaimed them aloud to the landscape around him like a poem or a prayer, for he took comfort in the fact that Jack too was often a wanderer.

Well, he put a little budget on his back,
and he set out.
And days passed,
and nights passed,
and weeks passed,
and months passed,
and he traveled along the road.

The young voice trailed off into the green woods to no response, not even an echo.

THIS BOY I'M SPEAKING of was a version of me, an early incomplete draft. I still have some of his teeth, and we share an inch-long scar—a deep cut from a horseshoe nail—just below our right anklebone.

The trail ahead forked at a big poplar tree, offering simple choices. Left or right? It was a simple time. But I knew even then that you could not just set out in one direction and necessarily get somewhere. You lived in the mountains as if cupped in a puzzle of unclimbable blue ridges and uncrossable black gorges. To travel through that place, you needed to know not only where you wanted to go but also that roundabout was often the only way to get there.

I pondered the choices. Each journey has two possible motions, two directions. Toward life. Toward death. It was like that for me, or at least it seemed so then.

I dropped the reins. The colt I had recently named Waverley in tribute to my favorite Walter Scott novel reached an unsupervised halt, hooves sucking into the mud. Rhododendron grew close on either side of the trail, and the wet glossed leaves nearly met overhead. When I looked up, water from my hatbrim ran down the back of my neck and onto the oversized wool coat my uncle had handed down to me. I pulled a map from my coat pocket and spread it open and rested it across Waverley's withers and studied the markings closely. Raindrops fell on the map, and I bent over to shelter the paper. My forefinger traced the way I thought I had traveled and stopped at the place I thought I had reached. The map was a real map, from a printer's shop, the result of a survey commissioned by some variety of government that claimed sovereignty hereabouts. My favorite part was a little box in one corner labeled LEGEND where the symbolism of the thing, its intent, lay revealed in pictographs. I had opened and closed the map so many times in the rain the past three days that it was already coming apart at the creases, and I rubbed at the rent places with my finger as if I could mend them back with a magic touch.

The land I had already traversed was displayed in fine detail regarding state and county lines, towns and turnpikes and traces, mountains and rivers. But westward, at a point about where I guessed I was, the map turned abruptly white and all the geographic opinion it ventured further was the words INDIAN TERRITORY, lettered rather big. No fading or tapering off. Everything halted all at once. So the lesson the map taught was that knowledge has strict limits, and beyond that verge the world itself might become equally unspecified and provisional. In my mind, the place thus rendered could be contained within no state and could contain within it no counties or towns. What mountains and rivers the geography held would lack official name and be whatever the few people living there chose to call them day by day. Brown River when you crossed it one time, Green River the next. Or just give it your own name, Will River. Put your impress on the land and see if you could force it to stay how you had decided to call it. The white landscape ahead was apparently open to considerable suggestion.

I HAD FEARED this moment of the journey since the first time I saw the map, five days before. The whole month previous, I had known something worth dreading was about to happen.

My aunt had begun acting coolish toward me. And my uncle, my dead father's brother, started cursing unrestrainedly in my presence as if I were suddenly a grown man. They had bought a rather fine young horse, new to the saddle. He was bay and had a beautiful narrow head and big quick eyes. At the trot he was fancy with wonderful suspension and hardly a break at the knee, but he was so newly broken to saddle that he often forgot his manners and went sideways if a leaf blew in front of him or a bird flew from a tree. He was full of his own opinions and paid little heed to the suggestions of others, in particular his rider. The tack that came with him was poor. The saddle was dried out and cracked and not much bigger or more comfortable than the hull to a big mossbacked snapping turtle. And also a pair of rush panniers and a leather budget as if someone were preparing for a trip.

Then, one unseasonable warm day, a man I did not know came riding up in a two-horse wagon to visit. He sat a long time talking with my uncle in the parlor. After a while he came out to where I sat under a budding apple tree trying to read a book in Latin, specifically Virgil, and I was to a particularly admirable line about the sun slanting and winter falling. The man had some years behind him. He looked as if he had fought at King's Mountain in the Revolution and still attired himself in the old style, at least as far as knee breeches and dingy stockings. Of course he wore his own thin white hair and not a powdered wig, and his hat was slouch-brimmed rather than tricornered, and he just had on regular low boots instead of the buckled shovel-nosed footwear in illustrations of the Founders, but still he carried about him a strong whiff of those old days, of Washington and Franklin.

The man reached out and shook my hand like I was a man. He asked questions about my schooling and said he had heard I was quick in the way of words.

I just said, Yes sir. There was little point denying it.

Then, out of nowhere, he said, Some people, if they saw an Indian in the woods, would be mighty scared.

I said, Not me.

And then, without further reference, he started talking about Indian country. The Cherokee Nation, where they still ruled. A sort of hole in America, bigger than most states but small in comparison to their old homelands.

The man said, There's every style of Indian out there. The most isolated and backward and ignorant fraction of their kind are mostly full-bloods, skin almost as dark as a buckeye shell. They don't know English from turkey gabble, and even if they did know it, they would disdain to speak it to you. They do the old dances and work the old spells and carry on like they still own the world. Come the dead of winter, they crawl in little mud huts not much taller than a clay bake oven, and they don't come out of their dens in spring till the bears do. Jesus is nothing to them, and the women run everything except for hunting and fighting. Their only law is eye for eye. They're so casual in the regulation of reproduction that all the parentage anyone can claim is the obvious matter of who their mother was. They don't even know there's seven days to a week and twelve months to a year. For them this wouldn't be March, it would be the damn Wind Moon.

And furthermore, the antique gentleman said, from old-fashioned Indians like that, they vary in every degree all the way to ones you can't tell from white men. Some of them have as high as nine parts in ten Scots blood, and might as well take to wearing plaid skirts and honking on the great pipes. Those kind of Indians own slaves and plantations, dress in tailcoats, eat off china plates with silver cutlery, and have grand crystal chandeliers swinging over their mahogany dinner tables. That rich bunch speaks English as well as any man among us and better than most. A lot of them can't even speak their own language.

He paused and said, You understand what I'm saying?

I said, Yes sir. Even though I didn't understand at all.

With that, he was apparently done describing the ways of the Cherokee, and he looked down the front yard to the paddock by the barn where the new young horse stood.

—That your horse? the man said.

—No sir. Not that I know of. They just got him.

—How old?

—Three or four.

—Which?

—Three, I believe.

—And not cut?

—No sir.

—So still a colt.

—Yes sir. If four's the mark.

—At four, he'll be a stallion. And maybe a good one, the way he's put together.

We looked at the colt together awhile, and then he said something strange. He said, Will, when it comes right down to it, not many men can afford to cross the woman they bed with. Not and live in any peace. I hope you won't think too bad about your uncle.

I studied on his comment and then just said, Yes sir. For I knew even then that it is often good to wait for events to unfold around you.

He went back to the porch where my aunt and uncle sat rocking and looking anywhere but my direction and not speaking with each other at all. I tried to go back to Virgil but could not attend to him. I watched the antique man as he crossed the yard and effortfully climbed the steps up to the porch and took a chair. He drew a sheaf of papers from the inside pocket of his coat. He talked and they listened. He went through the papers each by each and pointed out particular features with his index finger. Then they all rose and went inside, and I figured it was for a quill and inkpot to invoke the law and, as if by sortilege, foretell my life.

That night my aunt and uncle asked me to keep my seat after supper and dismissed their own children to bed. My cousins were ill-tempered ignorant little beings, a brown-headed three-year-old boy who had yet to utter a word of human language and a somewhat older girl barely more inclined to converse. I generally paid no more heed to them than to the yard chickens.

When they had trudged up the narrow stairs to bed, my aunt set a plate of cold cornbread and a glass of buttermilk and a sugar bowl in front of me by way of dessert. I crumbled the bread into the milk and sprinkled it with sugar and mushed it around with a spoon and began eating. We three sat awhile in the dim kitchen without talking, and there was just the sound of my spoon clicking against the glass. The flames of the cooking fire died out and the embers sighed and settled into a bed of ash on the hearthstones. A sphere of motes and minute insects vibrated around the flames of the pair of candles on the table. I pushed the glass away with one finger and held my face still, blanking my mind.

This is where they lay out my life, I figured.

—I can't hardly stand it, my aunt said. He's but a boy to send off like this.

She dabbed at her dry eyes with a wadded handkerchief.

—He's twelve, my uncle said.

She thought a moment and then added, Going on thirteen. As if that larger number had some further power to settle the matter.

My uncle pushed his chair from the table and went into the parlor and came back and set a big iron key in front of me and unrolled a map on the table.

—That'll let you in, he said, touching the key. And this will get you there.

He smoothed the map two-handed against the tabletop and set the pewter candlesticks on each end of the paper to keep it from rolling back up.

The key was hand-forged and fancy on the butt end, which was shaped like a lover's knot. The business end, though, was crude and had just two cutouts to bypass the wards, and anybody with a nail or a rat-tail file and half a mind could pick whatever lock it mated with in a matter of seconds. I looked at the key closely, for it seemed to figure into my future with some importance. But I did not pick it up. Nor did I ask where the lock might be.

I sat inside myself, awaiting the terms of exile.

As my uncle talked out the route, his finger limned the journey on the map, crossing wiggling rivers and climbing up what he said were deep valleys to pass through narrow mountain gaps. He told landmarks and described turnings. Left at such and such a place, right at another.

There were many such places. Which apparently meant that there were also many wrong turnings lying in wait as well. They all began to blur together.

And then when the map went white, he talked on but no longer ran his finger across the paper. I looked at the blank space, and the child in me thought for a minute that traveling through the territory so depicted would be like moving through a dense fog where near things lacked clear form or color and far things might as well not exist at all. But then I knew that the white only stood proxy for a real world, an indication merely that the mappists had not reached that far in their thinking. Still, I figured the place was the next thing to an undiscovered country and that what few people lived there were alone among the animals and the indifferent shapes the land took.

When he was done talking, my uncle looked at his wife and made the slightest outward gesture with his hands, like getting shut of something.

My aunt looked to me and said, Well?

—I've got a pair of questions, I said.

—Ask 'em out, she said.

—Am I now a bound boy?

—I wouldn't call it that, my uncle said.

—But there are papers, my aunt said. We've signed papers.

—It's seven years is all, my uncle said. And you'll be paid a stipend for your service.

So to the next question. It involved a fancy matchlock pistol that had been my father's. My mother used to take it to a window and show it to me, unlocking its wooden box and lifting the lid slowly as if within lay treasure. Light fell on a beautiful bright art object nested in blue velvet. The trigger guard was worked in scrolling, and the thumbpiece to the hammer seemed as big to me as a dogwood leaf. If I had to go out and travel the world alone, sole relic of a dead family, that pistol, stuck down in my pantwaist with just the beautiful sweet curve of ivory handle showing at my hip, would serve as fine passport.

I said, Might I take weaponry for the road? My father's pistol?

My aunt looked at me as if I were a fool. She said her opinion was that a gun would get me into more trouble than it would get me out of.

—You're off to be a shopkeep, she said. Not a highwayman.

At twelve, who wants to be given that news? Shopkeep.

I kept my face free of expression as a stove lid, but my mind visioned long decades stretched out before me to be passed, penned until death, behind a till.

—Knife? I said.

—Well, sure, my uncle said. That's more in the way of an implement. I've still got a big thick-bladed thing of your father's. You can take it.

I had no certain recollection of my father beyond his artifacts. Sometimes I thought I remembered a dark presence, a partial shape leaned down over me, no features, only a hint of the quizzical in the angle at which the head was cocked, a silhouetted embodiment. My mother had told me many times that when I was just a knee-baby I would ride all over the farm on my father's shoulders. And that's the size I was when my father drowned. He was crossing the Pigeon River in a wagon one day, and the whole rig pitched over on him in a heavy spring current and pinned him to the smooth stones on the river bottom and drowned the horse in the traces to boot.

My mother lived awhile beyond him, a decade nearly. And for much of that time she was still mostly a girl. I've counted out the numbers and that's all she amounted to when I was little. A girl, sad and lonely and vague, widowed and dependent, living among her husband's people. Of my mother, I mainly remember long stretches of days where we would be out from morning until dark running frantic pointless errands. All the way to town for a newspaper, halfway across the county to take a cake to someone she hardly knew who'd had a death in the house. But at some point, there were long stretches where she wouldn't go outdoors at all for what seemed like several quarters of the year. I'd bring in double handfuls of pale poplar blossoms to her room, then fat green poplar leaves, and finally yellow and brown ones gathered from the lawn to demonstrate the passage of time. She died of some consuming disease. I remember a lengthy period of wasting, hushed voices and darkened rooms, the sound of rattling coughs cascading down the steps, a black iron cauldron of blood-spotted rags boiling in rusty water out by the smokehouse.

Immediately after my mother was gone, some matter of financial beholdenness beyond my ken allowed my aunt and uncle to append our neighboring farm to their own, and so I was at once orphaned and dispossessed. For the nearly three years previous to my exile, they had continued sending me—out of guilt, I guess—to the school in town that my mother had chosen for me. It was taught by a learned and jolly Manxman, and he called it the Latin Academy. That was a grand name for what was just a spare room in his house. It was elevated into an academy, I suppose, by a bust of Horace sitting on the mantelpiece and a big Latin lexicon spread open on an oak stand. Under the Manxman's teaching, I could soon read anything you put in front of me, and moreover would do so with great pleasure. The conventions of grammar, both Latin and English, made sense to me, and I could parse most sentences accurately, even the great long periodic ones from the previous century. I read yellow and foxed copies of *The Spectator* as if they contained the most current and pressing thought. And I could do sums and knew the facts of the history and myths of Greece and Rome and England, much of which added up to how awfully murderous and lunatic a king will get to acting every so often. It all came to me with considerable ease. The teacher had started me on Latin in the second year, and already I could about get the gist of poems by that selfsame Horace. I still remember one about throwing stones at a lover's window in the night.

If we few little scholars had learned well and behaved for the most part of the day, the Manxman would break out a deck of playing cards in the afternoon, and we would gamble against him for striped peppermint sticks. He took his teaching of the rules and conventions and logic of all the common gambling games as seriously as the details of Latin grammar.

But now, the best I could tell, the Academy had been declared too expensive to continue, and at twelve—almost thirteen—I had been declared suddenly grown up. I was cut loose on my own. My aunt and uncle had arranged for me to be bound to the antique gentleman. I was to run a trade post out at the edge of the Nation. The clerk who had been running the post had just picked up and gone. Lit out for Louisiana or one of those other places out west. Savage Texas, maybe. And so a new clerk was needed immediately. As far as everyone besides me was concerned, my life was set.

The morning I mounted up to ride into exile, my aunt stood by the colt's shoulder trying to weep. The sun had not risen over the ridge, and the world was still grey and foggy. She gave me five dollars in silver and ten in Georgia paper money, a small iron skillet, and a folded piece of paper on which she had written recipes for fried chicken and biscuits.

The last words she said to me were these: Remember to read the Bible and pray and love Jesus and not fall in with the ways of the heathens.

I rode out from the farm and by sunup was passing through town down the main street. I could smell bacon frying from the hotel kitchen, and the blacksmith was stirring at his banked fire and laying on more oak. A young black girl went carrying a lidded chamberpot toward an outhouse. I was on the road and terrified.

I FOLDED THE map back into its pocket-sized rectangle and tried to remember all the turnings my uncle had talked out, and then I spit valiantly to the side and put a heel to Waverley and reined left of the poplar onto what looked to be the more promising of the two ways before me.

I rode on into the mountains with dark weighing heavily on me. On the early nights of the journey, I had slept at the cabins of people known to the antique gentleman, and he had given me letters to present them, saying to feed me and let me sleep in whatever place they had to spare, which meant the barn in most cases and a bare attic room in another. This would be my first night sleeping alone on the trail, and I was afraid of dark and tried not to think about it coming on so rapidly.

I stopped by midafternoon to allow plenty of time to make camp. The rain had ended, but the trees and brush were still wet when I found a piece of flat ground that backed into an overhanging rock cliff. The dirt under its shelter was dry and fine as sifted flour. The sound of moving water from off in the woods. By the trail, a little stand of grass just beginning to put out new growth after the winter. Opposite the cliff, an open wedge of a vista where a big tree had blown down and opened a gap. Seven layers of mountains faded off in diminishing orders of blue to the west. I stood and looked at the place and imagined it all pitch black, and I was afraid. Then I imagined the same thing with a fire blazing hip-high, and I expected I could put my back to the cliff and sit in the yellow light and wait for morning.

I had the advantage of it. I had to.

I untacked Waverley and watered and grained him and hobbled him where he could graze. Then I made myself a little supper out of the same bag of grain from which I'd fed Waverley. Boiled oats with brown sugar.

Part of my kit was a skein of hemp rope, which my uncle had shaken at me with considerable emphasis, saying, Without fail, hang your food from a tree limb to keep animals out of it.

Back then was a different time. Bison and elk had been recently killed out, but there was still a sight more bears and panthers and wolves than now, so I paid attention to my uncle's pronouncement. I took the rope and stood under a big pine tree and spotted a likely limb, stout and horizontal, about fifteen feet off the ground. I held the end of the rope drooping in my hand and wondered how I might loft it over the limb. First I tried to fling it. Took two steps of a run and threw the limp rope-end skyward. But it hardly went higher than my head. So I scoured the ground until I found a thin flat chunk of slate as big across as a dinner plate with spalled edges sharp enough to flay hide. I tied it tight to the end of the rope and reared back and, in the style of discus tossers, sent it winging mightily toward the limb. But I forgot to notice that I had my foot on a loop of the rope. Before the stone reached the limb, the rope stretched tight and sprang back, and the rock came flying straight at me, singing a dire whispery song by my ear. It hit the ground edge first and buried itself like an axehead in soft wood. I rubbed my forehead about where the stone would have hit had it come back a few inches southward.

—Reckon you're just required to attend without letup, I said aloud.

I went at the job again, with greater care as to foot placement, and soon had my budget and panniers swinging limp ten feet off the ground. Bears could bat at it until dawn and not do themselves any good.

I went looking for firewood, wanting a grand pile of it to shore up against black night. I hauled armload after armload. As I reached for a last fallen stick of oak, a copperhead newly awakened from its winter sleep, colored and patterned in brown-and-tan shades of old leaf fall, jacked its front end off the ground and struck at my hand. Its mouth flew open as if on hinges, like flinging open a valise with a pale-pink satin lining. The motion of the strike was a jerking lurch, more awkward than I would have guessed. When the snake saw it had missed its mark, it turned across itself and went flowing across the forest floor in retreat.

On idiot impulse, with no prior thought whatsoever, I did as I had seen an older boy do with a blacksnake. I grabbed the copperhead by its tail and cracked it like a whip. Its head flew off and hit the trunk of a redbud tree twenty feet away with the sound of a knuckle pecking on a door. I stood amazed. As I carried the snake back to camp, holding it near the bloody stub of its neck, the body kept coiling about my wrist.

Oats don't make much of a supper, so I gutted the snake out and skinned it and draped it across a green stick over the fire. And even then it still moved while it first cooked, coiling and twitching. When the meat fell still and became done, I cut it into pieces about corncob length and ate the white meat off the backbone and the keen ribs, thinking this: People say snake tastes like chicken and, by damn, it does.

Just before full dark, when it had chilled off enough to put on my uncle's wool coat, I went to piss by a thick stand of huckleberry bushes. I stood there unbuttoned with myself in my hand, all relaxed, eyes vaguely taking in the scenery. Out of the bushes twenty feet away erupted a young black bear. It was skinny from sleeping all winter and was only a few months past following its mama around and probably as scared as I was, but it came forward all in a rush, bouncing along, huffing air and grunting, and it looked much larger than the space it occupied. In mid-flow as I was, I could do little but hold out my left hand, palm foremost, and say, with a note of considerable urgency, Wait.

And, oddly enough, the bear did wait. It came to a skidding halt and stood still, looking confused in its expression like a dog justly chastised for bad behavior. I dribbled to a conclusion and went running back to camp, fumbling with the buttons of my britches as I fled, coattails dragging the ground behind me. The bear chased me a few strides and then lost interest and eased back into the brush and was gone.

At that point, sleep did not seem a possibility. I guessed that in this landscape the varieties of threat were likely not to fall entirely within the bounds of reason offered by rock and snake and bear. I had kept some coffee grounds and a tin pot out of the panniers, and I sat up most of the night drinking coffee, feeding the fire, watching the edge of dark for movement, and listening for the approach of killers and wild animals and the malignant supernatural forces said by many cultures to inhabit the wilderness. There was every kind of noise out in the woods, but mostly just the colt shifting about and taking deep, sighing breaths. I jumped every time he moved and expected to see a shape form up out of the darkness and loom and then come at me, and the least threatening thing I imagined was the young bear. I tried laying my father's knife naked-bladed on the ground beside me and practiced reaching to its elkhorn handle without looking. More often than not, I grabbed a handful of dirt. So I just took the knife up and held the handle tight and pointed the upcurved tip of blade at the dark.

Shopkeep, I thought. And maybe I said it aloud.

There were a right smart of boys my age sleeping in houses under a big pile of quilts with a mother and father bedded nearby. A great majority of boys were not squatting alone in the dark with a knife in their fist, without a soul in the world much concerned whether or not they made it alive until dawn lit up the east. I told myself that I would bury the knife deep into whatever crossed the edge of firelight.

—There won't be any call for Wait ever again, I said to the night.

A HARD RAIN fell during the early morning, driven on a high wind. But it blew from a favorable quarter, and the shallow ledge kept me dry. I slept many hours after the first grey of morning. When I stirred shivering from under the blanket, I found a blue day already under way and Waverley gone and my panniers as well. My budget, still tied to the rope, lay sodden on the ground, pasted with the blown petals of dogwood blossoms.

I rushed around all in a panic, looking in the brush for the colt or for a great bloody pile of wolf kill. But nothing presented itself.

And then I went looking along the trail for tracks and the story of theft or abandonment they might tell. But again, nothing was revealed. Any marks of hoof or paw or moccasin that might have been were all washed away. I remember having a great desire to yell at the top of my voice.

Help, I suppose, would have been the word. But I swallowed that impulse back into my chest and instead put two fingers to the front of my mouth and whistled loud and long, hoping the colt would whinny from down the trail and come trotting back. I did it again and again until my lips and cheeks were numb, and then I stopped and sat amid my bedding and looked at the white ashes of the fire, still smoldering and smoking.

I sat thusly through much of the afternoon. I cried some, thinking that if the normal ties and accouterments of human beings kept falling away from me at the rate they had been doing lately, I'd soon become not much different from that little bear out wandering alone in the woods. I came to the conclusion that I was too old to throw myself on the mercy of the wild and become a wolf child. There's a time in infancy when they will take you in, offer up a dark teat to your human mouth, and raise you in accord with their own lights, which would be both lovely and brutal. But I'd long since passed that time. Now wolves would give me a hard look, allow me one step to turn and run, then come charging to bring me down.

I looked through the gap in the trees and studied the view west. Little tatters of fog hung on the mountainsides here and there. The air was damp and fresh. It was a big green world, brightening up for spring. Another country lay out ahead of me. Blank as could be.

I spread what was left of my kit before me on the ground. I had my budget, the map and key, my long wool coat, my bedding, and the kettle and nearly a pound of coffee grounds that I'd kept out of the panniers the evening before. Some oats and two books wrapped by my own hands in an oilcloth bundle. A collection of Arthur tales and *The Aeneid*.

I looked around and all there was to add to this pathetic array was the sorry little turtle-hull saddle. I went and threw it off into the brush and figured the porcupines were welcome to eat it for the salt of horse sweat if they cared to.

That would have been a fine time to meet up with one of those magic beggars from the old Jack stories. Little wizened men who, if you give them a penny or a crust of bread instead of a clout on the head, will hand you an item—a basket or tablecloth or bowl—that produces a lavish spread of food on request. Like a big portable Sunday dinner that never ends. Fill Bowl Fill. But no such beggar presented himself.

As I've said, it is so often the case in life that you have but two choices before you, or at least that's all I've frequently been able to see. That day, it came down to these two: keep going and hope to hit the trade post before I starved or go back to the farm.

The farm was several days of backtracking away, and in the end I'd fetch up on my aunt's front porch. But it was not as if I could take back my old life. That was over. She'd just run me out into the woods again. So I spent one more knifepoint night under the ledge, and then the next morning I put my budget on my back and kept going west, hoping to find a way through the woods.

2

I'M LOOKING FOR A BAY COLT, I SAID. HE'S GOT AN INSIDE CALKIN broken off his right front shoe. I've been following after him for some time, but I can't see him here. I gestured to the cut-up roadway. Have you seen men go by with a string of horses?

—Might have, the girl said. A day or two ago. Might have seen them going up the river to where they always run their horses.

She squatted in the road drawing pictures with a sharp stick in the dirt, her dingy skirt draping about her feet. The girl did not even bother to look up at me, so about all I saw was dark hair falling to either side of her face from a strict white part. Scratched in the dirt around her were the heads of horses, their flowing manes and flared nostrils and arched necks thick with cords of muscle.

—I'm not to go there, she said. You'll have to find your own way.

—I didn't ask you to guide me, I said. Directions is all I'm wanting.

—It's pony-club trash stays there.

Everybody east of the Nation despised the pony clubs, which had been going on since shortly after the Revolution. It was what the young Indian men did when war became something they were not allowed to compete in anymore. They'd steal horses east of the boundary line and run them across the Nation, where their own law applied, and then sell them out in Tennessee or Alabama or Mississippi to white people not inclined to ask very many questions about the provenance of a fine horse offered for sale at a bargain price. At that point, the pony clubbers would steal some more horses and run them back in the other direction.

—How do I get to this place? I said.

—Three turnings from here. Left at a fork in the road, right at a bend in the river. Then start looking for a old track commencing next to a big hemlock and running hard uphill.

THE CABIN WAS set all around with mud and stumps. Set picturesquely atop a bluff overlooking the midsized river and a distant range of mountains. It was nothing special, an unpainted one-room dwelling lidded with curling grey shakes. At one end, a chimney of smooth stones hauled all the way up from the river.

Out in front, a man was digging a hole. He had been working some length of time, for he was in so deep all I could see was the top of his bald head. At rhythmic intervals, the metal end of a shovel sent sprays of red dirt flying onto a conical pile. I could hear loud voices and laughter coming from inside the house.

I walked up to the hole and looked down at the man. In there with him, he had a ladder of peeled poles lashed together with rawhide strips.

—Hey sir, I said.

The man stopped digging and turned his face up to me, but he didn't say anything. His face was round and white looking up out of that dark hole.

—I'm trying to find a colt that got away from me, I said. A bay, name of Waverley. Can any of you here help me?

—They's a bay colt around back, the man said. But I don't exactly recall him saying what his name was.

I walked around the house, and there was a stock pen with a dozen ill-sorted horses standing hock-deep in black mud. There was not the first sign of fodder, and the horses looked to have given up hoping for any. Waverley stood with his head hanging over the top rail looking at me. I went to him and started to scratch his ears but he pinned them back and wouldn't commit to recognizing me. I stood awhile figuring what to do, my eyes unfocused, looking toward a slatted springhouse beyond the pen and then off across the valley to the mountains. I went back around the house.

The man was digging again, and I stood at the lip of the hole and said, That's him. Who do I talk to?

The man stopped digging and climbed out of the hole, and when he did I could see that he lacked a part of one leg. Foot and shinbone gone. He walked on a wood peg fitted to his stub with a cup of leather and ties of rawhide strips. His good foot was stained with clay up above the anklebone, and the peg was muddy higher than that. He wore pants turned up to the knee but no shirt, and his shallow chest and upper arms were white as pork fat, and his forearms and handbacks were walnut brown. Despite his otherwise thinness, the man had a melon-shaped belly that lapped over his pantwaist. He stood looking at me, leaning on the handle to his shovel.

—Inside, he said. You need to talk to Featherstone. But I'd bet they's a right smart number of bay colts in the world that ain't yours at all.

—Is there any dinner in there? I said. I'm on my way to run a trade post in a place called Wayah and I've not eaten today.

—We've long since eat, the man said. I don't know if they've left anything.

He threw down the shovel and scrubbed his hands against each other to clean them.

—I'm not asking for charity, I said. I'd be willing to pay for my dinner.

—Oh, you'll pay, the man said.

I stood looking down into the hole. Red water was collecting in its bottom. Well or grave or what? I wondered.

We walked around back to the kitchen door. The man stopped and pointed down. Look at that, he said. That's a handy thing.

I examined the doorway and had seen such ingenuity before. It was a timepiece of sorts, a step farther back into the primitive than a sundial. A gouged mark in a floor puncheon. When the line between sun and shadow from the doorframe fell on the mark, it was noontide. All other hours were subject to speculation. It was not currently noon was all the advice the clock offered. I could hardly imagine how such a device might be called handy, for a similarly reliable report on the progress of the day could be had just by looking up.

The man walked on across the threshold, his peg beating like a little hammer on the floor. He disappeared into the darkness.

I stood at the door to the room waiting for my eyes to adjust, and a voice from inside said, What are you standing there for?

I said, I'm waiting for my eyes to adjust.

Another voice with a strong accent I could not identify said, What means adjust?

I reckoned it was a rhetorical question and held my peace until I could see a half dozen men sitting at a round table playing cards. Two women in calico with their hair loose lounged all tangled together on a pallet by the fire, flipping through a limp-paged book and laughing at its contents. The one-legged man hunkered on the edge of the pallet with the women.

I could not tell what any of them were. African. Indian. Whiteman. Spaniard. Nearly all of them wore moccasins, but none of them looked particularly Indian in feature or hue, though most of them were swarthy-complected, and some had straight black hair and some had curly black hair. Nearly all of them wore hunting shirts and leather leggings, and two of them had slitted earlobes. Some talked in English, and a few spoke in an Indian language, and one of them, upon losing at a hand of cards, swore in words that might have been West African, for I had once heard an old white-haired man curse in a similar way, and West Africa was where he said he had been stolen from as a boy. One man with skin as white as mine had a peculiar hairstyle with a wide border shaved bare above his ears and the upper parts grown out long and greased, standing in peaks like meringue and mostly grey but for a crest that was still reddish as the ruff down a boar's back running from his forehead to a brief plaited queue at the nape of his neck. A hammered silver ring pierced one of his ears.

They struck me as a bunch of people who did not know or care what race they owed allegiance to. I reckoned this was a place where blood quantum held lighter sway than in the outer world, and I judged that being a whiteman here might not be as great an advantage as I generally counted on.

The one-legged man looked at me and bobbed his head toward the table and said, That there's Featherstone.

He meant their obvious leader, the one with the hair-do. He was a man of about middle age, beginning to go stout through the barrel of his chest. He had thick freckled forearms haloed with ginger hairs, blunt hands with bulgy knuckles punctuating his short fingers. Every line of his face—eyebrows to eyes to cheekbones to mouth—was turned down. He had a thin strong nose and a high forehead and a chaw of tobacco lumped in his cheek. At close intervals he spit juice directly onto the floor. His clothes didn't give away much. He had on a collarless white linen hunting shirt buttoned to the neck, the cuffs rolled to the elbow. A red kerchief and a necklace of curved black bear claws shining across his chest.

—I need to talk to somebody about my colt that's out in your pen, I said.

Nobody even looked up from studying their hands. They were busy discarding and drawing and arranging their cards in tight artistic fans and holding their faces inert so as not to give away any of their thoughts.

I said, That bay Waverley colt's mine. Out back in your pen.

I waited, and when the hand finished, Featherstone put down his cards and said, Son, ownership of a horse is a thorny thing to establish anywhere. Here, it's well-nigh impossible. And besides, none of us is talking horses right now. That business has concluded for the day. We're playing cards.

I said, When could we talk horses?

Featherstone said, Regular business hours.

Another man said, That's noon of a morning till one of a afternoon, with time out for dinner. But we'd admire for you to join us at table if you've got any money for us to take off you.

Two or three of them laughed. And then one of them shuffled the cards in a showy precise way. He started dealing out another hand, the cards flying fast and sequential around the table, each card landing in perfect alignment with its predecessor until little discrete piles lay in front of the arrayed players. It took less time to do it than for me to tell it now.

I eased up closer to watch them play. They had a game of Lanterloo going, but they soon came to the conclusion that the doubling of stakes at every hand allowed for a loss of money faster than was strictly entertaining, and Featherstone declared that all the intricate fooling with the ivory counters was womanish.

So they switched to Put, and everything slowed down and concentrated.

After a while of watching, I said to the room in general, Have you got something to eat? Pinto beans? Cold cornbread or just anything?

One of the women on the pallet looked up from the book and said, See what's in the pie safe.

I went over to it and opened the punched-tin door and discovered a bowl of something grey and greasy and cold. It had set solid. A square-handled pewter spoon stood straight up in it.

I looked at the women and said, What is this?

I thought Featherstone was only paying attention to the cards, but he said, Groundhog meat and cabbage, with cow's-milk and hog-grease gravy, thickened with flour and the mashed little brain from the groundhog.

I tried to stir it with the spoon, but it rotated in the bowl as one chunk.

—Anything else? I said.

—Set that bowl by the fire and it'll loosen up after a while, Featherstone said.

—Is there not anything else? I said.

—They's some liquor in that pail, the one-legged man said.

It was more a tub, half full of greenish corn liquor. A tin dipper with a crook at the end of its handle descended into it. A brown pottery crock of springwater sat nearby. I knew that the water was meant to cut the liquor with, but the crock was full and gave the impression of long disuse.

—How often do you have to refill this water crock? I said.

No one even looked up. Featherstone lifted the corner of his mouth. Not another feature of his face changed. I understood that slight motion to stand in place of a grin. I dipped into the corn liquor and took my first swig of spirits, and it was like fire coals melted into a cup.

I asked the woman on the pallet what she was reading, and she said it wasn't her book, it was Featherstone's. She couldn't understand more than a few words of it. She tossed the book to me, and the first lines that struck my eye had to do with white bile and black bile and other such internal fluids, and when I flipped to the title page it read *The Anatomy of Melancholy.* I put the book down and went back to the card table.

A man in a turban, a black tailcoat, and fringed buckskin leggings stood from his stool and said, Here, boy. They might as well take your money as mine for a while.

I sat down at the table, and a player with his back to the western window—so that he had no more definition than a silhouette cut from black paper—said in a flat voice, You not planning to gamble on credit, are you?

All I could see of him in particular was that he lacked a hand on his left side. Just a blunt stub sticking out from his coatsleeve. I was thinking, I am in a land of partial folk.

But what I said was, No sir. I've got cash money. What game are we playing?

—We're switching to Blind-and-Straddle.

It was a game I knew and liked and had amassed great numbers of peppermint sticks playing. Featherstone, having the eldest hand, threw down a blind bet before the deal. He pitched out a little coin of some currency and denomination I did not know. It had a many-pointed figure like a child's idea of the sun on the tail face of it. Then the dealer shuffled and started tossing, and I found myself sitting at the round table with a pretty good hand of tallowy-feeling playing cards spread in my fist.

The doubling straddle bets that followed involved a great deal of talk and complicated agreements on currency exchange, since they were made in the form of several varieties of gold and silver coins from various states and nations. There were doubloons, guineas, livres, pistareens, florins, ducats, Dutch dog dollars, Scotch marks, Portuguese half joes, Peruvian crossdollars, and even one old smooth-worn bezant. The coinage of all those wide-flung nations converged at this frontier gaming house by some unimaginable but mighty power of commerce, traveling on long and crooked trails. Many of the gold coins had pie pieces sheared from them, and this led to disagreements over the fractional values of the missing slices. Also, bets were made with such slices, and then the argument became whether the fractions were nearer to eight or to four. Featherstone was the ultimate arbiter of exchange, and no one argued with his conversions, no matter how outrageously favorable to him they seemed.

When it came my turn to bet, I had little idea what a suitable amount might be. I reached in my moneypurse and separated the Georgia scrip from the paper with the chicken recipe on it. I laid down two of the paper dollars, and someone laughed and another two or three grunted disfavorable judgment. The silhouetted man said everybody knew how Georgia money had set the current standard of worthlessness and that I would have gotten about as far in the game if I *had* tried to play on credit. I picked the paper up and jingled my aunt's five silver pieces in my moneypurse and everybody settled down. I bet one of the coins and one man objected, but Featherstone picked it up and looked at it and pitched it back down into the pot and it rang against its brethren.

His verdict was that it would do, and the game went on.

When the hand neared a conclusion, four of my five hard dollars lay on the table, and I reckoned I was about to be done with gaming for the day. But when we showed our cards, I took the pot and they all laughed.

The lessons of the Manx schoolmaster stood me well in playing cards, and I kept on winning through the afternoon, and soon they all quit laughing. Featherstone and the one-armed man were the most regular defeatees. Piles of coins in confusing denominations rose in front of me, and I began worrying that the other players would decide to kill me and take my winnings and throw my body off the bluff into the river for the suckerfish to eat. So I kept close counsel. Refused provocation and sought to give none. When my money mounted into unseemly piles, I shoved handfuls of coins into my pockets to keep from offering too much reminder of my good fortune.

Twilight fell and the room became so dark we could not make out the marks on the cards. The first mosquitoes of spring were singing thick around our ears. Finally one of the women rose from the pallet on the floor and shoveled hot coals from the hearth into an iron pot and set it under the table and heaped doty wood on the coals to make smoke. Then she went about the motions of letting there be light. She stobbed a long stick in a crack between floorboards and angled it over the table and took strips of pork fat and wrapped them in loose-wove linen rags and tied them to the end of the stick. She blew up coals in the hearth and caught a broomstraw alight and used it to set the pork strips on fire. It smelled like breakfast. The air all around the table was thick with the rank black smoke from the smoldering doty wood, and the little flame from the pork lantern threw a halo around itself. All the things in the smoky shadows were just murk. For all her effort, the woman had created about an equal balance of light and dark. I still could hardly tell which spots on the cards were black and which were red, but at least the mosquitoes were driven back into the night.

THE TABLE BY now was made up of me, the one-handed man, three rivermen, and Featherstone. The rivermen had straggled in just before dark, bursting in the door all hilarious and blowing hard from the climb up the hill. The thighs of their pants dark and greasy, a stink of fish and brown water about them. The one-legged man and one of the women sat in straight chairs by the fire, drinking and giggling. The other woman still lay on the pallet asleep, her face to the wall and the dingy heels to her feet hanging off the side.

As the game went on, I noted that for any number of reasons of personal history and local custom, the other men treated Featherstone with a deference I found vexing. A lot of it was physical fear, for if there was any truth amid all the tales passing around that table, Featherstone had left a bloody trail behind him since boyhood. Also, they acted toward him the way my uncle did around the two or three rich men in our county. The cardplayers called him Squire Featherstone and Boss Featherstone and Chief Featherstone. But I couldn't square their deference with my current surroundings.

—Is this your house? I said to Featherstone.

Featherstone didn't answer, but the one-handed man snorted and said, He ain't got but three or four. This is just his hunting cabin. He comes out here to play Indian. He's built a plantation out on the Nation the match of any whiteman's in Georgia. Big house and slaves and fields of market crops and everything.

I reckoned that answer missed satisfying my curiosity, but I played on silently.

The men kept calling him Chief and Boss and Squire, and then at one point in the evening, one of the rivermen called him King Featherstone. I laughed, but when I looked around the table it appeared that no one else found the title funny.

So he's king here, I thought. And the more I thought about the big man, the more I grew dark-minded, for the older men I knew had fought a damn hard war to get shed of kings forever. And they were very convictional in their opinion that if the English wanted to cut the head off their king and then turn right around and bring kings back, that was their sorry business. Here, we didn't countenance kings and, God willing, never would.

I was just a boy, but the way I saw the table was that Featherstone and I were the major figures. The rivermen and the one-handed man were mere nothing. Spectators. I might add here that I had reached some nether end of exile and desperation and had been dipping into the green liquor now and then, and it was somewhat shaping my opinions to suit itself.

EVERYBODY ELSE HAD been dipping into the tub as well, and they suffered from equally clouded thinking. Featherstone was drunk to the point that he had gone past stupor back to strange lucidity. And when he reached that point, he began looking for a fight. That much was evident even in the provoking way he glared at the other players and the way he handled his cards and threw them down as if wanting to throw them in his opponents' faces. Much in evidence at his belt was a long cap-and-ball pistol of scrolled silver metal, with fancy scrimshawed grips worn bone-white in some places from handling and in other places greasy brown from hand dirt. It was pretty, but the pretty ones will kill you just as dead as the ugly. He spent a great deal of time making a show of adjusting its position against his groin.

At one point, he said he had probably put down ten or fifteen men more satisfactory than any of us. One more wouldn't signify.

At another point, deep in the night, one of the rivermen fell asleep with his head on his forearm but still holding his cards. Featherstone sorted through the deck and put four kings and a three in the man's hand, and four aces and a jack in his own. Then he kicked the man awake under the table and said, Either get to playing or quit the game.

The man roused a little and itched his scalp and studied his cards. He became suddenly alert. He bet big and everybody else soon folded but for Featherstone. The betting between them grew quite large, and in the end of course Featherstone won.

The man sat thinking a minute, and then he pulled a pistol and said, That's every penny I've got in the world and I might as well be dead without it. I hate to have to do it, but I'm going to kill you if you don't give it back.

Featherstone said, Calm down. There's no call for gunplay just because fate holds you in contempt. But I'll do this for you. On the next hand, I'll put up everything I've won off of you against that old worn-out pistol of yours.

—Hell, the man said. That sounds more than fair to me.

They went about dealing the cards, and Featherstone put down his bet, a pile of hard money glinting in the dim light.

The man sat dazed and unclear as to his next move. Featherstone said, Well, put your bet in the pot.

The man laid his pistol down on the mongrel pile of currency, and just as soon as his hand was back to his cards, Featherstone grabbed the pistol and covered the man and told him to get gone or be shot.

The man said, Yes sir. And I apologize for my behavior. And then he went out the door.

WE PLAYED ON long into the night. The women slept like a pair of puppies on the straw tick in the corner. At the table, money changed hands over and over, but I won steadily, and Featherstone lost. He became more and more agitated as the play went on. He rose once and briefly pistol-whipped one of the rivermen for winning a tightly contested hand.

In a dark hour before dawn, Featherstone put down a big gold guinea as a late straddle over a pile of Spanish and French silver. He said, Whoever picks up this guinea, I'll blow out his goddamn brains and leave him lay. He pulled out his artistic pistol and set it on the table in front of him and put his finger to the tip of the barrel and gave it a spin so that the bore and grip swapped ends a half dozen times.

—Who will tempt the wheel of fate? he said.

The atmosphere in the room was suddenly all hush and gravity. Everyone, Featherstone included, sat looking at the pistol as if it was a magic thing, even more potent than a cudgel in a fairy tale to which one could say Beat Stick Beat and have it smite enemies to their knees.

—He's powerful drunk, but that don't mean he won't do it, the one-handed man said. He folded his cards and rose from the table. He walked to the liquor tub and took a dip.

The rivermen at the table looked at each other and then folded and rose as well. Their thought was to leave the pot to Featherstone as tribute. I took it that this was a known ploy of Featherstone's when he had been losing. There were just the two of us left. The other men stood watching.

—You playing on? Featherstone said.

I reasoned that a wise man would walk away. But I was half drunk for the first time in my life and tired, and I was looking at three queens, a king, and a deuce. I firmly understood that combination to be a pretty good hand under almost any circumstance. And I was weary of Featherstone's ways. Something made me throw down the deuce and draw from the deck.

—What manner of fool are you? Featherstone said.

I sat looking at a second king. I fanned my cards on the table, face up. All around, everybody's expression changed.

—Now's when you lay down your hand, I said.

Featherstone spread his cards. A pair of fours.

Featherstone looked at his cards and then at mine. He started laughing.

—Why, hellfire, he said. You're the first one of these hens that ever called me.

I raked over the various specie with the crook of my hand and wrist. It was a bright and lively pile indeed.

—It's the rule of the game. You have to give me a shot at recouping, Featherstone said.

—Well, I said.

—We could play the game where if I win I kill you, and if you win you kill me.

—I thought that's what we just played, I said. And if I understand this game right, the object is to win something you want. I don't want to kill you.

—All right. How about the one where if I win you lose everything you've got, all your winnings, that horse you say is yours, the clothes on your back if I have a mind to take them. And if you win you get a girl of mine for yours. I've got one to spare. She's outside in the springhouse, for she didn't care to expose herself to this trash.

—Your deal, I said.

AN HOUR LATER I walked toward the springhouse. The narrow rectangle straddled the springhead and the first ten feet of its stream. It was built open-slatted to let air move through it. Candlelight shone yellow through the slats until I was near enough for the sound of my footsteps to be heard inside. Then the candle was blown out and only the moon shone down. I opened the door and stepped in. Shelves on one side filled with brown crockery. Milk jugs sitting up to their shoulders in cool water. The spring rose up from its deep source and smelled of wet earth and the stones at the center of the world. Whatever you believe and whatever god you pray to, a place where clean water rises from the earth is someway sacred.

But overlying that holy fragrance, and at great odds with it, was the clabbered smell of milk and cheese. Moonlight fell in bars through the slatted walls, and all I could see was the form of a girl in a loose shift dress. A table and chair, a book and a smoking dead candle. There was no color to anything, just the blue of moonlight and the black of shadow. The girl took a step back, away from me, and the bars of moonlight and dark moved up her form. I could see her pale bare feet below the dress. And then her wrists and hands, but not her face. Her head was down, hair forward.

I didn't know how to account for myself. Saying *I won you from your daddy in a card game* seemed a poor start.

The barred light glinted on silver bracelets circling her thin wrists. The only sound was the water rising from the seams in earth and the bracelets ringing against one another as she took another step away from me.

I was not a tall boy, and the hem of my long wool coat nearly swept the ground. It was warm and stout with a deep collar and wide lapels so that when I buttoned it to the top, it covered my face almost to the eyes.

It still had some of the lanolin in the wool and would turn a light rain, though in the sun it smelled strongly of sheep.

I'm cold, she said. She was shivering, and her silver bracelets chimed faintly.

I unbuttoned the coat and opened it wide. My winnings jingled in the pockets. I said, Here.

The girl stepped in close to me and I closed the coat around us. My arms circled her, and I put my hands on her back, the points of her thin shoulders, and then her narrow waist, though I could hardly feel a thing about her through the thick wool. She stood against me with her arms straight at her sides. She leaned her hard forehead against my own, for we were of a similar size. We stood together shivering. I could smell her scent, some attar or fragrant water. Lavender. I held her and it was like falling down a well.

I said, I've been wanting to do this for a long time.

At the moment that sentence fell spang from my mouth, I knew it was both foolish and true, though neither served as excuse for the other.

She said the obvious. You just met me.

—Nevertheless, I said.

—Nevertheless, she said.

I said, You're mine.

Of course, that girl was Claire. But I was not to know her name until some years later. I could have stood there and held her forever.

Except for my little sick mother, I'd had no experience with love in my life, neither incoming nor outgoing. Lately, since love had seemed an impossibility, I had steeled myself against it. But I held Claire, and that was that forever. Something was sealed. Desire abides. It is all people have that stands proof against time. Everything else rots.

She turned her head away and looked through the slats to the round moon shining through. She said, Wind Moon.

There was a sound outside. Stealthy steps in the dark. A number of people sneaking.

She said, You better run.

I was not at all ready to run, but she broke away and shoved me toward the gap at the low end of the springhouse where the water flowed out. Someone burst through the door. I scrabbled on hands and knees in the water, tiny gritted stones shifting under my palms as I bent toward the low sill.

A hand seized my collar. I wriggled under the framing, and the grey coat stripped off me like skin from a skeleton. I ran, zagging among dark grabbing figures until I snatched my budget by its straps at full speed like a horseman at a gander pull. Various confused bawls and yaps, the sounds of clamorous pursuit, faded behind me. I more fell than ran down the bluff toward the river, a dirty plummet broken by saplings, shrubbery, weeds, and wildflowers. And when I hit bottom, I ran lovelorn up the river road, my back to the grey dawn.

3

I WANDERED FOR DAYS THROUGH THE MOUNTAINS, FOLLOWING whatever paths led west, trying to remember my uncle's directions. I walked horse trails, footpaths, the runways of deer, and the remnants of buffalo trails nearly as faint as the sign ghosts leave in their passage through the night air. Not knowing exactly where I was going, I suspended expectations on time of arrival.

I bemoaned the loss of the girl, my horse, my coat, and my money. I didn't sleep well and had taken a cramping stomach ailment that frequently left me squatting in the woods, shitting and admiring the scenery. I was wrung out by the third day, twisted down to almost nothing. I thought I was hopelessly lost, though I kept walking a grown-over scratch through the forest so faint it might have been imaginary. It went climbing up a bold creek filled with green boulders and white water. A severe-looking dog emerged from the woods and crossed the creek and stood staring at me as if it expected something. I guessed it to be an Irish wolfdog or some like breed. Wirehaired and long-legged and colored like smoke. It stood panting in the trail with a ring of old grey hemp rope at its neck showing it had not always run wild. I said, This is a public courseway. You go whichever direction you will.

The dog looked at me as if I hadn't spoken, and I figured he was probably Indian and was unaware of the English language. When I set out walking, he fell in behind me like we were travel partners.

TWO DAYS LATER, I didn't have to ask if I had reached my destination. You couldn't miss it. The building stood just back from the wagon road. And there was a sign, a grey slab of shingle nailed to a stob pitched at a leisurely angle to plumb, big writing in red faded paint saying STORE. Which suggested the existence of customers. There was apparently a community nearby, but you'd never know it by looking. This was just the merest gesture of an outpost, a place marker set down in the wilderness.

The trade post sat on a little level patch of ground with a bold creek running loud to one side and big dark hemlocks growing serene and gloomy all around. It had been out of business since shortly after Christmas, and the board shutters on the windows were closed and an iron padlock big as a beef heart hung rusty from a hasp and loop. The first sprigs of ragweed grew from the packed dirt in front of the three steps to the porch.

Nevertheless, for all the apparent abandonment, two old men sat on the porch in straight chairs as if they expected business to continue any minute. One looked to be a full-blood Cherokee, and he sat with the chair tipped back on its hind legs and its post ends propped against the log wall, and one of his long legs stretched out across the floorboards and the other hooked by its heel to the bottom chair rung. He was looking right at me, and that was the first time I laid eyes on Bear. The other man was white and he was dozing, chin to chest, the slanting afternoon sun shining off his bald pate. He wore a grey wool coat thick as a saddle pad that appeared to be mine. It fell around his chair like a disorganized shadow. The man dreamed doglike, whining and grunting, his eyeballs jigging about under the lids, one foot thumping the floorboards.

Waverley stood off to the side in a disused corral with a pole run-in shed. He had his head down grazing on new grass, and I stood amazed, wondering how he had found his way here before me.

Bear looked at me without changing his posture or any other manifestation of his thoughts, as if twenty lost boys a day passed by this porch and one more was not worth even a quizzical expression. Bear wore his hair long and cut blunt at his shoulders, and it was about half grey, back then, but full to the temples. He had on hunting clothes. Long linen shirt, deerleather leggings. His moccasins were laced with horsehair, eyelet holes in-wrought with quills of feathers. Beaded bracelets, large rings in his ears. And a rifle, shot pouch, and powder horn arrayed at the porch rail.

The dog went straight to the porch and flopped down beside Bear's chair. He just touched the dog briefly between the ears, and it began wagging its hard tail against the floor like beating a drumhead with a stick. The other man came awake and threw back his head and ranted awhile in Gaelic, yelling out what sounded like curses and threats until spittle drops hung in his yellow chin whiskers. I'd heard the old language all my life, for our county was full of displaced Scots who still spoke it and a few who even thought in it. Such a great number of people got letters from across the sea that one of the qualifications for postmaster was to be able to read at least a little Gaelic in order to deliver the mail.

I thought it impolite to interrupt such a fervent tirade, so I just nodded a greeting to the big Cherokee and then sat on the middle porch step and figured to keep close counsel and listen first before I declared myself.

The Scotsman switched his language to English and began talking about Culloden, a story I had heard all my life in various forms. His voice fell into a solemn minor-key tone, as if the tale he told was a myth of origin, an explanation of how he came to be where he was, as I later heard the Cherokee tell of how Waterbeetle daubed up mud from the bottom of the ocean to make earth and how Thunder first made fire in the hollow of a sycamore tree. The man counted out in great detail the clans all arrayed on the field of Culloden and the colors they wore, noting the particular plaiding of the first line of Highlanders, the Camerons and Stuarts and Frasers. He squealed and wheezed to represent the bray of bagpipes, and he named the tunes they had played that day and described the brave men, greatly outnumbered but wild to fight, howling their battle cry. Then he told of how they scrugged their bonnets down low on their brows and made a headlong rush at the Angles and Saxons, saying it was exactly as Celts had done against the Romans at Telamon two thousand years before. And with like result. Heroes numberless killed down by cowardly and alien swords and, at the end of the day, their heads on pikes. And in the years following, the culture in disarray, the people forced into greater pilgrimages than even Moses and his Israelites made. The man spoke haltingly, almost bogging down at the end. As if the enemy language resisted him, like fording a river and trying to hold a line against the push of water.

Bear sat looking off into the distance, a long view through a cut between layers of mountains unfolding down a narrow blue valley. He nodded as if approving of the tale of struggle and loss, but he didn't say a word. The Scotsman rubbed his face with both his hands, and then he fell asleep again.

I said, Just so nobody gets the wrong idea, that colt is mine. And that coat too.

It was one of the few times I ever remember hearing Bear speak English, and he later claimed I must have been confused. But I remember clear as day him saying, Well, this dog's mine.

I said, Fine with me.

I dug through my budget and found the key with the heart-shaped butt. I put the business end in the keyhole and turned it. There was a simple rasping mechanical click and the lock sprang open like something alive. I swung the hasp and opened the door.

With the shutters closed, the place was lit only by the rectangular fall of light through the entryway. The room ahead was dim as the dens thieves are said to frequent in romance tales. The dusty floorboards gapped wide enough for snakes to rise through without impediment. I stood blinking a minute. Then I shuffled ahead, a hand held palm forward at hip level to keep from tripping over something. The smells of wood ash, cured meat, clabbered milk, pickle vinegar, old cheese, hemp rope, moldy harness leather, badly cured hides beginning to rot. Altogether, I thought, it smelled like death. Even before my eyes had opened up to the dark, I was appalled at where I found myself. This was not a store, it was some confabulation of smokehouse and henhouse and springhouse. Shithouse too, going by the smell.

Bear came in with an armload of firewood and got a yellow blaze going in the cold black fireplace.

He disappeared into the darkness, and I could hear him rattling about in the stock. He came back into the light carrying a bottle of dark amber Tennessee whiskey and a shot glass. He dug into a pouch at his waist and turned up a palmful of gunspalls and various coinage, including a George II farthing and a copper elephant halfpenny from the days of the Carolina proprietors. He set a coin on the counter and held up his whole hand of spread fingers to signify the number five. Then he poured out an amber shot full to the brim and held it to the firelight to admire its color a moment before drinking it down. When he had done that four more times, he sat by the yellow fire and began looking into it as if a scene from an engrossing play were unfolding inside. And not a comedy, from the look on his face.

So I'm bartender here too, I thought.

Bear started talking, and it sounded like he was telling a story, but of course I could not understand a word. After he finished, he stood and made some vague gesture of farewell and went to the porch and roused the Scotsman and peeled the coat off him and handed it to me. He gathered his weaponry, and the pilgrim Scotsman shouldered his pack. The dog yawned and stretched. The three of them went off down the trail, the dog running out ahead as if hunting, some brilliant thread of scent spooling ahead of him. I shook the coat, and the pockets made one faint jingle, a pair of coins representing the remainder of my winnings. I stuck my hand in the pocket and found a folded paper, a note in a big flowing hand. *We're even. Featherstone.*

—

IT DID NOT take me long to survey the stock. The store was hardly bigger than the parlor room of my aunt's house. What I found was mainly confusing, for I was accustomed to town stores at least partially full of manufactured goods, the shelves and cabinets stacked with tins and glass bottles and waxed-paper packages, a few of them from as far away as England and France. Bright printed labels telling what the things they contained were called and who had produced them, and remarks on their superiority to all other like goods, and little badges and devices, each unique, so that even the unlettered might know them when they saw them. Paper wrappers of soaps and candies, claiming that they were the sort enjoyed by the royal family.

Here, though, I found woefully little such stock from the outer world, and almost all of it was simple. Bolts of gingham and calico, plowpoints, bottles of ink, fiddle strings and fishhooks, packets of steel needles, gunpowder and flints, bar lead and bullet molds, axeheads, blank books and wool blankets, laudanum and coffee beans, pistols and palm-leaf hats and horse fleams. Of particular interest were the apparent anomalies for such a wilderness post, the sad commercial miscalculations of some previous shopkeep. A fine china tea service and several tins of rich-smelling black tea. A tarnished brass trumpet from which I could produce only a prolonged farting sound. Inexplicably, a full case of claret from Château Latour dating back almost to the previous century, which I remember only because later in life that is the red wine I most favored. And, most welcome, a little shelf of books that had apparently been unsuccessfully offered up to the buying public for some time, their brown leather bindings having blossomed with grey spots of mildew in the damp air.

The most part of the post's contents lacked any hope of name or emblem. Things were what they were, and you knew it or didn't. Rush baskets of muddy eggs all gone bad. Dried pinto beans. Dank earthen crocks of cloudy vinegar wherein shelled eggs half floated. Wheels of cheese grey with fuzz. Lard or tallow or some other fragrant grease packed in paired hog bladders and hanging from rafters. Baskets heaped with the forked roots of the magic ginseng. In one corner a tall pile of cured deerhides lay one atop another like a deck of cards swollen from being left out in the rain. Everything was some shade of grey or brown, and nearly everything smelled. I felt some other old world intersecting suddenly with the familiar.

I searched until I found a sack of oats and went out to grain and water Waverley. Whatever adventures he'd had in the past days, he looked none the worse for wear. I took the armload of books out onto the porch and wiped them clean with a rag and rubbed beeswax into the leather until the books looked better than new, dark as mahogany, the gold lettering of their titles shining like fire coals.

Morte d'Arthur. Tristan and Isolde. A Midsummer Night's Dream and *The Tempest* in individual volumes, and another thick close-printed volume containing all the tragedies. *Gulliver's Travels. Don Quixote* as reduced into English by Mr. Smollett. And Dr. Johnson's *Shorter Dictionary*, which included as an appendix an alphabetical account of the heathen deities.

When the books were clean, I lined them back on their shelf and figured they were about all the companionship I would have for a while.

I pared the mold from a big cheese and ate the inner slices with withered nubs of sweet dried fruit, the origin of which I could not identify though I guessed they might once have been plums or very old peaches. Long before it grew dark, I went and looked at the little sleeping room in the back. A full-grown man could have stood in the center and touched each wall with his fingertips. The narrow rope bedstead had a sour-smelling and brown-stained ticking stuffed with something that exhaled a deep animal must when I pressed my hand into it. I judged that I would not sleep a wink in this terrifying hole. I took blankets and a pillow out to the front room and made me down a lonesome pallet on the floor in front of the fire. Candles of tallow or beeswax being inordinately expensive and the woodpile being high, I supposed I would have only the hearth to read by.

I sat on the porch and observed the failure of the day with dread until it was nearly gone to black. Then I stretched out on the pallet and began reading the dictionary, taking it very slowly and forming each word whole in my mind in order to memorize it and also to conserve my few books into an uncertain future. I read going front to back, as if a compelling though knotty narrative were unfolding among the definitions and their rigid order. The firelight fell pleasantly golden on the page. It was a cool night, and the heat banking off the hearthstones felt good against the damp and chill of the cove. The sounds of wood combustion and the fall of water over creek rocks and the calls of night birds and the first spring peepers calmed my loneliness some. And really, what better company of a dark night than one of the smart dead Englishmen of yore? I just had to take care, as the fire burned low and I held the book closer and closer to the flames, not to drift off and drop it into the coals and send all those premium words up the chimney in a column of pale smoke. By the first grey of dawn, I had gotten to *bandit*, and then I fell asleep and did not wake until midmorning.

4

A MAN AND A WOMAN, FULL-BLOODS, YOUNG AND LOOKING LIKE newlyweds, came inside and stood. They wouldn't look directly at me, but I can't say that they acted shy. They seemed to have expectations of me. They just stood as if awaiting something, like passengers at a station when the stagecoach is overdue. I tried to talk to them, but they did not understand English, and I tried again and found they did not understand Latin. I waved my hands in gesticulations intended to have meaning leading to commerce. I pointed at various objects and made vivid facial expressions. I said the prices of various items and praised their qualities. But despite all my efforts, the people didn't comprehend a thing. For all the response I got, we might not have occupied the same moment in time. Then they left.

I waited awhile for them to return, but they did not. I went out to the creek and splashed about, turning over rocks to look for angry pinching crawfish and smiling salamanders. I built a little dam of rocks, and twisted up leaves to make ships, and sailed them on the impoundment and watched them be caught in the force of moving water and pulled to the lip of the dam and swept down to destruction. I thought, This world is a bottomless gorge.

—

I DIDN'T KNOW the proper way to do anything. But I studied the ledger from the last shopkeep and figured that writing down all the details of every transaction would be a good start. Mainly I needed to write down who traded how much of one sort of thing for how much of something else, since almost no one walked through the door carrying cash money. It was a trade post, and its commerce was mostly swapping the raw products of the earth like ginseng and animal hides for manufactured goods like gingham and hatchet heads and cook pots and plowpoints. Somewhere down the line, the ginseng and hides were converted into dollars, but all I ever saw was the raw leading edge of commerce as it first springs out of the ground.

Once a month or so, a pair of teamsters in an ox wagon would come up from the lowlands hauling new stock. Working together, we would unload that stuff into the store and then load the fragrant piles of hides and rush baskets of ginseng roots onto the wagon.

The teamsters said that some of the ginseng went all the way around the world in sailing ships and was sold to Chinamen, who ate it and believed it made their jimson stand up better. So I was just the second man in a long chain of people working to make that Chinaman stiff.

I wrote down in the ledger all the comings and goings of the objects that passed through the store, and sometimes I would also note what clothes the people wore when they came to trade or what the weather was that day or what their mood seemed to be at the time. How their hopeful expectation faded to resignation as they saw how little a basket of ginseng or a deerhide would bring when converted into cloth or axeheads.

VERY FEW WHITE people lived back in these remote mountains, and they were mostly misfits self-exiled to the woods and falling into only two categories, drunks and preachers. The latter category included actual ministers and missionaries and also all manner of backwoods social reformers, philosophers, and political theorists, men who came walking through the door with their eyes vibrating from the energy of their frequently crackpot beliefs, hardly waiting to state their names and shake your hand before launching straight into reforming your opinions on the Holy Trinity, the Apocrypha, the Whig Party, or paper currency.

All in all, I tended to prefer the drunks. A good many of the Indians had reached the same opinion and had become drunks themselves, Bear among them. When he was not off hunting, he came in almost daily for his shots. Nearly sixty, he still stood an unbowed six foot three inches tall. He paid mostly with deerhides and ginseng and credit like everybody else. But he was not like the others in that he was a talker. He always came in the door telling something in mid-story. At first I could not understand a word, but he kept talking relentlessly, and all I could do was listen.

Bear almost always brought the makings of a meal with him. He squatted on his hams by the hearth, cooking as if he were at a campfire upon the high ridges. He made every kind of thing but mostly soup. There was one where he stirred up a bowl of bird eggs and poured them into a pot of seething broth hanging over the fire from a crane. The eggs broke into pale yellow shreds like torn paper. He also made a thick soup out of roasted brown meat skins boiled with cornmeal. That one was my favorite. My least favorite was yellow-jacket soup, which Bear considered a great treat. The hard part was digging up the nest, but he had some trick about it so he rarely took more than a sting or two. He'd put the nest near the fire to loosen the grubs, and when they came wriggling out he'd pick them up one by one and drop them in a skillet to brown in hot bear grease and then boil them, and it did not make a pretty soup. In point of beauty and simplicity, his cockle soup took the prize. Pale yellow chicken broth afloat with pink rooster cockles like strewn rose petals. He would eat a bowl or two of whatever he had cooked and then take out down the road, leaving me with enough to eat on for two or three days.

I remember trying to return the favor by giving him one of a pair of oranges that the teamsters had left as a treat. Bear had not experienced oranges before, and he watched me eat mine before he started on his own.

It took him an hour to finish. He peeled it slowly and studied the differing sides of the peels and smelled them and smelled his fingers. Then he ate each section very slowly, sniffing each one before he put it in his mouth. He savored every moment of his consumption of that orange. When he was done he collected all the pieces of peel and dried them in the sun like deer jerky. A month later, they had lost most of their color, but they still held the ghost of the orange's aroma, and Bear kept them in a gourd sealed with a wooden stopper to hold in the scent that would have to do him until another orange made its way into the mountains.

BEAR WAS CHIEF in these parts. All the features of him—his clothing, his passion for hunting, his grasp on the unfolding world and its sad divergence from a clear sense of order and justice and beauty, even his hatchet-blade nose—were relics from the previous century. Down the creek not far from the trade post, he had a farmstead in the old style, with cabins and a winterhouse, cornfields and corncribs, a menstrual hut, orchards and corrals and lean-tos. And, because Bear was head man, he had built an old-style townhouse, the public building in which meetings and dances and ceremonies of a spiritual character took place. Also a great deal of lounging and loafing and gossiping and telling tales. The village itself, called Wayah, was nearly a mile farther downstream, after the creek had fed into the river.

The way I eventually pieced it together, the history of Bear's people was something like the following. In another century, these had been the kind of people that if you didn't watch out trespassing through their country, they'd make moccasins from your back skin, drumsticks from your thighbones, put your teeth in a dry turtle shell for a rattle to make dance music. Warriors, all of them, of either sex. If the men didn't kill you with hatchet or knife, they would take you home as a prize. Then it was the women who would flay you and set you on fire. And not by way of some precious venereal metaphor. The women would skin and burn you alive.

That was then. The people had been fighters, but after two hundred years of mostly losing to white men, the fight was nearly beat out of them. They had become dirt farmers.

It is tempting to look back at Bear's people from the perspective of this modern world and see them as changeless and pure, authentic people in ways impossible for anybody to be anymore. We need Noble Savages for our own purposes. Our happy imaginings about them and the pure world they occupied do us good when incoherent change overwhelms us. But even in those early days when I was first getting to know Bear and his people, I could see that change and brutal loss had been all they had experienced for two centuries.

Many of them were busy taking up white ways of life that baffled them. With every succeeding retreat of the Nation and every incursion of America, the old ways withdrew a step farther into the mountains, deeper up the dark coves and tree-tunneled creeks. It was not any kind of original people left. No wild Indians at all, and little raw wilderness. They were damaged people, and they lived in a broken world like everybody else.

The remaining game animals had become harder and harder to hunt by the year, for the simple reason that they had been killed down so far that some of their members—buffalo and elk—had entirely ceased to be. And the rest of the big animals—deer, bear, wolf, mountain lion—had become scarce. The people did not draw relationship between the tall stacks of stiff hides that went rolling off by the wagonload to Charleston and Philadelphia and the sudden lifelessness of the woods. It felt more like the end of an era, as if some mythic replacement was happening. The fierce old beings were dying. All those beautiful fleet animals falling away into history. And rising up in their places were just fat hogs and beeves and stupid greasy slot-eyed sheep, so fainthearted they sometimes died of fright merely from being shorn. Try to shear even a deer and it would likely cut you into jerk meat with its delicate black hooves. How bear and catamount would react to being shorn is not even a matter open to speculation. You'd die at the onset of the encounter.

With most of the wild game gone and war an impossibility, the whipped and embittered men took up farming, which had for all time been the province of women. The women, with their main jobs gone, became about as powerless as white women. Previously, the women had run the clans, but now the clans were failing and falling away. Clan law had itself become illegal. The old marriage ceremony had involved the man bringing meat and the woman bringing vegetables, and the union of the two had meaning far beyond just the individuals. Now, nothing made sense at all anymore.

Bear and his people were deeply bewildered by the strange new world forming up around them. It was a different country, where you had to own land by paper deed even to have a place on earth to be. Otherwise, you'd go wherever the buffalo and elk had gone. Everybody footslogging toward the Nightland together.

All the pressure of the new world was to scatter like white people and live on little lonely isolated homesteads instead of the companionable townships with their warm smoky townhouses and constant gossip and intrigues and friendships and quarrels and romances. Everything was changing, even clothes. Many of the people, men and women both, had forsaken their deerleathers and taken to wearing the same flimsy fabric as poor whites, except they liked to add a red or blue headband. Some of them had even forgotten their old names and went only by white sorts of names, like Sam Johnson or John Samson. Some of them mixed old names and new names, Walter Onion-in-the-Pot, for instance. A few of them, the older people like Bear, just abided by the old names.

But to be honest, some of their old names did not translate well into our language. Take Onion-in-the-Pot. That was a perfectly good-sounding name in their language and not the least bit ridiculous, but it renders poorly in ours. I guess we, being the victors, get control of the words, those denoting people and places both. Happily, though, a few rivers and creeks and coves seem to be resistant to our ownership. They persist in holding on to their old names even into the present. Cataloochee, Tusquitte, Coweta, Cartoogecha. Unfortunately, hardly any of the mountains have kept their real names, which is understandable since they make such grand ways to commemorate our dead politicians.

About ten years before my arrival, as the result of an unfavorable treaty, the boundary line between the Nation and America passed over Bear and his bunch like a dark cloud shadow and settled a half day's ride to the west. As part of the treaty, Bear and his bunch could choose between moving west with the Nation or taking a little deeded homestead of a mere few hundred acres down the river about ten miles in return for a whole world of land that had previously been theirs. It didn't take a lot of thinking. They stayed where they were out of deep affection for that unsteady and vertical and mostly empty piece of mountain country. They moved downriver to the new homestead for a few years and then a little way back up when Bear made a trade for another piece of larger acreage but with less flat ground. Moving was not a great hardship. No one owned much of anything at all. Log houses no bigger than barn stalls, so simple you could build one in a day or two. For furniture, maybe a table and chairs and a rope bedstead. Some tools and farm implements so simple their names rarely contained more than three or four letters. Plow, axe, hoe, adze, froe, maul. Also a few chickens and a cow. And some pigs foraging free range in the hills with identifying marks slit in their ears.

During this time of rattling around, Bear grew to appreciate the concept of private ownership of land, an essentially ridiculous new idea. A great many Indians had a ragged time coming to terms with it. Bear, though, saw the usefulness of land ownership, saw he could press it into service despite its flaws and its ultimate falseness, for indeed the fleeting nature of our instantaneous lives dictates that we pass through the land almost as briefly as water passes through us, and with no more real claim to possession. Bear began buying land, bartering land, working deals until he outright owned a small tract of about two thousand acres, a homestead situated so deep in the mountains as to be generally worthless. A little bit of it was good bottomland with rich dirt suitable for cornfields and gardens and orchards, but most of it was cove land with bold creeks and steep wooded slopes. Bear moved his people there—at that time a few hundred souls—and built a wattle-and-daub townhouse in the old style to focus their attention in the direction he wanted it to flow. Everyone settled along the riverbank and built their cabins and began going about life in the old way, dancing the old dances and believing everything they had always believed about the force of moving water and tall mountains. Bear took it on as his job to see that the world they inhabited remained recognizable.

WAVERLEY AND I rode past Bear's place and down the river to Wayah. The wind was coming toward me, so I smelled it first. The fragrance of woodsmoke, cabbage and beans cooking, hides curing, people smells, animal smells. All sorted together and not at all unpleasant but welcoming and comforting. It reminded me of my own membership among human beings, but in a sad distant way.

Coming in, I heard the crack of an axe splitting wood, the clatter of cook pots, laughter, chickens clucking, babies crying, and dogs barking. The accents of their voices sounded someway different from all the chickens and babies and dogs I had previously known. Grey smoke drifted among the trees and hung low over the river, and the last light fell through it parceled into scant downstrokes. People moved about conducting their lives at the end of day among cabins all huddled together in the narrow green cove. A pair of young girls went dragging a big limb of hickory deadfall home for firewood, the points of the branches scratching jittery marks in the dirt behind them like long lines of script.

It began raining slightly, faltering and inconclusive, and then it stopped. Bear's wirehaired dog, the color of fireplace ashes, went loping across the road without appearing to recognize me and then headed off past the corner of a fenced cornfield and into the woods like he was after something or had pressing duties somewhere in the distance and was late in their performance. Two boys shot long cane blowguns at a mark, and the darts fetched up quivering into a shake set up against a fodderstook. Three skinny brown boys stood thigh-deep in the river, wavering in their stance as their feet slid on the round mossy stones of the riverbed. They made a show of shooting fish with bow and arrow but were mainly roughhousing with one another and were lucky not to pierce their bare insteps with the arrow points. I could see them shivering in the cold water. They were about my age, possibly a year or two younger. Some of the people looked at me and some did not. No one spoke.

At every new sound and sight, Waverley went sideways with his ears pinned back. I talked steadily to him in a low voice to calm us both. We passed on through the village and went a considerable way out the other side until the road became a rocky trail pitching up nearly vertical alongside a whitewater creek toward the high mountains. It was almost dark when we turned and headed back.

Then the sun was gone and Wayah was the color of smoke. The slim poplar trunks fell straight and pale as string hanging from the dark sky. Amber firelight lit unchinked cracks in the walls of the bark-roofed cabins gathered at the side of the black river. It was becoming a chill evening. Nearly everyone was inside. A man loaded the crook of his left arm with firewood from the pile beside his house. The pale angled faces of the split wood shone bright in the final light of evening. I startled a woman pissing by the roadside. She squatted with her skirts discreetly fanned around her and smiled up at me with an open broad face as I rode past. A constant hum of human sound came from the buildings, the sound of a beehive pitched low, not even enough volume to overwhelm the river flow or the hiss of the woman's relief. A dog barked, and from way up the cove another dog barked in answer. Then they both fell silent, as if other than expressing greetings they had nothing to communicate. The river face was interlocked curves of black glass, motion frozen. Past the village, a last man fished with a cane spear. He stood posed with an arm cocked above his head. A pine torch stobbed into the soft dirt of the riverbank cast a yellow circle of uncertain light around him. One sharp motion and a brook trout, pierced to the root of its bowels, flashed silver in the torchlight.

A LONG BLACKSNAKE lived in an old oak tree down near the place in the creek where I dipped my water. My uncle used to say not to worry too much about snakes, poisonous or not, for they are more afraid of us than we are of them. That sentiment has not been borne out by my encounters with snakes, for many of them would rather fight than yield an inch. This one, as soon as I approached, would rear up from its home fifteen feet up in the tree where the trunk crotched into two fat limbs. It would hiss and flatten its yellow neck like a hood and offer to fight. I would fling stones and hope it did not choose to launch itself down on me. And as further sign of the contempt the local animal world held for me, during that entire first summer, a raccoon chose the second step to the porch as his nighttime place to take a big black oily shit, punctuated with various seeds and berries.

But in fairness I should add that not all animals disdained me. If I turned Waverley out of his corral while I was doing outdoor chores, he would follow me wherever I went, walking with his nose just touching the small of my back. I would cook him horse biscuits at the hearth, and they were just like people biscuits from my aunt's recipe except that I added a lot more salt and didn't wash my hands before mixing the dough.

THE LANGUAGE CAME to me fairly suddenly, and it was a good thing it did, for back in that whole white part of the map, linksters were few indeed, there being no more than five people who could render either language into the other. I listened hard to Bear and all the traders passing through the store, and within a few months I felt the words and their pattern begin to come on me and settle in my mind with great ease and gentleness. The words were just there in my mind. I didn't know how or when I'd gone from *tsis-kun*, the general word for bird, to *ka-gu'*, the particular word for crow. From *ani-tsila'-ski* to *awi-akta*, flower to black-eyed Susan. And then the proliferation of verb tenses—much more numerous and tedious than in English—began to make some sense, so that before very long I could talk and account for gradations in the flow of time without everything having to be happening right in the present instance.

Around that time, Bear's jokes began falling within the range of my understanding. Previously the only way I knew he was telling a joke was by his tone of voice and a certain cadence to his speech, and the only way I knew the joke was over was that he began laughing. But even after I could understand most of what he was saying, I still didn't think his jokes were funny. The characters were mostly animals, and the humor seemed to arise from their behaving exactly as one would expect them to do. Deer wary and frightful, bear ponderous and irritable. I tried to tell him my favorite joke, the one about the hunting dog named Old Blue whose main talent is his ability to hump raccoons to death after they have been shaken to the ground from their tree. Every old man swapping knives and pocket watches on benches outside county courthouses knows it, as do all twelve-year-old boys. Like certain personality traits and eye color and the shapes of one's fingers, the joke skips generations. It passes over the fathers, and the boys get it from the old men. The joke requires a great deal of careful preparation in the telling, particularly the magic division of its structure into three parts, three hunts. The dog's owner bragging endlessly to his companions about Blue's prowess must not be shortchanged. The first two hunts—recounted with attention to wood lore, weather, landscape, attire—end, of course, in the man climbing the tree and shaking down the coon, at which point Old Blue exercises his talents to their fullest extent. The result in both cases—dead coons. On the third hunt, after more excruciating detail, the dog's owner again climbs a tree to bring down a coon. He shakes the limb. But the coon, an extraordinarily large one, holds on and shakes back. The man slips from the limb. His laconic shout to his companions on the ground as he falls never fails to amuse me. Hold Old Blue.

When I finished telling the story, Bear did not laugh and looked more puzzled than amused. He asked what kind of dog Blue was. Any old kind of dog? A Plott hound? What? And then he had questions as to the name. For his people, the color blue denoted loneliness, defeat, despair, failure, loss. Why did the man name his hunting dog Blue? It was bad judgment and made no sense.

In other words, our two languages are not particularly suited to being rendered into each other. And so if you try to do it very literally, you end up with a lot of foolishness. O Great White Father. Many moons ago. Forked tongue. Firewater. Utterances like those of articulate and very pompous children. In the other direction, we sound equally foolish. All translations miss something. Some miss almost everything. Irony. Indirection. Complex metaphors. Straight-faced humor. Damped-down anger. The human touch.

ONCE I LEARNED to talk and understand, Bear had a great many things he wanted to say. A rush of stories poured out of him, personal history and belief. He held a certain disdain for agriculture and was one of the old-style Indians who found hunting and gathering a higher calling, a finer freer way of living than being prisoner to a little plot of tilled ground. Bear considered himself a student of the lives of the predators, and he numbered himself among them. Nothing in life suited him better than a chunk of meat cooking on a switch held over a hickory fire.

But a great upheaval and replacement was taking place among the animals. As the old ones disappeared, disturbing new ones arose in their places. Chickens were not even worth talking about. Bear still thought of them as new birds, provisional pending further evaluation. When he ate one he always expressed his slight approbation in a tone of surprise. Beeves at least had context. They corresponded with the general withering direction of the world in that they were understandable as a sad version of bison suffering under a bad spell of existence, in process of some terrible diminishment. The people would eat the meat of beeves, but generally without much enthusiasm. And as for milk, Bear considered it a nasty business. He never could learn to drink it. Nor were beeves the least bit exciting to hunt. They would stand in your dooryard and let you shoot them from the porch. What kind of hunting was that?

Swine, on the other hand, had no local precedent at all, but Bear talked with a great deal of excitement about hogs. He insisted that white men were kin to swine the way his people were to wolves, and the irrefutable evidence for his opinion was that hogs and white men had erupted into the world simultaneously and equally unexpected. He said the original white men to pass through the mountains were Spaniards wearing crested metal helmets and riding on the first horses ever seen. But despite their swift mounts, the white men traveled with exquisite slowness and enormous effort because they spent more time trying to keep their vast herds of swine and slaves all aimed in the same direction than they did actually moving forward. A few of the Spaniards' stray pigs escaped, but the people soon killed and ate every one of them. Then, several generations later, the Scotsmen and Irishmen brought hogs in greater numbers.

The old Celts' most brilliant idea in the direction of animal husbandry was to let hogs run loose in the woods during spring and summer and then to hunt them down like game in the fall. It saved work on the one end and provided entertainment on the other.

Free range animal husbandry began easy enough. Turn some young pigs out into the mountains to eat mast for the summer and hope you can find them in the fall when you're hungry and they're fat. The problem was, you could cut identifying earmarks in every possible pattern—smooth crop, half crop, swallow fork, under bit, under keel—and still, come hog-killing weather in the fall, a few rebels would manage to escape. Hogs smart enough to live through the winter multiplied without the interference of man and once again became violent hairy beasts. Given but a few generations, the survivors and their offspring transformed into an old style of swine, their bodies relapsed to a wild pattern. They got long-headed and grew red back bristles and sprouted long yellow tusks. Their temperaments became dangerously militant and bloody. Come some cold wet November a few years hence, instead of walking into the pen of a fat and muddy pink pig, smooth and inert as a river boulder, and burying an axe between its resistless ears, you had to pursue fleet fierce animals with the ability and the will to gut you open as they fled across the highest ridges. You did it at your own peril, like hunting bear or catamount.

And left to themselves in the wild, the pigs became smart. Bear said some of them even learned to catch fish. He swore he'd seen them plow their snouts in creek bottoms to turn up crawfish. In the spring when the redhorse were running, he said he'd seen boars wade out chest-deep and come dragging two feet of fish back to the bank and eat it whole, head to tail, while it was still flipping.

The upshot was, wild boars made excellent hunting. Men chased them with dogs, and it was a bloody business. Wounds and fatalities fell on all three sides. In the fall of the year, Bear could not get enough of it. He had bred boar hounds for many generations of dogs, and he remembered the best one among them with great love all these years later. The kind of love where pairs of tears form in the outer corners of the eyes but do not fall. The dog was the only one Bear had ever bothered to name—and that only barely, for all he could think to call him was Sir. It was a foreign word Bear had learned back in the Creek War, when he had fought under Jackson, and though the whites seemed to put a great deal of stock in it, Bear had never quite got the hang of using it.

Sir, the dog, was stocky, colored muddy yellow, with bright searching eyes. As to personality, Sir was strict and sage and settled, a good influence on his fellow dogs. And he possessed an unerring sense of direction home, whereas any of the others might take off following an interesting scent trail and never be seen again, not even having enough sense to follow their own smell back to the house.

During one desperate encounter on a long hunt up toward Big Choga, Sir had been gutted by a boar with a head the size and shape and color of a blacksmith's anvil. A swipe of tusks as long as knife blades laid Sir's belly open from his ribs nearly down to the testicles. Instead of mercifully shooting the dog, Bear cupped the wet pink-and-blue ropes in his palms, spilled them back inside, and stitched the bleeding belly back together with his kit for patching moccasins, which consisted of whang strips cut thin from a groundhog hide and a fat steel needle blistered with rust. Having done all he could, Bear laid Sir under the shelter of a poplar to die and then went on chasing after the anonymous dogs and the murderous boars.

Three days later, Bear passed back across the same ridge dragging an improvised two-pole sledge loaded with dripping hog parts, and there lay Sir, still living, a baleful look in his eye, a deep growl rippling his black lips like windblown curtains. Bear scooped him up in his arms and placed him amid the meat and pulled him home. Sir not only healed enough to go back hunting but was, if anything, more passionate than ever about the chase of hogs, as if every one of their kind that fell into death under Bear's rifle was Sir's personal retribution for never shitting effortlessly again.

ON DARK NIGHTS when I lay on my pallet listening to the sounds outside the window, I tried to match the names of creatures Bear had taught me to their various calls and signals. The peeps and creaks of insects and amphibians, a lone night-roaming skunk or possum crashing through the bushes as loud as a family of bears or panthers. Night birds in the trees. Martens and minks and other dark-goers stepping crinkly in leaves. One word bothered me especially. *Yunwi-giski'*. Bear said it denoted a cannibal spirit, an eater of man. Bear's people had lived here since some dim elder time and knew this place with an intimacy and depth that could not be improved upon. Why would they bother having such a word if there were no such things as cannibals in the immediate vicinity? Example in point: they had a word for a hog bite. Not two words, one word. *Satawa*. My opinion was that if hogs are biting you so often that you have to stop and make up a specific word for it, maybe lack of vocabulary is not your most pressing problem. The other thing that struck me is that this was a language with little interest in abstractions but of great particularity in regard to the things of the physical world. If they had a word like *Yunwi-giski'*, how could there not be its physical correspondent out roaming the night woods hunting for the meat of people?

But at such times, it always calmed me to remember the girl with the silver bracelets, to think of her scent, the way she stepped inside my big wool coat and shivered against me. Two forlorn children finding comfort with each other. More than once I went and buried my face in the coat's lining, and every time the smell of lavender was fainter than before. As if the girl who had stood within its compass was fading from the world.

WHEN I CAME to the end of the shelf of unsellable books, I began slipping a few additional titles into my orders. Thirty pounds of baking soda, six iron kettles, a mixed dozen of red and blue and grey strouds, shot and powder, five hoe heads, two plow irons and the associated collars and harness, a keg each of sweet and sour pickles, one slim copy of *The Sorrows of Young Werther* in the Malthus translation.

I was careful. A French dictionary and grammar in one order and *Manon Lescaut* in the next. If the antique gentleman noticed these oddities, he must have felt that a book now and then was not worth a quarrel.

THAT FIRST WINTER was horrendous. The first snow fell before the leaves were off the trees. Most of the month before Christmas was bitter cold. Mostly I remember that on the coldest nights, long past anyone's reasonable bedtime, I heated water over the hearth fire and dippered it onto oats and bran and drizzled the mush with dark molasses and carried the bucket out to Waverley in his run-in shed. It was a porridge I would not have discriminated to eat myself. I went out even when many degrees of freeze pushed faceted curls of ice from the broken ground of the store yard or when snow stood deep in the woods. Nights when it was crackling cold and the stars were hard points in a black sky and the snow squealed like mice under the weight of my feet. Such nights, I had to clear Waverley's water bucket by lifting out a silver lens of ice. I would hold it to the moon to view the fractured light and then spin it away to shatter against a distant black tree trunk. Waverley would bury his snout in the steaming oat bucket nostril-deep and eat with powerful messy suction until he was forced to come up for air. Then he would raise his head, oats in his eyelashes, take a long in-breath all the way from his belly, and then go down for more. All the while, his slow brown eyes looking at me thankful and happy. I would put my hand under Waverley's blanket of wool batting and waxed canvas, and, no matter how bitter the night, touching his shoulder was like palming a loaf of bread fresh out of the oven.

THERE WERE NOT many Christians among them in those years, and neither were they especially Druidic celebrants of winter solstice, so Christmastime went almost entirely unobserved except among the few families of converts. And even there was division. Some observed the twenty-fifth of December and others waited until Old Christmas. So the best I could do was split the difference and give gifts to anyone who came in the store on the first day of January by the new-style calendar. Everybody got a little bit of spice tea twisted up in paper or a few pieces of peppermint candy. I gave Bear a small bottle of good Scotch whisky, and he drank it immediately by the fire. He took the first shot in his usual manner: I poured a little into a cup and he threw it back at one go. Then he looked straight at me in startlement. He put his nose down in the empty cup and took a long breath in. And then a relaxing outbreath. Deep, deep in each direction.

He believed he would have another.

I KEPT THE ledgers by the new-style calendar—the names of the days in the week, the numbers of days in the month. But in my mind, those were beginning to mean nothing, and it was just the four seasons and the thirteen moons wheeling across the night sky that marked real time. Bear's people thought of the moon as masculine, which at first made little sense to me for everybody knows it is just natural that the sun is male and the moon female. But Bear said, The moon, he's like men are. He slips around in the dark. And by the old clan ways, that was what even married men often had to do if they wanted to sleep alongside of a woman and not a bunch of snoring, farting bachelors bunking in the townhouse. Men were in charge of war and the great woods and its animals, but women ran the clans and the household and the fields, and men entered those domains only at the pleasure of the women. There were men who never entered the houses of their wives except late of a night to ease in and crawl under the covers and be gone by daybreak.

SNOW KEPT FALLING beyond all reason. Then, one afternoon shortly after the New Year, Bear came riding up the cove on his little packhorse with his long legs dragging in the snow. Against my objections, he made me go with him to his place, for he said worse weather was coming. I rode Waverley in his wake back down-valley to his place, and I spent the majority of the next two months in Bear's winterhouse out behind his cabin. I don't know how I would have made it through that weather on my own. One after another, blizzards blew in from the north and spilled across the high mountains down into the coves. Howling wind, ice storms that broke stout limbs off the trees, snow that stood knee-deep for weeks at a stretch. Bear's winterhouse was a little tightly made structure of thick boards covered with a heavy layer of mud for insulation and then sheathed with clapboards to keep the mud from washing away. It stood on the earth square to the cardinal points of the compass. It was about the size to keep a few large dogs in, and you could not stand up under its low ceiling. If you wanted to change britches, you had to flop around on your back. You crawled or duck-walked in through a low door at one end. A fire pit stood at the other end, and since Bear was pickier than most, he had a smoke hole about as big around as a persimmon in the roof above it. A flat rock the size of a grave marker stood as fireback. Along both long walls stretched sleeping benches made of peeled poles and river cane, piled with smoky quilts and the hides of deer and one old buffalo of yesteryear.

The first time you crawl in one of those places the smell about knocks your head off. A ripe mix of smoke, meat cooking, the various odors of people, both the good and the bad. But you get to where you don't notice it at all. February we hardly stuck a head outside other than for toilet urgencies and to stomp through the latest fall of snow to feed and water the horses in their lean-to, Waverley all shaggy-coated under his blanket, ice hanging in his mane and tail like bright beads.

Day and night came not to signify. Our light was the fire. Smoke lay in a cloud above our heads, where it collected before going out the little hole. We kept housecat hours, sleeping three fourths of the day, and the rest of the time we cooked and ate and talked. Though he was not as shiftless as Aesop's grasshopper, Bear did not believe too overly much in hoarding up for winter. In general he relied on the favor of the Creator to get him through, but we did have basic food. We baked potatoes in the fire, made stews of corn grits flavored with bear jerky. We fried pancakes out of batter made with pumpkin or sweet potato and spread the crisp rounds with walnut butter or drizzled them with honey warmed by the fire. Snacked on popped corn and drank tea of dried herbs. Some nights, our dreams corresponded. I dreamed once of a circus, and over breakfast Bear described an impossible animal with a snake for a nose and great butterfly wings for ears.

Bear claimed there were old men and women he knew as a child who practiced a deep form of winter sleep and could den up nearly as long as bear or groundhog in a state of consciousness more akin to death than anything else. Those old ones would not eat or drink or dream or even rise from slumber to piss for nearly three months. But now the exact art of it was lost, like knapping flint into knife blades sharp enough to shave the hair on your arms.

Even without that lost art of sleep, our emergences into the world were so seldom and brief that it was hard to keep up with the changing shapes of the moon. Our limited powers of unconsciousness left us with long stretches of wakeful time to pass. We traded stories. Spearfinger. Uktena. How the Possum Lost His Tail. Jack and the Heifer Hide. Percival. And *Don Quixote*, which became a particular favorite of Bear's. By the time the deep snow began to melt, we had run out of known tales and resorted to making up new. The Old Man with Thirteen Young Wives. The Girl with the Silver Bracelets.

Then sometimes, to let our imaginations catch up, we would sit in silence for hours watching and listening to the fire. And at long intervals Bear would just come out with some question or statement.

—If you knew that tomorrow afternoon the sun would flame up and consume all the world, would you spend the time between now and then praising the beauty of creation or would you sit in a darkened room cursing God with your last breath?

—If tomorrow you came down with an illness that you knew with certainty would kill you, how many different things would you feel? Would relief be at all prominent among them?

On that latter question, when I opened my mouth to speak, he put his hand up and said, It is a mistake to answer too quickly. Then he said, Disease is nature's revenge for our destructiveness.

I also remember him saying, Interesting fact of creation: the deer has just enough brains to cure its own hide. No more, no less.

Now that's not exactly a deep secret. One deer brain is widely known to be exactly the right amount of brains to tan one deerhide. It's the way Bear said it that stuck in my mind. You knew he'd been studying on the matter and found the correspondence to be more than coincidental and convenient.

There was plenty of time for thinking in the winterhouse with the snow banked almost up to the low eaves and the world silent as death except for the little trance-provoking sounds of the fire. I decided that many of Bear's stories and comments shared a general drift. They advised against fearing all of creation. But not because it is always benign, for it is not. It will, with certainty, consume us all. We are made to be destroyed. We are kindling for the fire, and our lives will stand as naught against the onrush of time. Bear's position, if I understood it, was that refusal to fear these general terms of existence is an honorable act of defiance.

But when I tried to put what I had taken from his stories into an overall theory of fearlessness, Bear was uninterested in abstract expressions of life truths. He only responded by telling another story, The Origin of Strawberries. A man and a woman fall in love, which is always a good start. Then, of course, they quarrel bitterly. The woman flees from him. The man follows behind. So it is also one of the good stories of journeys and trails. Various things happen, but the man makes no headway against her flight. Then, taking pity on the man's yearning and despair, the Sun creates little green spring plants with crimped heart-shaped leaves and red heart-shaped berries and casts them in the woman's path. She picks the berries and eats a few, and their sweetness and their stains on her fingers and lips remind her of love and desire. She picks all that she can carry, and the strawberries bleed in her cupped hands. She turns back on the trail and begins traveling retrograde to her anger. She meets the man and holds the red berries out to him. He eats one, and together they follow the road home.

Then, as stories will do, one led to another, and Bear told of his first wife. She was named Wild Hemp and had died only a year into the marriage when they were both just seventeen, and he still missed her with a bitter ache even though that was way back in the bad times, the violent years after the Revolution, when Sevier's militia from the lost state of Franklin crossed the mountains and burned villages and cornfields and sent the people scattering away from the broad river valleys to hide up the dark coves. One of Sevier's men shot Wild Hemp down as she fled. Bear had never entirely found peace about it, and always in his heart there was a little bit of war still flaring all these decades later.

—Grief is a haunting, he said.

The first year after her death, he was agonized by her ghost, which—as the spirits of the loved dead so often do—manifested itself in the form of crushing despair not at all akin to poetic melancholy but more like the grim aftermath of a brutal beating that he reckoned he might not live through.

The newly dead are noted for their absolute lack of pity. Wild Hemp had a powerful desire for him to join her and did everything she could to hasten him toward her. For a while he felt ready to do it, to give up and follow Wild Hemp into the Nightland.

But he went ahead and did all he was supposed to do to fight back against her pull. He paid out large amounts to herb doctors and spirit healers, including the best of the bunch, an old woman named Granny

Squirrel who lived half a day's ride west. Primarily, though, Bear did himself good by going to water and immersing himself in the river every morning at sunrise throughout the year. He went even when big wet snowflakes fell all around him and disappeared into the black water without making even a brief dimple in its smooth face. And he went to water on spring mornings, when the river steamed and carried the fallen peach-colored blossoms of tulip trees and was skinned over with yellow pollen and the wormlike tags from oak trees, and trout held themselves still against the current and waited for food to pass by and their speckled backs merged with the color and pattern of the mossy stones on the riverbed. And also on late summer mornings, when the dawn sky was black and thunderstorm wind howled and rain was flung around sideways and maple trees turned the pale undersides of their leaves upward and lightning blazed its brief white light so bright that he felt sure he could see the insides of tree trunks, all the veins and long fibers running upward from the earth toward the sun. He went to water on autumn mornings, when red and yellow cupped leaves floated along, almost covering the river from bank to bank, and he could lie back in the chill water until his fingernails and toenails turned blue and look up into the nearly bare limbs and watch the final leaves release and fall and spin slowly down the quiet air. And sometimes for good measure he would go to water in the evening, when there was nothing left of the day but a yellow streak over Sunkota Mountain and the stars were lighting up in the indigo path of sky broken through the forest canopy by the river's passage.

All that year he marked the flow of time by the growth and wasting of moons, and he mourned the deaths of each of Wild Hemp's four souls in turn. And when a year had passed and her last soul, the soul of her bones, had died, she let up on her efforts to have Bear join her. He could feel her lift away from him. He decided to give up the worst of his lamentations and go on with life for the time being, but with the knowledge that a piece of him was missing and would never be recovered.

—

FROM THE TAIL end of winter into spring and summer, at new moons I would go nightwalking in an effort to put Bear's theory of fearlessness and defiance into practice. I'd strike off into the black trackless forest blinded. Offer my body to whatever harm this place might wish to do me. Try to see surviving the night not as suicide averted or botched but as proof that I could rest easy against the malignity or indifference of the universe and refuse to fear the world I occupied. A way to own it in the memory of my body. In the last weeks of winter I could look up and see stars through the net of twined tree limbs. But later, in summer, the canopy of the forest was so solid it might as well have been a pot lid, layers of thick wet leaves lapping over me. At first I would go into the night with my arms out before me and my palms forward, as sleepwalkers are said to posture themselves when they wander about on their senseless pilgrimages. I touched leaf and twig, trunk bark and rock face. Once, I touched a startled grouse that flushed up from low brush and then flared away, leaving me breathless, heart rattling away in my chest like a cowbell, with a memory of the lightest brush of wing tips against my palms.

At some point, I would put my arms down and just walk. Ducking when I supposed a limb was about to slash me at the neck, high-stepping over root and rock, wheeling away to avoid head-slamming a big hemlock trunk, skittering aside from any ground rustle that could be copperhead or rattler. Trusting that huffs and grunts and thumps were other than wolf and bear and panther. Let those sounds be the spirit forms of exiled elk or bison returned from wherever they went when they were all killed down. I would walk a thousand steps, in as straight a line as I could manage, and then turn square around and count back another thousand and see if I had returned to the store. I seldom succeeded. On many occasions I sat lost in the woods, waiting for dawn to light the way home, feeling that Bear would be proud of me for having fought the universe to a draw.

—

THE CHEROKEE GENERALLY found it beneath them to come into the store chaffering over the price of goods or the trade allowance you were willing to give for hides or ginseng. You'd name a price and they'd either take it or nod ambiguously and walk out. The few white customers, mostly proud old Scots, were about the same. But you could always tell traveling Northerners, for they were not happy unless they could force you through about three rounds of bargaining and come out feeling like they had beat you. If you started out by offering them the item in question gratis, they would most likely try to convince you to throw in something to boot. It's just the way they are, and they don't know any better. But that hardly helps when they're standing right in your face shouting their harsh and nearly incomprehensible brand of English like you're hard of hearing.

Case in point: one day about noon, Bear sat by the stove looking at the flames and sipping his third whiskey. A stout little Yankee man with a florid face and yellow hair in curls over his red ears came striding into the store like he owned the place. He was touring with a driver in a private carriage, having a big adventure in the far wilderness. He wore a grey suit of clothes spotted with red mud thrown up from the high wheels. Almost without transition, he began objecting to the price of both Cuban cigars and Jamaican rum, saying he could get either of them cheaper in New York City, New York. He offered to pay what he claimed the items in question would cost there.

I mentioned the obvious fact that we were not in New York City, New York. Nowhere near it.

But that one distant little frame of reference was the only one the man would acknowledge. I told him that rather than strike such a poor bargain, it seemed a surer way to make us both happy if he'd direct his driver to wheel the carriage around and ride him straight back up north where he came from. Or at least far away from here.

Over by the stove I heard Bear snort back a laugh.

Then damned if the Yankee didn't fail to be insulted but instead tried to offer me my original price on cigars and rum. And when I declined to sell at any price, he said, Boy, you will never succeed as a businessman, and the sooner I emerge from this benighted wilderness and cross to the upper side of the Mason-Dixon the better.

I said, Speed to your journey.

He left in a huff without spending a penny.

Bear sipped the last of his drink and said one word, *Ayastigi*. Warrior.

I said, I thought you didn't speak English.

Bear said that speaking and understanding were separate matters.

BAPTISTS CONVEYED AN offer to render the Bible—or at least a few of its most striking episodes—into the syllabary and supply copies of it to the people. Bear wanted me to read him some of the book before he decided whether to accept the offer or not. I more summarized than translated. He liked the story of Job, especially God's pride in his own handiwork in creating all the animals and the varieties of landscape and weather. Those features of the world were certainly noteworthy and successful. God's bragging about how well the nostrils of horses turned out struck Bear as some kind of truth about creation. He said that every being has at least one part that is of especial beauty, and his first wife had many such parts. As for the book of Job in general, he thought it was true enough that whatever power runs the earth sometimes beats a man down for no good reason whatsoever other than whim or black jest, but he also thought a good doctor like Granny Squirrel could work some medicine that would at least lighten the blows. Also, the story of the expulsion from Eden got his full attention, though his most persistent question was how big I thought the snake was. In the end, he said he judged the Bible to be a sound book. Nevertheless, he wondered why the white people were not better than they are, having had it for so long. He promised that just as soon as white people achieved Christianity, he would recommend it to his own folks. And that is the message I sent to the Baptists, which they chose to take as a yes.

—

ONE DAY ABOUT a year or two into my residence at the store, Bear left his cow-hocked packhorse grazing in the yard and came inside. His hunting costume carried about it the air of the antique. The hem of his rifle frock fell nearly to his knees, and below that, beaded buckskin leggings. Contrary to recent style, he wore his moccasins with the flaps turned up. He was all hung about with powder horn, shot pouch, hunting pouch. His hair was tied back at the neck with a strip of rawhide. He carried a long rifle draped casually over his forearm. I told him all he lacked was white skin and a flop-brimmed felt hat to look like Daniel Boone. But as was sometimes the case, a weak joke set him off on a serious discussion.

The long hunters from Boone's time, he said, were now old men, those who were not already dead. All they could do was spin winter stories about Kentucky and the big wilderness and the flowing blood of yesteryear. Elk and bison still numerous, and deer so thick in the woods that a single musket ball might kill two at a shot if they happened to be standing bunched together. The stories bore resemblance among them. Many featured a man closing in personal combat with a wounded bear and killing it in a manner like a tavern fight engaged in by a pair of drunks. If the man had a knife, then just as the bear's long-clawed forepaws drew closed around him to pull him apart like a stewed chicken, he plunged the blade all the way to the handle in the bear's chest and the animal bled out still embracing him like a lover. If the teller had a pistol, he discharged it into the bear's howling red mouth, thrusting the barrel past the yellow teeth and pressing the muzzle into the soft palate—the whiteman's suicide spot—before pulling the trigger. To prove the tale's bloody truth, the old teller might display raised white toothmark scars on the back of his right hand where it dragged through the clashing teeth on the way out. But that was a lost world of men and animals and freedom and death, and it would never come again.

What I thought was that while it might have been romance to those old hunters, really it was business. Hides and furs and feathers for the markets as far away as New York and London and Paris. And now the woods were as empty as church on Monday morning.

I said those things as best I could in his language, and Bear looked straight at me, all sharp-witted and thinking hard. I was not sure whether I had butchered the grammar or not. And I wondered whether I had found a workable replacement for the concept of romance and whether he knew at all about the existence of London and Paris.

Bear didn't say anything, only nodded a time or two and had his drinks and went off hunting.

But a week or two later he came down off the mountain, with a pitiful little batch of green hides draped over the horse, and sat on the porch and immediately started talking about how bad it is not to have a place in the world. Without a place where you belong, you have too many choices before you and therefore cannot go in any direction. It is a fine line between too few choices and too many. As he saw it, I had too much freedom.

—Too much freedom? I said. I'm bound with papers here to this one spot for seven long years. Any less freedom, and they might as well throw me in jail and turn the key in the lock. And if I light out and they catch me, they're liable to do it.

Bear clarified his point. He said he meant that truly living in a place means being tied to it in ways I was not. Having a place means being bound in many directions. To the land, the animals, and the people. By relations and even the names of places. Such ties are both comforting and discomforting. In some ways it is easier to be an exile than to have responsibilities. But also sadder. I had no bonds and was therefore lost in the world.

I said I was not lost. I knew for damn sure where I was. I was orphaned and then exiled from my own kind of people. And, by the way, piss on them if they wanted to send me off to the woods and make money on the deal. I was where I was, and I liked it just fine and could get along without them.

Bear said, Now, you be mad at your people all you want to be. And when you're done being mad, think about this. I'm offering to stand as your father.

Then he went inside, tallied up for himself what the hides were worth and deducted his five shots and drank them without a word further, and consulted only with the fireplace for an hour. Then he went out the door.

Well, my first thought was naturally that Bear would make a notably poor father, him being a frequent drunk and all. Also prone to disappear into the mountains for long stretches of time. But there wasn't exactly a line of people waiting to take an interest in me, neither fathers nor mothers. I also knew adoption was not a light thing for him. And it was not just a matter of him taking me on as a son. There was further scope and responsibility to it. The Cherokee were about the same as everybody else; they considered themselves the only people that mattered. The exclusive way to be one of them was to belong to a clan. Skin color or blood degree was not the issue back then. Belonging to a clan was everything. If you were born or adopted into a clan, you were Cherokee. Everybody else was an outsider. So when Bear made his offer it was not only between him and me, it was also a deal with his whole people and thus a matter of identity. For them and for me and for him.

Though for all the gravity behind Bear's proposal, there was no ceremony to it at all. I don't know what I expected. Maybe a knife slash across our palms and a bloody handshake that would make us part of each other forever. Father and son.

When Bear was next in the post, about a week later, to trade some marten skins stretched on hoops for an axehead, he didn't bring up his offer. He traded and drank and told about his hunting trip, which had been inconsequential except that a mountain lion had followed him for three days and at night he had to wake every hour and build up the fire to keep the lion backed off in the dark, for otherwise it was hard to sleep with the yellow eyes staring at him. Finally, I interrupted and told him I'd be honored to call him father.

Bear just nodded and said, We're dancing at my place tonight. You come too.

5

I HAD NEVER BEEN TO ONE OF THEIR DANCES. HAD NEVER BEEN INvited. But on still nights I had often heard the faint sound of drums rising up the mountain and continuing almost until dawn. Those had been lonely nights when Smollett's rendition of the *Quixote* was particularly welcome company, and the doings of the characters kept my mind from turning around and around until dawn, on aching thoughts of love and loss about my little dead mother and the girl with the silver bracelets or equally painful hatred for my aunt and uncle.

My first dance was held in the townhouse, so everybody understood it was Bear's party. Some of the women brought smoked duck meat and roasted venison and little rough cylinders of bean bread steamed in cornhusks with palm prints from their shaping still on the soggy dough when you tore open the wrapping. The drummers upended their various-sized drums and poured water into them to wet the skin heads. The fire in the middle of the floor was built high and bright, and it shot sparks to the ceiling and up into the starry night sky beyond the fire hole like a migration of fireflies. It threw amber light and cast shadows of the dancers against the walls.

I had expected that maybe Bear would make an announcement of our arrangement, but he didn't. Everybody seemed to know already and had made some adjustment in their thinking toward me.

I should pause here and say something about the townhouse itself. I have toured Europe and been to Chartres, Mont-Saint-Michel, Notre-Dame, and other such places. In other words, I've seen my share of architecture meant to scribe lines around a space on earth and a vault in air and declare it holy. Those constructions all succeed in their attempts at creating awe, at least to the farthest extent of human ability, however limited that might be. So it may seem ridiculous to add a ragged dirt-floored mountain townhouse of poles and wattle-and-daub capped with a low-hanging deep-eaved roof of cupped grey bark slabs to that list. But there it is, a space undeniably charged with spirit.

In the old days, a townhouse sat on top of a truncated grassy pyramid of earth, and it would have been a little more obviously magnificent. The peaked roofs of the townhouses stretched the lines of geometry to completion. But the people had long since lost the ability or the will to make new pyramids, and the remnants of the past were rapidly losing their angles. Wind and water had muted them into low round mounds.

Nevertheless, Bear's moundless townhouse was an interesting feat of architecture. The entryway was so low under the eaves that you had to walk bowed to enter—an enforced obeisance, a curtsy—through a kind of brief sunken vestibule, a baffled hallway. There were no windows. You emerged into a room of uncertain dimension, dark except for what illumination came from the fire and the small smoke hole in the tented roof. In daylight, a beam like a Jacob's ladder fell in a solid cylinder through the fire smoke and moved around the room as the sun arced across the sky. The air was thick with the incense of hickory, oak, chestnut, cedar, hemlock, fir. As your eyes adjusted, they revealed an expansion of vaulted space, aiming your thoughts upward. Of course, if you entered at night, there was just the fire, the yellow light waxing and waning, reaching out and falling back, touching the mud-plastered walls and the lowest radius of each converging roof pole. There was a power to the place. The earth floor, the circle of fire, the square of the walls oriented to the four cardinal directions of the world, the movement of light and dark, the four pitches of the bark roof as it climbed in its diminishing angles to the little round spy hole on the endless sky. At any rate, it worked on me as effectively as did, later, the stairway of the Medici Chapel or the dome of the Pantheon. A reaction of spirit as involuntary as a doctor striking beneath your knee with a rubber mallet. Or maybe it is only that we are so habitually inattentive that when some rare but simple geometry grabs us by the shoulders and shakes us into consciousness, we call our response sacred.

THAT NIGHT BEGAN with the social dances, the fire built high and bright. Old men got up and did the Gizzard Dance, circling the fire and swinging their bony asses to the music of drums and rattles made of gourds and tortoise shells. People sat on the benches lining the walls and ate between the dances. Later, some of the women did the Wood Gathering Dance, and toward the end of it a few men got up and went outside.

The fire had been left to die down and the room had become dark and shadowy. The people, by custom, let on like they did not know what was happening.

Some of the women began shaking rattles, and the drummers beat a fast ragged figure. Then a troupe of costumed Boogers erupted through the entryway. Ghosts and monsters. They were robed and masked to represent a caricature of outlanders of various skin tones, brown and white and black. The Booger Dance gave shape to the fear and loss the people had undergone since the arrival of such dangerous newcomers. The Boogers were figures of threat and carriers of despair, but the dance made them ridiculous. They rushed about randomly and violently, circling the fire and shouting in a made-up dissonant gabble meant to sound like various languages of Europe. But mostly they maundered as if seized by a fit of tongues, a dither of mostly vowels.

I was deeply aware, despite my new adoption, of my blood membership in the tribe of Boogers. One of them depicted an Englishman, and his mask was made of buckeye wood, painted chalky grey with a bright red nose and red cheeks, orange hog bristles for eyebrows and mustache, and a strip of boomer fur at the hairline. The eyeholes were cut with a suggestion of puzzlement to their slant, and the mouth was full of big blunt crooked teeth. A gourd-masked German talked like he was trying to rid his lungs of a rattling obstruction. An elderly Negro mask dark with charcoal had beard and hair made from tufts of thistledown. The Spaniard wore one of Bear's prized possessions, a rusty shallow-brimmed metal helmet with a crest standing like a cock's comb across the crown. The Spaniard's headpiece was usually on display atop a post in the corner. Bear claimed it had come down from an earlier time and was, in fact, the hat of the man who was the namesake for the deep hole a few miles up the creek, a place called Where We Drowned the Spaniard.

Bear's people had been rubbing up against other people for quite some time, starting with de Soto and Pardo and other such killers. As further memento of the Spanish *entrada*, Bear also had a small doll—a figure bearing only about as much likeness to the human form as a forked ginseng root and of nearly the same dirty color—which he said had been made from scraps of the drowned Spaniard's woolen underclothing, a great novelty back then in a place where sheep had not even been imagined. Though, truth be told, their own fabric woven from mulberry bark and hemp was much finer, and the mulberry had the added advantage that you could paint pictures on it. When Bear had first shown me his artifacts from the drowned Spaniard, I worked the dates in my head and said that the killing must have happened more than two hundred years ago. Bear said that exact calendars had not been kept back then, but indeed the Spaniard died in the creek a moderately long time in the past, though Granny Squirrel claimed to have been present at the killing and to remember it as clearly as yesterday, and she knew where the drowned man had been buried and whose pair of hands had held him underwater until he quit bubbling. But she'd never tell the killer's name, because she feared the white people might yet find a way to avenge the centuries-old death, righteous though it had been, for the Spaniard's behavior was atrocious.

The Boogers whirled and roared, and in their wake was a slight figure, draped in white sheeting cloth in the style of a ghost. It wore a mask over its head made from a great hollowed-out wasp's nest, leaving just the outer few layers of pale grey paper. The mask maker had stobbed a pair of forked twigs like antlers into the nest above the forehead. Deep black eyeholes had been slit in the bulb end, and the little hole at the funneled bottom where the wasps used to come and go was left to stand for a mouth. The mask was face-shaped and yet not a face. All it did was make glancing reference to faces, human and animal both. The pale wasp paper lay in wrinkles, dry and withered like the skin of the ancient dead. All in all, it was a frightening and strange vizard, blank and unreadable and vague. It struck the eye blurred, as if seen through water.

The drummers began a fast beat, the transient edges of the sound popping and decaying. The Boogers ran about the room gabbling their languages and flapping their robes. They lunged aggressively at people as if to slam and butt them, though at the last minute they always veered off on weird vectors, staggering one minute and prancing the next. The drums and rattles banged a hard rhythm. The Wasp Ghost spun in place with its arms extended, hands twirling and draped cloth streaming. Then it broke free and went about the benches peering into the faces of the spectators as if judging or searching. When it came to me, it looked long and hard and then went spinning off with its sheets flowing behind it to the far side of the fire.

Bear, as host, shouted at them: Who are you? What are you doing here? What do you want?

Dreadful Water, the man costumed as a Spaniard, was noted for his ability to break wind at will, and to each of Bear's questions he let loose a barking response that the women and children on the benches found hilarious. The Englishman kept opening his robe to reveal a great proud phallus made from the arching neck of a gourd, the head of it painted red with pokeberry juice. Every time he showed it, thrusting his hips and wagging it, the women shrieked in terror and then made humorous evaluative comments.

After a long while of chaos, the Boogers began settling down, like stirred liquid coming to rest. At the end of their swirling, they went and sat huddled together on a bench.

Bear went to them and made his inquiries again.

He spoke loudly in a stage voice to the room at large: Who are you? What do you visitors want here?

Now suddenly, after all their shouting, the Boogers would speak only in mutters and hums. They put their heads together and whispered unintelligibly among themselves, and then the Englishman, apparently their leader, gestured grandly for Bear to approach. Bear went and leaned to the mask, and all of us in the room were quiet, but all we could hear was a murmur.

When the mask stopped speaking in his ear, Bear stood and shouted in mock alarm, They say they come for fucking and fighting!

The women and girls squealed on cue. The younger men rose to their feet in fighting posture.

Bear made a patting motion with his two hands as if to calm them down.

He said to the Boogers at large, What are your names?

There was a murmur from the group and then the Spaniard, seated way at the end of the bench, muttered something. Bear went to him and listened again and very solemnly announced, He says his name is Enormous Prick.

The women laughed and some snorted in disbelief and one of the older women said, Weasel Prick, more like. Bear, unfazed, went down the row of the Boogers asking names. They were all to do with the nether parts, each filthier than the last, and not at all limited as to gender. Two words, a noun and a modifier, so make up your own. The permutations are not endless.

But when Bear got to the Wasp Ghost, he held his ear to the grey and frightening visage and then stood up and said a pair of sibilant words that I could not translate and neither could anyone else. They all looked puzzled and whispered among themselves and made it clear by their resistance to laughter that the name was a failure as an act of imagination. The last man, the Englishman, saved the day by delivering a name of such amazing genital filth that I do not dare to call it even in this cruder time. He brought the house down.

The drummers and rattlers started a quick fluttering rhythm, and the singers came hollering in with a lyric prominently featuring the English Booger's name in nearly every line. All the Boogers rose and began another dance, bending awkwardly and shuffling out of time with the music in the manner of ignorant outlanders poorly mimicking an actual dance. Everything was awkward—their footwork, the angles of their arms, the cock of their heads. Everybody laughed and I laughed too. But all I could think was that if I were called upon to take the floor, my dance wouldn't be any better than the foolish Boogers', a risible emulation.

As soon as the laughter tapered to a close, the drums struck up a tempo like a heartbeat at its limits of velocity and the Boogers all broke into a run around the fire, and then they went at the women sitting on the benches and on the floor, thrusting their hips and grabbing at the women's breasts and asses and humping away like boars in rut but in a mocking way. The Wasp Ghost, though, moved as if to a different music, slower. It peered into people's faces and made signals with its small hands that might have been meaningful to another race of people entirely. Meanwhile, the Englishman had come up with a great innovation for his red gourd penis. It had a hog's bladder inside, and he could squeeze it and water would shoot from a hole in the stem end of the gourd and squirt at the women, though mainly he hit the walls and the ceiling. The women howled and laughed, and one of them forgot for a minute that she was not supposed to know who was behind the mask and remarked loudly that Red Squirrel's real gourd neck, though much smaller, squirted only water too, and that was the reason he couldn't get no babies.

My first thought at that moment was to take notebook and ink flask from my satchel and a trimmed quill from my coat pocket and record the event on paper. All the details and my impressions of them. My delight and discomfort. The broad caricatures of the wood and gourd masks. The blurry frightfulness of the Wasp Ghost. The color of the firelight falling on the walls.

But all of a sudden I imagined my uncle and the other white men I had known in my childhood behaving in the crude manner depicted by the Boogers, farting and humping and grasping at everything their hands could hold and a whole lot more. And I thought about all the white men in the territory with little unacknowledged part-Indian babies running around, and nevertheless the profound superiority they felt over the Indians by blood entitlement.

I began laughing like everybody else, laughing so hard that I pitched backward on the bench and fell until I was caught by the wattle-and-daub of the townhouse wall behind me.

The drums and rattles reached a crescendo. The Boogers roared their final roar and rushed out the door into the night. The whole townhouse seemed to take a deep breath and pause.

Glad to be shut of them, Bear broke out a demijohn of popskull liquor and led the final bout of drinking, this being long before his later frequent vows of temperance.

Other dances followed, but they all seemed diminished by the departed Boogers. Beaver Dance and Bear Dance and Circle Dances where everybody joined in, even those as poorly skilled as myself. I was of the age where one feels overly conscious of failings at physical grace, and I tried to just sit and observe, but one of the older women yanked me up and shoved me into the crowd. I did the best I could, which, oddly enough, and entirely due to their generosity, proved to be sufficient.

When grey light was not more than an hour or two from showing through the smoke hole, it was time to do the Buffalo Dance and then go home. They danced the dance even though the last buffalo had been killed thirty years ago and its broad chalky skull with polished brown horns, fitted like molars in their sockets, was hanging from an old widow's barn up Hanging Dog Creek and the dusty hide covered Bear's bedstead.

Even before the Buffalo Dance was done, Bear wrapped himself in a blanket and fell asleep on a bench. The party broke up. It was a cold clear night, and when we all stepped outside, hot from the dancing, and stood about saying our good-nights, steam rose from us, all as one, and we were haloed in the moonlight. I put my wool coat on, and the hem no longer swept the ground but fell just below my knee.

Everyone set out walking down the creek toward the village, and I turned up the two-track wagon road that led home. The full moon was riding low to the west, and black shadows of trees stretched long across the pale dirt of the road. I had not gone much beyond the first bend when the ghost in the wasp mask stepped out from a stand of poplar trees, their trunks pale columns in the moonlight. The bulb-shaped face looked at me without expression, black eyes and wasp paper like the skin of a dead man.

Before I could catch myself I must have flared backward a step or two, a skitter just short of wheeling and taking to my heels.

The ghost laughed, and it was the sweet and unrestrained laugh of a girl.

—That was a pretty step, she said. I guess you've not had enough of dancing yet.

—Who are you and what do you want? I said.

I was halfway between scared and mad, and I had not at all intended to repeat Bear's formulaic questions to the Boogers. But they held within them the essential things you want to know from beings that erupt into your world and frighten you.

She laughed again and then said, We come for fucking and fighting.

She bent forward and took off the mask and set it on the ground. Her long hair fell forward over her face until she stood up and swept it back with a forearm.

The girl with the silver bracelets.

Of course I was stunned, but the world was a less populated place back then. You ran into people. Lots of land, few folks. The opposite of what prevails now. I wanted to say all kinds of things at the same time, but the last thing I wanted to say was, I won you in a card game.

—Do you remember me? I said. We've met.

—Don't get all inquisitive in a rush. Let's kind of sidle into this.

—There was a card game, I said. A game of Blind-and-Straddle.

—Hush, she said.

—I held good hands.

—Not another word on that topic. I mean it.

—Then what's your name? I said.

—It's Claire.

—Where have you been?

—Home in the summer. School in the winter.

—School where?

—Savannah this last year. Charleston before that. There was a little problem in Charleston.

I had all kinds of questions lined up, waiting to be asked. But she said, I've got to go. They'll be worried.

—They who?

—Relatives I'm visiting. I've got to go.

She bent to pick up the mask.

—How will I find you? I said.

—I'm going home tomorrow. It's far.

—Where?

She reached to the breast pocket of my coat and pulled out one of the turkey quills and flexed its point against her finger.

—Ink? she said.

I fumbled in my shoulder satchel and took out the little travel flask and was still feeling for the notebook when she stopped me.

She did not take the flask from me, but unscrewed the cap and dipped the quill into the narrow neck. She took my hand in hers and held it firm by the fingers while she drew a map to her home on the back of it, the split nib scratching and tickling.

—That's the way through the woods, she said, when she was done.

I held the back of my hand up to the moonlight. It was a mess of lines bleeding into the smooth topography of young skin.

—Is there not an address, I said, the name of the road or street? I'm not free to travel far, but perhaps we might write.

She dipped the pen again and capped the flask and took it from me and tucked it back into my satchel. On my other hand she wrote only four words—I could feel the pauses and the skipped spaces on my skin. When she was done, she tucked the quill back in my pocket and bent to the ghost mask at her feet and settled it over her head.

—Have you fallen in love with me yet? she said.

—I'm deciding.

—It's not a thing you decide.

There was a long silence and then she said, I didn't know if you'd made it out alive.

—I'm alive, I said, as you can see. But I don't know about out.

—I've got to go.

She turned and ran away down the road.

WHEN I REACHED the post, I built up the fire and transcribed the markings from my handbacks into my notebook, first the map and then the address, which read, in order of composition from wrist to knuckles:

CLAIRE

FEATHERSTONE

VALLEY

RIVER

I knew even then that she was something fatal piercing my life.

I WROTE TO Claire at least bimonthly for a while. Or, to be more precise, for an interminable stretch of slightly more than two years. And my voluminous letters must have been foolish beyond belief, an outpour of young feelings. My pride is not in the least bruised that Claire disposed of them. In fact, I am quite happy that they have long since ceased to exist. I imagine them balled up loosely in her fist and lit to ignite pine kindling for a February hearth fire. I, of course, kept all six of her single-sheet responses and have them to this day in a box. She answered me only quarterly, and her letters were highly impersonal, barely more than brief descriptions of the recent weather and the colors of the autumn leaves or the depth of snow or how cool the evenings had been for July. She was hardly present in them, and I was not mentioned at all except for an occasional perfunctory closing line hoping that my health had been sound.

I was not sure how I would ever happen to see her again. She did not seem particularly impressed that I wanted her, a fact I attempted to conceal in my letters but could not. It had been my understanding, both from reading novels and from some consonant feeling in my own heart, that women put a great deal of stock in the desire of men. And yet my desire had apparently been declared of suspect value. Not even the basis for a line of credit.

6

All of a sudden, when I was sixteen, everything changed. As I've previously said, successful old men like to look back at their ascension in the world and see it as an endorsing imprint on their brows, a mark from the thumb of God. But really, sometimes success just falls on you. Or you step in it.

The antique gentleman with the knee breeches who owned the trade post died. His son, named Junius, quickly ran the business into the ground so that none of the suppliers in either Philadelphia or Charleston would send us new goods. I hadn't been paid my little stipend in months. Junius came riding up one morning in a big boat-shaped Conestoga wagon heaped above the gunwales with all his possessions, at least the portable ones he could neither sell for cash nor trade against his debt with his many creditors. He was fevered with the notion of going out west to escape his failures and begin life anew. His destination was the farthest reaches of Mississippi. He could have taken a different route in his flight and left me high and dry, but he was not at all dishonest, just run-of-the-mill incompetent. He pulled up into the store yard sitting hunched on the seat board with long dark reins drooping across the backs of a matched pair of yellow oxen and with a fairly good ash-colored riding horse following at the end of a lead rope off the back. The canvas coverlid bulged out between the hoops in various geometric shapes, the points and angles and curves of his boxed and bundled things. A young black servant dressed in better clothes than his master rode with his legs dangling off the tailboard.

Junius stepped down and greeted me in considerable embarrassment, with only a brief limp handshake and a glancing look from his eyes. Then he drew me to the back of the wagon and shooed the boy off the tailboard and said, Pilfer about and see what you'll take for your wages that I owe you.

I climbed up and dug around in the dim internals of the wagon, and there was not much of interest in his clutter except for several boxes of lawbooks. I'd have been happier if they had been novels and poetry and plays. Nevertheless, they were books.

—I'll take these, I said.

—Good choice, Junius said.

I loaded the boxes off the wagon and onto the porch.

He sat doing sums in a ledger, his pen scratching fast against the paper.

—So we're settled on back pay and all? he said.

—Square and plumb, I said.

I was wondering what next for me, but I was just waiting.

—How much cash money have you got? he said.

—Not much.

—How much?

—A very little.

He made a sort of impatient forward rolling motion with one hand.

—About a hundred, I said.

—About?

—Maybe a little more. Hundred and twenty.

—Good God, he said, you've lived thrifty.

I shrugged. I had indeed lived thrifty, and I'd had a few little enterprises of my own. It was not part of my master's mission to deal in livestock, so I figured that making a little money buying and selling beeves and hogs with drovers passing on the way to the Charleston stock markets mattered little. None of my master's business.

Junius said, For a hundred and twenty, and that horse there in your paddock, you can just have this store and the one out on the Nation at Valley River to boot. There's not hardly any stock left in them, and I can't take the time to put them up for sale. I've got to get in motion.

—Nope, I said. I'm not trading my horse.

He looked back east up the wagon road as if any minute dark riders might round the curve in pursuit.

—Just the hundred and twenty then.

—For the stores and the time left on my papers.

—Sure. That too.

I went inside and collected all my savings—hard money and scrip both—from their various hiding places. I didn't even count it. I knew exactly how much it was. I carried it out in the bowl of my two hands. It was a little heap that in a fractional way represented the past four years of my life. All the way back to a gold twenty-dollar piece saved from my scrape gambling with Featherstone.

Junius didn't count it either. He spilled it down into a long leather moneypurse, and there was not much in its depths for my coins to jingle against.

He said, I would not have felt right leaving you unaccounted for.

I appreciated his fine ethics. But I was not a fool.

—Would you care to memorialize this transaction on paper? I said.

He wrote a fast contract, and we concluded it with signatures so big and looped and flourished that we might have been vying for a medal in penmanship.

He mounted to the driver's bench and whipped up the oxen, and the boy made a quick leap to the tailboard. The slack rope pulled taut against the good riding horse, and they were gone.

I stood in the yard looking at the contract, two dozen words and two signatures. All of a sudden the world felt a great deal more expansive now that I was no longer owned but an owner. No longer bound, at least not by paper.

—

THAT NIGHT I flipped through the lawbooks, reading here and there from several of the many volumes, and found that despite their mighty efforts toward incoherence, they were ultimately penetrable, at least after frequent consultations with Dr. Johnson's *Shorter Dictionary.* About all it took to be a lawyer back then was to have read the books and understood a little bit of them. And also to own a black suit of clothes and a white shirt of moderate cleanliness. For anyone even remotely sharp-witted, frontier lawyering was said to be a fine profession. The future suddenly rose up before me, bright as a red sunrise, like Jack meeting the old beggar with the magic tablecloth that produced feast after endless feast. As for the business, I knew something about how credit worked in such a fluid and uncertain economy. It was nothing more than paper stacked on paper, varieties of hope and speculation, handshakes and promises, moonbeams and horse shit, trust and risk layered one atop the other in thin strata like cards in a deck. And not much different from betting all you had on a shuffle and a deal.

Soon the post was stocked again and I was the proprietor, an independent businessman. And I now had an employee, a smart boy by the name of Tallent, just a year older than I had been when I first went into the mountains. But Tallent was not bound. I paid him for his work, though not much and most of it in the form of goods from the store and notes receivable held by me on men of reliable character.

It did not take me long to learn that money was not much interesting in itself. But it was plenty interesting in a secondary way, for what it could do on your behalf. It could, for a start, set you free and make a place for you in the world. In that new country, it began to be my understanding that getting what you wanted was largely a matter of claiming what you wanted.

IN THAT SPIRIT I soon left Tallent in charge and went riding toward Valley River. My intent was to get my new post there back in business and also to follow my map to Claire. By noon I was passing through a deep gorge in early spring with the leaves just squirrel-ear big on the trees and the river running hard and full, breaking white over black rocks. Somewhere along the way, I crossed the boundary between America and the Nation, but there wasn't a signpost or a rock cairn or even a stob in the ground to commemorate the frontier.

Waverley and I cut a stunning figure that day. I had sent measurements to a tailor in Charleston and had a good suit of black clothes made, including a fancy waistcoat in the hunting plaid of the Scots grandfather on my mother's side, its dim greens and dark greys and muted blues being more to my tastes than the clan's garish red dress plaid. And further contributing to our considerable flair, Waverley had matured into a stallion of beauty and spirit, with flawless carriage and movement. He was a bay almost to black, so that the only time you saw a difference between his mane and his coat was in direct sunlight. He shone like dark metal. His muscles lay in skeins and plates, reshaping themselves constantly all down the slopes of his body. And Waverley was not only handsome, he had impulsion. A horse either has it or not. Many horses suck back a little with every stride, and then before long you're bogged down, and you spend a great deal of time and effort kicking their asses in order to go. Waverley, all on his own without regard to the opinion of his rider, had a compelling desire to go, often at an alarming rate of speed. He had become worth quite a lot of money on the open market. People built houses for less money than he was worth. Of course, for at least two reasons, I would rather have cut off my left hand and sold it by the pound like pig trotters or stew bones than considered selling him. For one, it was awfully fine to ride around atop a horse of such head-turning quality. And for two, I loved him and believed he loved me. Together, we looked so fine that day I wished I could sit on a porch and watch us ride by.

For much of the way up the river, the passage was only a narrow ledge above the bank, alternately rocky and muddy, impassable to wagons for many months at a time. The walls of the gorge were so narrow and deep that we rode in chill shadows except when the sun shone straight down at midday.

Granny Squirrel lived in splendid isolation somewhere nearby. Up some cove or ridge where the trail climbed like winding stairs. If people wanted her medicine, they had to travel. It was said that she had a piece of clear quartz crystal the size and shape of a quail egg. A drop of your blood dripped from a finger onto one of its faces would tell Granny Squirrel all your life to come, the joy and hardship, victory and death. Some people wanted to know their future, and some didn't. I, for one, didn't. Is wolf or bear aware of impending death? No. Would wolf or bear be better for the knowledge? I tend to think not. Be as you are and then go on your way to the Nightland is my belief. But whether you wanted to know your fate or not was all the same to Granny Squirrel. She'd lived for two or three hundred years, had seen generations rise and pass. She took the long view, wherein most of the flurry of life meant nothing to her.

Down in the gorge that day, I passed only one other human being, an old man with skin the color of hemp rope camping in a bend of the river. I smelled his fire smoke hanging over the water for the better part of a mile before I got to his camp. The man was knee-deep in the river, fishing, and came out with his pants dripping and his feet bare and his big toenails pale and luminous as the insides of mussel shells. He fried me a pair of trout dredged in cornmeal, and afterward I made coffee and poured the man a cup, which seemed to be a great novelty for him. And he seemed mildly surprised that I was fluent in the language. He said his name was Walter Grey Fox, and he planned to live by the river all through summer and fish until at least the first snow in the fall, and then he would go to stay the winter with his last living son, five days' walk to the southwest. It did not bother him a bit to live by himself so long in the depths of the gorge, because the fishing was good and the river was musical, and travelers passed every few days and invariably appreciated a trout or two to break the monotony of the journey. We spent an hour together and parted as great friends so that if we had met twenty years later—which we did not—we would have embraced as kin.

It was far into the afternoon, the light falling at a low angle, when Waverley and I topped out of the gorge at a gap and then descended many miles down a long gentle incline, two thousand vertical feet or more into a broad green valley. That valley was, and still is, the most beautiful place I've ever seen. It was bounded on three sides by high blue mountains and divided down the middle by a slow river, but it stretched westward on and on without visible limits. As we passed through, the head of the valley was busy with the fields and orchards of homesteads filling the bottomland all the way to the first upslopes of the mountains, and then it was all big timber and coves and ridges sweeping to the sky. People everywhere worked newly planted corn and beans and squash. Little communal clumps of single-pen cabins lay scattered for miles down-valley. Some of the enclosing mountains were bald, topped with broad treeless swaths of long grass, and on one of these, Bear had warned me, a giant lizard was alleged to sun itself on sheets of exposed rocks, and he also warned that great red leeches the size of plow oxen still sometimes roiled the deepest holes of the Valley River.

The sky became deep violet with yellow dashes of light breaking between bands of black clouds hiding the sunset, and by the time we reached the trade post it was almost dark and a thin crease of moon stood partway up the sky. I did not even strike a fire but ate cold biscuits and water and spread my bedroll on the cupped porch boards. The post sat on a hill overlooking the river and valley beyond. I studied the view until night fell entirely.

WAVERLEY AND I came thrashing up a creek bank out of dark laurel with their long leaves in my hair and twisted in Waverley's mane and tail. Broken brushes of jack pine waved from under the wings of the saddle. We were like a small segment of thicket breaking free with violence from the general mass, to rise and stand alone in a vast bright clearing. I reined to a stop and let the milky sunlight sheet off us, liquid and warm, and pour into the ground. I beat the forest litter off my clothes with my hat and took a notebook out of my pocket and looked for the tenth time at the map I had transcribed from my hand by firelight two years previous. A turning had apparently been missed somewhere along the way. I looked around for a new direction.

Off in the distance across plowed fields stood an entirely unexpected sight, a tall columned plantation house situated in a river bend. Out back, various outbuildings, a slave village, more fields stretching into the distance, Africans moving in groups like shadows on the land. I knew such places existed, but I had never personally witnessed one before.

I had polished my boots to a high black sheen before setting out, but they were now covered in a chartreuse dusting of spring pollen from riding cross-country. I pulled a broken pine branch from under the saddle and whisked the leather clean with the fan of needles and rode on toward the big house, taking care to skirt the new-planted fields, the furrows still fresh turned, the broken dirt lying in pieces like potsherds, and the seeds of something yet indeterminable still germinating in the dark.

I rode to the house, and by the time I had alighted on the pea gravel of the circle drive before the front steps, a groom of twelve or fourteen, the color of an eggplant, had come out to take Waverley. He immediately pulled the reins over Waverley's ears and began trying to lead him off.

—Where you going? I said.

—Around back, sir.

It was the first time I had ever been called sir, and I was momentarily taken aback. The boy tried to go on leading Waverley away, but Waverley had other ideas and put his head back and went walking sideways and looking white-eyed. The boy held the reins by the ends, and it was like watching someone try to launch a very large kite in a March wind.

—Wait a minute, I said. All I'm wanting is directions.

—To where?

—The Featherstone place. I believe it's nearby.

The boy tipped his head at the white columns of the big house. Real nearby, he said.

I looked at the house again.

—I'm here to see Claire Featherstone.

—Somebody at the door generally does that. But they out back taking breakfast.

—They?

Waverley had settled some, and the boy renewed his efforts to lead him away.

—I'll give him water and some hay if that suits you, he said.

—Surely, I said. I'd appreciate it. And a cupful of oats if you've got them.

—We got aplenty of oats.

I looked up at the sun where it stood far up in the sky. Breakfast? I thought.

I went to the front door and knocked and waited. No one came. I walked around the side of the house, past boxwoods planted at the foundation, a brick chimney stack. Under a gathering of poplar trees stood a small dining table and chairs, blue-and-white dishes with remnants of bread and butter and preserves, a teapot and half-empty cups sitting in their saucers. I looked about and saw Featherstone and Claire off past a little fenced herb garden near an edge of woods. They were laughing. Featherstone broke off a branch of redbud blossoms and tapped her on the forehead with the flowers, a motion like anointment. They were dressed in the clothes of a plantation owner and his daughter, not as Indian horse thief or Wasp Ghost, and so apparently made easy transit between old and new worlds. Claire had grown up in a great many wonderful ways. She was a slim beauty, about my own height. Her hair was loose around her shoulders, and she wore a simple high-waisted shift that hung vertical but clung, where needed, to all the new curves of her form in heartbreaking lovely arcs. The neck scooped frighteningly low to reveal a creamy cloven expanse that I had to concentrate not to look at too closely. Such was the style then, at least among fashionable young women.

Claire introduced me as a young businessman she had met as a girl when she visited her distant relatives at Wayah. Featherstone did not seem to remember me in the least, and I did not think reminiscing about our card contest would be at all to my advantage. Nor would it be useful to remind either of them, however lightly and with a gentle laugh, of the scope of my winnings back then.

I was offered breakfast, and I said vaguely that I had taken mine already and did not mention that it had been more than four hours earlier.

Featherstone immediately led me into the house and began showing me through it with great pride of ownership, talking without letup about its features as we went. Like Washington and Jefferson, he had drawn the plan himself and had specified the design and material of its construction—all the way from fireplace stone to dining room chandelier, from the handles of the paneled doors to the brass screws with which they were affixed. The columns and glazed windows and the various pieces of mahogany furniture all came with stories of their uniqueness. The marble floors in the foyer coordinated intentionally with the colors of an enormous Turkish rug. The walls were plastered and whitewashed, only a little soot-streaked around the fireplaces. Wall skirting of delft tiles painted mostly in the oxhead style, but some depicting ships and milkmaids and postures of soldiers and unlikely flat landscapes with windmills in the distance, all of which Featherstone had specified, though the overall effect for me was that he had struck a good deal on odd lots and leftovers from the previous century. Some of his things seemed to have been chosen as much for their irony as their innate value. For example, the many fine crystal wineglasses upended on a hunt board had been made at Murano, the selfsame Venetian island from which worthless colored-glass beads had originated for nearly two centuries and were traded with the Indians for things of actual value like hides and pelts and feathers for the European markets. Furthermore, Featherstone's china came from England; and he found it humorous that the Wedgwood company had dug a particularly fine pale clay from a riverbank one mountain ridge east of where we now stood and hauled it across the Atlantic, dirt shipped way round the world. And then they did whatever they did to shape it and color it and make patterns on it and fire it into service pieces. And then damned if they didn't ship some of the transformed clay right back where it came from, to him. So much work and so many thousands of miles of transport to and fro. All of which Featherstone seemed to find of amusing worth all by itself.

Claire went along during the tour, an absent expression on her face, not really listening. She touched door handles and dinner plates with dismissive glancing brushes of her fingertips. She would not meet my eyes.

Featherstone said that aside from imported goods, he was a world unto himself. His enormous holding provided everything he truly needed and most of what he wanted. All the wood for his house and outbuildings had been cut and milled on the place. And the land produced the entirety of food for its population, excepting a few of Featherstone's favorite novelties like crystallized ginger and orange marmalade. He had beeves and hogs and every kind of domestic fowl in great quantity, and a fish pond from which big arm-long bass could be pulled at a moment's notice if that's what he craved for his dinner. Extensive vegetable and herb gardens grew in raised beds arranged in geometric patterns. He made all his own beer and some of his liquor, though he had given up trying to produce either rum or wine. In the latter case, all his efforts had proved entirely undrinkable and of a heretofore unknown color, both the reds and the whites. Every vintage a gritty and dreadful end to good grapes. And so now, to his disappointment, all his wine had to come from France in pretty little wooden boxes. It also upset him that the earth would not yield the right elements from which he could grind the pigments to paint his barn and outbuildings the particular shades of white he preferred. Nor did indigo grow well in this climate, and he resented having to pay ignorant low-country South Carolinians to dye the clothes of his slaves the color blue he thought looked especially fetching against a yellow field of ripe wheat. But to offset that failure, he pressed and baked brick from his own clay to special dimensions he found more aesthetically pleasing than any he could have bought elsewhere. He even forged his own nails, for God's sake.

Claire eventually drifted away down a hall as we went from one room to the next. It was all I could do to listen politely and not go following after her. Featherstone went on talking, gesturing toward objects of particular interest, the flats of his hands thick as puncheons and terminated with stout blunt fingers and opaque nails. He had forsaken his ear jewelry and shaven hair-do from back at the card game and now tried to fashion his greying hair after the high sweeping roach of Andrew Jackson, but it frizzed and crinkled as if singed. The pupils to his eyes were dark as pokeberries, a reminder that Featherstone was part Cherokee, though his hide was a slightly paler hue of white than mine. He wore the fashion of clothes current in Charleston and mentioned that, as a somewhat younger man, his conversion from breeches to trousers had been among the first, not just within the Nation but in the three-state surrounding area. On particularly Indian occasions, though, as a statement of identity, he topped his costume with a turban, as had become the fashion among Indians of several peoples, from Seminoles to Hurons. He subscribed to *The North American Review* and *The Allegheny Quarterly*, and every few weeks packages of books arrived from Boston. He reread his favorite book, *The Anatomy of Melancholy*, annually.

He was particularly proud of his study, and he saved it for last on the tour. It was all brown books and brown dead animals. The art of taxidermy, he said, occupied much of his leisure time. I stood admiring his work, and the gallery walls stared back with many reflective glass eyes in the mounted heads and bodies of everything that had thrived in the valley and its mountains. Buck, bear, and wolf. A whole panther, black phase, standing stuffed in the attitude of a scream. Owls and eagles and herons. Even a vole no bigger than a man's thumb. One corner of the room was filled with an entire section of hickory trunk, and a gravity-defying flying squirrel was mounted on a limb so that just the toe of one hind foot remained attached as it leaped into the air with the webs of skin between the legs stretched like wings for gliding and the bright chips of black glass set in its head for eyes looking toward the fireplace as if it had had enough of life and was ready to blaze away into the next world. Given pride of place above the brick hearth and heart-pine mantel was the enormous dusty head of a bull bison. It erupted blockish out of the plaster wall as if from another time, a lone straggler from a retreating bison army lost in enemy territory. Its old pelt was broken and peeling back at its neck to reveal a pale underlayment of unidentifiable composition. When Featherstone wasn't looking, I reached up and touched the broken place and could not decide whether it felt more like chalk or sawdust. And then I palmed the black nose, big as my spread hand, its texture like sand. On Featherstone's desk, an amber-tinted jar of glass eyes stared in jumbled sizes and colors, like a schoolboy's collection of prized marbles, frightening taws. More to my taste, stacked among the four walls of heads stretched shelves and shelves of brown books.

COMPARED TO WAYAH, it was another world at Cranshaw. But Featherstone was not unique. Inside the Nation's frontiers, land could not be owned. It was free for all. You claimed what you needed. Previously, back to the beginning of time, need had been defined as a little place for a cabin, small fields for beans and corn and squash, an orchard. Everybody the same size. Those were the rules Bear and his people still followed.

The white Indians, though, suffered under vast personal desire. In the years after the Revolution, Featherstone and a few others of his kind had arrived at the same new idea independently in various parts of their country. It was simple: claim all the land you want, not just what you need. They understood the changing times and the nature of property differently from their distant Indian kin, and they did not mourn the passing of the old ways, which were colorful but rather too strictly encompassing. In their view, everybody was not the same size. Nor was that a desirable way to live. The white Indians embraced the new ways like a fresh lover, and Featherstone was representative of his small class. He laid claim to several thousand acres of the best farmland in Valley

River, along with sweeping stretches of wooded mountain slope to the north and south. He named his place Cranshaw, which he understood to be a Scots name for something or other. He began farming on a large scale, not just for his own needs but for sales to distant markets. And he began running a toll ferry across the river, and also a gristmill and a smithy. As the money from his enterprises came in, he bought slaves out of South Carolina and Georgia and Alabama—at first just two or three and then dozens at a time. He set about building the kind of plantation house that white men so desperately desired. And, like his peers, he soon developed a reputation for ruling his holdings like a feudal lord in the beloved Middle Ages, which is to say with extreme violence and self-righteousness and absence of restraint toward any of his passing moods, especially pertaining to the under-people, which included nearly everybody.

There was a story about Featherstone, widely told up and down the valley. I heard it many times in following years, but I repeat it with the caution that I've had enough false tales told about me in print to discount every form of narrative by at least twenty-five percent. A sort of bunkum factor that must be accounted for in one's emotional ledger in the same way as spoilage or petty theft. Neither history nor journalism nor sausage-making is a pretty business. But here's the story, and take it as you will.

Years ago, immediately after the establishment of Cranshaw but before the death of his wife, while Featherstone was away traveling on pony-club business and his wife was off visiting relatives, his brother-in-law stole money from him. The man was a fool and a drunk, and he went into Featherstone's very bedroom and rooted around and turned up one of his money boxes under the bed. It had a fair quantity of gold and silver coin in it. Some have set the figure as high as four thousand dollars, which may or may not have bearing on how you judge Featherstone's reaction. When Featherstone got home and discovered his loss, nobody around the house owned up to knowing anything about stolen money. He raged around and burnt a house slave's hands in the cook fire to get the name of the thief. After the woman healed, she had scalloped patches of pink scars all over the backs of her hands. What she told Featherstone was that his wife's brother had been in the house while he was away and had given her five dollars not to tell and had also promised to cut her throat if she did. Featherstone gave the woman a round of butter to spread on her burns and said, I wouldn't worry about that threat for a minute, for he'll not live to carry it out. He went directly to the man's house and found the unspent remainders of his money. Then he dragged the man out onto the porch and beat him to death with his fists because, as he bragged later, he wanted the killing intimate, skin to skin, without an implement in the way, not even a buck-horn knife handle standing between him and that thieving bastard of a brother-in-law. And factor this in: Featherstone loved his wife with a consuming passion. That must not be forgotten. The first time I heard the story, I remember thinking that the wife was all the relation he had left in the world except Claire, who would have been only a baby at the time. And yet he killed the brother-in-law out of some sense of raw justice.

But that was then. With time, Featherstone mellowed, as men have a tendency to do. At least, that was the widely held opinion. Though mostly I think that any attribution of age-induced softening is more a matter of the generosity of others than a change in ourselves. It's one of the few sweet deals life offers: the older we get, the more we are forgiven the things we did when we were twenty-seven. Still, in Featherstone's middle years, when I was there to witness, he ran his holdings with a lighter touch and a certain contemptuous distance. Maybe he was a different man. These were certainly different times. When slaves offended, he disdained even to whip them and only rid himself of them by selling them off to Alabama or Louisiana. Despite all his holdings, he was a lone man. The only one he had left aboveground was Claire, and he loved her with a fierce and largely abstract love. So, looking back at my entry into Valley River, it is no wonder I saw Claire in the tall house as a maiden in a tower and myself as a despairing romantic loner, a Lancelot longing endlessly. And Featherstone, inside the tall plantation house, attractive and frightening. Arthur one day, Merlin the next.

—

MIDAFTERNOON THAT FIRST day, Featherstone sat at the head of the table. He had seated me between himself and Claire. He began Sunday dinner with the reading of a poem by Robert Burns out of a fat little duodecimo volume with the leather worn away from the feathered corners of its cover boards. He read the one about going no more a-roving, and the tone of his voice left no doubt in my mind that the poem stood equivalent to saying grace.

As we dipped into the platters of roast pork and fried chicken, the bowls of beans and squash and okra, the little china cups of chutneys and relishes, Featherstone began his examination of me.

Some of the questions were easy. Where was I from? Who were my people? How did I happen to be where I was? Where did I plan to go from here, both geographically and in the generality of life?

I told the approximate truth with no emotion whatsoever. You can just wear people out with your personal feelings. I said I was an orphan sold into the wilderness and had lived in Wayah for a long time, my people were Bear's people and I got where I was by hard work, and I was at the outset of a career as a businessman and a lawyer and I planned to read a lot of good books before I died.

And then Featherstone caught me off-footed and asked, When you pray, Will, what do you pray for?

—What? I said. Sir?

—A pony. More money. A new hat. Those sorts of things.

—I was taught that it is wrong to pray for anything that has to do with your own material well-being.

—So when you address your lord, all you allow yourself to do is ask that mankind improve itself or that it doesn't rain too hard in China?

—Or for a pure heart and a mind set free from desire.

—So what you pray for is death.

—Sir?

—Since neither of the conditions you mentioned is obtainable on this earth. Or have you not noticed?

Claire, at that moment, pressed a warm palm against my inner thigh under the table. A deep pull in her direction. She must have meant it as comforting, though it did not seem that way at the time. Not at all, in fact.

GOING ON SUNSET, we three sat on the back lawn in low wooden chairs with canted backs under a poplar tree. The chairs were aimed to look down-valley, a long prospect toward the blue west. Featherstone uncorked French claret, the bottle held tight between his knees. One quick expert pull revealed a stained cylinder of cork skewered on the screw. He poured the wine, red as melted garnets, into faceted stemmed glasses. The pale orange and cream blossoms of tulip poplars lay in the new green grass. He talked about the books he had recently read and discussed why he had admired them or not. Claire offered her thoughts on the books, which did not entirely coincide with his. He offered to loan me three of the best, and I soon sat with the little brown stack resting awkwardly in my lap. He asked whether I read *The North American Review*. I did not, but I resolved to correct that fault as immediately as possible. Featherstone notified me that he did not ordinarily trade at the post, his needs and those of his dependents being mostly met by his land, and otherwise he dealt directly with suppliers in Charleston or Philadelphia. But he wished me well in my endeavors, since the foundations of all nations rest on the stones of commerce.

I rode home late, a wavering inebriate in the saddle, moon and planets and stars layered dimensional and deep in the sky as if arrayed on the inside face of a funnel. Waverley skipped sideways at every tree shadow moving in the roadway. It occurred to me that the only times I had ever taken spirits were in the presence of Featherstone, and both those times to glorious excess.

Nine decades gone down life's twisty path—despite the depredations of time, the nights of thrashing sleeplessness until the damp sheets twine like kudzu around my ankles—I still remember, in the finest detail, the following blissful and fatally imparadised summers during which I fell irrevocably in love with the Featherstones.

—

I RODE OUT to Cranshaw every few days with the pretext of returning borrowed books and selecting others. I was fairly drunk on the riches of Featherstone's library and with the prospect of seeing Claire. In between visits, I read like mad late into the night so I might go back the sooner. And the books had to be read, for Featherstone quizzed me in detail about them. Even if I had been skilled at flimflam and filibuster—which, back then, I was not yet—that would have done me no good for, unlike many rich men, Featherstone had read a majority of the books he owned. In those earliest days, I rode out to Cranshaw along the river in the soft light of spring afternoons, and I rode back to the store under various diminishing phases of the Flower Moon.

Most evenings, Claire went out with me to where Waverley stood in the care of the young groom. I had learned enough to give the boy a coin with one hand as I took the reins from him with the other. After the boy left, Claire and I just touched hands.

—COME OUT TONIGHT, Claire said.

She took the box of writing paper she was buying and tucked it under her arm and started counting coins out of her moneypurse.

—Out? I said.

—Down below my window. But after midnight. Featherstone stays awake reading until then. One or two would be a good time. Come on foot. Don't make a sound. Be there.

—Be there for what?

—If you need to know, then don't come.

—Chilly night, I said. Blackberry winter.

—No night's too cold for a man in love. If that's what you are.

I put out my hand to take the coins, but she smacked them down on the counter like she held a very strong hand of cards and was placing a wager that could not lose.

—

IT WAS INDEED cold that night, the last frost of spring, and pitch-dark most of the way down Valley River. The half-lit Planting Moon did not rise until I had nearly reached Cranshaw, and I wondered if Claire had factored the time of its rise into her plans, waiting for days to order me there so I would walk through black forest to a secret moonlit meeting, feeling surreptitious and fraudulent in the night.

From a distance, the house was dark. Featherstone had put away his quarterlies, snuffed his candles, and gone to bed. I waited until the moon had climbed an hour into the sky and cast my shadow on the ground like a stain. And then a light was lit behind a second-floor window. A slim backlit figure threw open the sash, and I could see Claire leaning out into the moonlight. She held a leaf of paper the size of a folio page. She began folding it elaborately. I could see her hands moving very precisely. The flat paper became dimensional. She shaped it like a very simple bird, the head and wings and tail and sharp beak recognizable. And then she cast it out on the air. It glided toward me and passed above me, a pale shape against the stars. I chased it back toward the woods' edge and retrieved it as it landed in dead weeds. I looked back and the window was closed and dark. I took the paper bird and walked back up Valley River to home.

By the fire I could see that the paper was all written on. I opened it up carefully, taking the bird apart fold by fold, and found not a personal love letter but a copied-out passage from a then unknown poet. It had to do with childhood, springs and fountains, passion, mountains, autumn, and lightning. As if the writer had tried to compress the significant elements of my current life into a space of fewer than two dozen lines. In a much smaller hand at the bottom of the page, Claire had written a full bibliographic citation. Author, title, and details of publication. I read the poem over and over and then lay awake the rest of the night thinking about it and what it meant.

By the next morning, I had resolved to take up the challenge of her folded gliding bird. As a gesture of love, I had decided, it was not beyond improvement. For example, had it been me, I would have set fire to the paper before launching it into the air. And though I was moved by the poem the deconstructed bird revealed, I'd prefer to make up my own. So those were the elements I needed to work with. Flight, fire, poetry.

In the science section of one of the quarterly journals I had borrowed from Featherstone's library, I had read about how hot-air balloon flight worked and had seen an illustration of the taut bladder and well-dressed passengers waving from the dangling basket to the amazed crowds below. Astounding, yes. But it seemed a thing susceptible to miniaturization, a matter only of proportion, the lift of heat against the weight of balloon and basket. I pictured a dry leaf caught in the uprise of a campfire, a flake of pale ash rising up a chimney flue. So I ordered eight red silk scarves of the sheerest quality and a spool of fine silk thread from my Charleston supplier and began drawing designs for a withy basket and drafting a poem suitable for the occasion.

ON MY SEVENTEENTH birthday, as during the past several years, I firmed my mind to ignore the occasion. I went about my usual morning business, feeding Waverley and giving him a good brisk brushing until his summer coat glowed like buckeye. By noon only a few customers had stopped by to trade. Ginseng for gingham. Buckskins for plowpoints. The endless tedious round of commerce. Then Claire came driving up into the yard in Featherstone's cabriolet with the dark articulated top folded down like a stack of bat wings. I was sitting on the porch reading Powell's *Essay upon the Law of Contracts and Agreements.*

—I've made you a cake, she said. Get in.

I locked the door to the store, scratched a note in English and in the syllabary, and pinned it to the door. *Be back soon.*

Claire popped the reins and we went spinning off north, across the valley and up the wagon road that climbed along the creek a mile or two and then narrowed into a trail leading to the bald of the big lizard.

When we reached the end of the road, a wide spot beside the creek, the daily rain shower gathered over us with drops the size of pearls falling sizzling from the sky. I got out and hurried about raising the top to the cabriolet, but it involved erecting the framework and stretching the waxed canvas over the members and then attaching side curtains, and by the time I was done we were both completely wet and the hard rain had settled into a slow drizzle. The creek ran full and the fat leaves on the trees were glossed and dripping. A drift of fog settled down the watercourse and spread out into the tree trunks. It was a green world beyond any I've since known. Having read a number of books about the jungles of the Amazon and Congo, I'd stand amazed if they present a lusher face than that wet cove in July.

In our little dim chamber, we listened to the trees drip onto the canvas, and then we kissed a considerable while. At a point, a certain pitch of feeling, Claire leaned back away from me into the rolled leather, the pale stitching showing deep in the black upholstery. She breathed a long breath and then took a rush basket from under the seat, a blue-and-white checkered cloth covering it, and she tugged away the cloth to reveal a yellow cake with yellow icing that had slumped into a puddle around it from the warmth of the day and the jouncing ride up the creek. The body of the cake was fissured and falling into broken pieces. But Claire shaped it back as close to cylindrical as she could with her hands and elevated the icing into place with a thick-bladed knife from the basket, and when she was done it made at least an approximation of a layer cake. We ate in the cabriolet, cutting the mashed and lopsided cake with her knife and eating it from Featherstone's blue-and-white china with only our fingers for implements, since she had forgotten forks. The light was green under the wet trees, and raindrops still dripped steady off the boughs and fell in faint percussion onto the stretched canvas.

I held a last ragged delicious gob of cake in my hand. My birthday.

I sat a minute and then said, How did you know it was my birthday?

—Granny Squirrel told me.

—How did she know?

Claire made a slight twirling motion with her hands, a ghost move from the Booger Dance. She said, Same way she knows all kinds of things.

—You went all the way to her place? Half a day's ride to the gorge?

Claire said, This time of year, I like to be out and about.

LATE AUGUST, THE dogwood and sumac already red down by the creek below the store. On the porch, Claire reached into the neck of her blouse, her hand between her breasts. She brought out a little vial hanging from a rawhide lanyard around her neck. She bent forward and leaned her head down and swept her hair forward with her hand and wrist to pull the lanyard off. The nape of her neck was white, and I stopped her with my hand and leaned to kiss her there. She shook her head and tossed her hair back into place and held the vial up to me.

—You see this? she said.

—Hard not to, with you swinging it in my face.

—This will seal you to me.

—I'm sealed already.

—You're seventeen. Any pretty girl that smiles at you is the love of your life. At least for a short while.

I did not argue.

She reached to the waistband of her skirt and brought out a folded piece of quarto-sized paper. She opened it and the sun was shining on the face of it and I could see her inelegant jagged handwriting reversed through its back side.

She said, According to Granny Squirrel, I'm to say these words.

She studied the paper and read in a strong voice, as if to an audience of more than one.

Be sleepless.
Sleepless and thinking of me.
Wanting me.
Only me.

Change right now.
Change.
Now I own your thoughts.
I own your breath.
I own your heart.

Claire folded the paper and tucked it back into her waist.

—And furthermore, I'm to do this, she said.

She uncapped the vial and poured a powder dark as coffee grounds into the palm of her hand. About a teaspoonful.

She held out her hand and said, Breathe it up your nose like snuff.

I put my face to her palm and sniffed hard, and the powder went into me. I didn't feel anything but an itch in the nose, watery eyes, the brief sense of a sneeze coming on.

There was still some left in her hand, dampening in its creases. She looked at it as if somehow I had failed a challenge.

She said, I guess lick it.

The powder had no taste whatsoever, but her palm was salty.

—Now you're meant to always want me, she said.

I didn't doubt it, neither then nor now. I don't know what that powder was. Dried herbs and roots and mushrooms and fungus and bear gall ground in a mortar and pestle. Or something similar. I've never put much stock in the powder. But I believe the words entered me and changed me and still work in me. The words eat me and sustain me. And when I'm dead and in a box in the dark dark ground, and all my various souls have died and I am nothing but insensible bones, something in the marrow will still feel yearning, desire persisting beyond flesh.

THE RED SILK scarves I had ordered finally arrived in early fall. Just in time, for Claire was leaving before long for school in Savannah. I cut the rectangles of silk into wedge shapes and tried to sew them together into a sphere with an opening at the bottom, but I was downhearted when my handiwork turned out lumpish and not particularly globular, closer to a small ruddy flour sack than the taut elegant geometry I had imagined. Judging function over form, however, the awkward thing I made was weightless as cobwebs, and when it was held up to daylight you could read through it. I drew a picture of the kind of candle basket I wanted for it and took the drawing to the best basketmaker in the territory, a squat old woman with a face all scored with age but carrying the name of Rising Fawn. She wove the little basket exactly as I specified from oak splits shaved thin as paper, the warp and weft spaced wide to leave more holes than anything else. The basket would hold aplenty of candle stubs packed together, but you could cup it in your hand and it had no more heft than a good-sized sycamore leaf. I hooked basket to balloon with runs of silk thread and fired it up and held the sack above the flames with the mouth open to catch the rising heat and watched amazed as it belled out and lifted slowly into the air, exactly as it had flown in my imagination. I grabbed it down when it was head high and blew out the stubs and put it away to wait for a dry windless night when the moon was dark.

It had taken all summer to write a poem suitable to the occasion. In all honesty, I'll have to say that the final draft touched many of the same keys as the bird poem. But mine was briefer and more particular in the details of its imagery to Claire's specific features and to the exact geography of the valley. I copied my poem in my smallest hand onto a strip of paper and rolled it tight and tied it to depend on a long thread from the basket. And then I waited.

When Claire next came into the store during favorable weather and a dark moon, I said, Be at your window. After midnight.

I HUDDLED IN the dark below the yellow window, striking fire to the several candlewicks. When they were lit, I spread the mouth of the silk balloon and let it catch the heat. It rose like the spirits of the dead, a luminous red plasma ascending into the dark. Claire leaned out, black against the rectangle of her yellow window. She did not touch balloon or basket but reached and pulled the paper toward her and bit the silk thread through with her teeth and let the balloon fly on.

There was a breath of wind, a faint exhalation of the night, not even enough to stir the dry leaves on the ground. But enough to send the balloon drifting away from the house on a descending path. It floated off into the cornfield, only a few feet off the ground, glowing and mysterious, moving against the dark line of autumn trees. And then my balloon fell into a dry stook of fodder and collapsed and the basket upended and lit up like tinder and the fodder blades caught fire. Immediately, the stook was burning like a signal beacon out in the field, the flames standing thirty feet tall in the night and making a loud hissing sound.

I looked back toward Claire's yellow window and it suddenly went black. I ran and lay down behind a laurel bush. A light was lit downstairs. Featherstone, straight out of bed and backlit and wearing nothing whatsoever, came walking calmly out the door with a shotgun in his hands. He put it to his shoulder and fired both barrels out into the field, two booming reports with long yellow spouts of muzzle flash lighting the ground around him. I think he fired more as a kind of statement of selfhood rather than in hope of hitting something. And then he went back into the house. If I were a painter, I would spend a great deal of effort trying to capture that scene, a dark night sky with broken clouds, a fodderstook burning, a naked man illuminated in a halo of gun light.

7

As planned, Tallent and I swapped posts with the onset of cold weather and Claire's departure for Savannah. Back in Wayah, I didn't see much of Bear until hard weather drove him down from the mountains. In the winterhouse that year, with wind howling outside and woodsmoke lying thick under the ceiling, I listened as Bear told hunting tales from the months of my absence. It had been a series of seasons wherein all his solo jaunts through the woods were desperately boogered just short of fatality. He divided the narrative in three parts, no detail spared, for we had plenty of time. But I will summarize.

In green midsummer he was bit by an enormous snake, much longer than he was tall. The head of it was nearly as big as a dog's head, fangs the size of his pair of crooked forefingers. He thought snakes like that were long since gone from this world, but he was wrong. The calf of his leg swelled up as big around as the mouth to a bucket, and he couldn't walk out of the mountains. He lay under a rock ledge for days, taking no food but just drinking from a drip of water coming directly from a seam in the rock. The skin of his calf turned black and then split open from knee to ankle. It was two weeks before he was able to hobble home, thin as a cornstalk.

On the next trip, at the highest pitch of autumn, he had inadvertently shot and killed a grey wolf right at dusk, thinking it was some other animal entirely, a young doe or a long-legged hog. The light was very low, and he had been intemperate. Of course the sin of killing a wolf had invalidated his gun for further use. He tried cleaning it by filling its barrel with seven thin sourwood wands and soaking it in the river overnight, but still it would not hit a target. So he finally gave up his efforts and removed the lock and donated the piece to the children of the village to be used as a toy.

Then, on the very next trip, during a cold grey spell of early winter, he made camp at the lip of a cliff up in the high balsams. All he had for supper was a tea he brewed over his campfire from some frost-withered but nourishing-looking plant matter reminiscent of mushroom or lichen that he found growing in a rock garden nearby. A hard freeze settled in shortly after dark. Inexplicably and without precedent, the stars grew big as pine torches blazing across the sky. The full Snow Moon was a brilliant hole in the darkness through which another world became partially visible. It was a revelation worthy of strict attendance. Bear lay out on the cliff edge, engrossed by the amazing night and the long moon-grey landscape stretching off into a mountainous distance he had never before imagined. His mind being otherwise occupied, he let the fire burn out, and he failed to wrap himself in his bedding. By silvery dawn he could hardly feel his feet. He went to the little spring nearby and soaked them in its cold trickle, but he still lost one blackened toe on his left foot to frostbite.

—What a damn bad set of moons, Bear said. The worst hunting I've ever known.

With that, I changed the subject and told my love story from the summer. I went on for a day or two, between meals and sleep, doing the best I could to be entertaining with the material I had—the details of Claire and Featherstone, the beauty of Valley River, lavish Cranshaw, my anguish and desire concerning Claire.

When it became Bear's turn to talk about love, the first line of his story was this: I should have enjoyed an old age of quiet and respect as head man of my people, a wise voice in council, a strong tale-teller on winter nights. But instead I'm a fool and a subject of gossip and hilarity.

At that point I figured I was probably whipped in the contest of storytelling, and all I could do was listen.

Bear said he had fallen deeply and badly in love with a beautiful young widow largely on the basis of her pitiless and insatiable lovemaking. She was named Dogwood Leaf and also Sara. He could not get enough of her. And so when she insisted that, to continue, he had to marry her and her two sisters as well, he went right along and did it, for he still held with the old ways, even though the mixed-bloods and the white Scots Indians out on the Nation had declared that the old ways were swept aside and marriage ought henceforth to involve just two people, a restriction which had not prevailed before.

I should say here that Bear had been married quite a few times and was disinclined or unable to put a specific number to it. But to say he had numerous wives gives a possibly inaccurate impression. A pasha ruling over a harem or a cock treading a flock of hens in the farmyard. Some of the women he had left, and some had left him. It was about even. He held no bitterness toward any of them. And he still missed his first wife, Wild Hemp, with a bitter ache nearly fifty years after her death. When he thought of her, he was as forever young as she, for she would always be seventeen, and a great deal of love in him stayed back there.

Sara, though, was sensible enough not to be jealous of the dead, or else she didn't much care in what direction Bear's true feelings took flight. He married the three sisters all at one time, and they brought with them several widowed and spinster cousins, and a violent-tempered mother, and an old great-grandmother who claimed to have lived several decades past a hundred. So Bear was vastly outnumbered and much beleaguered by his many new women, who would gang up on him and overrule him in most decisions except in the traditional male areas of war and hunting, of which the former was entirely gone and the latter but a shade of the past and largely just an excuse for men to get away to the quiet woods.

Bear's women at least agreed with him in following the old ways, which dictated that the fields were the concern of women and thus fell under their ownership and were not his at all. And also the cabin and granary and of course the menstrual hut, which after years of abandonment suddenly began doing a brisk business near the full of the moon. If Bear ever ventured into the fields just to strike up a conversation with the women—for he had no interest in hoeing—they would run him out. The oldest woman, called Grandmother Maw because her husband had been the great Hanging Maw, was built low to the ground to begin with, and age had bent her practically double with rheumatism, so she was only about waist-high to Bear. Nevertheless, she went after him one day with an old flint hoe, hollering, No men in my corn. No bloody men.

Bear slept most nights in the townhouse, and when he couldn't stand it anymore, he went creeping by moonlight to visit Sara in the cabin on the off chance that she would agree to bed with him. And if Bear had little desire for the other new wives, they had none at all for him. One seemed not to be able to tolerate the sight of him and made angry biting comments about his every word or act, and the other treated him as a clown that God had created for her especial amusement. All three of the wives had lovers who came and went. These young men ate from the stewpot and disappeared into the sleeping houses at moonrise and were gone by dawn. All of the wives used the medicine formulas that armored them against falling in love, so their hearts remained free and clear. But they also worked the formulas that made men fall in love with them, so they had awful power. Bear was at a great disadvantage against them.

Soon, the lovemaking with Sara, which before the marriage had been frenzied and diurnal, suddenly slowed until it seemed to him that eclipses of the moon happened more frequently. And when she did take him on, he became the butt of jokes for days afterward, for the cabin where the women slept was small, like all the houses were at Wayah, and any sense of amatory privacy in such confined spaces was purely an illusion constructed from the decorum and reticence of the other inhabitants. But Sara's people—her mother and sisters and especially her grandmother—had neither. They'd talk about Bear's love sounds over breakfast soup and would contest with one another to see which among them could most closely mimic his groans. They made the sounds of boar hogs rooting in the ground, of groundhog whistles, buck snorts, crow calls. Bear would end up rushing from the house, either to sit all day sulled by the fire of his townhouse or to wander up and down the river no matter the weather in search of company and sympathy, in which case he would end up at the trade post, drinking and damning love in all its forms and wishing I were there to listen to him talk, for Tallent was a poor audience and didn't care a thing for stories, only writing figures in our ledgers.

8

THAT NEXT SUMMER IN VALLEY RIVER, I WAS NOT MUCH OF A BUSInessman. Nor did I crack a lawbook. Mostly I concerned myself with the slight weight of Claire's breast in my hand, the echo of a new poem from *The Congaree Quarterly* or *The North American Review* in my head, the mute colors of long sunsets, late suppers at Cranshaw lit with a great many spermaceti candles. Later, the spin of stars across the night sky as I rode home, for I never overnighted at the plantation.

Featherstone poured wine in great profusion that summer, and I knew enough of the trade by then to judge each bottle's considerable value on the open market. He bought only the best. Champagne in the afternoon and claret in the evening. He poured French wine like it was worth no more than the pure heavy springwater that rose cold and free from the ground. His library was also free, and I read from it with equal intoxication. Poe's *Tamerlane*, Byron and Blake, Brockden Brown's vivid ridiculous novels. Sidney's *Arcadia* seemed particularly to the point. Nothing made Featherstone happier than to see Claire and me reading, whether slumped in the lawn chairs on fair days or with a low fire going in the parlor when it rained.

On fair nights, Featherstone burned sparking head-high fires in the yard and sat at the edge of the light and drank the last of the wine and talked about astronomy and quizzed us on our current reading matter. When he eventually wandered inside to sleep, Claire and I went to the river and stripped to the skin and made squeaky love neck-deep in the cool water, with the morning fog already settling around us onto the black face of the river, my feet wedged deep between round stones and her legs tight about my hips.

Afternoons, Claire and I roamed the valley countryside in Featherstone's cabriolet and stopped when it suited us to grasp and fumble into each other on the tucked and rolled leather seats and also on mossy stream banks and out in the middle of the river on boulders with white water rushing on either side and rain falling at a slant from the sky and hissing around us or else the sun beating down hard and the river smelling like all of the valley—earth and stones and plants—had been steeped into a tea from the rainwater that ran down the slopes to make the river. We made love so often under the open sky that Claire became brown all down her breasts and belly and also her arced ass and faintly downed thighbacks. Previously, in May, all those parts had been luminous white, the ridiculous clothing of a young lady having been designed to ensure that under normal circumstances the only parts of her person the sun ever touched were the backs of her hands, on the occasions when she ventured to remove her gloves, and her face, when she tipped it out of the shadow of her bonnet's brim. I suppose I must have been equally brown, though all I remember is one uncomfortable night with my ass so sunburned I had to sleep on my stomach and the next morning surreptitiously rubbing myself with the juice of green tomatoes, which is a well-known palliative in such cases.

THE MORNING BEFORE summer solstice. I worked my hands down into the oak-split basket of dusty forked roots and stirred them around and judged them all to be sound. Poured them into the hopper of the scale and finger-tapped the weights from side to side until I achieved balance. Noted the weight and current value in the ledger beside the man's name. Flying Squirrel.

I said, You want credit or cash?

He stood looking down at the floor, uncertain. As if we hadn't done this about a dozen times recently.

—Credit, he finally said.

I wrote down fifty cents in the book and handed him his basket. He walked out and I followed him onto the porch. Claire was sitting in the store yard astraddle a horse I didn't recognize, bulging panniers behind her saddle.

—We're going to the bald and we're going to sleep up there three nights of the full moon.

—We are? I said.

She talked English, and though Flying Squirrel claimed not to understand a word of it, he looked at me funny and then went on out to the road and looked back again and walked away.

Claire said, Shut this place up. Get Waverley tacked and let's go. Come on.

—Featherstone? I said.

—Gone a-roving, not to return for a week at the inside. As much as a month at the outside.

I packed a pair of saddlebags and threaded the stock lock through the staple on the post door and clicked it fast and left a note. *Be back shortly.* Time was measured differently back then.

We set out on horseback up the trail to the Lizard Bald. Claire led. And all the way, I watched her hair fall against her back and admired the way it caught the light and shifted with the movements of her horse over the raggedness of the trail. The passway was full of rocks and went tacking up the mountain and we crossed the creek a dozen times. The leaves on the trees hung heavy and dark on the limbs from all the moisture. The whole world smelled like pulling a mossy smooth stone up from a creekbed and inhaling its fragrance. Toward midday the sky was like blue cloth faded nearly white from many washings, not a cloud in sight from horizon to horizon. By afternoon it rained out of black clouds like pouring piss from a boot, a common simile the tenor of which I have never understood. And afterward it was so foggy in the woods that you could hardly see your horse's ears ahead of you. Then the sun began setting, casting yellow and red beams through breaking clouds. Twilight went on for such a great while that you began to suspect night might not fall at all. If there was a time of year to be young and roaming the mountains, this was it.

We reached the bald at moonrise and built a small fire. We had decided not to cook and ate only water crackers with soft cheese and hot-pepper jelly I had brought. And four new peaches that Claire contributed, which we ate out of our hands like apples, fuzzy skin and yellow flesh both. And then we lay in a nest of quilts in the long grass and watched the Green Corn Moon ride slowly across the luminous arc of sky, looking so much bigger and softer than any of the winter moons that you could hardly believe it was the same orb. The horses grazed in the distance with the dew dark on their backs. I remember, sometime before dawn, Claire shrugging from the blankets all naked, her bare shoulders and tapered back blue in the moonlight, the tall grass silver and fallen over in long heavy skeins like a woman's hair. She wandered out to take in the view and came back under the blankets shivering, dew-wet all down her legs. We lay talking all night together until the first color of morning, and then we slept an hour or two, and when we awoke, everything below was a white ocean of fog. We boiled coffee atop one of only a few sunlit islands. And then the fog lifted out of the valleys and the folded world revealed itself and went on as far as the limits of sight permitted.

We spent three such nights sleeping out on the bald, living like angels, high above the corrugated world, bathed in various hues of light from dawn to dawn, privileged to be young at the highest pitch of green summer. We had taken little food and a single pot and a few blankets, but many books. Had it been rainy, we would have been miserable. The days, though, were blue. And the nights silver, lit by the briefest full moon of the year, arcing so bright across the sky that we read by it, both of us mad with words in whatever form, poems or tales. Sometimes we read to ourselves and sometimes to each other.

Much later, journalists and travel writers would discover these mountaintop clearings and find them irresistibly mysterious. Their summits were among the tallest in the East but not elevated enough to reach a tree line in this temperate rain forest. Some of the balds comprised scores of acres, wide bright meadows of tall grass and wildflowers, forming sudden dramatic openings to sky and distance out of the dark canopy of forest. Bear said all the balds were made by a giant flying serpent, and I've never come up with a better explanation of them, though I've tried.

Those three days and nights I had the best of both worlds, in that I had Claire and yearned for her at the same time. I looked down through the blue air, onto watersheds and dividing ridges and far ranges, and thought myself to be king of all that summer country.

Decades later in life, deep into aching middle age, I held deeds to most of the land I then saw, all the way to the longest horizon, stacks of papers saying all that summer country was mine. But of course, all the paper in the world was nothing in comparison to those three days.

UP ON THE BALD, young as we were, we sometimes tried to joke about marriage. But mostly the jokes didn't work. Age was not the impediment. Teenage brides were common. In fact, if a girl was exceptionally desirable, she frequently became bound to an old man of thirty-five or forty or even older who could give her a place in the world. Such marriages were business transactions wherein the bloom of youth was traded while it still had value in exchange for a life's security.

For us, however, the law was the issue. My state did not much care what mixtures or degrees of dark people wed one another. Among themselves they could go at matrimony however they saw fit. People in gradations of skin from the color of an eggplant to that of a chicken egg were free as the birds in the sky. But the state placed severe restrictions on whom a white person could marry. Minor fractions of darkness undetectable to the human eye were given significance to the extent that a drop of blood in a bucket of milk was sufficient to keep lovers apart.

Claire and I somewhat enjoyed the fact that the state prohibited us from ever joining in wedlock. Just talking about it made us feel like outlaws, which at that age seems a desirable condition. We'd break off kissing, lips all swollen and reddened, and she'd swear that the law suited her fine. She'd take nobody for a husband but a rich old man of vague race with money to burn. Some dusty-colored man with property and a big house with crystal chandeliers and suits of black clothes and hardly more Indian in him than she had. One drop of blood in a bucket of milk. Their children would come out so minutely fractional as to be a living confusion to the law. And when she was done with her fantasies, all I could swear fidelity to was bachelor freedom unto death. A long string of women stretching from here into withered senility.

And then, a minute later, we'd declare undying fealty to each other, and it seemed like bitter fetters to acknowledge the limits of the law.

—Does it address the Chinese? Claire said.

—I seriously doubt it, I said.

—So they wouldn't deny you a Chinese wife?

—Well, they've probably not thought of it yet.

—It's just a matter of time.

—Who you are is who *you* think you are, I said.

She leaned and kissed me as if I'd said something sweet and dear. But what young man wants to be sweet and dear rather than moody and mysterious?

She said, No, it's not that way at all. Most of the time it's who *they* think you are that matters.

I said, As long as we're dreaming, there's always Georgia. They'll marry anybody down there.

And it was true. Whatever mix of bloods the bride and groom had between them, they could cross the line and ride Georgia's pig-track roads to the nearest court town and find a drunk preacher or a sober magistrate willing to marry anybody in exchange for five dollars. That was the kind of place Georgia was. Wide open all the time. And then, of course—even apart from the laxity of Georgia customs—marriage was occasionally a casual thing on the frontier. People sometimes just said to hell with the state and called their own selves married and went on about their business for the rest of their lives.

—Maybe we'll get up in the morning and just go to Georgia, she said. No one would need to know but us, she said. It would be like a secret promise. We could just come back and go on as if nothing had happened.

—But we'd know, I said.

—Yeah, we'd know.

But we didn't go to Georgia, not the next day or ever. And I'm not sure how my life would have worked out differently if we had.

WHEN WE LEFT the bald, we came down Deep Creek, and for a while at elevation the laurel was still blooming. We could not allow a wide place in the trail to pass without riding alongside each other and letting our hands touch. At such a moment of conclusion later in life, I would inevitably have felt a sense of failure, an overwhelming gloom in the knowledge that days such as those three were done and gone forever. But back then I simply exulted in the false but glorious knowledge that life would be exactly this way from now on. I wasn't different from anybody else. I took youth as a special pact with God.

And as proof that endings were not endings, Claire reined up at a wide bend in the creek, a place of deep black water punctuated with green rocks, and went bathing. We both did. And afterward she lay drying in a patch of sun, stretched out long and naked, resting on her elbows, a spill of cream on a bed of green pigeon moss. Morning dew still stood in bright beads on the moss, and the creek water similarly beaded on her skin. Her nipples were drawn tight, stippled and cinnamon. She sat up and twisted the water out of her hair. And though I generally think that human beings are among the least beautiful of God's creatures—I mean, just look at us, and then look at fox or crow or trout—Claire at that moment was as beautiful as people get to be.

—You ever feel like an apostrophe? she said.

—An apostrophe?

—Just a little faint mark to stand in for something more complete. A place keeper. A convention. Barely more than nothing.

—No, I said. Maybe a dash or a hyphen sometimes. Now and then a set of apostrophes.

—I was not exactly joking, Claire said.

She slipped off the moss bank into the water and sank to her chin. She slicked her wet hair back from her brow and her face was pale and bare.

—You are not very happy, are you? she said.

—What?

—Alone. An orphan. Few friends. Only prospects. Which are rarely more lasting than yellow butterflies in September.

—I'm plenty happy. And I've got all the friends I care to have.

—Meaning you care to have—what, three? And one of those is a horse.

—People. They'll let you down.

EVEN IN OLD AGE, she recurs. I still dream about Claire at least twice a year. How amazing for a thing as vaporous as desire to survive against all the depredations of time, becoming, at its worst, a sad reminder that life mostly fails us. In some dreams she is just a fragrance. Sometimes lavender and sometimes clove and cinnamon, but also another scent dear to my heart. During those two summers, Claire had the habit of absentmindedly wiping her pen nib on her skirts, most of which were dark blue, so the only trace of her habit was the faint odor of ink around her.

SUMMER BEGAN WILTING to a close. Goldenrod and ironweed. Brilliant dry afternoons and the sun setting farther and farther south by the day. I had ridden from late afternoon into dark, heading to Cranshaw. That day, as they had done at summer's end since old times, the people burned brush off the lower slopes of the mountains. It made for better hunting, easier travel. Long into night, wavering lines of fire still climbed slowly toward the black sky. Smoke hung in the air all down Valley River.

It was going on midnight when I arrived, expecting a dark house and Claire waiting on the gallery. But Featherstone still sat out in his yard in a leather club chair, smoking a whole tom turkey over a glowing bed of hickory coals. The big bird was trussed with twine and skewered breast-up on an iron spit. Strips of bacon lay draped across it. Drops of fat stood on the browning skin like beads of sweat. Featherstone had his feet propped up on an empty wine crate, and he used another for a side table, on which sat a bottle of claret and a stemmed glass and a candle lantern and a pistol. He read from a book.

When he heard me approaching, Featherstone set the book winged open across his groin like a dead bird and rested his hand on the crate near the pistol without actually touching it. He looked toward the sound until I showed myself in the firelight.

Featherstone looked me up and down and then pulled out a gold Jurgensen watch as big as a biscuit and held its face to the candle lantern.

—Late to be calling.

—I told Claire I'd be by this afternoon.

—Then you're the very emblem of timeliness.

—I came from all the way down the valley. I'm thinking of buying another post down there. I went to have a look at it and was delayed.

Featherstone lifted his boots from his ottoman and nudged it toward me.

—Sit, he said.

I moved the crate to a quartering position around the circle of the fire and looked at Featherstone. He bent forward and tossed a dry hickory split onto hot coals, and the split flamed up yellow immediately. A streak of red bristles still highlighted his grey hair.

—I'm done with this book, Featherstone said. You can take it. See what you think. I think it's not bad.

Featherstone reached the book to me, and I took it and angled it to the fire and looked at the spine and then fingered it open and looked at a few pages of type and then closed it.

—I've heard of this poem and been wanting to read it, I said. *Don Juan.* I pronounced it as I understood the Spanish or the Mexicans might possibly do.

—Best I can tell, you say it different, Featherstone said. He rhymes it with *new 'un.*

I said the words experimentally. New 'un, Juan.

—It's about a fellow can't keep his peter in his pants. And you've been all anxious to read him. But I guess he stands for all mankind.

Featherstone reached out a small tin bucket with the handle of a paintbrush standing above its rim.

—Here, swab that bird and give it a turn.

I took the bucket by the bail and held it to my nose. It smelled of vinegar and hot pepper.

I dabbed the wet brush at the turkey with some delicacy until Featherstone said, There's plenty. Slop it on till it runs.

I did as told, and the dull red liquid sheeted off the slopes of the turkey into the fire and sizzled on the coals.

—Now turn it, Featherstone said.

—The bacon will fall off, I said.

—It's done its job. Crank away.

The spit was crooked into a handle at the end, and when I grabbed hold to give it half a turn, it seared a deep red stripe across my palm. I might have made some kind of momentary high-pitched acknowledgment.

—Shit fire, Featherstone said. I thought you had sense to use your hat or your coatsleeve or something to cover your hand.

I went to the black river and held my hand in the water but could not entirely drown the fire out of it.

When the turkey was done, we ate slices drizzled with more of the vinegar and peppers between thick cuts of wheat bread. And then we drank more wine and watched the coals of the fire. My seared hand burned on, and every so often I turned my palm to the fire and looked at the diagonal brand.

—Here, Featherstone said. A gift. Or rather, another gift consonant with the book. I'm all charity tonight.

He reached me a little red velvet pouch tied closed at the top with a pink grosgrain ribbon in the simplest bowknot. It weighed nothing.

I pulled one of the ribbon ends and fingered open the pleated top of the pouch and shook the contents out into my burnt palm. Three identical items. I knew what they were, but barely. Awful husks like shed snakeskins.

—Useful to stop the pox, Featherstone said. But also good to keep from getting babies. You soak them in water before use. And you're meant to wash them with some considerable particularity afterward.

I tucked the items back into the pouch and reached them back to him.

I said, No thank you, sir.

Featherstone grabbed my wrist in a fierce grip, first painful and then numbing. He was looking hard at me, a raptor eyeing a rabbit.

He said, Gentlemen keep them in an inside pocket.

He released my hand.

I tucked the pouch into my waistcoat, feeling mastered.

We sat a long time without speaking, and then Featherstone poured for both of us again. He said, I believe this past issue of *The Chesapeake Review* is their best yet. And I agreed.

But the more I studied the fire the more this seemed like one of the moments in life which, immediately afterward and for the rest of your life, you wish you could revise to your credit. It gnaws at you when you've failed yourself and can't go back and do anything about it. I could make a very long personal list of regretful moments. But this one would not be on it. I pulled the pouch out of my pocket and pitched the whole mess into the fire. The velvet smoldered a few seconds and then the guts flamed up quick and bright as pine shavings and died away.

—

VALLEY RIVER WAS busy with talk of the ball at Cranshaw. The party of the year. I awaited my invitation for days. No mail. Then Claire came by.

—He takes notions. Pay no attention.

—So then, I'm not to come?

—Ignore it. It's a few hours and then it's done. Let it go.

FEATHERSTONE'S SLAVES MUST have been making candles all week. Every window of the house blazed yellow. Men stood on the dark gallery talking. I could not see them other than when their black forms crossed in front of a window, but I could see the ends of their cigars stoke up when they puffed them, blinking here and there along the gallery like fireflies. And I could hear a mumble of voices, women suddenly laughing, and the sound of a poorly tuned spinet plinking some antique dance tune. A faint shuffle of feet. No fiddles and banjos for Mr. Featherstone's dance. Dancing room would have been made for the party, furniture cleared out, rugs rolled up. I supposed Claire was dancing now, someone's hand resting at the narrow of her waist or maybe a bit lower, at her hip bone or the soft place just below where her hip began arcing.

I felt just exactly as I had expected to feel when I set out from home. Exiled, bleak, an outsider lurking in the dark. And yet I had come anyway. It was a public road. Who could say no? And besides, I had been in a tragic mood for days, waiting for the invitation that did not arrive.

A majority portion of moon stood high and blue overhead, and I remained a long time burning in the road. A sad tune ran in my head like a circle.

Suddenly Claire was descending the steps, running across the lawn. Her fancy gown was green as the forest and scooped somewhat daringly at the breast. She was running right to me.

—Help me up.

I took a foot out of the stirrup and reached down a hand. She gathered the dress to mount, and as she leaped to the stirrup, her raised leg was all angles and curves above the black ankle boots. And then a glimpse of white chest and a darker depth, a scoop of shadow between her breasts as she rose toward me and swung on behind and her arms circled my waist. We were at such point of slim youth that we both fit in the curve of a saddle if we pressed hips tight together, which we did.

I gave a touch of heel and pulled right to make a show-off spin in the road, just cavalierly holding the reins one-handed. Waverley gathered himself under us and turned, pivoting in such a tight spin it felt as if his four feet would have fit on a stove lid. Then I gave a great deal of leg, and Waverley drove forward into flight.

We went hard down the road, riding double on a fine horse, the river road unspooling flat and sinuous and the wind blowing back Waverley's mane. I looked around and Claire had loosed her hair from its binding, and it too was whipping long behind, and her dress skirt was blowing back, flaring like a comet's tail, as if that sweep of hair and skirt was all the effect the resistance of the world could have on us as we streaked through the night in a moment that I could not then know was unrepeatable.

As far as I knew, we would go on endless. Youth and night and wild freedom and not one real worry yet intruding on our thoughts. Riding with the certainty that life could be a stream of such moments, a dream forever. I thought we could ride beyond the endurance or even the mortality of horses. Beyond the mortality of ourselves. All by virtue of velocity.

Waverley flew right through the ford in the river without letup, and the black water rose white around us as it parted and then fell behind. Claire leaned forward and put her lips to my right ear and said, Don't ever stop.

Remember, please, that back then there was nothing on the face of the earth faster than a fine horse at full gallop. Not one brute machine could outstrip it. In the places where they had railways, it could take four hours to go forty-five miles, at least so said Featherstone on the basis of a recent trip to Georgia. We were going multiples of that mechanic speed, ripping the night right down the middle in what now seems to me a last glorious expression of a dying world. We tore west down the valley through tunnels of close woods. And then we burst into open ground, fields overlain by infinite starred skies. The high ridges of the mountains flowed along to right and left in the moonlight. Waverley's stride was so long and elevated that we were only in contact with earth occasionally.

I could go on and on. But of course, eventually, we did have to break the spell and stop and let Waverley blow before his heart burst in his chest. And I had no doubt in my mind that if I had asked, he would have driven himself beyond the physically possible into death. His big willing chest went like a bellows between our legs, and I could feel Claire pressing against me, from her forehead at my hairline to the cusp of her at my hips. The moon was sloping west. Sad to say, we turned and started east. But slowly now, at a walk.

Claire said, Let me up in front.

She sort of pivoted some way that caused a powerful rustle and flounce of dress skirt but did not feel the least bit awkward. And then she was between my arms, leaned back against me, her hands gripping my thighs just above the knee for balance. I smelled her hair, fresh washed and scented with lavender. And I could feel a suggestion of the sides of her breasts through the dress where my forearms passed around her and pressed against her to hold the reins. I could feel her relax, a sort of deep softening breath against me. But I kept adjusting my seat in the saddle so that it would not be so apparent how rousing I found that current arrangement.

We went back toward Cranshaw, traveling retrograde to what I believed were our desires, about as slowly as Waverley could walk without coming to a full stop. But still, we eventually returned to the plantation house. Fiddles and banjos had been brought out after all, and there was a drunken buck-and-wing going to the extent that the whole place drummed with the stomp of boot heels.

There's not much left to tell about that night except that we dismounted and kissed a great long while. Her lips were chapped and she had rubbed lanolin on them and they were slightly rough and sticky. Close up, she had a faint odor of wool. And then the party began breaking up. Groups went away in the dark, heading up and down the river, in carriages and a-saddle and afoot. And before one of the groups had reached the first turn in the road, someone fired a celebratory shotgun blast straight up into the air. A yellow spew of fire gleamed fountainous up the black sky. Featherstone stood alone on the porch, a silhouette against the bright windows, and he tipped one finger to his brow in salute to me. Claire kissed me one more long goodbye and went back across the yard toward the house. I rode home. Or at least to the Valley River post, one of the places I called home. I kept Waverley at a walk all the way. I untacked him and rubbed him down with tow sacking and gave him extra grain and two little green apples and a big carrot, which he ate in one long suction from tip to feathery greens. I did not fall asleep until dawn.

A FEW NIGHTS LATER, Claire came to me just past sunset. It was raining and she was soaked. After her horse was settled in the corral, I built the fire higher and made a pallet of quilts and blankets on the floor in front of the fireplace. An autumn thunderstorm drove across the ridges to the west. The sky flashed outside the windows, casting brief light across the floor in blue trapezoids partitioned by the black shadows of muntins. Rain drummed on the shakes. We went at each other with incandescent yearning, all the bleak hopefulness of youth manifested in our grasping and clashing.

Afterward, Claire lay on her stomach with her forehead on her crossed forearms. I could have looked at her in the yellow light and smoothed my hand over the swell of her rump forever. But she soon sat up cross-legged with a quilt loose-draped around her shoulders shadowing everything but the foremost curves of her breasts lit by the fire. She sang in its entirety a recent song she had learned, "Believe Me, If All Those Endearing Young Charms." When she was done, she pointed out lines of lyric that she found especially rich in poetry, particular configurations of words that carried a freight of emotion for her. And also lines of risible sentimentality. And then when she was done, she sang "The Cavalier," a recent lesser song which I found marked by tedious excessive plot. A young man goes at night beneath a young beloved lady's window. He finds a rope ladder and thinks it is meant for him. But she has used the ladder to elope with someone else, though the mechanism by which he discovers this is left unexplained. On his way home he composes a song within the song. The refrain of his composition expresses the opinion that, as far as he is concerned, such ladies as his former beloved may go to Hell or to Hong Kong.

When we were done with criticism, we had a second go at each other. And then she reckoned she might spend the night with me.

—And as to your father? I said.

—Father?

—Featherstone.

—He's not my father.

—He's not? What is he then?

—I'm married to him, she said.

I could have died right on the spot.

—Married?

—It's complicated.

—Nobody ever said.

—Nobody ever said not. And I don't recall you asking.

I sat thinking a long time. I had made certain false assumptions.

I said, Have you ever slept with him?

—Yes.

—Well, that about covers it, then.

I rose to go. An awkward moment of poking feet into trouser legs, feeding arms into shirtsleeves. I was not sure where to go, since we were at my place. Nightwalking. Roaming out fearless into the malevolent universe. Running full speed into the dark until I slammed into something hard and jagged enough to open my head up. Spilling my pink brains, which apparently would be insufficient to tan my own hide.

—But he's never fucked me, if that's the question you meant to ask, she said.

She reached and took my hand and pulled me back down onto the warm quilts and told a story.

SHE HAD COME to Featherstone as part of a marriage arrangement, a deal under the old ways in which she was thrown in as an unwanted bonus. Featherstone had come riding along the road in front of their house near sunset one day. He was half drunk from a bottle of black Barbados rum that he had been nipping at all afternoon to ease the boredom of the journey between his plantation at Valley River and the new capital of the Nation—which was still mostly an empty field and hopeful marks on a plat map. A previous wife had recently died, and he had blood in his eye to take another. As he passed their farm, Claire's older sister, Angeline, was sitting on the bottom step of the porch, twisting the water out of her newly washed hair. It was a beautiful sight, and Featherstone said to himself, at that moment, I'll have to marry that girl.

There was no courtship to speak of, only negotiation. The mother was a widow and such a minor fraction Indian that she had blue eyes. She was thirty-five years old, still somewhat pretty, and eager to see if life had anything left to offer her. She set terms and stuck to them against all of Featherstone's counteroffers and bluffs, during which he threatened to walk away from the table. Finally, he agreed to her deal, the only one she had ever offered. Aside from a substantial cash payment, the mother insisted that to get Angeline, he had to take Claire, then a skinny girl of eleven. During that entire period, all the notice Featherstone took of Claire was that he once gave her a linty stick of striped candy from his coat pocket.

Featherstone did not come for them himself, nor did he send a carriage. An old African—with stiff arthritic hands, clawed and big-knuckled, holding the reins—pulled up in front of their house in an ox wagon. The canvas cover swagged in loose articulated arcs over metal hoops, the fabric grey and stained with use. It was the sort of conveyance in which you would haul dusty sacks of milled corn.

The man's sunken lids drooped over yellow-whited eyes. He spoke only fragments of English, and those few with a heavy West African accent, but he made it known that he was to fetch them to Featherstone. Angeline was disinclined to clamber over the tailboard of the miserable wagon and ride like produce to market. As far as she was concerned, the deal was off. This was not what she had been led to expect. Her new life was meant to be otherwise than this. But the mother would not hear of it. She argued that perhaps all of Featherstone's several carriages were in use that day. He had much important business to transact. They should all wish to accommodate, to show an attractive willingness.

Claire held her arms by their elbows, crossed and clenched beneath the narrow ribbed space of chest where her breasts would be. She looked off in the direction of a haystook by the pole barn where a pair of grey striped kittens played at hunting. They stalked and pounced on whatever small things moved in the loose hay.

The argument continued until, eventually, Angeline wore down. She fell silent. The mother said, Well, get on. The girls clambered awkwardly into the high wagon, and the driver poked the oxen with a stick. The pale blurred shapes of their similar faces and identical sharp grey eyes looked out from under the dark shadow of the wagon lid as they rode away.

After the wedding, such as it was, Featherstone, to his credit, had loved the older sister without reservation and taken her as his true wife, and Claire became a mere dependent, a daughter of sorts. Then after two years, Angeline died of yellow fever. Featherstone grieved her passing and had never, even after several years, come creeping to Claire's bedroom late at night.

—So why have you slept with him? I said.

—It is a complicated relationship, Claire said.

—Complicated?

—Yes.

—To me, this is complicated.

—What?

I gestured with both hands toward her, still sitting naked with the blanket around her shoulders.

She didn't say anything back in actual response but only asked what time it was. I went and looked at my watch, not yet a gold Jurgensen, and when I told her she said, They damn. She yanked her clothes on and went and would not allow me to ride even partway home with her.

9

THREE MORNINGS LATER, WAVERLEY WAS GONE. THE CORRAL STOOD empty and breached. The four peeled poles that slid into augured holes in posts to make a gate lay tumbled on the ground.

Not much was left from the old pony-club days, but some of the young men still ran stolen horses across the Nation to sell in neighboring states. And whenever some of the youngsters went horse stealing, they knew Featherstone would give them a place to overnight their string, and if they were in a real scrape they knew that, out of his stable of blooded horses, he'd provide the mounts for them to escape on. He saw it as a civic duty worth the risk to himself for the improvements pony-club outings effected in the character of the young men. So if you were missing a horse in Valley River, Cranshaw was the logical place to start looking.

THE GROOM WAS nowhere to be seen, and all the other slaves must have been busy. I could see a few of them building a run-in shed off at the back of one of the pastures and some others working in the apple and peach orchards on the far hillside. So when I walked into the stable yard, Featherstone was alone, tacking a mare. He wore his whiteman riding clothes. A dark coat, tall black boots, pale breeches, and a wide-brimmed Panama hat. At his waist a wide belt with a sheathed Bowie knife hanging from it.

Featherstone looked at me and said, Be with you momentarily.

He kept on about his business, working slowly with a great deal of fussiness in regard to settling the bit, a harsh twist of bright metal with long shanks, in the mare's mouth. He buckled the throat latch underneath her jaw, got the saddle all adjusted and the girth tightened and the stirrup leathers lengthened one hole on each side—and then, upon reconsideration, put back to their original positions. Finally, after some process of decision that—judging from the changing expressions on his face—could have gone either way, he added a martingale.

I stood and waited.

When Featherstone had mounted without the aid of a block and was about to ride off without another word, I said, I'm looking for that Waverley stallion of mine. He's gone missing.

—Haven't we already done this? Featherstone said. It was a long time ago. You were looking for a horse at my hunting place. Years ago.

—People's horses find their way into your corrals pretty regularly. It's why I came here first. Maybe you recollect mine. A bay stallion. You've seen him standing hitched in your stable yard about a hundred times.

—A lot of horses come and go. I don't pay much attention. But there isn't anything here that answers to your description right now. Not stallions, anyway. There's a horse over there in that third corral looks something like what you're talking about. He's a gelding, though.

I walked out to the corral and saw Waverley sorted in with a half-dozen little speckled horses of indeterminate breed. He still bled down the insides of his hind legs.

I stood there a minute and then started patting my pockets like I might find a pistol if I kept looking. And if I'd found one, I'd not have been able to hold back from shooting Featherstone out of the saddle where he sat. All I remember thinking was that I'd sooner die than let this pass. I declared it to myself as a vow.

I walked back to where Featherstone sat waiting, the mare bobbing her head impatiently and trying to back away from the bit.

—You care to climb down off that horse, I said.

—Great God, are you going to try to claim that gelding? I reckon there's hardly any horses between here and the Mississippi that's safe from being declared yours.

—That one's all I'm claiming, I said. Just about everybody between here and Wayah will bear me out.

—Oh, shit, am I ever in a pickle now. Up against a man with Indian witnesses scattered all through the big dark woods. That's just grand. I guess there's nothing for it but that I'll have to get me a few witnesses of my own. An even dozen shouldn't be hard.

He reached up and felt his forehead with the back of his hand like checking a child for fever.

—There, he said. I feel better already.

—Difference is, I wouldn't have to pay mine to back up a lie, I said.

Featherstone dismounted, and when he was good and off, standing with the reins in one hand and looking all bright and interested in where this might lead, I walked up to him and hit him square in the mouth with all I had. Still, I did not knock him down but just stepped him back two or three paces until he caught his balance. He dropped the reins and the mare went walking off unalarmed toward the other horses in the corral. His hat lay on the ground.

Featherstone put his hand to his mouth and bled between his fingers. He took his hand down and looked at the blood on it and then felt his lips and probed around his teeth with his bloody fingers. Then, so quick I hardly realized he'd moved, he'd yanked the broad upcurved blade of the Bowie from its scabbard. For a pair of heartbeats, it sang like a tuning fork as he held it to the light.

I wanted to take to my heels, but I stood inside myself and waited. I was unarmed and at least thought fast enough to say so.

He first looked like that fact didn't have a bit of bearing on his next act, but then he thought on it and said, I'll get around to killing you for this later.

He put the knife away and spit a red gob onto the ground. He pulled up a wad of grass and wiped his hands. It took him an undignified minute to pick up his hat and chase down his mare. He adjusted his hat on his head and mounted and rode away without looking at me again. The knuckles of my fist were already swelling, and the first two had split open like the skin of an overripe tomato.

DUELING IS A kind of courtship, codified and fraught with etiquette, but with the ultimate ceremony designed to effect the irrevocable parting of two lives rather than their wedding. The consummation serves to channel rage as marriage does the practice of sex, and with the same goal—to confine damage to just the two principals.

Now dueling is a thing of the past, and welcome so. But back then it was all the fashion, like an inexplicably popular new idea about the shape of hat crowns or the cut of lapels. Men of the dueling class, which is to say anyone who was a gentleman or wished to be considered one, often entered into affrays for the slightest reasons. Andrew Jackson, when a young backwoods lawyer across the mountains in Jonesboro, fought one of his several duels when his opponent expressed a poor opinion of Jackson's favorite lawbook. And that fight was not a singularity in regard to silliness. Men fought because one gave the other a look passing in the street. And they also fought because one *failed* to look at the other while passing in the street. Men held their honor like a wild bird's egg cupped in their hands, a beautiful little thin-shelled brittle thing, ready to break at the slightest breath of insult. But, of course, nearly every custom, no matter how risible, has its good points. So I'll say this for dueling, it worked a remarkable improvement on public manners, since knowing that any number of men you might encounter were willing to use pistols to address the slightest affront, and a small minority of them could snuff a candle at twenty paces, tended to moderate one's behavior considerably.

In the past four decades, the number of people claiming to have seen our duel firsthand has swelled to the point that one imagines a vast crowd requiring draft-beer vendors and women boiling peanuts and frying chitlins in black iron pots for their accommodation, as at the public hanging of a prominent murderer. And many of those claimants have told their stories of the day in great detail, some in print. The accounts vary considerably, and I have collected them over the years in my journals and in my memory. I, however, have never spoken or written about the *rencontre*, and neither did Featherstone or either of the two seconds before their deaths. And I don't intend to say very much here to set history straight, other than to make a few random observations, mainly about the preliminaries.

Featherstone waited several days, a week at least, before sending his initial letter by way of his second, a lesser plantation owner named Bushyhead. The lag in time was, no doubt, to educate himself on the etiquette of an affair of honor, the rules of which were many and widely published. Young men in Camden and Charleston kept copies of the French code in their pistol cases. After all, it was difficult to remember all the eighty-four rules off the top of your head at a time of some understandable nervousness.

Featherstone's letter, which I read while Bushyhead sat drinking coffee by the fireplace of the store, stated the obvious. There are offenses of such galling nature that one would rather die than let them pass unanswered. And he wrote that since I put so much stock in the ways of Charleston and suchlike places, he wanted to deal with me as a gentleman would do rather than just gut me out by the roadside as I clearly deserved. He said he would abide by any published code duello I cared to name. But after studying the matter, he wanted to recommend that we adopt the Irish rules, including the Galway addendum. He had discovered that according to those rules, it is well established that blows cannot be answered with words. So just an apology was out of the question. But the sensible and peaceful Irish suggest a way to avoid a fight to the death. In their view, the offending party in a case where a blow has been struck should not only make an apology on bended knee, like a suitor, but should then hand his own cane to the offended party. A beating of varying brutality ensues, entirely dependent on the character and mood of the offended. So you see, Featherstone concluded, we could easily resolve this business in a matter of ten or fifteen minutes without recourse to the field of honor and equality. He would await word from me specifying the time and place where he might beat me senseless with my own stick, after which our prior warm relation—nearly that of father and son, he wrote—might continue unabated. And in the role of elder and adviser, he suggested that in the future I not take the gelding of horses to be so personally symbolic. Then, a big showy signature. At the bottom of the page, he had added a postscript in a looser and perhaps later hand. It read, *What do you say we do as friends do and go have a drink together and not kill each other? A horse is a horse, even on its best day.*

I've heard of men who accepted challenges in their parlors with a bloody mind but then later, on the dueling ground, only discharged their pistols into the air and stood square to their opponent waiting to receive fire, saying afterward—those lucky enough to survive—that they had the courage to die but not to kill. I've never understood such men. They are not made for this world. They must either view themselves as saints or the duel as a finer alternative to suicide. For me, every time I saw the scabbed and puckered blankness at Waverley's groin, I still wanted to kill Featherstone about as bad as I had that day in his stable yard. And not just kill him but live to gloat about it for many years after. I pictured a bright summer day, the grass boot-top high, me a man in middle years with trousers unbuttoned, splashing piss off his headstone.

Of course, such happy visions were entirely different from actually believing I could accomplish his killing. In any other form of combat, Featherstone would have cut me down quicker than I could blink my eyes. But a duel with smooth-bore flintlock pistols at forty yards evens things out considerably. Back then, my aim was true, for I had a steady hand and had spent many a slow afternoon target shooting out behind the store at Wayah. And, too, Featherstone was more noted for his use of the knife than as a marksman, so I figured my odds to be even, or maybe a little better.

I wrote a quick note stating that I appreciated the information on how the Irish did things. It was always enlightening to learn about colorful foreign ways. But I had no inclination to apologize. Nor did I care to take a beating at his hand.

I left it at that and sent Bushyhead on his way.

The next morning he returned bearing the formal letter of challenge, which was phrased in the required exquisite diction. Perhaps it exceeded all requirements. It may have crossed some line into parody. The phrase *field of honor* figured repeatedly. The subjunctive mood was predominant. One periodic sentence of considerable magnificence, and with more than a whiff of the previous century, went on nearly forever, more than a page, before its grammar finally reached the payoff whereupon, if you were strict in your attention, you could figure out what the subject and the verb had been. But the gist of it was that certain offenses leave one's honor so fouled that the only solvent strong enough to cleanse it is blood. The letter concluded not with a challenge to a duel but with an invitation for an *entrevue.*

When I was done reading, Bushyhead asked if I'd say the letter aloud to him, and when I reached the part about an interview, he said, The only part I understood of it was Dear Sir.

I wrote back with the knowledge that though Featherstone might be intent on making a joke of the fight, I could still very well end up dead in a few days. I pressed my clerk, Tallent, into service as my second, and he shut the post at Wayah and came to Valley River immediately. He delivered my acceptance of the challenge.

The next day began a flurry of further correspondence. In one letter, despite the fact that he occupied the position of challenger and was not in a position to dictate choice of weapons, Featherstone demanded that we duel by war hatchet while tied together at our left wrists. He cited as precedent for the odd choice of weapons a famous duel by whaling harpoon at ten paces and suggested that we might as well also make history, or at least become notorious. When I declined to respond, his next letter simply read, *Blowguns at dawn!* Below that message, a bold flowing signature, written with a nib cut broad.

It was only when I threatened to post his foolishness on every wood fence in the Nation's capital at New Echota and to advertise it in every paper in the three adjoining states and *The Phoenix* as well that he settled on the customary matched pistols, of which I happened to own a pair, souvenir of an overly complicated livestock trade.

I showed them to Claire that week. The pistols were beautiful artifacts, all curved polished wood and glowing metal, and a great deal longer than you'd expect. Lying in their open-lidded wooden case, paired one above the other on the blue velvet lining, they looked like lovers coupling in a canopy bed.

I said as much to Claire, and she looked at them for quite some time and then said, Panicky bed.

She walked straight out the door and down the steps to her horse. I followed, trying to make her stay, but she mounted without a word, making an uncustomarily awkward hop and unbalanced swing of leg over the horse's back. But before she rode away she said, Between you and Featherstone, I am doomed to love asses and idiots.

The next flurry of letters picked at the details of the code, niggling over every detail. One letter expressed concern that our meeting lacked the necessary element of social equivalence to stand the test for a proper duello. *Even overlooking the disparity in our respective positions,* he wrote, *your choice of Second concerns me.* Tallent, he felt compelled to point out, was a mere shop clerk and, as such, clearly violated the spirit of equality embodied in the code. However, he reasoned, gone were the days when dueling was reserved for true gentlemen of the plantation-owning class. And sadly so. Now the institution had descended so far that every young would-be lawyer and peddler with social aspirations felt entitled to display an exquisite sense of easily bruised honor and demand to meet his betters on the sacred field. But he conceded that since we were in neither Charleston nor New Orleans, some latitude was called for. And perhaps, nowadays, even those bastions had been breached and concession held sway, for, he concluded, these were deeply degenerate times.

The letter seemed designed to provoke me into bringing to his attention the fact that I was a whiteman and he a sort of Indian, for pure white blood prevailed. I merely sent back, through Tallent, a brief note reiterating the time and place I had already specified.

As the day approached, I felt a kind of hysterical clarity. One moment I was tossing out witty comments to anyone who would listen and the next I was bent over, throwing up a grey spume of tea and biscuits into a patch of jewelweed by the back steps. Claire wanted to attend the duel, but Featherstone told her she was strictly prohibited both by her sex and by the rules concerning degrees of consanguinity allowed for spectators.

As I've said, accounts of the duel have accumulated over the years. They vary widely and are, each and all, in some regards suspect. Only three details appear without fail. The first detail is simply that Featherstone took a wound in the leg. The next, oddly enough, is that, to mark firing positions, my second scribed a line in the ground with the brass ferrule of his cane while Featherstone's drove a little wooden stob, hammering it down with the butt of his pistol. In none of the accounts is either duelist said to have objected to the lack of consistency, nor does it play any further role in the events. So why then, I wonder, did that particular detail—one which I do not remember and can neither verify nor deny—fix itself in people's minds as a necessary component of history? Third and finally, all accounts agree that the event happened during the first new moon in autumn, Nut Moon, with the apples all dead ripe on the trees, and hickory nuts and walnuts and chestnuts falling, and the leaves coloring. The month of the year when the world was created and time began ticking. Thus the first month of the new year is not in grey winter or green spring. Everything starts with the grace of approaching death.

As for the duel itself, I might fairly group the variant narratives into three categories.

The simplest and therefore most credible story is merely that the two men and their seconds met in a clearing beside the river at the first peep of dawn with the fog still settled in the valley and the light so low they must have been just dark shapes moving about making mysterious gestures at one another. Vague horses barely had shape at all where they stood across the road tied to trees. The customary wagon was present to haul home the dead or wounded. When the fog and the light had risen a little, the men began the excruciatingly slow and solemn rituals of loading the pistols and pacing off distances and marking the ground and taking positions. And, finally, the call to fire. One shot cracked, muffled by the fog. Hardly louder than an axe splitting a stick of kindling. Morning would still have been dim enough for yellow flame to have flashed from the muzzle, but the cloud of jetting grey smoke would have merged quickly with the river fog. And then, after a slight pause, a second shot. The result of the engagement in this telling was that Featherstone missed his target entirely, after which Will, at more leisure to take aim, struck him a light creasing wound on the inside of his upper thigh, akin only to a burn, a sort of branding, a red stripe that barely drew blood and did not even knock Featherstone to the ground but only staggered him a step and irreparably damaged a new pair of fine dove-grey breeches. At that point both men walked forward, shook hands, and declared the matter entirely settled with honor preserved all around. A frequent addition to this version of the duel is that Davy Crockett was among the spectators, having shown up unexpectedly the day before on a journey back to Tennessee. Crockett is credited with saying, at the conclusion of the events, that it never did make shit sense to him to tangle up the bloody business of killing with so much good manners. I will only say that I am nearly positive that I did not meet Crockett until at least a year later.

A second account, widely though more discreetly reported, was that the duel did not take place at dawn but rather at sunset, because word of the meeting had become widespread and a great many Indians, eager to witness this novelty of civilization, had camped at the specified ground by the river and cooked and danced through the night. When the duelists arrived in the fog of first light, they found a crowd already assembled, some of whom were drunk and many of whom had already begun laying bets as they would do at a ball game. Not wanting an affair of honor to become a carnival show, the parties discussed the problem among themselves and then announced that the duel was off and a reconciliation reached. The crowd, of course, was not pleased that the blood had suddenly drained out of the air. Amid the grumbling, the combatants departed and then reconvened at sunset after the crowd had gone home. During the preparations by the seconds, it is said, Featherstone went to Will and handed him a great lead ball, sized to fit a buffalo musket. Big as a crab apple is the most common simile. Featherstone said, Bite on this; it is meant to steady the nerves. Will was pale as death or the color of a cut peach, one or the other. But he had the presence of mind to roll the ball in his palm and hand it back to Featherstone, saying, Thank you, sir, but perhaps you should keep it as a spare in case you swallow your own. Meanwhile, the seconds were furiously thumbing through their copies of the code and found, as they suspected, that the principals are forbidden to address each other directly. They cautioned the two men that further communication would not be allowed. Will's second shouted, We insist that you both forbear to altercate further. He held up his copy of the code and jabbed a forefinger at the article in question. Featherstone's second, Bushyhead, simply said, No talking. None a-tall. Then, when the duelists took their positions and were given the call to fire, Featherstone stood his ground and let Will have the first shot, hoping it would be rushed and inaccurate, which it was. The bullet hit the ground at Featherstone's feet, throwing a spray of red mud up onto his dove-colored breeches and white shirtfront. Seeing the damage to his attire, Featherstone became enraged and rushed toward Will, either to fire at closer range or to strike him with his pistol or his fists. The moment Featherstone crossed his mark on the ground, however, Will's second, the clerk Tallent, acting in full accord with the chosen code duello, raised his own pistol and shot Featherstone in the thigh, dropping him like a poleaxed steer. Featherstone's second then thumbed through the code again and spoke the words therein suggested: I have been deceived and have come to these grounds in company with a coward. Featherstone was taken home in the bed of a wagon.

The third variant claims that in violation of all the various rules of dueling, the outcome had been arranged ahead of time by Claire Featherstone. She was seen every day that week, riding back and forth between Featherstone and Will, exhausting her horse in round after round of diplomacy. It was assumed she presented every argument she could construct to reconcile the matter without bullets flying. When she failed in her attempts to convince the two men to let sense prevail, she threatened the utter withdrawal of any affection she might still hold for either of them, slight as it was at the time due to their shared idiocy. Her love would be replaced by black hatred for the survivor should either be killed. That strategy eventually worked, and in the end both men agreed to let love for her take precedence over their hatred for each other and to discharge their pistols into the sky and call the matter quits. But at the moment when fire was called, Featherstone, in an exaggerated and silly preparatory flourish with his pistol, managed to miss the broad sky and instead, tripping the hair trigger prematurely, managed to shoot himself in the leg. The ball missed bone and went clear through the meat. The flow of blood was stanched with moss compresses, and Featherstone made a show of laughing and calling for a drink of rum all around during his treatment. He then mounted under his own power and rode home, but not before lavishly, and a-saddle, complimenting the courage of his young opponent in a tone of such carefully calibrated sarcasm as to come within a hairbreadth of inciting another round of dueling. One teller of this version adds that during the final preparations for the fight, Featherstone complained that Will was thin as a rake, girlish in figure, and offered little target, while he himself was strong and wide across the chest as a bull thus easy to hit. Will supposedly suggested that his own outline be chalked upon the front of Featherstone's black clothes and any shot of his that struck outside the lines be specified to count as naught.

I will only add that by my lights, dim as they may now be, none of the accounts summarized above is accurate and none is entirely lacking in fact. So readers may feel free to choose the story of their liking and consider it true history. After all, the exact nature of the incident is now unknowable. Everyone is dead but me. And my age precludes considering any account I might give as definitive. Something happened. Beyond that, nothing is knowable.

I SAW CLAIRE only once in the weeks after the duel, and that unexpectedly. Cold weather came early that year, and I was out for a morose morning ride in the novelty of snow with the bright leaves still on the trees. She was doing the same, and we met on a narrow byroad. Without much prelude other than a touch of hands and some sense of consonance between our moods and the falling snow, we fell together. When we arose, rearranging our clothes and brushing the snow away, the shapes of our bodies were printed in the snow like the angels children make by lying on their backs and flinging their limbs about. Big new flakes fell hard into our outline, filling it as we watched. But Claire angrily kicked away our sign as if a passerby might read it like a bear tracker and know every detail of our encounter. We stood close and I held her and she pressed her forehead hard beneath my chin. She smelled like woodsmoke, as if the night before, the first cold night of autumn, she had thrown cedar boughs on the fire and scented her dark wool cloak in the incense. It accorded well with her clove and cinnamon.

I reminded her that she had once chewed juniper berries as an experiment, though a failed one. Now kiss me, she had said. And when I did, the taste of her tongue made me jerk back in reflex. Which set her to laughing, and also to imagining other bitter combinations. Acorns and dried peppers. Crab apples and rosemary. Sumac berries and sage.

—That will be my goal for the future, she said. A mouth as sharp as a bee sting.

THEN, WITHIN DAYS, October was back to itself again, dry and sunny, and both Claire and Featherstone were suddenly gone, and no one at Valley River knew or would say where or for how long. The house was shuttered, but the business of the place—the fields and orchards and livestock—went on as usual under a nervous foreman who ran it as if Featherstone himself were hiding in the woods, waiting to pounce on any slight mistake. Some among the help said Claire was back in school, a new one in Virginia or Pennsylvania, and that Featherstone was off gambling and carousing for a few months in New Orleans and wheeling up and down the Mississippi on palatial white riverboats blazing all night with oil lamps. Others believed the two of them had gone off together, with plans to travel for a year or more in England and France and Italy. The only report I took as truth was that they had left with a great number of trunks sufficient to stay away forever.

I waited but received no correspondence from Claire. My inquiries to the various girls' schools up and down the seaboard all the way from Georgia to Maine bore no fruit. Which is an overly polite way of saying that the great majority of my letters went unanswered, and the few responses I received were rather too smugly pleased to inform me that if a young lady named Claire Featherstone were enrolled at their school, an exquisite sense of institutional discretion would prohibit them from revealing that fact to anyone inquiring by post or in person.

Claire was just solid gone.

I TRIED TO turn my attention to the law. I was not the first young man to plow my bitter ground with a deep share, turning lovelorn pain into ambition. And the frontier was just the place for new beginnings.

When I was first setting out as a lawyer, I went about it fairly part-time, having also my business responsibilities to my growing string of trade posts and my ties to Bear and his people. I entered the profession quite ill prepared, having only read law in my books and not ever seen it accomplished in a courtroom. And it was just like French, not at all what I had imagined. But I was a fast learner. And also my rates were low back then, for who wants a boy lawyer unless he comes cheap? There were a near-dozen county courthouses where I did regular law business, so Waverley and I spent a great deal of time in transit. I kept a clean white shirt and black frock coat in my saddlebags, and right before my cases came up you would see me spring freshly clad from the outhouse behind the courthouse. I stood in relation to regular attorneys as circuit-riding preachers are to ministers.

I never took cases of murder and rarely of assault or horse theft. Mostly I was a dirt lawyer, my specialty the buying and selling of land and the many complications and disagreements arising therefrom. And my practice was helped considerably by the idiocy of the state law that allowed anyone to file a claim on land, even if it was already occupied and filed on by someone else. Then everyone involved had to go to court to sort out the title. It was a bad law, but good for the lawyer business.

I noted that many successful frontier esquires had vivid personal styles that juries found entertaining and therefore convincing, and I tried to find one for myself. For a while I let my hair grow long in the back and shined it with pomade. I had a fancy waistcoat made of bright red silk and pointy-toed boots polished to a high gloss. I ordered Havana cigars in the largest size and would puff meaningfully at certain moments in my questioning of witnesses, as if I were thinking hard about their answers and could only come to the sad reluctant conclusion that they were lying.

There were days when court was like a knife fight. Debt collection and land ownership and whose hogs broke down somebody's fence all have surprising power to raise emotions to a high pitch. Nobody likes to lose, no matter what the stakes. Lethal threats were made right in front of judges. You came into the courthouse with your pistol in your pocket and left with it in your hand. Other days, though, court was a jocular affair, and the lawyer that prevailed was the one whose dry wit most often made the audience laugh.

I WROTE SOME poems during that time of Claire's absence. Of course I did. What young man of feeling does not? Furthermore, they did not remain forever in a private precious journal. The most romantic of them were published. Not enough to make even a slim volume, the pages sparely dressed with words, barely blackened between wide margins. So, without a collection, my works are scattered and lost to the reading public among old numbers of mostly discontinued periodicals: *The Chesapeake Review, The Congaree Quarterly, The Arcadian, The Allegheny Review,* and a few others of lesser note.

In the third number of the fifth volume of *The Arcadian,* my finest work, "To C——," was unveiled to the public. It was some poem. Better than a hundred lines long. In it, I promised my lost and presumably dead beloved *down all the ruins of time* that I would give my fortune (then largely nonexistent) and my place on earth (as marginal and remote as you can get) and pretty much everything but my left hand to once again *taste of her garnet lips.* (Why garnet? Because I had recently found a large one in the creek behind the Valley River station and was quite proud of it.) Between those semiprecious curves of flesh, her teeth shone like pearls, her breast as white as moon in June. The poem expresses a great deal of *'tis* and *thither.* Gloom and mystery. I'm afraid I might have used some phrase like *Now, still grave, speak.* That sort of sentiment.

I reckon there was such a shortage of poems back then that the quarterlies would set into type just about any rhymed writing you cared to send them. The price of postage was all that stood in the way of becoming a poet. In summation, you might say that my poems did not breach the citadel of the soul. I'll just leave it at that. Except to say that, in fact, favorable notice was taken in some discerning quarters. I had a few appreciative readers, and my abandonment of poetry was not welcomed by all.

ONE OF THOSE YEARS, when dead winter had set in and I had retired with Bear into the winterhouse, I remember walking out one day for a breath of fresh air. I had to break snow knee-deep to reach the creek. It was covered over with grey ice, and through it I could see black water rushing underneath. What a mournful day it was. I took my knife tip and carved Claire's name in the ice and then wrote down what I thought the date was, though I could have been as high as a week wrong, one way or the other. And thus the year wheeled back around to yet another grim commencement.

PART THREE

. . .

removal

1

THE FIRE IN THE CENTER OF THE TOWNHOUSE WAS BUILT SMALL, burned down mostly to coals with blue and yellow flames rising low and sporadic from checkered and nearly consumed logs of hickory and chestnut. The pole benches all around the walls were crowded with people, and the children sat or lay on the packed earth floor. They nearly faded into the darkness, except for vague blurs of faces, the pale movements of hands. Bear stood and walked around the fire and used the light to his advantage—like an actor moving in and out of the yellow glow of footlights—revealing and then retreating.

He began the council with a confession. From his long and somewhat error-prone life, his greatest regret was that long ago he had let old obsolete hatreds mislead him into fighting under Jackson during the Creek War. He regretted fighting against other Indians, even though the Creeks had been enemies of the Cherokee long before the first whiteman erupted into the world. Even more, he wished deep in his heart that he had not squandered the opportunity to kill Jackson back then, for they had stood an arm's length apart on several occasions, and it was well known that Bear always had a quick hand with a knife. During that time he had witnessed Jackson order a boy soldier shot for insubordination. The offense was failing to obey a command to pick up some chicken bones littering the ground. The boy did not do it immediately but waited until he finished eating his dinner. By necessity, the firing squad killed the boy sitting on a log, for he was too terrified to stand. On the other hand, after the fight at Horseshoe Bend, Jackson's men cut bridle reins from the back hide of dead Creek warriors and collected their noses to verify the numeration of dead. On those actions, as opposed to a matter of chicken bones, Jackson had no comment one way or the other.

Jackson had long since announced his intention to remove all Indians to the West. A date certain had been set, and though it was many seasons away, it was rushing toward them. Some of the Scottish Indians on the Nation paid little heed to it. They believed in their ability to make a deal. But Bear had seen Jackson at work. The Old Possum was implacable, and he meant to put an end to Indians.

—End-times are tricky things to deal with, Bear said.

He moved out of the light, gliding toward a dark corner where his voice would be deepened by the intersecting walls and project sourceless into the vaulted and dramatic space. He reminded the people of the great comet years ago, before the memories of many in his audience. Its tail stretched across half the sky, and it had fallen through the night for weeks. Then over and over for more than two months, the old and dying earth shook until one wall of the townhouse had fallen away and the roof collapsed. Holes opened in the ground and filled with bad water. Hens were shaken from their roosts onto the dirt, and treetops swayed though there was no wind whatsoever.

Shortly thereafter, an old man reported that one afternoon he was sitting by a fire in his cabin yard when a tall man came out of the woods. All his clothes were made of green leaves, big sycamore and poplar leaves fashioned so that they lapped one another like snake scales, and he had his head covered with a broad hat of waxy laurel leaves. He carried a child in the crook of one arm, and he claimed the child was God and God was fixing to destroy earth soon unless the people returned to the old ways and gave up clothes of woven cloth and guns and plows and nearly all metal whatsoever, and quit growing yellow corn and went back to real corn—the old mottled ears—and stopped grinding their kernels between the stones of water mills and went back to pounding it into meal by hand in log mortars, and resettled the old towns and rebuilt the townhouses on top of the mounds and recommenced observing all the old sacred festivals and dances in the squaregrounds at the foot of the mounds. The Green Man laid down all these conditions, and God offered no additional opinions on his own but just kicked his bare feet against the air and pulled at the leaves of the man's tunic and looked around as if seeing everything he had made for the first time, and his attitude was one of surprise and delight.

Soon a prophet named Dull Hoe weighed in with his vision. Dull Hoe was a man who did not just visit the spirit world but resided there nearly full-time and only experienced this world as a vague troubling dream. On a lonesome journey into the mountains, he had seen black riders come across the sky on their mounts and light to rest on a high peak, Tusquitte Bald to be exact. Their leader was beating a drum, and the whole world vibrated to its urgent rhythm. When he quit beating, he started talking, and his words matched up with the story of the Green Man and God. Stop following white ways, don't break the bones of corn in hideous and violent machines, forswear all metal, wear hides not cloth, be wary of the wheel in all its forms, see the plow as an enemy, dance the old dances. Die otherwise. For a great storm was coming soon, with hailstones as big as hominy blocks falling from a black sky, killing all the whites and anyone else who did not go to refuge in the highest mountains. The world would be wiped clean. Afterward, the disappeared deer and elk and buffalo would return from wherever they had gone, and the people could go back to living like they used to, all the beauty and blood of the old ways restored to them.

Soon, belief in these visions and revelations became widespread, and trails from the foothills up to the mountains began filling with pilgrims. They went to the high balds and camped in the long grass and waited. There was not a date as exact for that apocalypse as Jackson had given for this one. *Soon* was all the Green Man and God and the Black Rider had said.

When the people had been up on the mountaintops so long that by anyone's reckoning *soon* had long since passed without any sign of a cleansing storm gathering on the horizon, they journeyed back down to the same hopeless world they had fled.

Bear, who then as now lived in the mountains and kept mostly by the old ways already, had not followed the pilgrims but watched all of it with despair. What he believed then was that Green Man and God were not going to save him or his people. And he believed the same now. There would be no regaining what was lost. A world once gone was gone for good.

And neither would war save them. The Creeks had fought with Jackson and lost half their people. Choctaws had been cut down likewise. So fighting was out.

How to survive? How to save the broken fragments of the world? Those were the pressing questions. On the Nation, some of the people had decided that becoming as much like the whites as possible was the way. Washington and Jefferson had told them that to survive, those were the only terms. And the white Indians of the Nation had gone at it to the best of their understanding. They now had their own laws and head chief and bicameral legislature housed in a big townhouse, and a supreme court and even a national academy and a museum displaying the long culture of the people. Also a newspaper, *The Phoenix*, printed in the syllabary. All situated in the capital city of New Echota, which was platted out and in progress of construction. And that was all fine for those people out on the Nation, but it hadn't changed the Possum's mind a bit.

In Wayah, Bear didn't think he and his people could turn white no matter how hard they tried. But he didn't much want to try at all. He wondered if you could be said to have survived if at the end you didn't even recognize yourself or your new life or your homeland. Do you dissipate like a drop of blood in a bucket of milk, or do you persist, a small stone tossed into a rushing river?

One choice that lay before them was to go west as Jackson had commanded them to do. But if the western territories were as fine as they were made out to be, the white people would soon come and take that land away from them too, for it was the nature of white people that they could never be satisfied.

As Bear saw it, his people had only a pair of things in their favor. The first was their land. It was so difficult and beautiful that nobody wanted it but them. Most of it lay inconveniently vertical. It was hard to farm. You couldn't cut a wagon road through even the easiest parts without the greatest difficulty. It had no gold. It was wet and foggy and rainy a great deal of the year. But nevertheless it was theirs, both by heritage and by deed, nearly a thousand acres of it anyway, which Bear conceded was not really much land at all. But it had the advantage of belonging neither to the Nation nor to any whiteman. It was on paper under his name. His view was that they needed a great deal more such land.

Then he told another story, of his journey to Charleston and his discovery of the workings of the law and how he found a way to use it in his favor, like an axe, by keeping its sharp edge turned away from himself and his desires. Blossom, the girl he had redeemed from slavery, was among the people in the townhouse. She was now a stout woman of middle age with a half dozen children, most of them grown. Her hair was parted in a strict line down the top of her head and was threaded with white. She spoke up and told how splendid and terrifying the court was and how, nevertheless, Bear and his lawyer had swept all before them and set her free.

Bear looked at the crowd and waited in silence long enough for them to grow uncomfortable. Then he said, And now the second thing we have is our own lawyer, who is one of us. Me and Will can save us.

Everyone looked at me.

I wanted to run far away from the kind of fight Bear was proposing. But what I did was stand up beside Bear in the firelight and say that at least I'd give it a try. Go to Washington City and see what I could do in our behalf.

—

DAYS ON HORSEBACK east to the nearest town with stage service. Days on the stage to the railhead. Then flying along on the train for two days at dizzying speeds occasionally approaching twenty miles an hour to the state capital. And after some business there, on to navigable water. And then lazy days floating in a riverboat to the coastal port, followed by a sailing ship up the Atlantic and past Cape Henry into the Chesapeake, and then another riverboat for the final stretch up the Potomac.

On that first trip, I was so excited about train travel that for the first fifty miles after the railhead, I sat up front in the locomotive conversing with the engineer and the fireman and helping feed wood into the firebox. And in turn they shared their dinner with me, fat yeasty bread rolls and thin beefsteaks seasoned with a great deal of crushed black and red pepper and seared fast in a dry long-handled iron skillet heated nearly red-hot over the fire.

I was delighted by the variety of towns along the way, whether I stopped for the night or just for an hour of rest and food. I remember overnighting at a tavern in the hill country, where homesick Irish fiddlers and pipers and drummers played their music until almost sunrise. There were towns noted for pig cookery, where they dug pits in the ground and built fires in them and let the wood burn down to red coals and then put in the pig and buried fire and carcass together in red clay. When the pig was disinterred the next day, it would be chopped or hand-pulled to shreds and dressed with vinegar and hot peppers and served with salty dollops of cornmeal fried in lard. Cookery in each town was somewhat different from the next. One place, full of little stout Dutchmen, had the finest sausages I had ever eaten, cooked over hickory coals and served with sauerkraut and brown ale drawn from brown glazed crocks cooled in the creek. Another town had a tavern where they alleged the T-bone beefsteak had been invented, though I did not see how that claim could possibly be true since beeves had surely gone around with that part of their insides for quite some time.

Down along the coast, everything smelled of fish and salt water. I spent a night in a town where the wild hogs came down onto exposed mudflats at low tide and ate little pale crabs, crunching them like chitlins. More pleasantly, in Wilmington I found a waterside place that took pride in their cool grey oysters pulled fresh from the sea and arrayed still quivering in their opened shells and eaten alongside glasses of straw-colored wine from France. The first time I dined on oysters, my enthusiasm embarrassed my tablemates. I slurped down two dozen in quick succession, and even after I could eat no more, I kept now and again between swallows of wine lifting an empty half shell to my nose and sniffing the pearly cup to remind myself of the existence of this marvelous and completely unexpected food.

I was raw to that flat country of piedmont and coastal plain. So when I boarded the first riverboat of my life—a sort of broken-backed sternwheeler in bad need of scraping and painting, a watercraft disappointingly far removed from my imaginings of the grand floating palaces of the Mississippi—I wanted to be taken for a young man of substance, traveling with a certain style.

I was met on deck by a little lean purser even younger than myself.

—I'd like your best cabin, I said.

—Best how? the purser said.

—Largest, finest, cleanest, brightest. Those sorts of things. Your best.

—They're all of a kind.

—Surely some of them have some superior features. For example, better views than others?

—Winders?

—Yes, I said.

—They've none of them got winders. Lets in bugs. Every cabin here, you walk in and shut the door, it's like you've shut your eyes. But if I was to cull, I'd say, the way the air flows, maybe fore is better than aft. You smell less of everybody's chamberpots in the morning. The way the cook fries breakfast, it's hard enough to take sunrise as it is.

—Book me a cabin to the fore, then.

—You'll not be sorry.

—

SHABBY AS IT WAS, there was almost nothing about the paddleboat and its passage eastward toward the Atlantic that I did not like. Churning down the broad brown rivers of the coastal plain, tying up at night at some backwoods landing with torches burning globes of yellow light against the black night and turpentine barrels and cotton bales stacked high on the dock and the slaves working shirtless and sweating and singing mighty rhythmic songs while they loaded the goods onto the boat. Sun rising yellow through fog hanging so thick across the water I could hardly see the green jungle we passed through. Or the big cleared fields planted with indigo or cotton, their dizzying furrows running in converging lines to a distant flat horizon unlike any I had ever seen before. I could hardly sleep for fear of missing something. Booming down the river through all that coastal area with its pine savannas and cypress swamps cut through by guts and creeks—which were not at all like creeks where I came from but were just tidal ditches of black mud and stinking salt water, but they seemed exotic and like the places that travel writers got all worked up over in the quarterly journals I favored.

The riverboat cabins were hardly bigger than tipped outhouses and not much better smelling, with their sleeping pallets stained by every fluid the human body is able to produce and unemptied chamberpots and poor ventilation. And they were so close and hot in the summertime that on the few nights when the mosquitoes were at all calm I preferred to sleep on deck, swinging in a string hammock and watching the moonlight fall on the river and the dark woods pass above the steep sandy banks.

Contrary to the purser's assessment, I found the food excellent, though supper might be no more complicated than a good fish soup with little beads of yellow butter afloat on the surface of a thinnish milk broth, accompanied by fine-crumbed corncakes and little gherkins, heaped bright green on a white plate with the stained vinegar pooling underneath.

The passenger list was shuffled up at each stop down the river as people came and went from town to town. In that part of the state, the men all talked in a certain style, with their lips run out and pooched up in front of them so that they reminded me of hens gabbling right after they have laid an egg. They were without exception wild for gambling and would sit up all night in the little salon playing cards and swapping money to and fro among themselves. I played seldom and carefully and quit early, for I did not care to lose much money. But I haunted the salons until late, having discovered that the ladies on board found me exotic. At the supper table one evening, the tall and thirtyish wife of a somewhat younger little indigo factor listened to my very brief and reluctant accounting of my life and then said, Imagine that. From the far mountains. An orphan adopted by an Indian chief. Intimate with Nature. And yet a lawyer and businessman and now an Indian chief himself. And so well-spoken. And on his way to Washington City to lobby Congress and the Jackson administration on behalf of his people.

I said, Well, I do wear shoes and can count to twenty with them on and everything, but there are lots of chiefs. It's not like being president. More like mayor. And I'm just the chief when it comes to business and law. My father Bear's the real chief.

Late that night while her husband was still at cards, the indigo factor's wife pecked on my cabin door with a knuckle, and we had a fumbling and fully clothed congress rather less than fully reclined on the miserable pallet. And then she straightened her clothes and smiled and kissed me a glancing blow on my cheekbone. She said, You might consider just letting people think a chief is whatever they imagine it to be without further correction. It will work better for you. Then she eased out the door. The whole thing had taken three minutes. But from then forward, I elaborated on my life a bit more fully and romantically during dinner conversation, and if anybody wanted to call me chief, they were welcome to it.

WASHINGTON CITY WAS being built on a landscape of utter insignificance, a mudflat by the river barely elevated above sea level, with a midsized southern town arising on it, with the distinguishing addition of a few scattered half-formed classical temples of enormous scale, in such a state of partiality that it was hard at first glance to tell whether they were falling or rising. Hogs ran free range right into the edges of town. The raw new city amounted to not much. And perhaps that was the point. Any gesture of accomplishment could stand tall, for it would lack further reference or perspective beyond itself. In such a place, the pale dome of the Capitol could loom high as Mont Blanc from the mud riverbanks, and the men who peopled it could consider themselves Goliaths.

Congress was in town, so Washington City was a busy place. Most of the principal streets were paved with cobbles, so there was always a racket from the metal hoops of carriage wheels clashing against them, and at night the calkins of horseshoes struck sparks off them. The unpaved road up the hill to the Capitol was like a winding stream of black mud, such an axle-deep mire that drivers mostly forsook the roadway and set out cross-country directly up the slopes of the hill, which had become cut like new-plowed ground with the parallel tracks of wheels and the cupped prints of horses and mules right to the Capitol steps.

I ARRIVED GREEN as a barrel of June apples. Since I was there to represent the Cherokee, I dressed the part. My idea of what an agent of the Indians, a member of a clan, a business chief, ought to wear for meetings with government officials expressed itself fully only on one occasion, my first visit to the office of the secretary of war, where all Indian business began and most of it ended. I wore a silk turban in the style recently adopted by many of the eastern Indians for occasions of high seriousness. Mine was deep purple and patterned with yellow figures of pineapples. I had on a regular black frock coat, but my waistcoat matched the turban, as did the cravat securing the neck of my starched white shirt. On my feet, beaded buckskin moccasins, laced to the knees and fringed along the outer seams. It was a splendid outfit. As I walked from my hotel to the War Department, people on the street took little note of my odd display, for the town was full of various kinds of outlanders, everything from Creeks to Turks.

When I arrived at the office, Secretary Cass did not offer a chair but stood looking at me a long time, and then he said, Sir, I don't wish to take up any of your time just now, when you so clearly have appointments with hatters and cobblers. Perhaps you could arrange to return after those obligations have been met.

I said, No, Mr. Cass. I have plenty of time right now.

Cass again looked at me silently for a long uncomfortable span of seconds. He finally said, Let me be clear, then. I was trying to avoid saying that you look the fool. You're not the first young man ever to do so. Come back when you don't, and I'll be glad to meet with you and hear your business.

I flushed red to the hairline and got up and gave a little one-inch head bob of a bow and left.

—THEY'RE WEARING THEM with wider brims and rounder crowns of late.

I put the narrow-brimmed creased-crowned specimen back on its display block.

—One of those new sorts then, I said.

—I can have it done in a week, the hatter said. He wrapped a tape measure around my head and said, Excellent. And I wondered, but did not ask, how the size of my head might be worthy of such a superlative. That began the period of time when I refused to wear any outfit in which the hat failed to correspond with the clothes.

I had first taken a room in a boardinghouse that was cheap and bleak and not at all well situated and was popular only among the youngest and least influential congressional aides and other useless wayfarers. I soon moved to the famous Indian Queen, even though I could not really afford my long stay there. But it was popular among young men of bright prospect and also various Creek and Cherokee and Seminole legations come to Washington City to negotiate treaties. Sam Houston had been a regular before he fled to Texas, and the management still talked of him with sad affection. Nothing could ever again match the times when Houston was in residence at the Queen and held court late into the night in the lounge, often until the first flicker of dawn, for he didn't sleep well in the dark and liked to pass the night drinking and talking and listening to fiddle music. He only went to his bed when daylight began rising, and then at midday he arose all red-nosed and puffy and ate a vast dinner of beef and began conspiring. All the chambermaids and desk clerks agreed that those were the days, and it had all been downhill since.

I RETURNED TO the office of the secretary of war as soon as my embarrassing entrance into politics could be corrected. I had since visited every fine tailor and cobbler in the city and had acquired all the wardrobe I could afford. By any standard, I looked irreproachable.

I thought my argument was simple and unassailable. Bear's people were too small and remote to be of interest to America. And there were the deeds Bear and I held to the land we occupied. Our land was not the Nation, it was America. Private ownership of land was intended to mean something in this country. Real property was a bond as strong as blood. The dissolution of the Nation and the exile of its people to the West had no bearing on our situation, for we owned our land outright.

—All Indians? the secretary said.

—Yes.

—Some would say that fact is all that matters.

—My argument is about ownership of land, not blood.

—How many Indians are you representing? the secretary said.

—We have never been more than a thousand souls. A little village called Wayah. Existing independently outside the Nation for many years.

—But all of them Indians?

—Yes. All of us. Mostly full-bloods.

Cass sat looking at me, at the hue of skin visible outside my clothing—my face and neck and handbacks—judging blood degree. And he was an expert, for every fraction of Indian in existence had passed through his office.

—You're white, the secretary said, not inflecting a question at all.

—Yes, I said. Adopted.

—And only a thousand of them?

—Well, fewer of us than that.

—How many, then?

—Five hundred, about. Or somewhat fewer.

—Let's say four hundred Indians. And not a one of them with the vote.

—I vote.

—So the entire tally of electors is one? Why should I bother?

IN A WEEK, armed with only a few letters of introduction, you could meet everyone of political or social consequence, right up to the president. It was a small town. I made the rounds, office to office. I talked with seat-fillers in various departments and agencies. Met with many young representatives, and even a couple of old regal senators, one of them the famously contentious John C. Calhoun. And I soon saw how the business was done but realized I did not have the money to do it very well. I took men of influence out for suppers and drinks, but I could not offer any more in the way of inducement. And more was what the situation called for. I was left to stand on the logic of my argument about the sanctity of property ownership. And in Washington City that did not amount to anything.

I went from office to office, and the men who inhabited them would sit and listen, but I could see wheels turn and the teeth of interlocked gears engage behind their eyes. They soon ceased listening and began wondering how agreeing with me might benefit anyone who mattered. In particular, themselves. Everybody I talked to came to the same conclusion as the secretary of war. Why bother? I'd ask them for their support, and they would look me in the eye and go off talking on some vague other heartwarming topic, with the sincerity of a dying man addressing Jesus. They were artists of misdirection as sure as any thimblerigger shifting his three shells and one wizened pea.

But at least Calhoun saw some prospect in me, or some element of entertainment. The senator had coffee brought in and we left off business and talked more generally, as elder to younger. At some point in recounting my brief history, I mentioned that I had taught myself French with no other help than a grammar and a dictionary, for there were many books in that language I had yearned to read, in particular Rousseau's *Meditations of a Solitary Walker* and the Abbé Prévost's *Manon Lescaut*, either of which, by the way, I would have considered entirely worth the effort, and so it was like I got Voltaire thrown in for free. When I arrived in Washington and heard the language aloud for the first time, it was a great disappointment to find that I could not understand a lick of it. Nor could any of the young aides to French diplomats understand me when I tried to speak. The short of it was, French didn't sound a bit like I thought it would. Calhoun said it was without a doubt the nastiest-sounding tongue practiced by any known people on the round globe and he himself spoke a very little of it, only what he could remember from his classes at Yale many years ago. But he would pass along a trick he had learned, which was this: you couldn't go far wrong if you pronounced every single word of the language as if it were a child's euphemism for the private parts.

I WENT TO the White House with a letter of introduction from Calhoun, who warned that it might have more the opposite effect since a rift had developed between him and Jackson after they won the election of '28 and Calhoun had become Jackson's vice president and then resigned in a quarrel over the issue of nullification, there being no stronger supporter of states' rights than Calhoun.

But you couldn't say Jackson wasn't warned about the temperament of his second in command, for Calhoun had also fallen out similarly when he was vice president the first time under Quincy Adams.

Calhoun's nature demanded that he buck against anybody who sat above him, and yet he never managed to get himself all the way on top. It was more than clear to everyone in Washington that Calhoun and Jackson, though both old men, were still violent as fighting cocks at their cores and would very much like to kill each other. So it was a wonder to me that they didn't find themselves out of an early morning by the misty Potomac squaring off in a pistol duel. And it is a shame they didn't, for they would have put Burr and Hamilton in the shade as a piece of history.

Calhoun's letter in pocket, I walked up to the White House, past the paddock where Jackson's horse stood switching flies and dozing, and on through the door. I searched down long corridors for someone to whom I might present the letter. Finally I opened a door and found the old murderer himself in his office, holding forth to a small gang of cronies, most of them young men about my age. Jackson was stretched out on a chaise, alternately talking and sucking on a pastille. The pleated skin around his mouth opened and closed rhythmically as a bellows. Flattering portraits notwithstanding, Jackson looked older than he was, sixty-five or thereabouts. He had indeed the pointed face, tiny blank eyes, and sharp snapping teeth of a possum. He blinked his little vicious dark eyes beneath his upreaching, pyrotechnic white hair and registered scant interest in me beyond an assessment of how difficult I might be to kill in a formal pistol duel or an impromptu tavern knife fight, both of which he had successfully fought in his youth and middle age.

When I presented the letter and brought up my business—launching quickly into the details of citizenship and ownership of land—the look in Jackson's eyes suggested he might have a killing or two left in him. But all he did was raise one hand and give a dismissive gesture in my direction and then begin talking around his pastille about his new boots. He wiggled his feet down at the bottom of the chaise to highlight them. His opinion was, the new boots were close to the finest he had ever worn. Whereupon all the attending young men, in turn, commented favorably on their every superlative feature, from heels to lacing. I judged the heels too high to be strictly proper for a man but kept that opinion to myself and occupied my mind, during the round of praise from the cronies, in looking at Jackson's head and thinking that, between them, Jackson and Calhoun had the two most alarming manes of hair I had ever seen on white men. I qualified the judgment in that way because as a boy I knew a few old Indian warriors who still sported coifs from their youth way back in the previous century, styles that involved plucking half one's head with mussel-shell tweezers and letting the other half grow long, festooning random braided locks with colored beads and silver fobs and making part or all of the remainder elevate in spikes with the assistance of bear grease. But in a contest of extravagant hair just among white men, Jackson and Calhoun would have split the prize. They hated each other and yet continued to share their lofty hairstyles, which struck me as having all the features of placing exploding possums on their heads. Of course, they were both from South Carolina and thus given to strange enthusiasms.

WHEN THE LEADERS of the Cherokee, Chief Ross and Major Ridge, came up to Washington City to lobby against removal, they were a source of deep racial confusion to those in power. Chief Ross, the head man for the whole Nation, was as white as any congressman. And Major Ridge, though dark-skinned, dressed somewhat better than all but the richest senators and carried himself with an arrogant attitude that created a suspicion that he was of superior intelligence. Both men were wealthy plantation owners and almost equally powerful within the Nation, which was a new and uncertain country set inside America like a reflection in an imperfect mirror. I had been to New Echota many times and was never sure whether it represented a grand experiment or a pathetically inept confidence game.

Chief Ross had more Scots blood than anything else—seven-eighths majority of it, in fact. He was a short man who spoke Cherokee so poorly that he would not attempt it in public, nor could he even read the syllabary. But he was a sharp and close trader in business and politics, and a prideful little man who parted his hair just above his left ear and carried the long remainder up and over to the opposing ear in an attempt to cover the barren ground of his bald pate. He used a fragrant pomade, and the comb tracks were straight as bean rows traversing his scalp.

Major Ridge, who had been given his rank by Jackson back in the Creek War, had his boys with him, both approximately my age. Young Ridge was the only son, and the other was a nephew, Elias Boudinot, who had been born Buck Watie but had decided to take a name that better suited him. Boudinot and young Ridge featured themselves to be darkly Byronic figures, an image countless young men—myself included—held of themselves.

Looking back upon my first meeting with them in the social room of the Queen, it seems like we should have gotten along. For some now unaccountable reason specific to young men, we didn't. I knew all about them, though, for they were somewhat famous. Major Ridge had sent them to Connecticut for their educations, and when they could read Latin and write fluently in every verse form common to the English language, they came back to the Nation dressed to the teeth in the latest fashion, riding in matched cabriolets drawn by matching teams, and married to matching white wives, all four of them unimaginably young and burning to make progressive reforms in every department of life you could name. Education, child-rearing, government, literature, journalism, cuisine. Upon arrival in the Nation, the two young Yankee brides were reported to look pale and stunned but game for the new lives they'd chosen with their brilliant and exotic new husbands.

The people of the North are very open-minded and so much more advanced than we are. All they did to one of the girls when it became known that she intended to marry an Indian was burn her in effigy on the main street and chime all the church bells of the town hourly throughout the night. She was sixteen or seventeen, somewhere in there. The next morning, which was a Sunday, she got up and dressed in her best clothes and walked alone straight through town, past the grey and still-smoking ashes of her pyre and into the church, where she sat on the front pew with her face set and let the congregation all glare hatred at the back of her head for an hour. She left that afternoon to meet Boudinot nearby and be surreptitiously married by a sympathetic preacher, and afterward they set out south with young Ridge and his equally stunned bride.

It took them the better part of two months to make the journey back to the Nation, because they paused on the way in New York City to watch a few plays and in Washington City to go to parties attended by members of both houses of Congress.

I don't know what the girls were expecting when they reached the young gentlemen's ancestral home. Wigwams and feather headdresses, maybe. What they found on arrival was the plantation house of Ridge's family, hundreds of acres with slaves working vast fields of cotton and tobacco, moving down the rows like the shadow of storm clouds settling over the land. And inside the big house, white tablecloths and silver and china in the dining room. Presided over by a stout big-haired patriarch who went by the title of major and wore ruffled shirts and waistcoats and anything else white men were wearing in America.

All of which is to say that for the Government, Chief Ross and the Ridges were unsatisfactory Indians and hard to deal with. Silver trinkets and talk of the Great White Father got nowhere with them.

Though Ross and Ridge shared the same goal, the survival of the Nation, they hated each other more than Calhoun and Jackson did. Somewhere deep in their minds, they both imagined a future in which the Nation would become a state, a new star on the striped banner. Governor Ross or Governor Ridge living in a new executive mansion.

When their delegations arrived, I half expected Featherstone to be among them, but he was not. Lobbying must have seemed a little too much like real work, though I could have set him straight on that fear.

Both Ross and Ridge viewed me with a great deal of wariness, since I represented Indians living outside the Nation, and when I tried to suggest we join ranks in our efforts, each man let me know I was on my own and warned me not to muddy their waters with my little problems. Nevertheless, Ridge and I drank together some nights in the Queen and got along just fine when we were not talking business. But I made Ross nervous because I spoke Cherokee with a degree of polish, while Ross could barely comment on the weather, and even that topic was limited to the current moment, since the chief's understanding of his people's language was limited to the present tense.

I MET CROCKETT through the agency of Calhoun. Crockett was then at the height of his fame, at least pre-posthumously. When I knew him, he was a figure of folklore; it took the Alamo to elevate him all the way to myth.

It was considerably more difficult to arrange a meeting with Crockett than with the president. In preparation, I bought *Sketches and Eccentricities of Col. David Crockett* and went to a coffeehouse and settled in to read. Well, the story just got the more unbelievable the farther I proceeded. And then I reached this line: *Here roamed the red men of the forest, free as the breezes which fanned their raven locks.* I put the book down and tried not to let it color my view of the man, for Crockett had no say in its production. Writers can tell any lie that leaps into their heads.

I had at least gotten far enough to learn that Crockett and I held in common the experience of being bound boys, though in Crockett's case he had violated the pact his father made by running away from his new master, a hog drover, on their first journey together. Boy Crockett had dared either man—master or father—to try enforcing the contract. He backed them down. At least that's the story the book told. And for me, it was as Romantic as all of Byron's poetry put together.

Our first meeting was in his office in the Capitol and we got along like equals, even though Crockett was old enough to be my natural daddy. He soon began coming around the Indian Queen late afternoons for a drink and a visit. He was going through a spell of malaria about then. His color was like wood ash, and his eyes were dark and swollen below the underlids, and he was sheened with sweat even in the cool of evening. Like anybody else of good sense, when he stayed up all night drinking, he favored Scotch whisky of the highest quality, as long as somebody else was buying. He was a hard man to keep up with for more than a day or two, but I liked him and hated to miss good and useful entertainment. So I did my best, which meant showing up to listen night after night and providing a bottle of Macallan's no more than once a week, for to do so more often would look needy and also wreak entire havoc on my wallet. One useful thing I learned from Crockett on those nights was to alternate my Scotch with glasses of chilled mineral water, preferably from the mountains of Virginia.

THOSE DAYS, it was hard to be noted as a character in Washington, what with Crockett strutting and flashing about town being the wild frontiersman. I liked him a great deal but I had no desire to become Davy Crockett's understudy, his sidekick, his young buddy. However, I was around him enough to think that *being* Crockett in those days would have been pretty fine. Crockett had the attention of everyone. When he entered a room, it felt like the candles would all flicker out from the breeze created when every head suddenly turned his way. Even in a great pressing party crowd, everyone knew exactly where Crockett was at all times. If he went outside to piss, word of it spread from one end of a ballroom to the other before he could button up and get back indoors. What made me truly like Crockett was noting, in moments of a public nature, a sad discontinuity between the upcurve of his smiling mouth and the bleak deadness of his eyes. And also that Crockett knew it to be a flaw in his public image but could do nothing to correct it other than, when outdoors, to cock his hat so that it rode low on his brow, its brim casting deep shade to the bridge of his nose.

One day, drinking in the lounge of the Queen, Crockett noted that there had been a withering attack on him in one of the morning papers. I asked if that sort of thing bothered him, for back then it would have bothered me a great deal. Crockett said, Oh, I'm a big target and easy to hit, so there's no honor in it. Every newspaper jackass with a pen and half an hour of unclaimed time gets to take a shot.

—

I SOON LEARNED that the public galleries of the Senate chamber were an excellent place to meet ladies, both young and youngish. What I desired was Claire, but the gallery ladies were better than lone bachelorhood. In the streets most days, I could not help staring hard at passing strangers in case one of them might be Claire, visiting the capital with Featherstone.

I met the famous actress Mrs. Chapman at a small party in the house of a senator from one of the upper states, a squat dark little man with almost no hair and only a dense chin beard for compensation. She had grown up in Charleston, had succeeded Fanny Kemble as the principal female lead of *High, Low, Jack . . . Game,* and was the talk of the town. Wherever she went during the day, all traffic, both pedestrian and vehicular, came to a halt to watch her pass. She was tall and angular and beautiful, and a soft warm light seemed to shine down on her, following wherever she moved. But, constantly and a little awkwardly, she tried to step just out of its beam, and thus she went about with a dodging motion, as if always apologizing for herself. All men and most women found her sidling manner charming in the extreme.

While the party went on in an adjoining room, she and I circled awkwardly around a long dark mahogany table burdened with china platters filled with various delicate foods. Our orbits were duplicated in a great rippling framed mirror on the wall. Both of us eyed the little special doughballs filled with meat, the dense rum cakes and dark mincemeats. My attention was drawn to a dish of fig pastries, each no bigger around than a gold dollar. Mrs. Chapman claimed to have handmade them herself. I ate one and offered the bland opinion that it was especially good.

She had been told I published poetry, though regrettably she had read none of it. She mentioned that she knew a vastly famous old Boston writer, who had told her he could not get through a day in any peace unless he had written a specific quantity of lines. Otherwise, despair.

She paused and then mentioned the exact melancholy number. It seemed unimaginably large.

I pictured the old grey man sitting at his desk scribbling as frantic as a farmer beating out a wheat-field fire with a wet tow sack, shedding strands of white hair in a momentous backlit explosion from his nimbus of beard and coiffure, tossing the dense blackened pages over his shoulder into a pile of paper as great and conical as a haystack. It seemed to me that onanists must feel the same way. Not happy if they are unable to practice their special art daily.

But aloud I said, With me it's the other way around.

She nodded politely and composed her face as if my comment were something worth serious consideration and not just a piece of smart-assery, for which generosity I found her even more lovely.

I met Mrs. Chapman at other parties and was initially only polite to her, given the Mrs. attached to her name. But I soon got the distinct impression that Mr. Chapman, whoever he had been, had long since passed to another world, or at least to an unimaginably distant state like Ohio or Illinois. And also, stunningly, that Mrs. Chapman was twenty-two. My age exactly.

When I discovered this fact, I brought it up at a dinner. We're the same age.

I regretted the comment as soon as it fell from my mouth.

She said, Many are. But let's agree to make a special pact of it.

In short order, Mrs. Chapman and I began seeing a great deal of each other. On Sundays we often went riding, usually to view the stone locks on the towpath of the Chesapeake and Ohio Canal. Or to the George Town heights to look across the river in the direction of Alexandria and on back to the Capitol across the thin scattering of homes and government buildings. I took her to see the portraits of significant Indians from the various peoples displayed in a chamber of the Department of War. We met at the sorts of parties where the music and dancing went on until past midnight, and then supper was served. At one party held at the house of a noted art collector, Mrs. Chapman and I danced not a step but spent time going from canvas to canvas. We decided to bypass landscape, my usual favorite, and also still life, for she did not find bowls of grapes and apples very interesting. We chose to examine only portraits that evening. Most of the faces gleamed up from brown darkness, bathed in a flattering buttery light, eyes liquid and searching. We studied them one by one and guessed in which of the two basic categories the persons belonged, preachers or drunks. At another party, we created a minor scandal by dancing every dance exclusively together. It was a fancy ball where only the eldest senators were excused for arriving *en habit de ville*—a phrase I overheard Calhoun use in begging the pardon of the hostess for his failure to find a suitable costume. That year, getups of Asian flavor were predominant for both men and women, though there were also the usual scatterings of pirates and gauchos and Indian maidens and chiefs, so I found an unexpected use for my purple turban and tall moccasins. Mrs. Chapman was living alone in a townhouse with only two or three servants, and when the party broke up deep in the night, I accompanied her home in her carriage. I walked back to the Indian Queen shortly before dawn with only the late-night packs of half-wild dogs roaming the streets for company, the Corn Tassel Moon almost full.

And then with little warning the play's run was over and Mrs. Chapman was off to another city, and I moped about the riverbank for days on end and neglected my correspondence to various departments of government and back home to Tallent. I wrote a poem rather more about my moping than about Mrs. Chapman, and it was published in *The Chesapeake Review*.

After the pain subsided, though, I became more assured in the presence of congressmen and lobbyists from Boston and New York City, who seemed particularly polished in mixed company. I took pleasure in noting that few if any of them had run up against Charleston women. And also, my invitations to parties increased. I was out to dinners and dances at least five nights a week. That year, the fashionable younger women—and a few of the older—wore their breasts cinched down low with vast creamy expanses of skin exposed by the low scoops of their necklines. It allowed a fine appreciation of their breathing. Crockett was philosophical on the matter. Things change, he said. There's nothing you can count on. Come back in a couple of years and they'll be wearing them high, hove up nearly to their chins.

A lobbyist for rice growers, a wealthy plump middle-aged lawyer from Savannah, was said to live a complicated life. I did not know what that might mean other than a girl proving to be married when you thought she was not. But then I spent some time around the man and noted that his black body servant rarely left his side and spoke in a rarefied English kind of accent he had learned in Bermuda. There was a way about their eyes meeting, a way their hands touched in the passing of a teacup, tones of voice in speaking to each other. Complicated.

THE CITY WAS ripe with brothels. When the Congress was in session, the houses were full from dusk until dawn. Those who could afford it went out whoring, drunk and lustful, at least a night or two a week. The old senators, most of them fat as beeves, rolled up in their carriages just as soon as the sun went down, and then in very short order they rolled home to bed. After that, right through until dawn, the younger representatives came and went. And also all the scavengers and predators, the diplomats and agents and lobbyists like me, drawn to the scent of blood and money and power the city throws out.

One night, I played the old Washington hand, giving a walking tour to the clerk of a new senator just arrived from some little hard-shell Baptist-ridden town in Alabama. The clerk was enormously delighted to be staying, to his complete astonishment, at the famous Indian Queen Hotel, and he could not stop talking about it as we walked. The air carried the smell of the river and the mudflats. Every brothel we passed was tinkling with piano music and breathing out its own particular fragrance of perfume and sweat into the evening. I looked over, and the clerk had tears of joy in his eyes and a look of rapture beaming on his face.

—Perhaps we might choose one to enter? the clerk said.

—Perhaps we might, I said. But farther along.

A few blocks later, it was my pleasure to introduce the clerk to an entire roomful of exquisites, both young and not. Of course, that was back when men joked about the pox as if it were a runny nose.

IMMEDIATELY UPON MY return to Wayah, I engaged in a three-hour-long ball game in which my nose was broken by a blow from a racquet. Truth be told, it was my own racquet. I made a desperate stooping dig at a grounded ball, and somehow the long webbed stick rebounded from the earth. The haft of it struck me hard, square across the bridge of my nose. A veil of blood streamed down my lower face. I went to the creek and stanched it with cold water and went on playing. I understood the injury as justice. Punishment for my time among the Washingtonians.

Bear was a spectator that day. He sat on a big downed log with a raucous group of old men drinking from a shared bottle. When the game was over and my team had come out on the bottom, Bear asked me whether I had won or lost in the bigger game against the Government. All I could say was that the ball remained in play.

WHEN I NEXT visited Valley River to check on the post there, I was told immediately upon arrival that Claire and Featherstone had returned during my long absence. An hour later I stood on the gallery, Waverley with reins looped over a rail behind me. A round brown woman of indeterminate race opened the door. I reached into a breast pocket and took out one of my cards, printed at excessive expense at the same Washington stationers that now made my journals. Please present this to Mrs. Featherstone, I said. The woman looked at the face of the card and ran a finger over the raised lettering, and then she turned it over and looked at the blank back with equal interest.

—Who? she said.

—Mrs. Featherstone. Claire.

—Oh. She don't need your little pasteboard, but I'll tell her you're calling.

She handed back the card and shut the door in my face. There were chairs farther along the gallery, but I went to the steps and sat down with my back to the door. It was a still day, and I could hear voices inside. The woman came back to the door and said Claire was not receiving visitors. I asked when might be a more convenient time to return, and she said, There's not likely to be one.

2

IN THE SOUTHERN MOUNTAINS, A *HELL* IS A BAD STRETCH OF LAND, a hard place to get through, a laurel thicket so vast and dense that men go in and can't find their way out and die there. In other parts of the country, it's the section of town with all the bars and whorehouses and gunfighters and knife fighters. Not the Hell. A hell.

That's what the immediate future looked like it was shaping up to be. And no clear way through, at least none that I could see. No way to come out the other side feeling noble or even whole anymore. And plenty of ways to come out ashamed and disappointed in yourself for the remainder of life, with stories you wouldn't even care to tell drunk. But there was no direction to go other than forward. Bear had set his mind and heart on staying in his mountains, and nothing could change his mind, certainly not government decrees or new lines drawn on maps or old lines erased. Mountains were home, and that was that. Bear said that every time he had been to the flatlands, he felt like he might slide off the end of the world, for there was nothing upright to stop him from the void. He said being in a place without mountains was like riding in the bed of a careening wagon without side rails.

I loved the old man and would do anything for him, and also I believed that Bear's people had as much right to decide where they cared to live as anybody else. Maybe I should have packed up and gone to Washington for good, used my friends there to find a position. Put that Wayah Town behind me. There are many who can make new selves at a moment's notice. Slough a skin, dismiss memory, move on. But that is not a skill I ever acquired.

If the soldiers came marching into the mountains and began collecting everyone on the Nation together and taking them off to the West, I had little faith our sheaf of inconclusive letters and vague legal papers would stop them from coming on up to Wayah and emptying our coves too, deeds or no deeds. But I kept working, tirelessly and without hope. I made the long journey to Washington and back three times during those years, each time with a stronger presentiment that all my efforts would be futile. No argument had helped the Nation. Chief Ross and the Ridges had constructed years and years' worth of arguments, and nothing they did or said changed a thing. Sympathetic lawmakers ranted righteous opposition to Jackson and then moved on to more pressing matters. The Supreme Court rendered a decision siding with the Indians, and Jackson said, Now let them enforce it. The Court, a toothless and ultimately corrupt bunch of old men, backed down.

The Ridges and their followers stalled as long as they could, but before the axe fell they made a desperate and almost actuarial calculation to determine their best chances of personal and financial survival. Helping them in their decision was the old major's very concrete experience, all the way back into the previous century, of fighting both for and against white men. Before white men, war of Indians against Indians was very bloody and sometimes cruel to the limits of human imagination, but it was a near relative to the ball game, a form of sport. These new white people took all the fun out of war and just won and kept winning, as if that was all that mattered. Major Ridge had seen firsthand what wonders of domination can be accomplished by the overwhelming and single-minded application of force, and finally he and his bunch of supporters conceded defeat.

One winter night in New Echota, a small roomful of wealthy Ridge men, Featherstone among them, huddled about a white paper centered on a candlelit table and autographed a secret nighttime treaty, selling all of the Nation to America under the most favorable terms they believed they could get and agreeing for all their people, without consultation, to remove to the new Indian Territories. When the group had finished putting their names to paper, one of them expressed the opinion that they had just signed their own execution warrants. And of course he was right.

The treaty, as drafted, contained a provision to allow the richest Indians to stay, keep all their holdings—land and houses and slaves—and become American citizens. Unfair, yes. But I was all for it, since it meant that Claire and Featherstone could remain at Cranshaw, and just her proximity offered hope, for time back then seemed long enough for anything to happen, even the softening of a heart inexplicably hardened against you.

When the treaty reached the White House, however, Jackson ranted against any exemptions whatsoever. He wanted all Indians gone, no matter how rich or how white, and the provision was stricken from the final document.

The Old Possum finished out his eight years and began rusticating outside Nashville, a hermit in his Hermitage but still savoring the sweep of his hand across the land even in absentia. Van Buren followed him and his Indian policies like a swimmer caught in a riptide.

In the year before the Army arrived, the members of the Ridge bunch began leaving the plantations they had built, the mills and ferries and stores and printing presses, and pulled out to the West, taking a few of their house slaves with them but leaving most to follow later. Some of the paler among the rich Indians might have been tempted to cross out of the Nation and melt into the surrounding white populations, but the bordering states, Georgia in particular, were vigilant in arresting fugitives of whatever blood degree and deporting them to the West under conditions suitable only for convicts.

Major Ridge and his wife chose to travel out to the new Nation by riverboat, quickly and uneventfully. Boudinot and young Ridge and their Yankee wives made a happy jaunt of it. They trotted to the new

Nation in fine carriages drawn by strong healthy horses. Even under such leisurely conditions, their trip took a mere month, the young couples enjoying the fine dry weather of a southern October and the spectacular change of colors and fall of leaves as they crossed Tennessee and rolled through the Ozarks. It being fashionable among gentlemen at the time to be naturalists, Boudinot and young Ridge noted in their journals the passing varieties of wildlife and plant life. They even took time from their journey to visit the Old Possum at his Hermitage, which, when I heard about the visit, struck me as being not entirely required by the etiquette of the situation. And the more I thought about it and imagined their conversation, the more disturbed I became. But the Possum always had something about him that moved many folks his way, like the wind pushed them or gravity pulled them in his direction.

Back on the Nation, Chief Ross fumed and litigated on against America and, of course, denied the legitimacy of the Ridge agreement, rightfully pointing out that the Ridges had no authority to sell even an acre of Nation land to a non-Indian and had in fact committed a capital crime in doing so. When Ross's efforts all continued to come to nothing, he soon began striking deals of his own to have America pay him, by the head, to move all the people to the West by overland routes. Vast caravans of Indians and slaves, accompanied by soldiers and missionaries, emptying the old Nation and filling the new one. America took Ross's low bid and got what they paid for. The trail where they cried.

LIKE MAJOR RIDGE, Featherstone chose—in his words—to eschew the toilsome overland route to the new Nation in favor of the more comfortable water passage, where one might eat dinner at a cloth-covered table and take a morning shit through a buttock-shaped hole in a sternward outhouse overhanging the passing brown river face all a-churn from the turning paddle wheel. Contrary to his wishes, Claire remained behind to pack their belongings. Clattering silver service, footed trays and platters, tiny salt bowls, and endless flatware. Wedgwood dinnerware and Murano crystal cocooned in yellow straw. Many shelves of books and bureaus of folded clothes laid rectangle by rectangle in wooden crates. Her goal was to be done and gone before the soldiers came.

The night before his departure, Featherstone built a midnight blaze of his collected works of taxidermy, a nightmare bonfire on the lawn. Generations of dusty animals large and small combusting quick as fatpine kindling, their blank faces looking out of the fire, scenting the spring air with an autumnal odor like burning the bristles off a butchered hog. The next morning Featherstone set out for the West on a sort of middling-quality horse which he planned to sell at the river before embarking. His only baggage was a pair of bulging saddlebags filled with dress clothing, all the way down to gloves scented with frangipani for the riverboat salons and a great deal of cash with which he planned to begin life anew. When the poor Indians arrived, he'd be there waiting to profit like most of the other rich Indians.

No argument had worked for the Indians on the Nation, not even the white ones, and I didn't expect anything to work for Bear's brown people either. But Bear had put his hope in a fistful of deeds, and his faith never wavered. At that time we had Bear's thousand acres, which he owned outright, and my more extensive land, which I controlled mainly through a series of notes and IOUs as interlocked and tangled and messy as an old weathered osprey nest. I held one of my tracts by such convoluted means that a second mortgage on a prime field hand figured prominently in the deal. I lived in fear that if one twig was pulled from it, the whole nest would collapse and fall to the ground. But it held and grew.

Bear kept close watch over all the dealings, and at one point he asked if I knew what the difference between us was.

—No, I said.

—Seems to be, there's two kinds of men in this new world the white people are making. Ones with payments and ones without. You're a man with payments.

The year before the Removal, Bear and I between us could fairly accurately claim control over about ten thousand acres. It was a fraction of what our holdings would become a decade later, but enough to form a confusing principality, existing outside the Nation and inside the state. With inhabitants of unclear citizenship and all possible degrees of blood, but so remote from the state capital that nobody in government much cared who we were or what we did way out in our doleful coves.

Just to see what might happen, I sent a carefully worded claim of state citizenship for all of Bear's people to the appropriate department down in the capital. The response was worded in such exquisite bureaucratic cant that it took me three readings to decipher its meaning. The best I could tell, my claim was not accepted, but neither was it rejected.

Though Bear and I had sat up late nights for years planning the future—hoping and despairing over it, resolving to fight against it all we could—most of the people didn't at all understand what immediate threat of losing their homeland they now lived under. The doings of the larger world, even Jackson's will to put an end to Indians east of the Mississippi, seemed as distant and uninteresting as wars conducted by the King of Siam. A lot of our people had never been farther from their own farms than the top of the most distant ridge they could see. They were like everyone else; all they truly knew was locked in the body. The diameter of their world was tightly drawn, just as it was for most of their white neighbors, and its topography was confined to the coves and ridges and watercourses they had seen with their eyes and walked with their legs. Whatever larger geography they held in mind was theoretical. So the distance to the West was entirely abstract, as was the length of time it might take to traverse such unimagined space and the danger that might wait along the way.

DURING THE MONTHS leading up to the Removal, letters and reports flew back and forth between Washington and the earliest representatives of the Army. And on both ends of the transaction, I had ways to get hold of scrivener's copies. A case in point:

Memoir Relative to the Cherokee Nation within the Limits of N. Carolina and its Immediate Vicinity, by W. G. Williams, Capt, U.S. F. Grs. Febry 1838.

—

Preparatory to a Report based upon the data procured by Instrumental Survey, it occurs to me that you may be pleased to be made acquainted with a few particulars in regard to the country in which we are operating; and which have come to me, in the form of memoranda, through the notes of the assistants under me and from my own observation. In a country like this and at a season the most unpropitious for surveying operations, it is natural to suppose many difficulties have been encountered.

In pursuance of my instructions, I will advert to such circumstances as may pertain to an estimate of the resources of the Indians of this district, in the hypothesis of an attempt on their part to evade the stipulations of the Treaty in reference to removal. Previously to entering upon this as a question of numbers, physical strength, interest in the country they inhabit, their means of subsistence & ca. I will remark briefly what has occurred to me as to the moral disposition of the Indians in relation to this subject.

Poor, ignorant of economy of time, or money, cultivating the soil for a base subsistence, they prefer the chase of the deer or deer idleness to more useful employment. It is but natural to suppose that the love of home is a paramount sentiment with the Indian whose range of ideas is too limited to stimulate him to enterprize beyond his immediate vicinity and who is moreover attached to the grave of his ancestors by feelings of superstitous veneration. This natural sympathy is kept alive by the appeals of those interested in their opposition to a removal and by the representation made to them of any thing but advantage in such an arrangement. Influential Chiefs and some white residents among them, stimulated by sordid views and either feeling or pretending to feel for their situation encourage every proposition adverse to their own true interest and the wishes of the U.S. Government.

Under such circumstances the result of our observations is that the great mass of the Indians in this section of the country are decidedly hostile to emigration, and what is to be lamented, the hope of remaining is kept alive by false representation to a degree that is truly surprising. It is, therefore, to be regretted that these delusions of false hopes will only be dashed to the ground at the very period when it will be necessary to carry out the conditions of the treaty, and it is much to be feared that, referring to general principles of human nature, an irritation of feeling may grow out of their sudden disappointment and incite them to acts of desperation. Had the conviction been fully and universally impressed upon their mind that they must go, they would long since have accommodated themselves to the idea and been prepared to meet their destiny.

In regard to the locale of the Indians in the mountain district much may be said in its adaptation to their mode of warfare and for the purposes of concealment. It would appear obvious that if they could provision themselves in these fastnesses of nature, and possessed arms and ammunition, they would be enabled to oppose every formidable resistance to any attempt to dislodge them, for it must be considered that they have the range of not merely the mountain region within the territory now occupied by them but that of a very extensive bed of mountains, so sparsely inhabited by whites as to offer them a secure and inaccessible shelter from invasion and yet a fertile field for their predatory incursions.

It would appear obvious from the nature of the ground, that the most effectual mode of reducing Indians would be by compelling them to come in by the pressure of want and privation. To effect this object it would be necessary to secure the vallies in which their farms are situated and seize at once the grain, cattle & swine they may have on hand, on the slightest exhibition on their part of a hostile intention and the immediate occupation of these vallies could place us in the attitude to carry this plan into effective operation. They would thus be driven to the mountain fastness, where it is true, they would be almost inaccessible to attack, but at the same time they would be destitute of provisions and the necessary appliances of war. They would be obliged to have recourse to hunting for food and could not therefore embody to any extent and might be met by small detachments whenever they emerged for purposes of procuring the provision by hunting, necessary to their existence.

They are very illy provided with arms and ammunition. It is thought that there are not more than 400 rifles among them, and those for the most part useless or in bad repair. They have bows and arrows and an implement called the blowgun, which they use for the purpose of killing small game, at which they are expert. This might be regarded as contributing some what to their resources in that respect.

I herewith send a sketch of the country above referred to in which the principal points are laid down with accuracy and very different in position from that exhibited on previous maps we have been able to procure.

I am, Sir, with respect
W. G. WILLIAMS CAPT. U.S. Top Ensgn.

THE SOLDIERS FELL on the land like calamity. Down by the river, on an expanse of flat ground, they razed away a vast canebrake in a conflagration that looked for a short span of minutes like the end of the world. Red fire and black smoke rose to the top of the sky, and for two days grey twists of cane ashes kited on the wind and then rained down on Valley River. For days after that, all you could hear was the ringing of axes as the soldiers cut and limbed pine trees. Teams of yellow oxen snaked the straight trunks out of the woods. When the soldiers had a great heap of timber, enough to build a whole settlement of cabins, they dug a huge rectangular trench and sank the butts of the pine trunks and erected them each by each like a giant pale fence to make a palisade, the logs with the bark still on but white and sharp at the tips as trimmed pencils. Two bark-roofed blockhouses projected from the walls at opposing corners like crude bastions from which you could fire down upon attackers on either of the two sides they each commanded. Loopholes opened high in the walls, which suggested the existence of banquettes inside to stand on and move from one loop to another to fire. A sally port opened on the side of the square they considered the front.

From up the hill at the trading post, looking down across the river, there was a dream geometry to the place. A flat of bottomland cut to red mud by men and horses, the unbroken brown face of a broad river running straight and then curving away, green mountains rising in steep pitches to the four cardinal directions. The log fort sitting dark and squat in the middle like a lump of black wax impressed with the seal of fate.

From that point forward, everything changed entirely in the village. The enlisted men were let out only on rare occasions, and then they would cross the river in rowing boats and climb the hill and pay whatever price was asked for any kind of brownish popskull liquor whatsoever, as long as it was vaguely reputed to be Barbados rum or Tennessee whiskey. The officers, though, seemed to have a considerably greater scope of personal freedom. Most days of the week, they hung about my trading post. The officers drank all the Moët's and Macallan's Scotch that could be kept coming by the wagonload up the roads from Charleston. There was, understandably, a considerable markup, and the officers seemed compelled to announce that they could buy it back in New Jersey for half that price. I taught the young clerk minding the till to say, Well, maybe you'd better go back to New Jersey then. At least the wooden wine cases made fine bookshelves when stacked in a staggered fashion along the walls of the store's sleeping room.

GREEN CORN MOON, the weeks leading up to the summer solstice, had long been one of my favorite stretches of time. But not that year. From the post I would wake up and take my coffee onto the porch and if it wasn't too foggy or rainy look down across the river to the fort and watch little groups of soldiers sally forth shortly after dawn to search the mountains and collect Indians cabin by cabin. In the afternoon I watched them march families and old folks into the holding pen that the fort had become. Late afternoons I could smell the smoke from their cook fires rising, and then by dusk the young officers began coming up the hill for their drinks and an evening of conversation.

Many of them were contemptible, but I guess no greater portion than the generality of people. A few, though, resembled actual human beings and seemed shaken and saddened by what they were doing. One of these latter officers was a young lieutenant named Smith. He was a slim blond-headed fellow, gangly and not yet in complete control of his big hands and long feet. A few years younger than I was, but when you're that young two or three years still seems significant. He would talk as deep into the night as I would listen, telling me about his day and every flicker of thought and feeling that had crossed his mind.

I remember one evening in particular, but I'm not sure why, for it was about like all the others. Smith said they had ridden out from the fort shortly after dawn to go round people up and escort them back to the stockade. Smith rode half asleep with his reins loose and his pipestem clamped between his teeth. A column of four soldiers, if just four could be called a column. The young lieutenant and three enlisted men, boys from Ireland and Philadelphia and Charleston. Their job was to work their way upriver and clean the Indians out of the mountains cove by cove. About all Smith had previously been trained to do was salute, and the three enlisted men had been taught the additional skill of sponging out cannon barrels after they had been fired.

The days were all alike, Smith said. Circle their houses and give them half an hour to collect only what they could easily carry and then herd them down the road or trail to the next farmstead and do the same there. By dusk, they'd have thirty or forty people walking ahead of them, carrying bundles of blankets and pots and precious worthless little objects, portable things to remind them of their former lives. The people all walked away from their homes fearing what their new lives held for them. A very few cried and a few made grim humor of their situation, but mostly they went wordless with their faces composed into an expressionless mask, as if they had placed a large wager on whether or not they could conceal any hint of their thoughts or emotions.

Tagrags and offscourings and white trash followed behind the little column with the attentiveness of buzzards circling a kill. The whole bunch of followers smelled of armpits and ramps. Then, as each farmstead was vacated, they would rush in behind the soldiers to collect livestock and possessions left behind. There was nothing to be done about it. Sometimes the rabble fell upon a place so soon after vacancy that the owners could look back and see them trying to straddle a plow mule or struggling to lead away a reluctant hog by a rope around its neck or flailing about in the farmyard chasing old big-breasted and flightless hens that ran squawking with their wings trailing in the dust. Sometimes out of exuberance the followers would set fire to a place after they'd emptied it. And at the few places that had wells rather than springs, some wag among them would drop his trousers around his ankles and take a shit down the hole to spark general hilarity.

That morning, Lieutenant Smith's party had ridden up a green cove, their first mission of the day to roust out an old woman, a widow living solitary in a cabin with tied bundles of sage hanging stems-up under the eaves of her porch to dry, the cabin hemmed in by fenced garden plots, corn and beans and squash growing in her fields, chickens scratching in the yard, straw skeps humming with bees, carefully pruned apple and peach trees busy putting out fruit. A bold creek cutting through the middle of the farm, running clear over mossy stones. In every direction, mountains hanging like green curtains from the sky.

This particular old Indian woman had her grey hair pulled back into a fist-sized bun, and she wore a greasy apron over a blue skirt that fell in limp folds from her wide hips. When she saw who they were and what they had come for, she went into the cabin and came out very quickly with two blankets and a little black pot. She spread the blankets on the porch floor and folded some of the herbs and the pot into the blankets, and with a quick knot she fashioned a shoulder sling of the bundle. Then she stopped and insisted on feeding her chickens before she was taken away.

Smith wanted to tell her not to bother. The chickens would not live out the morning but would have their necks wrung and be roasting on a spit for someone's dinner. But he guessed she did not understand a word of English, and perhaps the longevity of the chickens was not her point of concern but just her stewardship, maintaining it until the last moment. So Smith squatted on the ground with the other soldiers and refilled his pipe and smoked. One of the enlisted boys, an Irishman, said that other than for the hue of her skin the old woman looked much like his last sight of his grandmother when he was a boy. He told how he and his family had been set to sail for America, and they had gone from Galway out past Spiddal for a last visit. The Irishman recalled how his grandmother had refused to acknowledge that the journey meant she would never see any of them again in this life. When they got ready to leave, she had said, Be off with you, then. Said it in a tone as if they would be back in a week or two. And then she started feeding her chickens from grain she held basined in her apron.

The rabble that followed the soldiers to loot the farmsteads stood off at the edge of woods and waited.

The woman moved about the dooryard casting crumbled bits of dry leftover cornbread onto the ground with a rattling motion of her hand and wrist, like shaking and throwing dice. The brown chickens gathered and so did wild mourning doves. The birds mingled together and scratched the ground with their tripartite toes and ate the crumbs of bread, and then the chickens scattered across the bare ground and the doves flew away, their wings beating with a sound of mittened children clapping hands. The woman struck her palms against each other twice, with a hard brushing smack.

It turned out she did speak English, for she said in a loud clear voice, I spit on my past. Let's go.

And then she shouldered her bedroll and walked off into exile.

Her house was afire and black smoke rose to meet the low clouds before she made the second turning in the trail. But it was all the same to her, for she didn't look back.

At the end of such days, Smith said he went to sleep with a bitter taste like ash from a coal fire in his mouth.

But at some point, he said, it was just a job. And as with any job, you can become accustomed to it. Six days a week, get up before dawn and go out and beat the bushes for people and dispossess them of everything they have and march them away to the holding pens. Neither Smith nor the boys from Ireland and Philadelphia and Charleston were ever cruel. They marched nobody away with a bayonet point to their buttocks. And what did it matter about burned houses and slaughtered animals? Smith asked. Everything of value was noted down in his ledger. You could do the accounting with your eyes shut, for every place was materially the same. One cabin with puncheon floors and stick-and-clay chimney, one hewed-log corncrib, a bed or two, one table, a few rush-bottomed straight chairs. Various house clutter, basins, spoons, and dippers. A weeding hoe, a shovel plow, a short-handled axe. Hasp and staple, collar and hames. The American Government would pay them for what they lost after they reached the West.

By that point in the night, all the other officers had wandered back down the hill. Lieutenant Smith was left sitting with a flat inch of Moët's in his flute. He needed something from me, and I was afraid it might have been absolution. But I was no preacher. I've always numbered myself among the drunks. Absolution was outside my range of talents or responsibilities.

I said, So the gist of your story is that you worry how many times during your rounds you can note knife cuts in wooden doorframes to memorialize the heights of children at various moments of infancy and still find it poignant?

—Something along those lines, Smith said.

—Go home, Lieutenant, I said. Or at least back to your tent. I'm done with commerce for this evening.

—

I FLURRIED ABOUT, always a-saddle. Letting constant motion stand in place of actual achievement, everything done half-assed, both tending to business and to the heart. Back and forth on the daylong ride between Valley River and Wayah. The roads were filled with uniformed Federal soldiers and heavily armed Tennessee mercenaries dressed like bandits and hired just for the summer by the Government to roust out Indians. The bandits' cook pots hung behind their saddles, clashing like unpleasant bells as they coursed along the roadways. They were all draped about their chests and shoulders with powder horns and shot pouches.

I rushed to Cranshaw, after I heard Featherstone was gone, and found Claire bitter amid the wreckage of packing crates, slaves milling about directionless, fields untended, ragweed knee-deep among the cornstalks, suckers overwhelming the tomatoes, squash and pumpkins and melons growing tiny and pale as babies' fists in the shade of rampant chickweed. What to say to her other than Love me, love me. Don't go. Stay with me.

She would not even accept an embrace in the dooryard but stood all rigid and looking off toward the river with her hands clasped tight behind her back.

At the fort, the growing population of prisoners, many of whom I had known since boyhood, sat in the dirt of the stockade drinking liquor bought from a cart one of my clerks tended just inside the gate. People drank deep to achieve immediate stupor. And why not? Who was I to deny them comfort? Denial was what the Army was for. If you can't get drunk when your entire world comes crashing down around your feet, why did God make alcohol to begin with?

And then back outside the Nation in Wayah, I found Bear awake long nights in his townhouse, plotting out the organization of a new miniature world in the pattern of the vast old one. Divisions of governance no bigger than cove bottoms but assigned the names of lost clans. And not even all of them, only Long Hair, Paint, Wolf, and Deer. Also,

Bear was pensive and mournful over the state of his troublesome marriage to Sara and her grievous sisters, and the two endeavors, politics and love, were part of each other, both necessary in his attempt to rebalance a world gone wrong, to try to get back his time again.

I WENT BACK to Cranshaw, feeling hopeless and foolish at my desperation to make one more try to reach her. Expecting nothing. But Claire ran to me. I had hardly looped Waverley's reins around the hitching post when she came rushing down the front steps and fell into my arms. I didn't spend a second wondering what it meant or how I felt about it. I just held her tight and let myself be happy and hopeless and free of further desire, in case that moment was all we would ever have.

I stayed at Cranshaw three days that were like a compression of our two summers back in green youth, except that Featherstone was absent and the place was being taken apart. Packing crates stood in stacks in the emptied rooms, their walls bare of paintings.

I started out trying to be discreet in front of the help, but Claire did not care what tales the servants might carry to the West. The first evening at dinner, she straddled me in my chair, her dress in a bunch around us. A woman came in bearing a tray of pork loin and roasted new potatoes and little lettuces killed with bacon grease. Claire did not even lift her face from where it was pressed in the space between my neck and shoulder. After that, I quit worrying and let desire rule.

We sprawled on the broad river rocks at noon, and the sun scalded our buttocks as in days of yesteryear. We drank too much of Featherstone's best wine. We drove the carriage at high speed along the valley roads at any hour that suited us from dawn to midnight. Claire was beautiful, beautiful. Every single part of her.

One night we built a fire in the yard in the old black circle. I recited to her from memory my old poem "To C——," taking care to note that it had actually been published in *The Arcadian*. All the way through, line by line, we laughed like idiots, especially at the conclusion about lips of garnet. We both traced the outline of her lips and said the word *garnet*, as if it were the most ridiculous word in the entire English lexicon.

On the third night, we fell asleep fully clothed, exhausted. I awoke in the dark. Claire was gone. Nothing but a dent in the pillow, flapped-back sheets. I went looking for her. Traversing the long dark upstairs halls, keeping my bearings by brushing fingertips against the plaster walls. Then down wide steps to the parlor. Partway there I saw her moving across the dark room without a candle. Gliding silently, keeping her bare feet close to the oak floorboards so not to stumble. Her hands out at waist level, palms forward, to touch doorframes, table corners, chair arms, crates of packed china, trunks of clothing. Everything displaced, unfamiliar.

The mullioned parlor windows were grey. A thick slice of the Ripe Corn Moon stood framed above the western horizon. Enough light to shape the ridges against the sky, enough light to know that though the mountains are not permanent, they are persistent. Claire reached the front door, crossed the porch, walked down the lawn to the riverbank. The slow water moved almost without sound.

I stood in the doorway and watched as she undressed in the moonlight.

Even in full summer, the complete attire of a fashionable young woman constituted such an elaborate layered array of pleated and ruched and lapped fabrics that it was like taking something small and precious, an art object, from a series of beautiful protective cases and pouches. A thing of wonder, but only to be admired briefly and then shut carefully away again. Claire finally descended through the layers to a doeskin summer corset, light as a second layer of flesh, the color of chamois and trimmed in green satin. She shed it onto the frothy hummock of pale silk and bombazine and linen and stood pale and slim in the moonlight. She walked into the river. Going to water.

Ankle-deep, she stopped, wavering. The surface of the river before her was black, bottomless. But when you reach the point that you no longer trust the world, you live in never-ending fear. She walked on, wobbling and uncertain, the arches of her feet shaping to the round stones of the river bottom. When she got shoulder-deep she looked up into the strip of sky the river cut through the trees, a mirror of the river's shape. Stars overlapped stars down a vertiginous well. She bent her knees and sank below the water.

THE LOADED WAGONS stood lined in a train outside Cranshaw, ready for the journey west. Claire sat for a long time on the tailboard of the last wagon, leaning forward with her hair covering her face. Her blue skirt draped in her lap to outline her thighs, a shadowed valley between them. Polished ankle boots dangled in space. She gripped the edge of the tailboard so hard her knuckles went white. I reached out and ran my finger across the four knobs of bone. I wanted to kiss them, but when I tried to pull her hand to me, she pulled it away.

Claire leaned back and shifted the mass of hair from her face with a raking motion of wrist and forearm. She stared at me hard, lips parted. She touched my face and said, I want to remember how you look, at least for a while.

—Send some thoughts this way to fill this empty place. I put my palm on my chest.

—What a silly thing to say. Just get in.

—I can't. I'm needed here right now. I've worked so long for Bear, for our people. Things are at such a state they could fall apart in a moment. I have responsibilities.

Claire turned her palms up, held her hands out.

—What about Featherstone? I said.

—We can deal with that when we get there. He might not be exactly what you think he is.

I hesitated. I'm not proud to report it. It was my Lancelot moment. Hesitate to get in the cart, and you are lost. Maybe every life has one moment where everything could have been different if you'd climbed on the cart.

Claire looked around at Cranshaw and said, I would have burnt all this down at a word from you.

The driver looked back at her. She tipped her head in the direction of forward. West. He whistled a sharp note down the line of wagons, and the whole train lurched forward. He popped the reins on the mules' backs, and they pulled. The rig creaked into motion, the narrow wheels broke free of the mud with a sucking sound.

Claire rode away as the condemned ride the final cart to the gallows. But I was the one condemned.

I thought then that if she would look up and say one more word, I would turn my back on the life and the place I had made, on the people who had taken me in as an exiled bound boy when no one else in the world wanted me, and I would follow her anywhere. But she lowered her head and her hair covered her face, and that was the end. The driver began whistling "The Girl I Left Behind Me." They turned the bend in the road, and all I had left to look at were the parallel tracks in the mud leading off into a future that had sideswiped us all.

Now I think, What more could she have said? And for so long I have hated my nature for failing to say what I felt. And most of all for not acting on it. You live with such choices until you die. They eat at you like heartworm, coring you out until you are just a skin enclosing nothing. A balloon filled with hot breath.

That moment has haunted me all my life. Her sitting on the tailboard of the wagon, going away, the driver rattling the reins and the mules pulling and the wooden members of the wagon rubbing and rattling against one another as the wheels rolled through the mud. Claire bending her head and her hair falling over her face like drawing curtains across a bright window. And me saying nothing. Doing nothing. I was a young man, but I believed my best life was over.

3

I RODE BACK TO WAYAH, THROUGH THE GLOOMY GORGE, WITH THE feeling that the whole world was splitting apart. Bill Axe sought me out immediately upon my arrival. He was a half-blood and lived on the outskirts of our land. He urgently needed to tell me about a visit to his homestead by a little party of pilgrims. We sat by the fire in the trading post, and I listened to his story.

They arrived at Axe's place before dark, carrying the odors of journey in their clothes and their hair and on their skin—scents of morning dew beading the leaves, the dust of the trail, the droppings of animals, sweat, and woodsmoke. They had come down out of their home on Nantayale Creek and followed the river through its narrow black gorge where the water ran white between great smooth boulders and the walls were so high and close that the sun only shone at midday. They came out the lower end of the gorge into the open valley, where they could see the big mountains standing blue to the north like a wall marking the ultimate limits of the world. Somewhere in their eastward progress, they had crossed the boundary line and had left the Nation and entered America and become fugitives.

There were about a dozen of them, men, women, and children—three generations of Charley's family. The youngest boy was named

Wasseton in honor of the first president, and he led a little small-boned packhorse loaded with a lumpy burden of food and pots and blankets. Equipage for living out in the high mountains for some time to come. A dog loped along with them, and she was of such antique configuration that she might have been a recent convert from the tribe of red wolves hunted nearly to absence by whites who could not abide their existence and also by Indians recently forgetful of the old pledge never to kill them due to the close blood relation between wolf and man. The dog carried her triangular head hanging loose, almost touching the ground, and her nose often pulled her out into the woods on some fascinating scent-path.

Bill Axe's cabin stood in a clearing of tulip trees above the north bank of the river. A fire of red cedar logs burned on the ground outside the house, and the smoke in the air smelled like incense. The slant light of afternoon fell in broken beams through the yellow leaves and straight trunks. Axe sat asleep in a straight chair by the fire with his hands folded in his lap and his chin on his chest. Everyone but Charley stood off in the trees and waited. Charley went into the clearing, walking effortfully on bowed legs like an old horseman, though he had seldom ridden.

Charley touched Axe on the shoulder with two fingers and then stepped back.

Axe looked at Charley and rubbed his hands down his face to compose himself for wakefulness. Charley was the color of old polished cherrywood. His face was marked with hard wrinkles, running horizontal on his forehead and vertical on his cheeks and neck, and they were deep enough to lose a handful of river pearls in the folds. He was a short man but broad at the shoulders, stout through the barrel of his body, round-headed and big-handed. He wore a red bandana, blue calico shirt, brown linen britches, and greasy deerhide moccasins without beading or other ornament. His hair was going grey and he wore it blunt-cut below his ears where his wife, Nancy, trimmed it monthly by gathering up the excess at the back of his neck in her fist and lopping it off with one swipe of a skinning knife. He was only about sixty, but he looked eighty and was a grandfather several times over.

Axe said, You're taking the wrong direction. The soldiers are riding up and down the river looking for runners.

—I'm not going, Charley said. I'm abiding by the old lines.

—They're wiped clean away. No more boundary lines. No more Nation.

—I'm not going.

—A man can't live in the woods. They've emptied out. Everything's gone. The deer and bear and turkey are on the way to wherever the bison and elk already went. Far away. Where you're going.

Axe argued that the whole slab of mountain range, all the southern slopes, the cuts where the creeks drain down to the rivers, the dry ridges leading up like ribs to the long crest of the chine, are indeed a vast and convoluted piece of terrain. But not endless. And a man cannot crawl under a rock and disappear. Much less a family, three generations extending from Charley down to members not yet weaned and still wavery on their feet. Nor can such a group turn themselves into bush fighters and bandits.

Charley said again, I'm not going.

During the day's walk, the boy Wasseton had shot several squirrels from chestnut trees with darts from a cane blowgun taller than he was. The boy said he could smell squirrels, especially on damp days. At a distance of ten paces, Wasseton had driven long shaved hickory darts through their skulls with a single plosive breath.

Some of the women skinned and gutted the squirrels as handy as shucking an ear of corn and ran them through from ass to mouth with sharp birch skewers and set them to roasting over the fire coals. Nancy mashed pinto beans and mixed them with cornmeal and wood-ash lye and rolled the mixture between her palms into little loaves and wrapped them in scalded fodder blades and held the packages together with thin strips shredded from fodder blades and tied in neat knots. She simmered them in a black iron pot. Axe's wife brought out some chunks of yellow squash and cooked them at the edge of the fire until they softened up.

When the cooking was done, the squirrels looked awfully little with the hair and skin off, but they were sizzling brown and shining with grease. Their grimacing mouths shone full of long yellow teeth.

Charley's people sat by the fire with Axe and his wife and ate the meal off wood trays with cane-stalk implements. Charley had a pattern to eating a squirrel. He kept it on its skewer and worked back to front, eating the little hams first, each by each, and then he went at the body meat, eating it off the ribs as if it lay in rows like corn kernels. When he finally got to the head, he broke it off and put it in his mouth and worked it around for quite some time like he was gumming tobacco. And then when he was done, he reached in a finger and pulled out a bare little skull and showed it cupped in his palm like it was a fine achievement, his own creation worthy of favorable comment.

Nobody said much of anything during the meal. But later, when Charley's people had made camp in the clearing and fallen asleep, Axe and his wife lay in bed and talked quietly in the dark about how they might gracefully rid themselves of these dangerous guests.

And after Axe was finished telling his tale, I too wondered what varieties of woe Charley might bring upon us when the Army came searching. I had known Charley a little since boyhood and felt disoriented in a world where a subsistence farmer and his family could become transformed into dangerous fugitives.

THROUGH VARIOUS CHANNELS, bits of copied correspondence continued to fall my way.

Lieutenant H. C. Smith to Colonel Haden

—

Your favor of the 24th instant of August including your orders to find and "put into motion" toward the Indian Territories the fugitives said still to inhabit this region was duly received, and I have done my all to carry your wishes forward. But I am afraid my efforts have produced little gain.

You refer to assistance reportedly given to the fugitives by the few bad white men scattered among the mountains, but I have yet found no evidence of such assistance. At every white settlement of five dog-trot log cabins and a frame church, the inhabitants congregate to tell us of great masses of Indians hiding high in the mountains. They fear them and fervently wish us to rout them out. But we cannot verify their tales, and tales are all I believe them to be.

We have searched both sides of the Little Tennessee and about ten miles up the Tuckasegee, marching long days, though of little mileage, tracing every rumor and tiding mongered hereabouts. The land is unimaginably rough, and in the laurel thickets five hundred men could hide from a thousand in an area of exceedingly small scope and we have found nothing. We went up the Nantahala and from there we searched Snowbird, Buffalo, Hanging Dog, and Beaverdam, days and days of travel in terrain whereupon our horses could not find secure footing and we often had to walk them, and all with the result that we found but some old thatched hunting camps and one Indian man so blind he could not travel, and during the whole time of which heavy rain was falling from a dark sky and the autumn leaves yellow and red in the trees and slick on the ground. There is a great deal of mast, mostly chestnut, but little or no game to be seen as it has all been hunted out to near barrenness, buffalo and elk thirty years gone and deer failing fast, and many nights we have had to make do with our dry provisions. I do not see how this place could support a lone man in the wild, much less a large population of fugitives.

The men have been in ill temper and poor health. They cough and their clothes and bedding are wet constantly and in camp they hang them on stick frames to scorch by the fire, but the dews and mists and rains of morning wet them again. On the trail the men frighten themselves with phantom dangers that they imagine lurk in the forest. They cannot see ten feet beyond the passway, and they invent ambush from every fall of limb or call of bird and I have had to threaten to severely penalize any man who fires indiscriminately.

Frankly, sir, I cannot understand our continuing concern with this land and its inhabitants either white or red. The Indians are ignorant beyond all reckoning and the whites too, mostly the dregs of Scotland and Ireland fled here for lack of alternative. The country is no better than a jungle of unpracticable mountains cut through with narrow coves and deep gorges, being generally precipitous cliffs falling directly to unnavigable rocky rivers. Beyond the river vallies the little flat ground is filled with thickets of azalea and laurel almost impenetrable to anything but a deer or an Indian and them crawling on their knees. Its only value to the white settlers is as a range for cattle and swine and the country must become much more thickly inhabited before it will be used for that, and if in the meantime the small number of fugitive Indians who presumably now occupy it are left undisturbed the worst injury which can arise from their continuing presence will be the loss of a few hogs and a little corn to the whites in the vicinity, who I should point out purchased all they have of both from these very Indians.

THE YARD OF THE stockade was packed with people, internees. Too many people in too little space. Families had staked out futile claims to a place on earth by spreading blankets on the ground. People sat in small groups talking. Some lay curled up, knees to chest, trying to sleep. Children wandered about, aimless and blank. Personal goods and clothing lay scattered about. It looked like the aftermath of a train wreck. The smell from the toilet pits brought tears to my eyes. Up against one palisade, a minister sat with his ass upon a crate that had held wine bottles. The stunned look on his face suggested that his imprisonment had come as a surprise to him. He was like a lot of them down on the Nation; he thought becoming as white as he could would protect him. Look white, dress white, act white, be white. He had his black slaves and a few Christian Indians fanned around him, listening to some of the pronouncements of God on the subject of how people ought to act. The Commandments were, as always, especially favorable to the rulers. The minister's skin was as white as the thin pages of the Bible open on his lap. He had on a dusty black frock coat and a white shirt, and he was locally celebrated for holding a degree in divinity from Princeton College. About all the Indian he could have had in him was a half-blood grandmother, but that was enough. If he were Negro that would make him an octoroon. The words for blood fractions went even smaller than that, down to the thirty-second part of dark blood that in some states still disqualified one from the many entitlements of being white. But primarily, the preacher was a citizen of the Nation and not America, so he had to go.

As I wove my way through the yard, overhearing a thin slice of the sermon, I reckoned the slaves must be doubly stunned, seeing how their Indian masters were suddenly powerless and stripped of nearly every item of private property except for themselves.

The day was bright and blue, but at the far end of the stockade I was shown into a room with the shutters pulled, a square of space dim as evening. Colonel Haden was a big hog of a man, with biscuit crumbs in his whiskers and gravy stains down his shirtfront. Though it was going on noon, he sat behind a table littered with breakfast dishes. White plates with smears of dark yellow where the yolks of soft-fried eggs had run and congealed. Cold coffee and cream skinned over in a cup. A decimated round of warm butter slumping on its dish. In a rambling sort of way, the colonel was talking out a letter to a young scribe, who sat at a corner of the table and scratched fiercely at a sheet of paper, trying to keep up with the rapid flow of words.

I stood and waited, and in a minute the colonel lost his place in his own thoughts and fell silent. He looked as if he needed a nap or a drink. He picked up the coffee cup and rotated the contents and set it back down. The scribe used the pause to correct an error in his transcription near the top of the page. He scraped at the words with his penknife and then shook pounce on the bad spot and rubbed it with agate and rewrote the colonel's sentiments accurately. In the meantime, the colonel had lost interest in the letter and had begun lighting a pipe.

He looked up at me from his puffing and said, You're the lawyer?

—At times.

—Well, whether this is one of those times or not, I'd like you to listen to something and then hear what say you in response.

He shuffled among the scattered papers and came up with a sheet that he studied to himself a moment and then handed to the scribe.

—Summarize the relevant sections, please.

The scribe read the several pages of the letter through in silence. He looked out the window for a minute of deep contemplation and then, all at one fast swoop, said, During the period of detention, this Cooper sold the Indians popskull liquor at prices that would buy a whiteman bonded Tennessee whiskey. His young clerks traded right by the stockade, where they were penned until the cart they sold from was ordered to be confiscated. After that, they sold liquor from their persons, in coat pockets and satchels. He is said to be a man of such make that he could preach temperance out of his mouth while at the same time digging in his pocket to make change for a bottle and not see any conflict between the two actions. These Indians were about as low as you can get to be. Nevertheless, he sold them liquor in any quantity they desired and could afford, from the demijohn to the noggin. And under his influence they became drunk as lords and about half of them spent their days laughing and the other half sitting with their backs against the stockade palings and their blankets over their heads, either passed out or crying. He was ordered again to quit selling, and he not only continued to do so but raised Cain about our authority to set conditions on him. He was banned from entering the stockade until the primary departure. Unfortunately, this Cooper is also a sharp lawyer and has long been under the spell of an old chief in these parts, and they have overmastered their fraction of Indians for quite some time. And whenever he is not here going buck wild, full Indian in language and customs all the way down to playing their deadly violent ball game, he's in Washington City dancing at fancy balls and bootlicking every wheelhorse and crony in the Government, which is why his bunch of Indians get to stay in their homes unmolested while all the rest are hunted up out of the woods like hogs in the fall. He has written a great raft of lawyer letters to his Washington City friends complaining that we had no right to deny his legitimate business and furthermore claiming he is owed a substantial reimbursement for vaguely specified expenses, some related to food and other supplies he says he gave the Indians after we failed to meet their basic needs. In conclusion, what are we to do with him?

When the scribe fell silent, the colonel drew on his pipe and puffed smoke. He took the letter from the scribe and tossed it back among the clutter.

—Any speculation as to the correspondent? the colonel said.

—Apparently not one of my well-wishers, I said. Perhaps some green young lieutenant unacquainted with the facts.

—Major Cotton, he said. He picked the letter up again and studied the signature and said again, Major Cotton.

—I'm shocked that a man of such rank is so misinformed, I said.

The colonel waited awhile, entranced by the smoke rising from his pipe. His timing was impeccable. Finally he said that he did not intend to altercate. And under no circumstances would he consent to my outrageous claims for reimbursement of expenses. But he had a counteroffer. A deal for services as guide and translator that only I was in a position to render.

—We intend for you to help us bring in the runners, the colonel said.

NEXT MORNING, I watched from up the hill as the fort emptied out in a sad parade. Soldiers on horseback, wagons loaded with provisions under their canvas coverlids, Indians and their slaves following afoot behind, children walking and babies being carried. Everything was a shade of brown, the people and their clothes, horses and wagons, and even the muddy road itself.

And this was not a singularity. There were other such forts scattered about the old Nation, each host to its own drab procession heading out to the West. A whole country shed of its people in the course of a summer.

TWO DAYS LATER, back in Wayah, I sat in the dim midday townhouse with Bear.

—You talked with that colonel? Bear said.

—Haden's a detestable old sow. His nose was so far up Jackson's ass for so long he couldn't smell honeysuckle, even if you presented him with an armload of blossoms. He needs to be gutted, and I had about half a mind to do it. Right through to the backbone with a Bowie knife, which I had on my hip.

Bear's face did not shift one way or the other.

—No? I said.

—That kind of thing, you can't get away with it anymore.

He said it sadly, like the world had been unalterably diminished.

—The colonel asked for our help, I said. He doesn't dare come within three days' ride of here under any circumstance. Too rough and dangerous, and none of them know this country in any detail. I'm to be their guide. I made a deal.

—For what?

—Certain considerations in regard to our situation. He gave me his assurance we'd be left alone, our deeds respected and any uncertanties as to citizenship ignored.

THERE WAS HARDLY any autumn that year. At the end of the dry summer, one black storm after another came ripping across the ridges, and by the end of September the trees were nearly stripped of leaves and the rivers were full to the banks with red water. The Nut Moon had hardly made an appearance during its cloudy month. Bright autumn, normally the driest month of the year, was like a new unsatisfactory season interjected into the year's round, warm and wet and yet the tree limbs stark as shattered glass against the grey sky and the goldenrod and ironweed and joe-pye weed all beat down to brown trash on the ground. Nothing colorful at all except for a few stunted pumpkins still glowing in the fields and a few persistent apples hanging red in the skeletal orchards. The Harvest Moon arrived like it intended to be about the same.

All through that unsettled weather, I rode with Lieutenant Smith and his soldiers, scouring the coves for fugitives. There were ten boys, all from big towns. Not one of them other than Smith had yet passed twenty. None of them had ever fired a weapon except in training or for amusement or in highly amateur attempts at hunting. They were baffled and frightened by these wet dark woods and mountains that went on and on, with more twists and folds and dangers than a Minotaur-infested labyrinth. Besides the Indians, bear and wolves and panthers still roamed all through these forests. The fact that the boys had seen no animal bigger than a groundhog failed to ease their minds. At night when the sky was blanked with clouds and there were voices coming from the creek noise and every odd sound out in the woods could mean death, they slept poorly. Most mornings they arose at dawn, wet and unrested. All day they searched the coves for fugitives, going up and down the many convoluted rivers and branches and creeks with names that were hard to pronounce and so impossibly resistant to spelling that the lieutenant would sit by his candle flame at night writing his reports and cursing loudly each time it became necessary to render one of the Indian watercourses into a phonetic approximation of English.

And for our relentless searching, two weeks of it, all we found was one old man, nearly blind and living alone, who said his name was Hog Meat and that he was nearly a hundred years old. They believed him, for he looked every day of that age, and I vouched for his harmlessness and frailty. He stood in the entryway to his cabin with one hand holding back the greasy deerhide that served as door and the other hand visored over his cloudy eyes, looking out to where we sat our horses in the rain. The lieutenant did not even bother to get down off his horse but said, That old man won't live out the winter. Perhaps we should let him be and give him some cornmeal. So we sorted through our packs and gave the old man food and then we let Hog Meat be. As we rode away from the house, I was thinking that a man's in a bad way when fellows younger than your grandchildren get to decide how your life goes from now on out.

Then one morning we rode up unexpectedly on sixteen fugitives camped right out in the open by the river with no apparent thought to concealment. Old men and women and children. They were starving and weaponless but for one rusty shotgun with no loads and a bow with only three arrows and a blowgun with a handful of long darts whittled from buckeye wood and tufted with thistledown. They put up no fight at all. The Irish boy took the bow and arrows from the man who held them, and the fletching of the arrows was rumpled and gapped like the feathers of a wet chicken. The Philadelphia boy broke the blowgun into three pieces and threw them into the fire. After being fed some beans and cold cornbread, the captives told where another dozen runners were hiding near the forks of a river two or three days away. So the lieutenant decided to divide his men, sending part of them back to the fort with the prisoners, and now it was just the five of us to find Charley's people and bring them in.

WE WERE CAMPED beside a strong-running creek filled with mossy boulders. Big woods rose black all around. The hobbled horses had finished eating their oats, and they shuffled and whickered nervously off in the dark beyond the firelight. I lounged with the three boys around a small fire that pushed back the dark only to arm's length. The lieutenant was sitting a little distance away with a candle lantern, writing up his report for the day.

The boys were cooking a supper of potatoes and bacon and cabbage, a grey mess that was just rising to a boil in a pot hanging from an iron tripod. A pile of chestnuts lay roasting in the outer ashes. The boys sprawled in their uniforms and overcoats on ground cloths waterproofed with wax. Their saddles and rolled wool blankets served as backrests. Wet wrinkled boots lay with the open ends to the blaze in hopeless effort to render them dry, if only briefly, so that in the morning the boys might not have to start the day with cold sodden footwear. They sat with their wool-socked feet close to the fire, steam rising from their toes.

—Well, fuck all, the Irish boy said. His name was Perry.

He had reached into his saddlebag and come out with a wooden stem and the shards of a yellowed clay pipe bowl cupped in his palm.

—Busted all to fuck, he said. My last one.

Perry pitched the pipe shards off into the dark and put the stem in his coat pocket until such time as he could buy another bowl or at least come upon a corncob he could core out and fit it to. The other two men were smoking with great concentration and looking at the fire.

—Anybody got a loaner? Perry said.

Neither man spoke.

Perry settled back against his bedroll. The man next to him reached out his pipe and Perry wiped the stem against the back of his wrist and took two draws and passed it back. The man held the bowl and looked at the stem and then made a show of waving it across the flame of the fire to clean it.

—I heard when we're done here it's Florida for us, Perry said.

—I heard Canada. The border, leastways, said the Philadelphia boy.

—One or the other, I guess. But I'm pulling for Florida, Perry said. They say it stays warm all winter and there's plenty of fish to fry.

—Where I'd like to be right now is Charleston, walking down Dock Street, the Charleston boy said. And then the Philadelphia boy said he'd like to be walking down South Street. When it was Perry's turn he said Galway, walking down Quay Street to the waterfront right at sunset to watch the light fall away from Inishmore across the water. He had not seen Galway Bay since he was nine years old, and he never expected to see it again this side of the grave.

I was reading a Washington Irving book about the western prairies by candlelight reflected.

Smith, finished with his report, came over and said, Perhaps one of you might stir that pot. Smith was barely older than the boys, but he did his best to act confident beyond his years and experience. He had the habit of including the word *perhaps* in nearly every order he gave. Perhaps, Private Perry, you might build the woodpile a bit higher before dark. It was an affectation he had not picked up at the Military Academy but had acquired all on his own, either in an attempt to be elegant or else to blunt the edge of command and make himself more likable to the boys under him by suggesting that the action he was requesting might be entirely optional. I had noticed that the boys had taken the word into their own vocabularies and used it frequently and not without irony when they were out of earshot of the lieutenant. Perry, perhaps you could try not to burn that bacon to a cinder. Perhaps next time you might walk a little farther away from camp to shit.

Perry dug the spoon into the grey mess and turned up the burnt bottom, black as cinders.

The boys were not cooks. Pretty often, their idea of supper had been to wrap a few strips of bacon around a green stick and hold it over the fire and try to get it brown without lighting it ablaze. I, on the other hand, enjoyed trailside cookery and even traveled with a coffee grinder and green beans, which I roasted in a dry skillet until they were black and sweating a sheen of oil. That night, I told the boys to toss out their charred cabbage. I cooked the best quail any of them had ever tasted. I'd been lucky enough to shoot four that flushed up out of an old weedy cornfield. I put pieces of apple and onion inside the birds and cut bacon in little slivers and shoved them between the skin and the breast. I rubbed a mixture of dried sage and salt and red pepper between my palms and let the dust fall over the plucked skins. Then I cooked the quails slow and patient on spits over a fire burned down to red coals. And I was not content with just the quail. I sliced potatoes in thin rounds and arrayed them pinwheel fashion in an iron skillet and daubed the top with butter and some more bacon slivers and lidded it and let it cook slow over grey coals until it was done. I cut it like pie and flipped the slices upside down on their plates, and the top was crisp and brown, and the inside was soft and had almost melted. I wished I'd been able to shoot a bird apiece, but it came out close enough.

The soldiers ate in total silence until their plates were empty but for a scattering of fine clean bones and a few little grey shotgun pellets, and then Perry wiped his mouth on his sleeve and said, Great God. And the rest of them agreed entirely.

Perry said, Every single time I try to cook chickens they end up with the feet burnt to charcoal and the thighs bleeding raw, and hardly any of it what you'd properly call done.

I said, You ought to see what I can do with a beef tenderloin.

THE NEXT AFTERNOON we made camp in the rain.

—Wet day, Smith said.

It had rained since dawn, rain falling white against the trees.

—We're famous for our moisture, I said.

Smith and the boys were miserable. I, though, had spent enough years in these wet woods to know how to do. I kept a set of clean dry clothes in an oilcloth bag. At the end of a day's travel, I'd strip out of my wet clothes and wash in the creek and then dress in my dry evening attire. Come morning, I'd put the traveling clothes back on, wet and cold until they warmed up to body temperature, but that was better than being miserable all the time. Another thing I did that people chose to interpret as an eccentricity was to take an umbrella into the woods for especially wet days. If I was afoot, I would wedge the handle between my knapsack and back, leaving my hands free, and I guess it did look a little strange to meet up with me on the trail.

Perry had taken off all his wet clothes and was naked under his grey wool blanket, which he wore cowled over his head and drooping to his white shins. He went and addressed himself to the fire, standing close, his back to the other men. He opened the blanket and baked for a while.

—I'd take it as a favor if you'd lap that blanket shut before you turn around, the Charleston boy said.

It might have seemed strange to me that these hapless boys should form the sharp edge of national policy, had I not moved among the men who made that policy.

I went to check on Smith, who had built his own fire. He sat in his underwear cross-legged on a blanket with his coat draped over his shoulders like a cape and his boots unlaced and flapped open on his feet. He finished his smoke and knocked out his pipe bowl against his boot heel. His wet clothes hung limp on a tripod of sticks near the fire. His hat was off and his blond hair stood in points, and every once in a while he would rake his fingers through it as if to smooth it down. His little mustache, faint even in brightest daylight, was invisible by the fire. He looked forlorn out there in the woods in the dark. I had brought along a bottle of good Scotch whisky, and in the spirit of conviviality I offered to share it.

—Strong stuff, Smith said after throwing back a shot.

—Smoky and strange. A taste of peat, which as I understand is a sort of swampy mossy kind of plant that the Scots and Irish collect and dry and make fires from, as settlers on the prairie burn buffalo dung. A cord of dry split hickory must be a thing of absolute wonder to such people. But to return to the point, the whisky is extremely passable.

Smith reached to his canteen to cut it, but I would not hear of it. It was necessary to draw the line somewhere.

—Either drink it or don't, I said. If you're going to water it down, you might as well be drinking the piss Welch sells at the tavern.

Smith deferred to my judgment and drank the whisky slow and careful. Something about its brown and musty taste carried a tinge of retrospection, and after two pours, Smith began recounting his life—at least his boyhood and youth, for that is all he had to tell. His father an old veteran of 1812, his mother somewhat younger but now dead. A bout of drear military school. And then, after four pours, he told that every day in these impenetrable woods and mountains left him terrified. He didn't know a thing about them and did not ever care to know. He wanted to go home. His greatest wish was to operate a store selling clothing, men's and women's, of the most recent fashion.

—Then go, I said. And do.

—I'm to make this my life and advance in it, he said. A career.

—Made by whom?

—My father. All the people of the town.

A bound boy, I thought. And then, damned if I didn't pop right out and say it aloud.

Smith started to get his back up and then thought better of it. He said, I'm meant to come home someday with honors. But they're not going to be gained here. It would make one's feelings about this go down easier if they had put up a fight. As it was, they wept. In the camps, some of the women killed themselves. There's no honor here.

—They already had all the fight beat out of them some time ago.

—Were they any good at it?

—Fighting?

—Yes.

—Now and again, they were. They were once a fierce people, but they're long since worn down from losing.

—Could you go tell that to the boys? Smith said. He was tired, and the whisky had hit him fast.

I went over and said, Boys, this is not your country, and I guess you feel uneasy in it. But it *is* my country. Colonel Haden is fond of referring to the people hiding in these mountains as fugitive warriors. But Charley's no warrior. I know him. He's a dirt farmer. An old man. Tomorrow will go fine. Nothing to keep you awake fretting. Sleep hard and dream of your sweethearts.

The next morning by the fire, with coffee boiling and side meat frying, Smith got all proper and priggish and said, I fault myself for an excess of frankness last night.

What I wanted to do was slap him down a bit with wit and words. Grammar and vocabulary as a weapon. But what kind of world would it be if we all took every opportunity presented to us to assault the weak? I said, It was the spirit of the evening and the Scotch whisky. Think no more of it.

And at least Smith had sense to say, I thank you.

WE LEFT THE horses tied a half mile down the river and moved up as quietly as we could through the thick ground layer of frosted leaves. Smith lay behind a blown-down hickory trunk glassing the camp. The other three boys were farther back in the woods, sitting with their muskets beside them. Two of them started loading pipes, tamping tobacco with their thumbs like filling a posthole. I looked at the final few leaves on the trees to see the way the wind moved, and then I looked at Smith, who kept his scope to his eye and made no attempt to keep the boys from lighting up, so I motioned back to them with both hands like pushing something down to the ground and they stopped.

Charley and his people had camped on a piece of land where two rivers joined together. It was a configuration of terrain that had an old appeal to the Cherokee and to the people before them. In the old days, they had usually built their mounds and villages in such places, both for practical reasons of defense and agriculture and flat ground for dances and ball games, and also because watercourses held spiritual import for them. I always thought it a sign of their generosity that they found water spiritual even in a land so wet that water is more often a nuisance than anything else.

An old hemlock grew on the highest part of this piece of land. Its stout trunk was still six feet through at head height, and the ground underneath would be soft, hundreds of years deep with a bed of its needles and the loose black earth into which the needles decay. Charley's people had built insubstantial shelters under the tree, a tentative-looking pole shed and an arbor, both lashed together with vines and roofed with brush and leaves and pine boughs. Provisional structures that would fall apart and melt into the ground in a few seasons. A dying fire sent up white smoke from its bed of ashes, and Smith said he could see muskets propped against the hemlock trunk nearby. Everyone in camp still seemed to lie abed, though the sun had been up for nearly an hour.

That worried Smith. He thought it was a ruse, and he began whispering about ambush and his plans to avoid it, all of which were unnecessarily complicated and impractical and based on the assumption that these baffled and powerless people—whose country had, as if by conjuration, dissolved beneath them and been reconstituted far off on some blank western territory—would put up a fight. I rose from behind the hickory trunk and started walking into camp, and as I went Smith was saying something to me in a hissing whisper inflected like he thought he was issuing orders. I looked back, and a vigorous plume of vapor puffed from Smith's mouth.

I went on and walked into camp and got between the people and their guns. I collected the two muskets, old worn trade pieces, where they lay propped against the hemlock trunk. They were loaded and cocked. I took out the caps and put the hammers down. I went and sat by one of the fires with the muskets on the ground beside me. There was a woodpile, and I stoked the fire and motioned for Smith and the boys to come on in.

They jingled and crashed and thumped their way into camp and everyone in the two shelters woke up and rose fully dressed. Charley walked partway to the fire and stopped.

—Hey, Charley, I said. Sit down here where it's warm.

Charley looked at the muskets on the ground and grinned and said, Hey, Will. He came over and sat down.

—I don't expect we're going to have any trouble here today, I said.

—No trouble.

The soldiers stood spaced out. They had their muskets aimed generally at the bunched people. I didn't know all the names. Just Charley and Nancy and their grown boys, Nantayale Jake and Lowan. And the boy Wasseton and the married daughter Ancih, and a few other women. There were several children, all wakening and hungry and crying. The women drew them together and the younger children stood behind the women and leaned out to look from behind the barrier of calico skirts that were thin and pale from long wear. Smith went and looked in the shelters for weapons and found none. He came back out and sent two of the boys off to fetch the horses.

I didn't see Ancih's husband and said so to Charley.

He said, George is out hunting. Gone two days.

—With anyone else?

—Maybe some others. Maybe alone.

I told Smith what Charley had said, and Smith said, We'll wait awhile and see if some more come in.

—They are not likely to come in if they see us, I said.

—They either will or they won't. We'll sit here today and start walking them out in the morning. And by the way, don't ever ignore my orders again.

I was fairly furious at his high-handed manner and the assumptions he was making about how the lines of authority ran within our little party. I started to remind Smith that I was not under his command and had not taken a cent in pay from the Government and would do as I pleased and call my own orders. I managed to hold my tongue but resolved within myself that all Smith had to do was utter one more word and I'd mount up and ride away and they could discover their own route out of the mazy mountains and wave hand signals in the air to communicate with their captives.

But Smith looked tired and white-eyed with fatigue and the nervous strain of this woods duty, which had been confusing and frightening to him. His fatigue made him look every bit as young as he was, maybe younger, and I remembered that he was so fresh out of school he still remembered how to read a little bit of Greek. I thought about the previous weeks of travel and camping, how Smith didn't sleep well in the mountains, jumping at every sound of falling leaf and foraging possum. Every morning he awoke twisted in his blankets, more exhausted than when he went to bed. I had once been like that myself. As a boy alone in the world, I slept best after the first grey of dawn began rising and dissipating the fear that collected in the dark. Now I found the woods narcotic. The blacker and noisier the better. Bear's old lessons in fearlessness and my own experiments in nightwalking had brought about the transformation.

I decided to exercise a certain amount of sympathy for Smith's nervousness and said, A day of cooking and eating and resting by the fire wouldn't hurt any of us. And then, in the casual tone of bidding good morning to a stranger you pass on the roadway, I said, Do not fear the universe, young lieutenant.

Smith did not have a response, and when the boys returned leading the horses, I turned my attention to the food. Smith and his boys had the inevitable potatoes and bacon, a partial sack of flour with little yellowish miller-moth grubs working in it, and a few bruised cabbages. I had a pannier full of my own stores, not caring much for army victuals. Cured ham, lard, salted butter, white cornmeal, dried beans, grits, dried apples and peaches, porridge oats, dark sugar, cinnamon, black tea, green coffee beans, and a small hand mill to grind them. Also a tin of ginger candies and a bottle of good Tennessee whiskey. And Havana cigars wrapped carefully in oilcloth.

I put Perry to work helping cook while the other two stood watch at the edge of camp. Smith sat looking at the fire in a daze. Charley's people went back into the shelters and talked among themselves, and then Charley and Lowan and Jake came and squatted by the fire. I roasted coffee beans and directed Perry in the assembly of a big pot of porridge with dried peaches minced in it and flavored with a profligate amount of cinnamon and dark sugar and butter. The children ate it and became all big-eyed with wonder at the taste, and the soldier boys, including the lieutenant, were not far behind in their appreciation. I took just a little of it in a tin cup, and mostly sat drinking coffee and enjoyed watching the people eat. All in all, it was a companionable breakfast. Charley and I talked and Smith sat listening as if he expected to catch a word now and then.

Charley said, Where we going?

—Where the Nation is going, I said. You live on the Nation.

Charley said, I'm abiding by the old lines.

—You've got to quit thinking that way, I said.

—Then where we going?

—Going west, I said. A long way.

Charley made an exhaling noise between his teeth and lips like a long string of F's.

Later in the afternoon, the soldier boys squatted on the ground, gambling penny stakes on tic-tac-toe, the grids scratched in the dirt with the point of a knife. Perry did not have a firm grasp on the logic of the game; otherwise no money would have changed hands as every game would end in a draw. As it was, he played as if the outcome were as random as casting dice or flipping a coin. He, of course, lost steadily and seemed to think the other two possessed enormous luck. After a while, I went over and said, Look, son. Put your marks where I say.

After a few games, with me whispering, Top left, bottom middle, Perry saw what he'd been missing. Goddamn, he said. There's nothing to it at all.

The Charleston boy looked at me and wiped the last grid away with a sweep of his palm and said, Hell, I could have won tobacco money off him from now on out, but you've boogered that all up.

SMITH, OF COURSE, wanted to assign watches through the night. But I told him that he had not the least worry that any of Charley's people would make trouble, and besides, I'd about rather have Lowan or George cut my throat in mid-dream than sit awake in the long hours between midnight and dawn. So Smith assigned me the first watch, from just after sundown to bedtime, as if that had been his plan all along and my objecting to the watches had nothing to do with it. And Smith would take the last watch, from around four to sunup, which left those three boys to stand the worst of it. Smith reckoned to keep them awake two at a time, letting one always sleep, spelling one another every couple of hours.

Supper that night was beans and bacon and cornmeal mush fried crisp in lard. Charley's bunch mostly took their food to the brush arbors to eat, and maybe it was just the food but they seemed unaccountably happy. They talked and laughed and seemed able to let their larger circumstances not weigh on their thoughts for now. Content to let worrying wait for later.

The soldier boys ate their supper and then tried to get in an hour or two of sleep, but they just rolled around in their blankets and muttered to one another. Smith and I sat studying the fire and Smith had almost nothing to say. I left him and gathered a fist of cigars and the bottle of whiskey from my packs and went to Charley's fire.

They were telling tales, and I nodded at them to keep on with what they were doing. Sometime when no one was looking, George had slipped back into camp to share the fate of his wife and children. I passed out cigars to the men, and we lit them with a twig caught alight in the fire and passed the bottle around. Charley was doing most of the talking, telling a hunting story from the days of elk and bison, neither of which anyone in attendance but Charley had ever seen. He made them epic animals in his story, inhabitants of an old better world not to come round again. He then told about his lost farmstead at the old mound village of Cowee, before one of many disastrous treaties had driven him and his family west to Nantayale. At Cowee, he had been noted for his success with apple trees, which over the years he had planted at the spots where his outhouses had stood. Apples grew on his trees huge as dreams of apples. That Cowee house was old, from the time when they still buried dead loved ones in the dirt floor, but Charley could not remember exactly whose bones had rested near as a lover beneath his low sleeping platform. Then, without transition, Charley told how Nancy tailored his pants. She would have him lie down on his back on a smooth patch of bare dirt outside their door. She would take a stick and trace the outline of his lower body as children trace their hands. When she was done marking, Charley got up carefully, and Nancy would scribe lines to show his waist and the bottoms of his pantlegs. Then she'd lay out pieces of rough wool or linen she had loomed herself and scissor two pieces to match the pattern on the ground and stitch them together. In Charley's telling, it was a miraculous process, at the end of which he suddenly had new pants.

And then Charley told a new story from the past month, another hunting tale. He had been out alone under a low sky, moving up a narrow cove north of here into a deep closed landscape, a cut in earth so sharp he sometimes had to walk the creek like it was a trail because the cove walls narrowed and rose straight from the lapping water of the creek edge. He had a sort of lidded forage basket or creel woven from oak splits on a strap across his shoulder, and when he came to a place where the cove widened and there was a flat woods floor for a stretch, he looked about at the dry stalks and frost-burnt leaves of low-growing plants. He stopped and got down on his knees and dug in the black ground with a stick and then with the tines of his stubby and spatulate fingers, the knuckles swollen like galls in a blackberry cane. He didn't use the broad-bladed knife or the hatchet that hung in leather scabbards from his pantwaist, though they would have made the job easier. They were each sharpened keen enough to shave his forearm bare, but he would rather damage his hands than his tools.

He dug elbow-deep in the dirt and then came out with a root, pulling it from the ground as if he were a fisherman with his hands plunged in muddy water grabbling out a heavy and reluctant catfish. His catch went into the creel with its fellow roots, and Charley closed the lid as if they might otherwise escape. Some would be for eating. Some for making tea. Some for medicine.

He stopped at midday and struck up a small fire from pine shavings and oak sticks. He boiled creek water in a kettle and set it off the fire and steeped rounds cut from a piece of ginseng root. When it had made tea, he drank it out of a tin cup he kept tied to his rope belt with a smaller loop of rope. That was his dinner.

Charley sat by the fire a long time thinking about food. The trees were nearly empty. The thorny chestnut husks had fallen and the nuts had been eaten every way there was to eat them. Raw and roasted in the fire and made into bread. The leaves of the poplars and maples and chestnuts lay on the ground, and at night the bare limbs cast jagged moon shadows across the rocks of the river. Just the oaks held out against the cold with a few yellow-brown leaves left rattling in the wind. Wasseton had darted all the squirrels within a mile of the camp with his blowgun. Their slim charred bones and tiny skulls were mixed with the white ashes of the fire pit. Also the long column of spine and the many curved keen ribs of a big rattler that Wasseton had hit right in the soft underside of its head as it rose up in striking posture and then finished off with thrown rocks until it lay twisting, head crushed, in the leaves. There seemed to be few turkey or quail or even songbirds left in the woods. No hares or coons. The horses were long gone—traded to Axe, first one and then the other—during late summer and early fall. All they had brought in the trade was a puzzlingly small quantity of beans and cornmeal and a few pumpkins and cabbages. At this precise moment of the fall, since the beginning of known time, passenger pigeons had arrived in great clouds, their masses like a dark river flowing southward down the sky, settling into the bright-colored woods for a few days like a dense grey fog of bird meat. And in the past, Wasseton would dart them out of the trees with his long blowgun until the muscles of his diaphragm and stomach became weak from the effort of deep and sharp exhalations, and his six hickory darts became heavy and dark with blood all the way to the thistledown fletching. He could reliably drive a dart through a pigeon's head at nearly the distance he could throw a rock. But this year the pigeons came only in ones and twos, and then after a few days they were suddenly gone altogether. All Wasseton could provide for the group was one feast of birds roasted over coals. For the children, one little leg apiece like upside-down water drops of meat. Small split breasts and bony backs for everyone else. Then, only a day later, nothing but watery grey soup of feet and necks and gizzards. The woods refused sustenance. One day, all anyone had to eat was a clear broth made from a single goldfinch, so dilute you could have gotten as much flavor from dropping a stone into the water.

Though Lowan and Jake and George hunted daily, they had failed to kill a deer for the better part of a month. All the meat left now was a little venison jerky, just tag ends and scraps that served no purpose beyond flavoring a pot of cornmeal soup. Charley remembered that last deer, a fat buck. Half of him they'd eaten fresh, and half of him had been shaved into thin strips and hung from drying frames to jerk near the fire. Charley had gone out of camp to piss one night, and as he came back the hanging meat with the firelight coming through looked like bloody curtains. Before sunrise three mornings earlier, Lowan had killed a possum with a pouchful of babies. They stewed her and roasted the little ones on sharpened sticks over the fire, and the little ones were hardly a mouthful apiece. And that to feed a dozen people. The women and children had no energy and they hardly spoke. They spent most of the days sleeping under the brush arbors or sitting wordless by the fire. Winter was falling soon, and they would need more shelter. If they were this hungry now, just after the fall of leaves, what would it be when the Bone Moon came? Beyond looking for a cave, Charley had no plan for winter. The days of the year were too evasive for planning. They fled shapeless before him. The future held no hope. And he had already abandoned fearfulness. All he could do was exercise an attitude of still acceptance.

Charley's fire would have fit in his pair of hands, and when it began dying he covered it with dirt, for it is a bad and unbalancing thing to put out fires with water. He walked away from the creek and began climbing a dry ridge to cross over to another cove whose creek he figured to descend toward the river and the camp. As he walked, he scuffed his feet in the deep leaves just for the companionship of the rustling sound. The poplars, simplified by having shed their broad palmate leaves, stood as bright vertical slashes against the brown hillsides. Charley curved around a cropping of rock and climbed steep to the crest of the ridge and then pitched down the sharp slope toward the next creek. There was a joy in descent, in suddenly finding the pull of the earth acting consonant with your needs. He barely took note that the sky was closing down over him, becoming a grey press of moisture.

It began raining hard, straight down, as if the air had turned to water. All he could do was squat under a stand of rhododendron with his blanket over his head and wait. For a while the long glossy leaves turned water away from him, and then suddenly they did not. Water fell in runnels from the leaves onto the chalky ground litter under the shelter of the rhododendron and pooled at his feet. Charley's blanket and clothes became heavy and sodden. Then, at the point when he became wet to the skin, the rain tapered away to nothing but dense fog.

Charley rose from under the rhododendron and twisted the water out of his blanket and set out again downhill through the foggy dripping woods. He walked at a smart pace, and before long came to the creek and turned downstream. This was not his home country, and he did not yet know it well, but he reckoned he could reach camp and the heat of the fire long before dark.

Deep woods are haunted places in the fog. Light comes from everywhere at once, shapes shift, and sounds are muffled and magnified unpredictably. As Charley walked, he began to feel a presence in the woods, a sense of being watched from out of the fog. He spun and looked behind him and saw the blurred black shape of what might be bear at the edge of vision. If so, it stood square to the ground looking his way, motionless. It was probably a tree stump or a wet rock.

Charley started walking downhill again, and the fog thickened as he descended into it. He was partly blinded. The big trees were visible only halfway up their wet trunks, and the creek was a muffled rush off to his left. He could not even see the far bank, just a ribbon of dark water and the mossy rocks rising from it. All color was damped down to shades of grey. The passway lay narrow and slick underfoot, and his best idea for navigation was to keep the creek within hearing to his left and not climb any ridges to the right. By doing so, even a blind man would strike the river eventually.

He walked on down the winding creek, passing a white cascade and a deep black pool. But the thought kept weighing on him that a bear would be awfully good eating about now. A bear with yellow fat lying three fingers deep over the red muscles from a long autumn of gorging on chestnuts, hickory nuts, acorns, and huckleberries. Tasting sweet and dark like a rendering of the forest. Meat to last into the next moon. Cooking grease for the entire winter. A heavy fur for the children to sleep beneath when snow comes. Long curved claws the color of charcoal for his grandchildren to auger holes through and string into necklaces and keep as relics to remember Charley, evidence of his existence long after he was gone. He could see them showing the claws to their own grandchildren and telling the story of the day he came walking into camp bloody to the elbows, bent from the weight he packed over his shoulder, a great bear haunch in a black bundle made from its skin. And then how the women started cooking the meat and the men all followed Charley back up the mountain to finish butchering the bear, and then how they all sat about the cook fire for days, eating until their bellies hurt.

Charley stopped and turned back around and saw a motionless

square shape, a dark interruption in the luminous fog. He took out his hand axe and knife and felt their heft and looked at their edges, honed bright with spit and a flat river rock. Charley reckoned his tools might suffice to kill this bear. Men had done such things before, or at least people told stories of killing bear in close combat. He had never actually seen it done. But in the stories, the men had always first wounded the animal with bow or gun and then let it bleed awhile to weaken.

The famous Bear Drowning Him, now mostly just called Bear, was said to have gotten his name when he was still a boy by killing the master bear of all this territory, wounding it first with an arrow to the lungs and then fighting it with a knife in his fist until they both streamed blood. They brawled down a hillside and then to the river's edge and then onward until they were waist-deep in the water. They closed awkwardly together, neither finding much purchase against the round slick stones of the riverbed. But the boy drove a blade deep in the bear's vitals. And then the bear lurched forward and pressed the boy down under the water with his full weight. All that remained visible was the muscled hump of the bear's back breaking the dark surface of the river. But at the last moment of Bear Drowning Him's strength, the bear died. It went still and lay with the water flowing around the bulk of it in a pair of smooth curves. The boy came up and slung the water out of his hair, and he still had the knife in his fist, the blade shining and clean from the water.

The bear was claimed to have measured a full arms' span across at the ass. Even deducting for decades of exaggeration, that was still a big bear. Even now, when Bear wanted to cut a dash for children, he sometimes exhibited the parallel welted scars across his back and ribs where the claws had scored him to the bone in their last embrace. Bear had narrated the story to Charley's children several years ago when, on a hunting trip, he had spent a rainy night in their cabin. Bear loomed over them at his lean excessive height and told the story, and the children looked up and listened in amazement. And then at the climactic moment, Bear turned to a quartering position and pulled up the tail of his long hunting shirt, and the skin was becoming creped and hanging loose over the bones, but the scars were bright as ropes of rubbed silver, relics of an accomplishment that could be taken to the grave and perhaps beyond.

There was a slight shift of wind from up the creek, and it carried an odor like wet dog. Charley began walking back toward the dark shape. He talked to it in a low voice.

He said, Come to me. Come to me. And then he sang the bear hunter's song: I want to lay them low on the ground. Low on the ground.

He reckoned that taking nothing but a cup of bitter tea without honey for the entire day was about the same as the hunter's fast of the old times. He had the hatchet in his right hand and the knife in his left hand with the edge up for good ripping after a deep belly stab. He said again, Come to me. And then he said the last prayer before the kill: Let the leaves be covered with clotted blood, and may it never cease to be so.

Through the fog, Charley could see the bear's ears and tan muzzle. It made a bouncing motion with its front end. Charley took it that the bear was willing to fight. Without thinking much about it, he took two running steps forward and let fly the hatchet. It was a deep throw, all the strength in his old stout body expressed in a flow of movements calibrated so that the hatchet would make two revolutions in air before burying its blade in the bear with great force.

There was the sound of a solid blow struck, but he could not see what he had hit. The bear did not charge but made a single plosive utterance, a huff. It wheeled and ran uphill at amazing speed, crashing through a stand of laurel and disappearing into the fog. Charley stood and listened to the cracking of limbs and imagined the working of the massive hams and buttocks. Big muscles that would make good eating. He sheathed the knife and went and retrieved the bloody hatchet where it lay on the ground and took off running hard.

Charley was like the bear in his squat build, his power all settled in his ass and thighs, and he ran lumbering but strong, and his short legs were good for climbing. For a while he could take his direction by stopping for a second and listening to the bear moving ahead of him through the leaves. But when Charley grew short of breath and slowed to a walk, the bear soon outdistanced him. He stopped to listen, and there was silence, even when he opened his mouth wide to aid his hearing. But he could follow the trail of disturbed leaves and broken branches and blood, and when there was no sign, he chose his forward path only by guessing how the bear would react to the flow of terrain and the way the forest plants might serve as obstacle or cover. At intervals he found gouts of blood on the forest floor and broad smears against tree bark to confirm the correct working of his imagination.

He moved in the bear's wake all afternoon, climbing without letup. The blood led on, but thinned down. Bleeding out or healing up.

Gouts became drops. Drops became rare as garnets cupped in fallen leaves. Step by step, footprints lay lighter on the earth, fainter and fainter as if the bear were slowly elevating into the sky.

Charley went at a near trot, bent double to look for fading sign. He climbed out of the coves where colored leaves still hung on the trees, through a region where ferns and vines had grown fountainous through the summer and were now melancholy and dying as far as the eye could see, and then along the dry ridges, and by dusk he was rising through a forest of bare trees grey as winter toward the ominous balsam forests draped black across the highest ridges, a world of shadow and hush, where every step fell muffled by the soft foot-bed of old brown needles. He hoped he would not have to cross that boundary, for the only time he had done so a giant owl had glided silent and big-headed right past him in the half dark that was day under the balsams. The owl's face as big as his own and pale as the moon. A bad sign. Not the word you wanted spoken to you out alone in the high mountains.

Charley went on upward, one red drop at a time until the sign died entirely before him. He went casting forward until that direction became hopeless, and then he backtracked to the last drop of blood and began circling, making wider and wider rounds without success. He looked up into the trees and the sky beyond, for it seemed as if at some point the bear had spread wings and taken flight. He followed a rill of water no wider than his hand back to its source, for it is widely known that certain springs offer entrance into the world underneath the world, a refuge. But there was no sign of bear along the rill. Charley kept searching until it was so dark he could not tell one kind of fallen leaf from another. He sat with his back against a tree and looked up through the bare winter woods toward the highest peaks and sent out a prayer to the bear and all his animal brethren, speaking aloud without hope or despair. Saying that since the beginning of time, animals have willingly sacrificed themselves to the needs of people, have given us their pain and blood as a gift along with their fat and meat. Don't stop now.

He waited by the tree until dawn for the outcome to his prayer. Ready with knife and hand axe in case a dark shape separated itself from the night and came to him, offering him its life.

When Charley returned to camp the next day, it was with neither a bloody haunch over his shoulder nor a heroic story to tell. He had only his creel of withered roots. He set about peeling and slicing them and brewing a pot of bitter tea the color of strong urine.

Charley concluded his hunting story by saying that until this night by the campfire with the tobacco smoke and brown whiskey, he had not spoken a word about his lost bear to any of his descendants but only whispered about it to Nancy the night of his return as they lay on their bed of hemlock boughs, and she held him and brushed his face with the big knuckles of her fingers and told him that he had tried but failed and sometimes that is all the victory we are allotted.

4

THE EVENTS OF THE FOLLOWING DAY HAVE BEEN THE SUBJECT OF a certain amount of speculation over the years, both in print and as mere gossip. Some say I did not join the soldiers and Indians when they headed out down the trail because the Indians had warned me something might happen. Others have said that maybe I felt crushing guilt and stayed there at the forks of the river under the big hemlock to reflect in solitude on my recent actions. I'll set the record straight, though it is not in the least to my credit. My recollection is that after a long stretch of camping in the woods with soldiers, I had enjoyed about all the male companionship I could stand and began wishing for the company of women. I calculated that it was but a half day's ride to Welch's Tavern, at least for me, knowing the shortcuts and going at a good clip on a fine horse. With Smith's party moving at foot pace, I had time to drop in for a night with Welch's accommodating female employees before catching back up the next day. That, to the best of my remembrance, is why the mounted soldiers and their pedestrian prisoners left after daybreak, Smith navigating nervously by the little scrap of map I had drawn for him. And that is also why I did not arrive at the killing ground until the morning after and had to piece together what happened from the sign on the ground.

—

THE CLEARING IN the woods where I came upon the boys hewn to death was hardly bigger than the stage of a theater, a brief and roughly circular interruption in the dense forest. I commended them to what god they claimed and then walked about the perimeter, observing the order of the scene.

The boys lay spaced apart, and the ground was marked everywhere with sign of what had taken place. Of the several interpretations that were possible to make, this is how I shaped a narrative from the attitudes of the dead boys and their scattered effects and the scripture on the ground that the skirmish had left.

Skirmish is such an airy-sounding word. It could very well be near kin to words like *cotillion* or *promenade*. But the men who die in these little inconsequential fights are just as stone dead as if they fought at Hastings or Culloden or Sharpsburg. A quarter century after this bloody moment memorialized on the ground, I, as a middle-aged man, engaged personally in more than a few skirmishes, and I found them to be desperate and ugly encounters, gunfire spluttering in pulses, men yelling curses, brief confused silences between outbursts. And when they're done fighting, men lie dead and dying, stunned and bleeding and pale. Other men go on calmly about their business. Those are the winners. The losers leave their dead and wounded where they fall and flee in vomitous panic.

In this ugly little encounter smeared on the ground before me, it looked like one of the men, let's say Lowan, struck high, a hard and solid hatchet stroke opening Perry's head from the hairline to the teeth. Perry fell face down. The phrase that might be used by someone who has never seen a man die is that Perry was dead before he hit the ground. But that's not always the way it happens, even with your head opened up, and I'll leave it at that without further detail. At nearly the same moment that Lowan made his move, another man, George maybe, must have taken a two-handed swipe at the Philadelphia boy and buried the hatchet head deep at the junction of his neck and shoulder. The blade had caught hard in the bones, buried as in a dry log butt. George would have yanked at the handle but could not make it come loose. Philadelphia wanted to fall and went as far as his knees, but George kept yanking him upright, trying to get his hatchet out. Philadelphia grabbed the handle just behind the head and they disputed over it, and even then George could not retrieve his hatchet. Philadelphia fell forward and lay dying, half propped up by the handle and grabbing desperately at the ground. Simultaneously, Jake had struck at Charleston's head, hoping to lay him out quickly, but it was a glancing blow and only staggered him and raised a peel of scalp over his ear. Jake closed with him and struck again and hit more with the flat than the sharp part of the blade. The joints of Charleston's knees let go and he collapsed like pleated cloth straight to the ground and did not move further.

I was just assigning theoretical parts for the killers. The dead and their wounds, though, were certain. As was the fact that the killings took place outside the Nation and on our territory. I've never been much of a one for prayer, but I looked at the dead boys and prayed that in the future it would be the likes of Jackson sprawled on the ground and not poor boys with hardly two pennies to rub together dying for the foolish ideas of greedy old men. I heard horses in the woods and went and collected the three and tailed them one to the other for travel.

WHEN I REACHED the fort a hard day's ride later, I found Smith alone in his pale pyramidal tent. He sat drafting his report atop a little folding table, and the ground at his feet was littered with balled sheets of paper. A half-full bottle of whiskey and a half-full glass stood side by side on his desk. The luminous brown contents of both vessels rocked with the effort of his writing. He looked up, and he did not seem happy to see me. I sat in a camp chair and waited for what he had to say.

Smith became suddenly occupied with the tedium of writing. He trimmed a fresh quill with a penknife, dipped into the inkpot and scratched down enough words to make a few sentences, and then immediately balled up the sheet and tossed it on the ground as if paper grew on trees.

Smith rose and went to a trunk and took out another glass and poured me a drink from his bottle. He turned his chair my way and sat leaned forward, holding his whiskey glass two-handed between his knees. When he looked up at me, tears were brimming at his lids. He said, These goddamn fucking mountains. I wish I'd never laid eyes on them.

I asked the obvious. What happened?

Smith said it all exploded so fast he still wasn't sure what happened, exactly who did what. It began when Charley's wife, Nancy, had grown tired. She fell back to the end of the group and then stopped. One of the soldier boys dismounted and went to see what was the matter. There was some kind of altercation, and the other boys dismounted as well. From that point, the bloody little moment unfolded in less time than drawing five breaths. Hatchets appeared from under blanket cloaks. Honed edges flashed in the sun. Smith, still mounted, tried to loose the flap of his holster to get at the pistol, but his fingers just twitched at the simple device of button and eyelet. He saw the three boys cut down while he was still fumbling. His spit turned to mucilage, tongue stuck to the roof of his drying mouth. He couldn't piece together who committed what act of violence.

The women and children stood watching, emotionless and completely still, grouped in near symmetry so that the memory of them would stay with Smith all his life, coming to rest in his mind like a family portrait. Perry and Charleston lay still, and Philadelphia, bleeding heavily, made motions with his hands like trying to get a grip on the earth. There was an awful lot of blood in the brown leaves, and the men with the hatchets turned in Smith's direction.

It was not as if he thought about it. Thinking was not what the moment called for. His heels jerked back into a kick and his hands loosed the reins and the rowels of his spurs cut and drew blood. The horse gathered himself low on his hindquarters and then galloped off downhill with Smith riding loose and his elbows sticking out and flapping like he wished to take flight.

—At least sometimes that's the way I think it was, he said.

—Might have been that your horse wheeled and bolted as you were trying to unholster your pistol. By that point, it was too late to save anybody but yourself anyway.

—Might have been. I can't say.

—And might have been that if I'd come along with you I could have said something that would have mattered.

—There wasn't time to say anything. Everything happened all at once.

We poured another drink and sipped without further comment, neither of us truly believing the generous interpretation of the other.

Without even a courtesy clearing of throat, the colonel's little scraggle-haired scrivener came into Smith's tent and said, Both of you, right now.

As we neared the door of the colonel's office, Smith slowed and entered behind me. The colonel sat at his table behind the leavings of a boiled-beef dinner, the plate rim-full of grey juice afloat with fat pearls of congealed suet. Two spermaceti candles burned in pewter holders. The whites of the colonel's eyes were the color of the suet, and he looked at me a long time before saying, How did it ever occur to me to send you two out together?

—They were farmers, I said. You've rousted out thousands of them without incident. How were we to know these few would put up a fight?

—You worthless little shitheel, he said.

—You took all they had. People get pushed too far, they lose their heads.

The colonel touched a forefinger into the cold grey juice in his plate and then put the first joint of the finger into his mouth. When he was done tasting, he scrubbed at his greasy finger with the thumb of the same fist. He looked at the working of his hand as if it were fascinating.

He said, Speaking of loss, you're about to lose something too. Land and people and everything. If I need to do it to catch the killers, I'll send in all the Army necessary to clean every Indian out of here, no matter whose land they claim to live on. Your land included.

I looked around at Smith. He still stood behind me, and he was looking off to the side. No help at all.

I said to the colonel, What about our previous agreement?

—Things change.

I could feel everything falling apart. Bear and everyone who had taken me in as a boy, walking away to the West. Claire gone. I guess my face looked like a map in process of erasure.

The colonel waited and watched. Then he said, If there were an easier way, I'd be willing to entertain offers.

—What do you need? I said.

—The killers. Every one of them delivered to justice.

—For what purpose?

—I recollect that you're an attorney. The language of the law is not a mystery to you. They've committed a capital crime. What end does that suggest?

—And our people?

—Not an issue if I get the killers.

—And what about any other fugitives hiding up in the mountains?

—They can stay or go. All I'm interested in is the killers.

I paused to think but then realized that not much thought was required.

—All right, I said. I'll bring them in.

The colonel took the time to look at his plate and thumb it, sloshing, to the far side of the table. It left a shining trail across the desk like a slug's passage. He said, I guess next you'll want cash payment for your services?

I told him that what he was asking might well cost me my life, and that he hadn't enough Federal money at his disposal to compensate me for its loss. Furthermore, I said that if I was to die I didn't want to go under the ground as a hireling. It would be as a free agent or nothing at all. And contrary to the devout belief of his Yankee people, money was not the engine that wheeled the stars across the night sky.

The colonel smiled at my foolish lack of skill in negotiating. He said, No money at all?

—None.

—I believe we have reached a deal, he said. You have a month from today. Bring them in and we're done with each other. And none too soon. One day later, and I'll wipe all of you away to the Territories.

—Care to memorialize this agreement on paper? I said.

The colonel laughed as if I'd told the joke about Old Blue the coon dog. He motioned me away with flicks of his two hands. I backed directly into Smith. We jostled and regained balance and went to stand together by the door. The colonel and his scrivener huddled together whispering, and then the scrivener sat at the end of the table and dipped his quill and began writing.

BACK IN WAYAH, I told Bear all the details of my recent past. The travel with the soldiers, the capture of Charley, the killings. I concluded by showing him the colonel's letter and translating it for him, explaining in detail its guarantee that we and any innocent fugitives now on our land would be left alone if we caught Charley and his people within a month. Minus my day of travel from Valley River. Otherwise we might well be wiped away to the Territories.

Bear looked so old, everything about him drawn smaller except his knobby fingers. He sat without a word for a long time and smoked a long-stemmed clay pipe down to ash. He said he believed that you could think about our situation for a month and come to the same conclusion, for our dilemma was simple. What we had before us were two bad choices. But there was nothing unique about that. So often in life, all the option Creation grants us is either shit or go blind. The short of it was, Charley's people had put us in danger. We hadn't killed anybody, except in our dreams, but we would be punished just the same by reason of blood identity. That's why Wild Hemp had died back in the last century at the end of the Revolution. Her red blood. She hadn't raised a finger against either Americans or English and could not even tell the difference between them and was confused by why they were fighting each other to begin with. They looked much more alike than we did in regard to the Creeks or anybody else you could name. But she was shot down by the Americans nevertheless. And the only reason for her death was that Indians had sided with the English, and the English had lost. Wild Hemp died as a result of forces she didn't understand or even acknowledge. Dead in the dirt, the most beautiful being ever created. There was no justice in the world anymore. All you could do was try to go on living as a form of vengeance, to keep your memory alive as long as possible. For as soon as Bear died, the memory of Wild Hemp would pass entirely from the world, never to be retrieved again. As if she had never lived.

The end of Bear's thinking was that Charley had made a choice for all of us, and Bear did not agree with that choice and was not bound by it.

—Let's bring him in, Bear said.

Hunters had reported to him that people were hiding somewhere up among the highest mountains, starving and cold and sick. Lichen's bunch. Several dozen fugitives from at least three generations. Bear said, We'll start tracking Charley from here. You go up and find Lichen and get his people down with us to help. Do it before Charley gets to them.

—So they don't join up? I said.

—The fewer people we're hunting the better.

I WENT ALONE through that unsettling autumn weather, on foot through rough and ragged country for many days scouring the coves and creek banks until I tracked Lichen's band to a cave up under the peaks of the highest mountains. I won't tell every lone camp and miserable thought that crossed my mind those days except to say I lay awake every night, flat on my back, watching the stars transit through the tree limbs and wondering if Claire had made it to the West and fearing she had not. The word *bleak* would pretty well describe every element of those footslogging days. I'll just say that I walked a long way and finally tracked Lichen's bunch to their cave. Perhaps I should also add that with every upward step I feared that when I found them they would kill me and leave me in the deep woods for the wolves to break apart.

THE FIRE WAS burning low and a layer of pale smoke thick as meringue settled against the ceiling of rock, unable to find a passage out. A thin brown dog rose stiffly and stretched and circled and then moved a few inches closer to the blaze. The cave held the heat of the wood fire close. People sat far back from the flames and were only dark shapes. I couldn't see the faces of the people around me and knew them only by their voices, but I had known some of them since I was a boy. The generations surrounding me were as desperate as you can drive people to be. Babies crying in piercing tones, elders coughing with a deep rattle in the lung. They were a band of fugitives living hard and pressed, starving and hopeless, but together in body and purpose. All I had to offer them was five pounds of dried beans and an ugly deal, but necessary and without reasonable option. I didn't know where to begin arguing with these people. They had survived beyond fright into glazed and fatal blankness.

I started with a rant against the whole sweeping weight of the modern world that was poised to fall on them. After which it would just keep moving forward like a wave on the sea, oblivious to individual pain. I used every tactic of rhetoric I had learned from Bear and from all the smart dead English writers I treasured and from all the days in court, teasing out disputes about land titles and property lines and whose cow broke down somebody's pasture fence. All those experiences stood me in good stead, at least to the extent that I convinced Lichen and his people not to kill me.

The concluding sentence to the first stage of my argument was this:

Come down and help us track the killers and be welcome to join Bear's people. Have peace. How can you argue against peace?

—Peace, Lichen said. White people wipe their ass on the notion of peace every day. Don't come all white-faced telling me about peace. You people spit on peace.

—Not all of us do, I said. I don't spit on it. And furthermore, I said, if he wanted to call me white, that was his privilege. But I took my clan membership to heart. I went by the old rules. If you were a member of a clan, you were an Indian. As to peace, I said, I had spent most of the past few years trying to find a path to it. The entire direction of the new world, though, was against peace. So it was an honorable thing to fight against the world. And I had done my best to be a warrior.

Lichen said I was not the issue. He could not be at peace because soldiers had hunted them like wild deer. A year ago he had a wife and child, a woman he loved and a brave bright-eyed boy. And because they would not become slaves and be told where to live, they were left to starve upon the mountains. He had buried his child, and then shortly thereafter he had buried his wife. And this was his own country. How could that be right? Hunted like animals in your own country. Every man and woman with him had a similar story. So Lichen would agree neither to come down from the mountains nor to join in the hunt for Charley. They had known each other since boyhood. There was no precedent for hunting your own people like game. And so he scorned my proposition.

Bear had guessed at Lichen's response and had suggested that at some point I might need to tell the tale of U'tlunta. Spearfinger the Monster. I sat by the fire and told the story that everyone already knew. But I fleshed it out and used the best features of the language to make it live anew. I told how Spearfinger had been one of our people, a respected old woman until she went bad and began shifting shapes and became covered in scales as hard as plates of shale that no knife or arrow could break. She grew a forefinger like a spear point and poked everyone she met to the heart, men and women and children. Then she opened them up and ate their livers. She brought threat and disorder down on the people. They didn't ask for it, she brought it. She went through the mountains singing a song, and it was pretty if you didn't listen closely to the words, for they were all about eating people's livers. Spearfinger forced the people to band together and find a way to kill her. They chased her through the mountains, and then they dug a pit and trapped her in it. A bird told them where to aim their arrows between the scales of rock to strike her heart. Her death was a sad victory for the people, for Spearfinger had once been one of them. But she had left them no choice.

At the end of the story, I paused. Five dramatic heartbeats. I could feel them beating in my wrists and temples. I said that by killing the soldiers, Charley and his people had brought similar threat of annihilation to all our people. And, similarly, we were left with no choice.

In the end, Lichen's people came on down to Wayah with me. Along the way, we collected a few more fugitive stragglers. After eating from the community stewpots nonstop for two or three days, Lichen's men joined us in searching for Charley. We scoured the rivers and creeks and streams like hounds after foxes. Charley and his family fled before us like driven deer or quail flushed to the guns by beaters.

5

I WOULD LIKE TO MAKE THE CONCLUDING ACT OF CHARLEY'S STORY an epic and tragic tale. But almost nothing in life is epic or tragic at the moment of its enactment. History in the making, at least on the personal level, is almost exclusively pathetic. People suffer and die in ignorance and delusion.

Late in the fall, during the final diminishing parings of the Hunting Moon, I pieced together the rest of Charley's story from what Nancy and Lowan and George and Jake told me. And from another long night by a campfire with Charley. It seemed important to me to let them all bear witness. I heard five separate stories that did not entirely correspond, but I believe I understand something fairly close to what actually happened, at least a few fragments, and that is better than most of what we know of history.

THERE HAD NOT been a plan to the killings. When Lieutenant Smith had failed to uncover the hatchets in his search of the shelters, the men figured they were not responsible for calling attention to them. The next morning, as the soldiers prepared to drive them away, the men hid the hatchets under their clothes with no notion other than that edged implements might become useful. No deadly plotting took place among them. They just figured it was better to be armed than disarmed. They also reasoned that a hatchet, like a knife, is both weapon and tool, and for all they knew, the Army allowed its prisoners to keep their knives and hatchets.

The only point of unanimity in their stories was that during the day's march, when Nancy grew tired and dropped back, one of the boy soldiers prodded her forward with either the blunt end of his rifle barrel or the sharp end of a bayonet fixed beneath it. At which point the men righteously objected and drew their hidden hatchets.

After the killings, the horses bolted off into the woods and then stopped and came back and milled about in confusion, stepping awkwardly on their fallen reins and whickering among themselves. Charley's people consulted, and decided that the horses would be an impediment up among the trackless peaks, and so they left them standing nervous and confused with the dead boys.

The women gathered the few items that would help them in their escape. Weapons, leather goods, saddlebags, tin pots, and dirty linens. Then they went running upward into the mountains. Even at that desperate moment, they knew no altitude was high enough to offer sanctuary or refuge.

AT SOME POINT in their flight, Charley stood drawing breath, watching old Nancy and the nursing mothers and the little children and the younger men struggle up ahead of him toward the ridgetop. Thrashing through newly fallen leaves that lay knee-deep on the legs of the younger fugitives. Babies cried, though all they had to undergo in regard to suffering was to be carried jostling across broken ground in their mothers' arms, pressed against soft breasts that had ceased to give milk. Far behind them, trackers rose up the slopes of the coves and drew nearer by the day.

There is romance in the lone fugitive. But when babies are involved and exhausted young mothers and grey-haired elders with swollen finger joints, being a fugitive is just terrifying and hopeless. Not flight but slog. A desperate passage through a landscape rising against you, the beautiful world you love suddenly risky and dangerous.

Charley opened his mouth wide and cocked his head, listening for the sounds of the manhunt, but his own people made such a racket that he couldn't tell how far away the runners might be. The numbers of the hunters had grown by the day.

To flee or hide or surrender? Those had been the decisions someone needed to call. And it had fallen on Charley to make the call for all of them. It was a weight shifted onto him by reason of age alone, for he knew he had no particular wisdom left in him. And also because he was stout enough to bear the unwilling responsibility toward all these people climbing ahead of him, none of whom would be gathered here starving and in flight but for some urge he once had on Nancy's body.

We are all mad when we are twenty. And because of it we cause pain farther on down the road. And then, if we are not weaklings, we have to take possession of our old madness and try to soothe its issue.

Charley's littlest ambulatory grandchildren, the shortest boys and girls—each bearing some reference to his particular hands or hair or nose or slant of eyes—churned lattermost against the gravity of the mountain. He heard them wheeze in their effort. Dead leaves and black humus and pale pipe plants broke apart under their struggling feet. They wanted to live and so they climbed.

Charley wondered why his people possessed such unreasonable desire. To live is to suffer. And they were doing plenty of both right that moment. If he could have swiped his hand across the world and made every one of them not ever have been at all, he would have done so.

But being goes on regardless.

Charley placed both hands in leverage against the place where his knee joined his thighbone. He lifted one foot in front of the other. His whole body disagreed against the downpull of the mountain. With considerable effort he came shepherding behind them all.

—

THERE WAS A great deal more to Charley's story. He talked and we drank most of the night. You can tell all kinds of stories in the space between dark and dawn. I'll skip forward to a point that I remember very clearly. Charley said the blanket bundle in his arms was airy as if it had been stuffed with cornhusks. Death seemed to have diminished the boy. The wind howled out of the northwest and carried the winter's first pellets of snow. Charley went alone, climbing through hardwoods, their leaves cupped and holding the little bit of grainy snow that had fallen to the ground like salt in a hand. He climbed up into a stand of gloomy balsam fir to a ragged rock face streaked with dark ribbons of seepage and hung with long icicles and encrusted with scabbed patches of bright orange lichen. Jaggy stones of all sizes lay scattered on the ground, sloughed off the rock face. The passway across the ridge crest bent around the face and went on forever into the north, a thin wavering line that had carried trade and war as long as there had been people to walk it.

Charley squatted, and his knees made a crackling sound like dropping an armload of firewood. He opened the blankets and lifted the weightless boy in his hands and laid him on the frozen ground. The boy had been dead less than a day, but the skin was grey as wood ash and his long black hair seemed unaccountably full of pale dust. He was naked and already arranged by the women into fetal compactness. Naked because other children needed the clothes. The soles of his feet were a color of white that Charley had never seen before, even on a whiteman. The boy's arms and legs were bone thin, and the elbow and knee joints looked enormous. Charley circled the calf of the boy's leg with just his thumb and index finger and there was room to spare. Charley's grandson had lived five years.

There were no digging tools to be had, so the burial would be in the fashion of a stone barrow. Charley stood up, and his knees made the firewood sound again. He began carrying rocks and stacking them over the boy, working first with the largest ones he could heft, making an effort to think only about their shapes and how their angles best fit together and not about their weight. The stones were cold as blocks of ice, and his hands were soon numb and his fingertips were bleeding from small cuts. He worked until he had sweated through his clothes and something in the small of his back had given out and prevented him from standing up straight. He carried and stacked stones without stopping until he had built a tight mound to chest height, sufficient to keep out wolf and maybe bear, and imposing enough to invite every passerby to add a stone to the top of the pile.

When Charley was done, the snow was falling again in little grains, rattling in the tree branches. He went to the rock face and broke off the end of an icicle and put it in his mouth to melt. It tasted of the minerals in the rock it had passed through. He wrapped the blankets from his grandson's bundle around his shoulders and began walking back down the trail.

EVERYTHING HAD GONE WRONG, but how could it not have?

After days of chase—down creeks, over ridges, up coves—the hunters were right behind them in the grey open woods. They had spread themselves up each slope of the cove and came on relentlessly, driving Charley's people forward. Charley was aiming his family toward a laurel hell that went on and on, close and convoluted like a vast cavern. But it was a long way there.

The younger women and the children and Nancy sat down in the leaves and could go no farther. The children no longer wept. They were all silent except for their hard breathing. The runners in the distance made a sound like a rising wind below them. Nancy told the men to go on, Charley and Lowan and George and Jake. But not Wasseton. She would keep him with her. The Indian trackers would certainly not kill women and children, and perhaps the soldiers would spare them as well. The men stood a better chance of escape on their own.

Charley looked at Lowan and George and Jake, and they seemed to have no opinion on this matter or any other. Their eyes were dead and hopeless as polished river stones. Wasseton began to object that he was not a child and should go with the men. Without getting up from where she sat, Nancy turned and slapped him hard across the face where he sat beside her, striking him twice, first backhand and then with her hard palm. Wasseton blinked back tears and shut up.

Way down the cove they could hear a long cackling laugh. It sounded like a puppy barking. Charley nodded to Nancy. He and the younger men began climbing away.

—Not together, Nancy said.

Charley turned and nodded again. He and the three younger men flared off from one another, Charley taking the path straight up.

AT NIGHT, sheltered deep in a thicket, Charley built a small fire and slept warm. The next day he did not even get up off the ground where he had slept. He lay all day by the ashes of the fire with his mind blank, wishing he would die here and never be found. White bones gnawed by porcupines. He did not know what would happen to his family. He liked to think that Nancy was right, that neither the trackers nor the soldiers would kill women and children, but who could know? He might go on to the highest ridges and follow them northeast until he was far away from the hunters. But then what? It was said to be nothing but white people up there now.

Everything had fallen away from him. First his house and animals and crops and neighbors, then his family. Now white voices and Indian voices both hunted him. His own people running him through the woods like an old boar.

IF YOU ARE in the mountains alone for some time—many days at minimum, and it helps if you are fasting—the forest grows tired of its wariness toward you. It resumes its inner life and allows you to see it. Near dusk, the faces in tree bark cease hiding and stare out at you, the welcoming ones and also the malevolent, open in their curiosity. In your camp at night, you are able to pick out a distinct word now and then from the muddled voices in creek water, sometimes an entire sentence of deep import. The ghosts of animals reveal themselves to you without prejudice toward your humanity. You see them receding before you as you walk the trail, their shapes beautiful and sad.

Charley had reached such a point when he went to sleep under his blanket up on a bald. He woke up under three quarters of the Hunting Moon with frost silvering the grass and the cuts of the creek drainages through the mountains etched out below him in blue light. The bald was thick with feral hogs. Dozens of them. They rooted with their flanged snouts and long tusks for something in the ground that they savored, some grub or minuscule rodent. The tusks of the boars were like pairs of long dirks that would lay you wide open. The ground they passed over looked like it had been turned by plows. The hogs went about their work all hunched forward. Most of their bulk was in the thick muscles of their necks and shoulders, and this was further emphasized by the ruff of red bristles that roached up like porcupine quills from the base of their skulls and tapered away along their backbones. Their hams thinned off as lean and long as the hind legs of a Plott hound.

Charley was too weary to hold any hope of killing a hog with just a hatchet. But he was in a sort of strange mood, and so he walked out slowly among them, and the stout blue shadows they cast across the bald merged with his own. He passed his hands across the red bristles on their backs and talked to them and said he required nothing from them and only wished them well in their endeavors. They paid him little attention as he stroked their backs, only arching slightly against his palm like house cats. When he had touched each of them, he bade them good night and went back and lay down under his blanket to sleep.

But just at the first point of slumber, he had a dream of falling and gave out a little yell. And when he did, the hogs broke to run, and the direction they went was right over the top of him. What he found himself under was a grunting squealing eruption of hogs, a resurgence of the wild. Their sharp hooves left him looking like he'd taken a beating with a war club. When the stampede was over, he was bleeding and bruised, but nothing was broken.

—

IT WAS A bad time of year to be a fugitive living off the land. Charley overturned creek rocks to find crawfish, and one by one as he found them, he pinched their whiskered heads and snapping foreclaws off between thumb and forefinger and ate the tails and whatever hind legs remained while they still pulsed in a last attempt at flight. He made no effort to separate meat from shell, but crunched them together between his back teeth and swallowed them down. He dug roots and brushed the dirt off and ate them raw as apples. There were still a few wormy chestnuts and hickory nuts on the ground under leafless trees. One day he caught a trout by spearing it with a sharp hickory stick and ventured to light a fire no bigger than he could have cupped in his hand to sear it over. When he was done with the body, he held the head in his mouth and sucked until it held no more flavor than his own spit. His bowels suffered greatly from such diet. He squatted under the canopy of rhododendron and felt that his insides were being twisted like a dirty dishrag.

He wished he had a great double-barreled gun as long as he was tall with which to kill whoever he could until they overwhelmed him.

ICED STREAM BANKS, frost-burnt pigeon moss, a cold sun setting down a metal-colored sky. Heavy-timbered steep land. No scrap of it horizontal enough for a short man to sleep on except where a damp gravel bed rose a handbreadth above a creek shoal. The sky was overcast with such thick low clouds that the sun did not even make a bright spot through them, and there was no way to gauge the progress of the day.

Charley put his back to a big chestnut tree and slept sitting up, forehead to knees, cowled in his blanket. The next morning after he awoke, he sat motionless a long while trueing up his mind. Then, suddenly, the sound of runners coming close. He had no time to hide and just squatted with his back against the trunk of the tree and became utterly still. He fixed his eyes on the ground between his feet, for it is the meeting of eyes that most identifies prey to predator. Hunters bloomed out of the fog and ran past him without letup. He could have reached out and hit them with a stick. Then they were gone, and he rose and fled upward.

The white sky was entirely free of birds. Charley looked down the long view south, grey mountains lapped and stacked to the end of the world. He stood at the edge of the vast laurel hell, feeling the hard cold that spilled down the slopes so gently it did not even stir the leathery leaves that overlay one another dense as a wall in front of him. But the cold seeped through the weave of his clothing and chilled him deep in his joints. The laurel could feel the cold too, for they were beginning to curl their leaves into themselves in long rolls that looked no more alive than strips of deer jerky. Under the canopy, as dense as a canvas tent, there would be nothing to eat whatsoever other than two lumpy pocketfuls of chestnuts and hickory nuts he had picked up the day before. Charley pinched the last little bit of fat at his belly and judged he could live only a short while longer on water and nuts. He shook his big stoppered gourd to check if it was still full from the most recent creek. He parted laurel boughs and they rattled against him as he passed through their gates at a stoop.

It was as if he had entered a cave mouth. The day immediately dimmed to twilight, but stained green, and he moved through it as if crawling across the bottom of a slow deep river. Dry dead laurel leaves under his hands and knees and feet were thick as nutshells. They clattered against one another like potsherds when he moved.

He went on and on, walking stooped when he could, but mostly crawling where the tangled trunks and limbs left no choice. After dark, he ventured to strike a little fire no bigger around than the mouth to a bucket. The runners would have to be on top of him to see it through the brush. He wondered where Nancy was tonight, and all the children. At best, they were captives beyond his power to redeem. He leaned over the fire as close as smoking meat, trying to get warmth.

When he woke up in the night, the fire was dead. He waved his hand in front of his face and could not see a thing.

He heard them coming, following his trail, which must have lain behind him in the dead leaves plain as if he were dragging a plowpoint.

It was a chase suited for an old man, very slow and mostly on hands and knees. Charley moved jittery as a crawfish. He crawled over dirt like powdered ashes, trunks and branches spreading all around bare as old bones, broken-down skeletons.

When he paused, he could hear them coming. And he guessed they could hear him too.

So he tried just sitting, looking with unfocused eyes at the various parts of the laurel in its dim green light.

There was a long silence, and then the hunters spread out and moved forward and began circling around him. Many of them. They made no effort now to move silently, and the sounds of the men crawling in the ground litter and of the laurel boughs brushing and sometimes breaking against their bodies came from all sides. It sounded as if the thicket itself were closing around him, the limbs tightening and reforming from wild tangle into something much simpler, a harsh-spoked wheel with him at the hub.

The first man to reach him was only a few years older than Wasseton, and he came crawling forward out of the half-light with a knife between his teeth and an awkward long musket on a strap over his shoulder banging against every limb and trunk.

Charley still sat, breathing deep. He looked at the boy and said, Hey. And then he looked more closely and said, You favor a man I once knew. He went by the name of Dull Hoe and sometimes John.

The boy sat up and took the knife out of his mouth and wiped the spit against his britches. He said, My grandfather.

The boy took two strips of deer jerky from a pouch and reached them to Charley.

—They'll be wanting your blades.

Charley handed him his hatchet.

The boy said, We caught the others some time ago.

Then he made a sort of bow to Charley, at least to the extent possible given that they were both sitting. An acknowledgment of Charley's will to live.

LIGHT SNOW CAPPED the highest balsam ridges, a bright band between the grey slopes and the dark sky, and it did not melt away until nearly midday. In the bend of the river, there was a grassy piece of flat ground with just a scattering of old grey birches and a few big rocks. The river was high and thick and red with the clay it was carrying. I stood on a hill above the bank and saw it all from some distance, so that all the men were remote and small, actors on a distant stage beyond earshot. I had not slept in more than a day.

Across the river I could see the fire circle where Charley and I had sat up talking all night.

Guards stood over the prisoners, who sat under a birch tree with their bound hands between their thighs and did not talk, even to one another. The younger men—Lowan and George, Jake, and the boy Wasseton—wore brown felt hats, and old Charley had on a white head-cloth tied in a band around his forehead. They all wore moccasins and britches and shirts of linen and faded red calico. The women and little children stood together, off to the side, guarded by a pair of young soldiers.

Lieutenant Smith and another officer huddled together and there was a long period of talk between them, and then they seemed to argue. Smith made broad encompassing motions using the whole of both arms, as if to implicate the wide landscape in the coming actions. The other made little jerky emphatic gestures with just his fisted right hand and kept his left in his coat pocket. Among the hunters from Lichen's bunch, disagreements appeared to run in many different directions. Voices were raised and lowered and raised again, though I could not make out a word of what passed down below me. Two Indians shouted at each other and then locked up and fought on the ground until soldiers waded in and grabbed them by their arms and snatched them apart.

Two other Indians went and propped their muskets against a rock and walked into the forest and did not return. No one tried to stop them.

Several of Lichen's hunters began working at the loads to their muskets, fooling with shot pouches and powder horns, checking the pans and priming. Smith watched them and then took a rundlet from his saddlebag and drank a long pull and stoppered it back and put it away in the bag. Then he took it out and pulled again at it and just kept it in his hand.

Soldiers stood Charley and the boys up and walked them out near the riverbank and left them standing there in some confusion. The Indian hunters, including Lichen, went and stood near Charley and the boys. I could see them talking. Then just Charley talked and tried to make gestures with his bound hands. The hunters backed away and raised their muskets. There were two shooters for each of the tied men, and it was arranged so that one would aim for the head and the other for the heart. Smith walked over and pulled Wasseton from the group and led him away toward the women.

I saw the flash of powder in the pans, the leap of grey smoke against the background of dark trees. A great bloom of red blossomed on the white forehead band of Charley's turban. Then—only after the four men began falling, knee joints gone limp—the reports of gunfire arrived across the river where I stood watching. The sound had crossed the water and climbed up the ridge like a rushing wind, but still in arrears of what sight had already told. When the brittle crackle of shots reached me, not appreciably louder than eight dry sticks breaking, it seemed allied with the brevity of life, with time, the sound we make as we fall through its abyss into darkness.

PART FOUR

. . .

the nightland

1

After the nation had been wiped away, the empty land was not even left for a moment to draw breath. State surveyors had plotted and platted it in preparation for a mighty land auction in the spring. Down at the capital, someone had drawn the street plan for a county seat to erupt near where the empty fort stood, the ground still beaten smooth where the people were collected and held before transportation to the West. Squatters and claim jumpers began streaming into the white space on the map even before the auction. And of course there I was, my string of trading stations already in place, ready to sell them everything they needed and a lot they didn't at elevated prices justified by the distance goods had to be transported and by the lack of competition. I expanded all the posts and began calling them mercantiles and brought in a wider range of stock, for I knew the trade would not just be hides and ginseng for gingham and axeheads. And too, I was already buying land like God wasn't making any more of it—which He wasn't, for otherwise we wouldn't have had to shove someone else off to make a place for ourselves.

—

THE WINTER AFTER the Removal was a hard one with a great deal of snow. It often piled halfway up the door of the winterhouse and the wind howling blue out of the north. Bear and I would be inside warm as loaves baking in a clay oven. Nearly all we talked about that winter was loss and land and love. Maybe if we'd known there wouldn't be many more Cold Moons together by the fire, we'd have talked about something else. The meaning of life or the nature of God. Maybe not. We were in pain, and that has a way of focusing one's attention. We still could hardly talk about what had happened to Charley and the boys, and the part we had played. I was all broken by Claire's absence, and Bear yearned desperately for Sara, who was holed up not a quarter mile away in the cabin with the other women. I argued that her proximity made me the winner in degree of anguish, but Bear declared physical distance irrelevant. The obstacles of time and space were as nothing compared to a heart hardened against you. Also to be tallied in his column of despair was the fact that Sara had recently produced a baby, which was clearly not Bear's, for it had reddish hair and pale skin. Very quickly it grew four sharp front teeth from its pink gums and would bite like a snapping turtle onto any extremity that presented itself, though unlike the implacable turtle it would let go if you just popped it lightly on the top of its head rather than having to wait for a clap of thunder.

We dreamed powerful and vivid dreams during that blizzard and we told them to each other in great detail. In my dreams, Claire never made an actual appearance. She was a force akin to gravity or magnetism drawing me toward her through various landscapes and through the corridors of buildings that were somewhat like the Indian Queen Hotel and the Capitol in Washington City. I searched and never found. Bear's dreams, though, all ended in full consummation. He bragged shamelessly of night emissions as profound as those of a fourteen-year-old boy.

It was Bear's contention that if you want to know who is dreaming of you, just look at who peoples your own night world, for there's a confluence to the flow of dreams. I could only hope that Bear was right and that out in the unimaginable West, Claire woke up every few mornings with her pillow in a wad and her bedclothes damp and twisted, and that she went about with a haunted empty feeling that bruised the day blue until well past the dinner hour.

When we became exhausted with the subject of hopeless love, we turned to land. Bear had begun studying on the matter as soon as the great auction of the Nation was announced. In the winterhouse, I tried to show him my paper map of the territory printed by the state. The rivers were drawn crooked as life, but everything else was cut up into perfect squares and rectangles that bore no resemblance to the ragged and often vertical terrain. Bear looked at my map a minute but then rolled it back up into its cylinder and began to draw his own in the dirt of the floor. He squatted on his heels and swept his palms in broad strokes to smooth the dirt, and then he sharpened a stick with his knife and sat a long session scribing interlocking rivers and creeks and ridges, working from physical memory of walking them over a lifetime. He progressed from the large to the small. Rivers to creeks to branches to streams, going uphill all the way back to their sources. Thin lines and thick, continuous and truncated. Real places and speculative places. The Great Leech Place, the Great Lizard Bald. When he was done he had covered most of the floor with topography. He studied his work for a long time and then eased carefully to the fire so as not to step on anything important. He made tea and built the fire brighter and studied his map some more. And then he began talking, cataloging all the land he wanted to acquire.

—Make sure to get that Beaver Creek land, he said, jabbing at the marks on the ground. That's some good land. And Snowbird, all that rough land up in there. Elk Creek, from the river up to the source on both sides, all the way to the ridges. All that sidehill land around Hanging Dog. That whole Buffalo drainage.

On and on. When he was done, he had laid out a place to make a stand, a homeland in the image of the world of his youth, where we all, in our heads, most truly reside. A little bit of river-bottom farmland, good water, and a large proportion of mountain hunting land considered very nearly worthless by whites. Coves and creeks and ridges, all steep and jungled. The kind of place most people say has no value except to hold the rest of the world together. Bear's plan was to undo all he could of the past and draw his people together again into townships. The bad years after the Revolution had scattered them into the mountains, where they lived isolated up coves, an unnatural way of doing, at least for the Indians, though the immigrant Scots seemed to like it fine. His new world would, of course, be on a smaller scale than the old, a plan enforced by our inability to buy three or four million acres of land. As is the case with all of us in life, what Bear would settle for was not as encompassing as what he wanted, but it was a great deal better than nothing at all. His dirt map was a claim of ownership on a space of earth. Not his claim alone, but his people's.

As he saw it, the imagining of a homeland was the hardest work. The buying of it he took as a small matter delegated to me. Like he could just think it so and I would make it be.

THE AUCTIONEER WAS a hen of a man with a big prow-shaped barrel to his body and a little head with tiny close-set emotionless eyes peering out at the world from atop his long sharp nose. He chanted numbers in a rapid rhythm like song, if chickens sang. We bidders made minute gestures with fingers and chins and eyelids and elbows. My sign was a double tap of forefinger to cheekbone. The signals were of such great but ambivalent significance that when the parcel in question—eight hundred acres of steep woodland—was finally knocked down with a sharp rap of wooden mallet on tabletop, half the drunks in attendance snapped into wakefulness and hadn't a clue whether they had bought land or not. The whole crowd let out a cheer, for it was the last parcel up for bid. I went to the table and signed the papers on that final parcel and left the courthouse.

I walked down the main street. In the afternoon light the clapboard buildings and the muddy street and muddy board sidewalks looked antique. The little mountain town, though, was so recently settled that the cemetery held only an unlucky few markers rising off-plumb from long grass, like death was an idea that had failed to catch on. The main street sloped off to a river and afforded a vista of an old townhouse mound. Rain and time had begun smoothing its pyramidal angles and its entry ramp into a general round pile. The Indian village that once spread all along the river had been gone since the Army burned it down during the Revolution. A cornfield stood in its place, the new crop only a green haze along the furrows. The townhouse too was gone, though it had stood and been occupied by an old firekeeper when I had first ridden through this valley years earlier. I remember sitting by the fire drinking herb tea with him and eating peaches from the new crop, and we spat the peach pits into a hole in the dirt floor where one of the posts supporting the roof had rotted away.

When I reached the hotel, the bar was filled with men celebrating the end of the long auction. It had taken almost two months to sell off our state's portion of the Nation, and I had bought all of it I could afford and a great deal that I could not.

I ordered a cup of coffee and a shot of Scotch whisky at the bar and carried them to a big round table crowded with buyers. They were all listing their acquisitions and detailing their victories and defeats in a swirling conversation, voices overlapping one another around the table. Drinks came in a steady stream from the bar. Stabs of light angled through the seams in the closed shutters and made Jacob's ladders in the thick smoke of pipes and cigars. I was tired from the long bout of commerce and only half listened. When the men were done bragging on themselves, one of them said, We've not heard from Will, and he bought more than all of us.

—More in quantity, another man said. But mostly what nobody else wanted.

—Some of it's wasteland so steep a red hog couldn't traverse it, someone said.

—How much did you buy?

—I don't exactly know, I said. I bought what I needed to buy.

—But how much?

—In acres? I said.

—What else measure would you use for land? They don't sell it in quarts.

—He's awfully cultured and drinks French wine and reads their books. He probably keeps track of his holdings in arpents. Or else he's bought so much he goes by the square mile.

—I don't know for sure how much, I said. I haven't added it up yet.

—Man's bought so much land it's not worth his time to bother counting.

—It was a right smart of land he bought. In old Europe, they've made countries out of less territory.

—Dukedoms at least.

—Principalities.

One man raised me an ironic toast, To the Prince of the Goddamn Indians.

Someone else said, The Duke of the Wasteland.

Glasses clinked together.

Everybody drank except for one man who declined. He said, Andy Jackson spent his whole life trying to get shut of Indians and the goddamn Nation, and Will's trying to put it back together. I'm not drinking to that.

The table had reached a high pitch of drunkenness one degree short of pistol-pulling time. They were at the point where men need a clear direction pointed out to them or else they become dangerous.

I raised my glass and offered a toast, not to the old Nation or the new but to the sanctity of private property. It was a popular concept and received the approbation of all in attendance.

When I reached my room, late into the evening, I sat amid my piles of papers and tallied my recent purchases and added them to my previous holdings and was somewhat stunned to find that the sum could fairly be spoken of not in thousands of acres, or even tens of thousands, but in hundreds of thousands.

It was every kind of land. Not everything Bear wanted but a lot of it.

I had bought whole chains of mountains, long ridges, and the entire runs of several bold creeks along with the slopes that drained into them. Every penny I had made from business and law was gone. And still, only a minority of the transactions were straight sales. The majority involved promissory notes, loans supported by other loans, kited checks, and lines of credit cosigned by figmentary personages. None of it tallied. I had constructed deals of such complex usury that I didn't even understand some of them. But the next morning when I rode out of that town, my saddlebags bulged with contracts and deeds and notes. I had transformed Bear's imaginary dirt map into a great convolution of interlocked promises memorialized by a cascade of paper into a vast tract of actual mountain land.

THREE DAYS AFTER the auction closed, Bear and I went walking up the cove to Granny Squirrel's cabin. The bold creek ran white over green rocks and the trail was muddy from spring rain. Bear was dressed in his best old-time fringed buckskin shirt worked with beading of red and white. And contrary to the law of things that says old folks, no matter what height they once attained, will end up squat and humped and hobbled, Bear stood tall and lean and straight, and he walked with a long loping stride that left me puffing trying to keep up. He had pulled just a part of his long hair into a plait terminated with a large amber bead, and the rest was let to swing free about his shoulders. He carried a long rifle drooped across his left forearm, but it was more as a fashion accessory than as a weapon, a defining implement that made him feel young. And it was important for him to feel young, for we were on a mission of love.

Granny Squirrel's cabin was about the size of a pony stall, and the roof shakes were as mossy as the creek rocks, and it was pressed down into the head of the cove as tight as a tick in the intricate folds of a hound's ear. Speckled chickens moved in a body across the dooryard. Red peppers hung in lapped strands from the porch rafters to dry, for she liked her food with a great deal of pepper and sage to the point that no one else would eat it, and that was the only secret of her longevity that she would share with others.

We stood in the trail and Bear called out greetings and the old woman came onto the porch and billed a hand at her brow to study her visitors. She motioned us inside with a two-beat gesture of her first and middle fingers.

She was cooking bean bread. The little room was filled with the smell of wood fire and the imminence of food. We sat beside the hearth and watched the light shift in the embers, and for a long time nobody said anything. Granny Squirrel had the manner of many conjurers, all aloof and held within themselves and proud of their particular notion of enchantments.

When the bread was ready and we were busy unwrapping it from damp fodder blades and scalding the palates of our mouths, Bear told her our mission. He knew she could write in Sequoyah's syllabary and that she kept a little book of her formulas. She had traded for the blank books at the post. Her clients had reported that she sometimes consulted their pages as she worked. He had little interest in the doctoring parts of her knowledge, for he had never been sick a day in his life, and at that time neither had I. So she could keep the ones such as When They Piss Like Milk; When Something Is Causing Something to Eat Them; When a Tooth Comes Out, to Throw It Away With.

But we'd pay whatever price she asked for the love formulas. To Make a Woman Lonely; To Protect Against False Thinkers; When They Flee from You, to Make Them Return. Those sorts of things. We needed help. We were love-struck and in pain always. Endless running pain, perfect and inexhaustible. We were impaired and wanted fixing. Bear was stricken with love for a harsh woman. And as for me, I either needed something to make my distant love come to me or else to release me from my anguish over the loss of her.

—Too costly to do it that way, Granny Squirrel said. I don't much care for writing, so I charge steep for it. Real steep. But I can work the formulas without you having to buy the book. What's the names of these women?

I blurted out Claire's name, and Granny Squirrel started shaking her head immediately.

—I'm the one set the spell on you to begin with, and mine don't come unstuck easy. I'm not saying you're a goner, but don't raise your hopes too high.

When his turn came, Bear didn't care to call his tormentor's name. He said, This job will take some doing. Some long trying. And I'm not wanting to journey up here and pay you every week for another go at it. The way I see it, I can either hire a man to plow my cornfield every spring, or I can buy a plow. I'm looking to buy a plow.

He reached into an old bag that had once been a shot pouch and drew out a spray of silver coins and fingered them out into a rainbow array on the tabletop. He elbowed me, and I started digging in my pockets and added a greater pile of specie and a thick fold of notes.

—No paper, Granny Squirrel said. I've got no use for it. But she began raking the silver with a hook of hand and wrist to the table edge and down jingling into her lap. She said, You understand this might be no more use than buying a key without its lock? Sometimes it's more than words.

Bear and I went walking back down the cove, me carrying the rifle and him with the little book in his hand like he was carrying a live coal back to a cold hearth.

Bear's formulas went on and on for many pages in the little book. One by one, I read them to him, and he repeated the words. Let her be marked out for loneliness. Let her be blue. No one is ever lonely with me. I will never become blue. That sort of thing. Then he did whatever action might be required to go along with them, one of which had something to do with splinters of wood from a lightning-struck hemlock tree. Amazingly, they took effect almost immediately. Sara again veered toward him, and before long she was sexing him down well and frequently. This lasted all through spring and summer and autumn. He never slept in the townhouse, but only rested there during the day to build his strength for the nightly bouts. He spent the afternoons watching the fire and drinking a great deal of ginseng tea, figuring if it worked on a Chinaman's pizzle it might well do the trick for him. He stuck close to home and was happy and tired all during the entire life span of the tree leaves—pale spring nubs, big wet green fleshy July spreads, sepia withers falling in tight spirals and long glides down a deep-blue autumn sky. And then, when the first snow fell, that was the end of Sara's desire for him. Things went back chill between them like it had been before. No more feats of love for Bear.

Bear tried taking her little presents. Bundles of pine fatwood split into fragrant kindling. Bead necklaces and silver earbobs. A ham of a deer. Nevertheless, she offered nothing in return.

And when he tried doing Granny Squirrel's spells again, they failed utterly.

One November afternoon by the fire, he complained at length about being cut off from the pleasures Sara had to offer and reminisced fondly about the stirring, lengthening nights of early autumn.

I said, Indian summer. I meant it funny, but he was not aware of the term, and when I explained it to him he failed to see the relevance. The ironic tone was never one of his greatest strengths.

As for my formulas, during those three seasons after our pilgrimage to Granny Squirrel, my erotic life consisted exclusively of an experiment in projection of thought across distance, a thing Granny Squirrel claimed would occasionally work and sometimes wouldn't. Sad but true. There was no telling, really. It was like so much of life: nearly hopeless, but you must go ahead and try.

What I was to do was train my mind to throw its force westward, thinking toward Claire these brief expressions: Come to me. Come to me. Can't you hear me? Can't you hear me? Thinking the words over and over through all my daily rounds until they said themselves, whether I was waking or sleeping, like a constant drone or a chiming in the ears, calling across the incomprehensible and ghost-ridden distance between us. Come to me.

Despite all my efforts, Claire failed to come. At one point I became so desperate I went back to Granny Squirrel. She prescribed various courses of herbs and going to water and scratching the skin of my chest and arms with trimmed turkey quills until I bled. I performed all her cures one after another and then all together, and still Claire had not come to me. And neither was I free of desire for her. As a last effort, late in the fall, Granny Squirrel suggested finding a hollow among rocks along the banks of a river bend, a place all full of little sticks and shredded leaves and dead insect husks formed by high water into a shape like a bird nest. Then boiling the entire nest in a pot to make tea and drinking it for four days while otherwise fasting. I did as she directed, and the only result was that I emptied myself in painful wrenching spasms from both ends. After all that failure, she said perhaps my only hope was to become a conjurer myself, a sorcerer's apprentice, and work nonstop in my own behalf. But when she held two beads between her thumb and fingers and let them move themselves around, what the twiddling told was that I lacked the aptitude and qualifications to become a conjurer. She would not state what those attributes were, but there was no doubt I didn't have them. She suggested that I brace myself against failure.

Two days later, the stage came sloshing into town, a freezing rain just beginning to glaze the canvas of the lowered side curtains. The narrow tall wheels sank so deep into the mud that the spokes were stained red halfway to the hubs. I came out of my office into the street, and the driver handed me down a letter from Claire, soiled from months of travel. Even his gauntlets were wet and muddy, and the places where he held the letter pinched between thumb and forefinger came away dark and wet. I broke the seal standing in the rain. It was dated near the equinox and arrived on the day of winter solstice. I scanned down it with the rain falling on its face. It was about like the few others I had received since the Removal, written as if to a mere acquaintance. *How are you? I am fine.* The new Nation was a little hillier than she expected. The new plantation house was nearly finished to the exact plan of the first, and Featherstone insisted on calling it Cranshaw. And so forth. Not one blissful memory or hint of yearning for me.

The letters had begun at the rate of about one a month and then dwindled gradually to one per season of the year. Each one becoming slightly more distant in tone. I began to dread their arrival and had suggested in my last letter that if she was so intent on receding from me, she should write each succeeding letter in a smaller and smaller hand until at some point, even with the aid of a magnifying glass, I could no longer make out the words, and then she would be gone.

2

THE FIRST OF MANY JOURNALISTS FELL UPON US THAT NEXT SUMmer. He was a skinny, tallish Yankee with a big head of curly dark hair, and his black suit was worn to a green shine at his elbows and cuffs and the seat of his pants, and he did not even carry letters of introduction. He was writing a travel piece about the southern mountains for a magazine I had never heard of. I can't remember whether it was a monthly or a quarterly. All we were to him was just a day's rest on the trail and a brace of paragraphs in his article. Which was lucky for us, because we—and by we, I mean Bear and I—were unprepared to answer his questions about Charley and exactly how he came to be dead and we came to still be living in our homeland instead of displaced to the West.

I told him how the wealthy white Indians on the Nation had referred to Bear and his people as animals with names. But by a set of legalities and treaties and circumstances too convoluted and ironic to be easily explained, Bear's people—who were the most pure-blooded and traditional in their habits of all the survivors of the original clans, people for whom the concept of private property held no meaning and who offered a great challenge to every sect of invading missionaries, whether Baptist or Quaker, because they did not even have words in their language to correspond with the concepts of sin, repentance, grace, heaven and hell, damnation and salvation—had come to live outside the boundaries of the Nation on private property to which they held legal deeds. Bear had set up a world of his own on his little parcel of land. And it backed up onto a vast and beautiful range of mountains so wild as to be unowned. On the Nation, no one held deeds to property because all the land was, by their customs and laws, held in common. But Bear had papers. And except for the singular fact that white people put great stock in them, he held them in so little regard that otherwise he would have balled them up and used them to light a fire or to wipe his ass. I talked on and on and hoped to muddy the issue about Charley in particular, for his manner of death troubled me a great deal and had darkened Bear's mind as well. I used the difficulty of translation with Bear to deflect questions aimed directly at him.

But after the Yankee journalist had departed, Bear and I agreed that blather and indirection would not always work, particularly after Bear had passed to the Nightland and I was left on my own. And given Bear's advanced age, his passage was not an unforeseeable event. So Bear and I spent a long night figuring out how best to tell Charley to the future. Not his history, his story. For that is what it would become, a narrative, with our help or without it. I'd learned something in that regard from my time with Crockett—the way he became a barely recognizable character in print, either for the better or the worse. Similarly, somebody would give Charley's final days a created shape and meaning rather than leave things the way life actually overtakes us, which most of the time is just one damn thing happening after another, all adding up to confusion. So Bear and I figured that if the story was going to be told by somebody, we might as well go ahead and do it ourselves. Bear had learned enough about the way written history works from my readings and summarizings of Herodotus and Thucydides and Caesar, and by his firsthand encounters with the Old Possum, to know that it's generally the victors who get to make up the stories and furthermore that they have a great deal of leeway in regard to adherence to facts and especially interpretation and opinions, not to mention outright lies.

We sat around the townhouse fire deep into the night, me drinking a little and Bear not at all, for this was during one of his temperance periods. We told Charley stories different ways to each other, trying alternate versions for how they might play. My tendency was to make up too much, to lay the plot on too heavy. Politics and machinations in excess. As a narrator, I had an overconcern with the *why* of people's actions, when really the *what* is largely all that matters. So of course it was Bear who came up with the idea of leaving everything exactly as it was, telling the story straight through just the way it happened, but flipping it with the underside up. It would be Charley who sacrificed himself for the good of his people, not the other way around. Nothing else needed to change. Charley chose to give himself up in return for the promise that the rest of us could remain. It made a better story and was certainly better for Charley.

—He'll be like your Jesus, Bear said.

Coming on toward dawn, Bear told his version of Charley complete from start to finish in great detail, touching up the dignity and tragedy, giving it a high degree of shine. And it was so good that about all I could think to add was a little *Et tu, Brutus?* touch at the moment before execution. It was not much of a creative contribution, but I'm proud of it nevertheless. And later, the journalists ate it up. My part goes like this: Charley looks at Lichen, the head of the firing squad, and says, We have been like brothers, and yet you are to do this to me? Lichen just nods his head. Then the blindfolding and the shooting play out pretty much without further writerly intervention. The End.

We tried the story out on Lichen the next time we saw him, and he liked it so much he nearly convinced himself that it had happened just that way. Like brothers we were, he said.

All during that time, we were busy seven days a week re-creating the world on our expanding boundary of land. The old clans were gone except vestigially, which is to say that most people could remember which one they would belong to if clans still meant anything. So they took enthusiastically to Bear's plan of organizing his territory by laying out various townships with the names of the old clans. Each would have a small townhouse wherein local business would be conducted by consensus rather than the majority rule that I favored. The old townhouse at Bear's place would be enlarged and reserved for issues of wider scope.

Bear believed that if we make the world around us a better place to live, our inner selves can't help but come along for the ride and we'll get better too. Sometime in the far bright future, we would all live in a world of saints. And who's to say he was wrong? Certainly not me, at least not vociferously. So I arranged the building of the new townhouse and suggested that a school and a church wouldn't hurt, in regard to our relations with the outer world. The latter two whitewashed buildings were identical, except that the church was capped with a little gesture of steeple at the door end of its gable. Of course, I immediately hired a teacher and a preacher, nearly indistinguishable young men from Baltimore with no better prospects in life other than come to what must have seemed the ass end of creation for a rate of pay that amounted to little above room and board, and forced them to live together in a one-pen log cabin so small they shared a rope-and-tick bedstead. The two were so much of a size they could share each other's clothes, three black suits identifiable only by degree of fade to grey.

Bear and I also established a volunteer firefighting corps in the village, calamitous grease fires being a constant fact of life. But he drew the line at police, saying that he thought more highly of his people than to believe law enforcement was needed. And it was my idea entirely to designate a shelf of books in the post as the beginnings of a library, the books loaned out gratis until the time of the next full moon. Because we needed money to fulfill Bear's vision, we started business enterprises as well, a gristmill, a blacksmith, a saddlery, a shop for constructing wagon wheels and barrels, et cetera, et cetera, all the way down to a gunsmith and a shop wherein women made fine handcrafts, baskets and woven materials and the like. In little more than a year, we had built an entire town based on an abstract idea of the minimum requirements, a few little log and clapboard buildings standing on either side of a road I called Main Street.

It all worked as planned. There were meetings and dances in the townhouses. Children learned to read and to cipher, and some of the people listened to sermons and sang the Methodist hymns with considerable enthusiasm, though many did it phonetically. More money came into the community from the new businesses, and that is nearly always good. Everybody got a piece, including me. And things did get better in very tiny increments.

JUST AS BEAR and I had suspected, the writers kept coming. We were too exotic a story to let be. They wrote about the last vestiges of the old ways. Our land accumulating at a frightening rate. Old Indian chief and young white son carrying out a plan to hold their place on earth against the forces of progress and the wishes of the Government. The first few writers were mostly a novelty and a welcome diversion. But each one was a little less charming than the last, and pretty soon they were just a nuisance. By about the fifth or sixth, I quit taking most of them seriously and just made up answers to their questions as suited my mood. And Bear acted like a house cat that disappears when strangers come visiting and pops back out when they're gone. I told one of the writers that our fields were so nearly vertical we planted our corn with a shotgun and had to breed a race of mules with legs shorter on one side than the other for plowing. And when he asked how we transported the corn down off the mountain, I said, In a jug. He appeared to believe me, so I was encouraged to go on and tell him that every church in that corner of the state, except for our Indian congregation, either conducted services speaking entirely in tongues or else took up serpents as recommended by Jesus. Both the writer and I had taken a few rounds of Scotch at the time. The story appeared as fact in a well-known national periodical, along with the obligatory descriptions of the beauty and ruggedness and unmatched remoteness and mystery of our mountains.

Of course, several of the preachers from the better churches in the nearest county seat were particularly angry with me, and the Episcopalian lit into me directly from the sanctity of his pulpit. Also, a newspaper editor took me to task in his paper, addressing to me an Open

Letter expressing his outrage at the shame I had heaped on the region in much the same terms as the preachers. Moral outrage was apparently the order of the day. But I didn't pay too much attention to any of them on the grounds that some preachers live to be angry, and the newspaper was of the other political party from mine. As to the Episcopalian in particular, I had always believed prayer ought to be conducted on our feet rather than on our knees, since God seems in all other departments of life to require us to stand upright and account for ourselves. I immediately dashed off a letter to the paper in question, saying it was a sorrowful but true fact that some people, mainly newcomers to the region, fail to appreciate the subtleties of frontier humor; however, such lack of taste was not sufficient grounds to evoke an apology from me.

Just to show I had not been cowed, I told the very next writer passing through that Hog Bite—humped over poking a stick in the dirt to plant squash seeds as we passed his garden plot—was performing a very powerful conjuration believed to affect weather worldwide. Every mark he scratched and hole he poked had enormous significance. If there were typhoons in Calcutta and drought in Italy, blame Hog Bite. That story too was immortalized within the covers of one of our higher-class monthly periodicals and was later cribbed by yet another writer in a quarterly of nearly the same water. So for a time Hog Bite was famous, at least among our better-read visitors, and he began charging as high as twenty cents to re-create the sacred weather ritual.

OF COURSE I took some of the writers seriously, the ones who might be useful and the ones too sharp to be trifled with. I will let one example stand for many. His name was Langham, and as a writer he specialized in mountains. His descriptions of a walking trip through Europe, titled *Views Afoot; or, The Alps and Pyrenees Seen with Knapsack and Staff*, had been well received, and I may even have read it. But several years had passed since his last book, so he had been forced to set out on another journey, though he lacked enthusiasm for hard travel. He had ridden up from Charleston, intent on following the mountains north as far as he could stand to travel, going it alone without guides but with a thick sheaf of letters of introduction, including one from Calhoun.

So the next morning I saddled Waverley for a brief ride to tour Langham around. This was a few years after the Removal, and Waverley had become an old gentleman horse, nearly deaf, with silver around his muzzle and threaded in his black mane. His hip joints rose angular beneath the skin, but he remained bright-eyed and eager to be lunging forward, so much so that I had to rein him back to a walk as we set out. We started at the old trade post, childhood source and root of all our fortunes, and then rode into Wayah, where I displayed the new enterprises to Langham: Indians shaping barrel staves and riving shakes and tanning hides and even, a couple of them, forging plowshares and the complicated mechanisms of muskets, the locks and other such parts. Blacksmiths beat musical rhythms on red metal as we visited their shed. The silversmith shop turned out passable earbobs and necklace pendants and the like, and a weaving shop produced good stout cloth from wool sheared from our little mountain sheep, spun into thread on drop spindles, and woven to broad goods on handlooms. And there were nimble-fingered women shaping oak splits into closely worked baskets of all shapes and sizes. Markets for all these goods had been found in both Charleston and Philadelphia as well as in the nearby towns, and thus the village was, as I pointed out to Langham, the state's largest center of manufacturing and commerce west of the foothills, a distinction perhaps only of local interest, since every time I traveled, no matter where I went, I was told that a certain mercantile or tavern or hotel was the largest between Washington and New Orleans. Of course, I showed Langham the schoolhouse and the church. And I mentioned the temperance society conceived by Bear when he began to fear that the drinking of ardent spirits sank any people of whatever color into a state of degradation and violence.

Bear himself I used sparingly. A brief appearance, scripted and dramatic. This was during his waning years.

The next day, in Langham's honor, we played a ball game, and I took a turn on one of the teams. His description of it, in his book *The*

Alleghenies by Horseback, is accurate enough. The players wore the nearest nothing. Greasy buckskin breech coverings so tiny they would hardly have served to cover a clutch of eggs. No footwear or leggings or shirts. A few players wore cloth headbands and kerchiefs, but that was foolish; they gave handholds for tackles. There were few rules to the game. You first had to come into possession of the little deerhide ball by way of the stick, catching it in the webbed pocket or digging it from the ground. Then you could palm the ball, throw down your stick—or fling it at your nearest pursuer—and run for your life toward one of the goalposts before you were knocked down in the most brutal way. There were no limitations on violence other than that it was frowned upon—but not forbidden—to scratch like a woman. And bringing a ballcarrier down by dragging at the breechcloth was supposed to be outside the pale, but when it was done and resulted in a man revealed in all his deficiency, great hilarity ensued both in the crowd and among the players.

The teams walked toward each other from either end of the ball ground, yelling that their opponents were the veriest quaking rabbits and eunuchs. They whooped war cries and shook ball sticks like they meant to kill one another, and when play commenced they nearly did. The ball was pitched in the air and everyone went for it with a great clash of upraised sticks, though the ball nearly always fell through them to the ground. Then they began raking for it in the dirt and grabbing the sticks of other players to snatch them away. It was a great confusing huddle of men, and the ball was no bigger than a walnut, so the spectators could hardly tell what was happening until a ballcarrier broke free to run.

Players slammed into each other, running flat out, and the sound was both the wet slap of skin and the deeper thump of three or four hundred pounds of meat and organs colliding. Then they wallowed on the ground, skirmishing with each other even though the ball had passed on to another man and he had also been knocked down so that at any one time there might be three or four wrestling matches going on, totally unrelated to the scoring of points. The ball was small enough to put in your mouth, and runners often did just that, sprinting to the goal and then fingering out a slobbered ball and holding it aloft to the delight of their supporters.

It was a sport in which the referees carried long stout whipping sticks and used them with great enthusiasm as they saw fit against the players, thrashing red stripes into pairs of combatants who had wallowed each other around too long or whaling indiscriminately at all the players when the game bogged down into a great pileup, wherein men bit and choked each other and pulled hair and twisted fingers, and the ones at the bottom just hoped not to smother.

Writers invariably found the game charming, and Langham was no exception. I played moderately well that day and was particularly good at the technicalities of stickwork, though I lacked the sheer speed of the younger men in running the ball. When the game ended, I bled from several minor wounds on the shins and forearms and sported a long red scratch from temple to chin—and was, no doubt, grinning from ear to ear with the joy of the game even though my team had lost.

The day after that was Sunday and I took Langham to church, where we all prayed to the Savior and were as sober as deacons. The entire service was conducted in Cherokee, so I acted as Langham's guide and translator, hovering close to him as his shadow in the pew, whispering the words of the sermon and hymns into his ear, and he was struck by the oratorical skills and poetic flourishes of the speakers.

Langham and I parted as friends, and when his book was published I recall thinking that the chapter devoted to Wayah was more sympathetic than I could have hoped for. He retold the story of Charley exactly as I told it to him, and he portrayed the village and the surrounding lands as a successful social experiment and Bear as a figure from another time, worthy to be cast in bronze. Langham reported, accurately, that I was increasing our land holdings at a frenetic pace, particularly in areas formerly within the Nation. Where the money came from, he could not tell, only that my holdings were already vast, with no signs of me slowing down.

Then, unfortunately, he delved deeper. My life to that point, he wrote, was a captivity narrative turned inside out. But whereas in a previous century Mary Rowlandson and many others had been taken forcibly by the Indians, family killed, terrified, transported into a howling wilderness, I, on the other hand, was thrust out into the wilderness by my own people, my family already dead, myself already terrified. And instead of wishing for deliverance from the savage wilderness and restoration back to my home, I made a home where I found myself.

Near the end of the chapter, Langham quoted Calhoun, who had apparently told him that, though I had the money to live wherever I chose, I did not do well for long in the outside world and could only make excursions into it for a few months at a time. Any longer, and I began to experience qualms and panics that did not abate until I retreated to my distant outpost.

The chapter's final lines go something like this:

And yet when you see him there in the wilderness, it is hard to say what he is for these people. Certainly he is described by them as counselor, guide, business agent, solicitor, friend. But he seems among them rather than of them. Though he grew to be a man among these people, there is a sad isolation about him, a sense of truly belonging to no place, neither this nor any other.

3

FOR QUITE A FEW YEARS, THE MONEY CAME ROLLING IN LIKE THERE was no end to it. Growing numbers of mercantiles, real estate transactions, investments. And I still practiced law, but only to the extent that it involved the conveyance of land titles. I built a fine house, not at all on the model of Featherstone's Cranshaw but more like Jefferson's Poplar Forest, which I had visited on an overland trip to Washington City, the old genius dead and gone several years and the pretty little summerhouse occupied by a family who did nothing but complain about its inconvenient features and brick up its tall windows one by one until it had begun to look like a bastion without a fort. My house, though clearly under the great man's influence, was a little larger than Jefferson's and made of native river rock rather than brick, and it exhibited a few modest improvements in the areas of fenestration and galleries. I drew the plans myself, and for an entire year men within a twenty-mile compass earned their livings hauling rocks and cutting locust fence rails and riving roof shakes. Pastures were cleared, stumps yanked like molars from the earth by teams of oxen, the black dirt of the former forest floor planted in grass. A stable built for Waverley and the string of fine saddle horses I planned for its dozen stalls, a kennel for my half dozen good bird dogs. Artistically arranged garden plots plowed and planted for vegetables and herbs and flowers. A fishpond dug and stocked with trout and bass, so that when I wished a fry-up I could have it at a moment's notice. A man worked an entire week hewing a watering trough from a great block of stone, and then other men ran piping of hollowed poplar poles from a hillside spring forty rods distant so that Waverley could have a constant supply of fresh water.

When the place was done—all but the hanging of chandeliers, which had not yet arrived from Charleston—I moved in, thinking I had finally made a true home and would inhabit it fully and leave it only when six strong men hefted my coffin to carry it to the upper pasture for burial next to the plot I had in mind for Waverley, who spent his days resting in the shade of a dogwood tree except when he occasionally chose to dash from one diagonal of his pasture to the other at a high rate of speed with his tail in the air as in days of old, chunks of expensive new turf flying in the air behind him. I can admit now that I entertained the pipe dream that circumstances would someday lead Claire to live with us and eventually join us in the upper pasture so that in some way our night ride together long ago might never end.

The house was finished in late May. There followed an entire June of unequaled wetness, weather so foggy and chill I kept a fire going in the parlor hearth night and day. I sat on the front gallery most days, wrapped in a quilt against the damp, reading Ovid and Simms and some other things not distinctive enough to have lodged in my memory. The pages soaked up the damp in the air and became limp as dishrags, and the bindings swelled and buckled. When I tired of reading, I watched the rain fall onto the river's black face. Or the red cows, standing bleakly in new green pastures, all facing the same direction, with the rain beating on their backs and dripping from stalactites of mud hanging from their swagged bellies. On especially bad days, fog lay so thick in the valley that I could not see the poplar trees growing on the riverbanks, though I could hear the flow of water rushing against the rocks. And then wind would drive the fog off the river and up the cove, and rain fell heavy and sloping, streaking the air like dirty twine.

A daunting number of people worked about the place. Some lived in the house and others in outbuildings. I noted that they all lived rich lives to which I was merely tangential and that as long as they kept working, the place could go on just fine without my being in residence.

AT THE END of the month, I packed a pair of fat panniers and rode out on a new grey mare. Waverley ran the fence line at an arthritic trot with his head up and ears pinned, offended at being left behind. All I could do to comfort him as I passed was to say aloud what a good and handsome horse he was and how when I returned we would go riding up the gorge together.

For the next few years, I lived, you might say, in transit, bedding in taverns and boardinghouses and hotels and the private estates of business and political acquaintances. Mail waited for me at my regular stops, correspondence from the indispensable Tallent. He supervised the young men I had working for me in the various mercantiles and other enterprises. They were smart boys, every one, ranging from fourteen to seventeen and none of them bound by papers. They worked for wages and could quit whenever they cared to go.

I traveled frantically those years: Savannah, Charleston, Wilmington, Washington, New York, Philadelphia, and many lesser points in between. I had a map darkened with lines of ink tracing my routes until the scribble looked like letters to an imaginary language. I went horseback, stagecoach, sailboat, railroad, and steamer. Living one night at a time in hotels and taverns and camping in the woods when I had to. Feeling every afternoon as the shadows got long that I was without a home in the world. Roaming and blue. Most of the travel was purposeless, carried out in exactly the desperate spirit of fleeing from pursuers. It was romantic, in a certain sense. Especially if you're not the one doing it.

Out in the wider world, I behaved about the same as did many other youngish southern men who were rich and free before the War. We hunted and gambled and went to dinner parties and dances, and in whatever time was left, many of us lawyered and some of us were elected to public office, jobs that were not particularly time-consuming. We took horses as a religion and could talk endlessly about their physical features and abilities and personalities. The worst of us could fill an entire dinner's worth of conversation just detailing his best mount's style of jumping and its manner and attitude as it approached a fence. We would walk a mile to catch a horse in order to ride a hundred yards, and we traded horses among ourselves as intensely as poor men do pocketknives.

The Washington parts of my life were mostly cold business, conducted for the benefit of Bear's people and myself and, I believe, in service of fairness and justice in general. I had learned the ways power flowed through that city, the big channels and the creeks and little streams, and I could navigate all of them to my favor with the help of friends I had made in years past, though I missed Crockett and was saddened to see Calhoun turned old and grey and a little foggy-headed.

In Washington those days, winning or losing each skirmish was a side issue. The main idea was to keep your pieces in play. I had learned ways to leave things unresolved for years using various strategies, none of them lacking brass. I'd fight fifty confusing little actions in all directions in order to win the main battle. And I never let up.

For example, though the War Department still wanted to send us to the Territories, I kept the Government occupied with the argument that it was only fair that Bear's people should share in the payout for the land of the old Nation. Why not? The circumstance that Bear's people owned their land and hadn't been living on Nation land at the time of the Removal was beside the point. And if America doesn't stand for property rights, what does it stand for? The land of the Nation was our heritage, ancestral homeland. Sacred places, et cetera, et cetera. Lost for all time. And—by the way—what land is not sacred? It all is. It's all sacred or else it's all just fit to be shit upon. It is impossible to construct an argument to prevail against that last assertion, and also hard to live up to its strict requirements.

And, too, I claimed Bear's people were owed the same payment that all the other Indians from the Nation got paid for travel expenses to the

Territories: $53.33 a head, plus six percent interest, compounded annually. The fact that Bear's folks had not made the trip west did not faze me one whit. It had no bearing on the argument. And the interest, especially, kept my attention, for the years since the Removal just kept rolling on.

When I wasn't meeting with someone in a position to help advance our cause, I sat at the desk in my room at the Indian Queen drinking cup upon cup of black coffee and writing letters to members of Congress and assistants in various agencies and undersecretaries. A loopy line of ink, stretching on and on, referencing the past and demanding a future. Memory and hope spinning out in an endless trail of paper. It would have been easy to see all those blackened pages as something highly abstract, having at best a specific reality expressed only by other paper in the form of currency. But the reality was otherwise. It found its truest expression in something as fundamental as dirt. Land. And, ultimately, the life—plant and animal and human—that can exist atop it. I never let that slip from my mind.

All in all, I didn't win or lose during my stays in Washington. As I've said, that was not entirely the point. But I kept our ball in play, and during that time our territory expanded and became fairly autonomous, at least as much as the modern world allows.

DURING THIS PERIOD of rambling, I was out one Saturday night in Charleston, searching for entertainment. Streets full of people. Many choices, both wholesome and otherwise. I declined to enter a flea circus said to have performed before the previous king of England. I pictured the king as some fat sot, a wigged geezer humped over a little table of tiny trapezes, teeter-totters, tightropes, carousels, and upright wheels. The old man with a great magnifying glass in his hand, one eye squinted closed and the other swelled big as a turkey egg by the curvature of the glass, the iris watery blue and the rest yellow as tallow and cut through by blood vessels zagging about like red lightning bolts. I figured all those splendid particular fleas that had fallen under the royal gaze must surely be dead, for even fleas of extraordinary talent live short lives. So what was the point?

Farther down the street at a small theater, I paid a steep fifty cents and went in. The audience shifted about in wooden chairs. Oiled floorboards squeaked against their nails. Directly, a young man in a vaguely military jacket of blue wool with gold buttons and piping on the sleeves came onto the stage and lit the gaslights and turned the flames up high. Metal mirrors focused their yellow light on the closed stage curtains, which depicted a brilliant scene of blue ocean and a three-masted sailing ship moving athwart broken lines of whitecaps. The house was left nearly dark, and it was so quiet you could hear the hiss of the gas burning. A string duo—banjo and fiddle—took position at one end of the stage. The narrator, in a cream-colored suit of clothes and a floppy black tie, emerged and stood behind a lectern at the other end. The curtains juddered open and revealed a canvas stretching across the stage between two great spools taller than a man. Enormous letters of a shadowed three-dimensional character spelled out BRAVARD'S MAMMOTH PANTOSCOPE OF THE MISSISSIPPI RIVER, the words surrounded by ornamentation meant to suggest ancient scrolls. The musicians struck up a solemn tune and then, out of sight, someone turned a crank. Gears engaged with a clatter, bearings began grinding just audibly beneath the music, and the canvas began moving slowly across the stage, feeding from the full spool toward the empty. The painting was claimed to be three miles long and would take most of the evening to be displayed.

The narrator bellowed out, Behold the mighty Mississippi.

The first scenes depicted a steamboat, its decks and galleries and long salons all populated with very particular portraits of the passengers, each rendered in ways to identify their class and occupation. Tinners, glassblowers, ventriloquists, gamblers, cutpurses, dentists, and all variety of merchants and confidence men; planters, traveling ladies and their handmaids, fortune hunters, and actresses hardly more virtuous than harlots, judging by their appearance. We in the audience were meant to imagine ourselves among those pilgrims, journeying down the river, encountering at each moment the dangers and temptations of travel.

The spools kept turning, and riverbanks began passing by. We encountered other steamboats, one of them aground on a shoal and brilliantly afire, and then we passed a broken pair of stern-wheelers in the cluttered buoyant aftermath of collision. The many passing towns were said to be rendered in perfect accuracy, each with its church steeples and white houses and docks for wooding and taking on passengers and cargo, and the narrator said each of their names and told something distinctive about them, even if it was only that the citizens were noted for their cheese making or their honesty.

The musicians played a sort of ambling leisurely theme for peaceful scenes of rolling down the river. But when the boat passed a tepee encampment of Indians on the river's upper reaches, the banjo player took out a small drum and struck a simple four-beat pattern with emphasis on the offbeat. Later, as scenes of a barn dance scrolled along, the fiddler played a jig. And farther down the river, when slaves danced outside their cabins, the banjoist took a solo turn.

The skies, I thought, were particularly well done. Yellow moonlight through blue broken clouds, sunrise through thin river fog. Blue days and grey progressing in a rhythm suggesting actual life. Black storms formed and then lightning forked down, all enhanced by clever manipulation of the lamps and colored filters, gauze screens and reflectors. At appropriate moments, smoke was made to drift across the stage to suggest fog.

The river went on and on, in all its variety and sameness. It made you want to travel, to be on the open road, to pass through numberless towns, each different in some barely discernible way from the last. To meet people who would aid your passage or oppose it. To weather the weather. To feel the curve of the continent passing under you. The slow flow of landscape changing from one expression of itself to another. Salt flats and pine flats, mountains and rivers. And of course there was the matter of Claire existing somewhere out in the territory beyond the Mississippi enriching the show.

When the Pantoscope had spooled to its close with a view of the skyline of New Orleans, my approbation knew no bounds. I leaped to my feet and applauded until my palms were numb.

NEXT MORNING, I mounted up and rode out. I journeyed west through sand hills and pinewoods and cane creeks and palmetto flats. And then there was wasteland and cypress swamp, flat and watery country where the trees that grew were bearded with grey moss hanging from every twig. It was country that drew up night fears and blue thoughts. On the scant dry ground beneath the trees lay the dim-lit runways of wild horses, wild pigs, and red wolves. The season grew increasingly buggy, and in camp I unsuccessfully tried burning cow dung and bark and noxious vines to keep off the various bloodsuckers. Then I met a black-haired, dusty-skinned family of wandering Melungeons who showed me how to make a dark and fragrant paste of lard and herbs and fish parts, which at least kept the mosquitoes off, and afterward I slept a little better. Though even then, I spent more than one long wakeful night in the swamps, my shotgun across my lap, gators and bears and panthers coughing and grunting and splashing in the night and sometimes their eyes shining bright as stove coals where they circled round the edge of the firelight.

When I came out the other side of the wetlands to where people were again, there stretched before me as far as eye could see great flat fields of cotton and indigo and the occasional bog of rice. Great packs of slaves worked them, all under the watch of mean little white men on horses.

I went westerly through such slave country for some weeks until I passed into a territory of little dusty one-street towns scattered about in clearings among the vast pinewoods. I just rode on through the towns, rarely even stopping to ask their names. In one such place, there was no one about and the only sound was my horse's hooves, muffled in the dust of the street. A hearse painted with glossy black lacquer came toward me. The harness of the four horses was adorned with faded black ostrich feathers. Though I found myself vaguely embarrassed by such a show being made over something so common as death, I nevertheless pulled my horse to a stop and removed my hat. As the hearse passed, the driver nodded to me, and I could see an open coffin through the glass panels. A glimpse of pale skin, the sharp-nosed profile of a young woman, and then it was gone.

I rode mornings, slept at noon, shot game birds and squirrels for supper, then rode on until just before dark. I kept up an infrequent correspondence with the trusted Tallent. Money and letters pertaining to my businesses were to await me at specified banks in the larger towns.

In the open country, people sometimes put me up for the night, and I slept in every kind of house from plantation mansion to trapper hut, and the inhabitants of the one seemed as ignorant as the other and there were not books to speak of in any of them, only religious tracts printed in the poorest manner on paper hardly more permanent than crepe. The people seemed to get less interesting the farther I went. But during every day of travel I watched with endless fascination the varieties in the way land could shape its contours and what bearing water and weather had on it and what sorts of plants and animals could love it or at least tolerate it enough to grow from it.

As I traveled onward, I noted in my journal the passing road signs stating the next town of destination and the mileage to it. In particular, I began counting and recording the bullet holes in the signs, always wondering if the number signified something about the town designated. Did twelve holes warn of something that three didn't? Did an unblemished sign portend a city of angels? Did a sign shot to scraps on its post suggest an upcoming hell, a slaughter yard? The farther I traveled, the more I believed myself capable of understanding hidden correlations that might be presenting themselves.

The Southwest seemed a sorry and benighted place, and each small town had its pit of bloody sawdust wherein chicken fights and dog fights and man fights were played out for wagerers. So I angled northwest and cut across a corner of Mississippi, a scrub state, intolerably flat, to which I paid no more heed than it deserved.

By such route I thus came somewhat unawares upon Memphis. I rode into it at night and it was lit up like Judgment Day, full of folk surging all through the streets right down to the river. I found myself somewhat disconcerted by such population. It was not an entirely cheerful thought to find so many people unexpectedly extant out here in the West. There was music of fiddle and banjo and guitar and piano coming from the doorways of saloons and whorehouses, and the first place I walked into for a drink was full of near-bare women, their clothes so skimpy there was not enough cotton among them to wad a rifle load, and they made it clear to any who entered that they were willing to gap their legs for a drink of liquor or any state denomination of paper dollar, even Georgia money. Neither Washington nor Charleston had entirely prepared me for such a place.

I took a room in a hotel, and during the days following I found that in a town like Memphis the people act like every day is court day. They just milled about in great numbers and drank and whored and listened to music. At night, the big riverboats blazed with lamplight, and their bright tiers of decks jittered in long reflections across the black expanse of the river.

Money that should have been banked for me had not arrived. I waited for it day after day. In the afternoons I would walk down by the river to a sort of bar, a dirt-floored, thatch-roofed lean-to, and sit at a table and read my old boyhood copy of *Werther* and drink warm beer and watch the white riverboats churning slowly against the current toward St. Louis or booming downstream to New Orleans. Black smoke from their stacks so thick as to make shadows on the water. It was my belief that beyond the Mississippi little existed but empty landscape and Claire.

Little brown frogs lived in the mud of the riverbank, and pink-headed buzzards fell in drunkard angles from the sky and stepped through the mud to eat them, and sometimes the commerce between the two parties went on right at the legs of my table. I would stay until the light on the river's dull red face fell toward evening and my book became unreadable. Besides, I had read it so many times over the years that the brown leather was dark from my hands and the gold lettering on the narrow spine was entirely worn away and I about knew the words by heart. The margins were scribbled with penciled thoughts of yesteryear, nearly all of which I now disavowed and judged to be juvenile.

The great river parted the country like a gash in meat. The immense space lying beyond its western bank felt like a frightening vacancy drawing things toward it, and the contrary part of me wanted to turn away and ride back home. Another part of me wanted to cross the river by whatever means available and just keep on moving across the wild land and see what it offered or threatened day by day until I died or fetched up against the Pacific in California Territory.

One day, fairly drunk, I put a thin leaf from a river cane in *Werther* to mark my place and went to the water's edge and stripped to my linens and set out swimming. I suffered under no romantic idea that I was swimming to Claire. How pathetic that would be. Travel a significant arc of the continent out of mere longing and then possibly find yourself unwelcome at journey's end.

I just wanted a Byronic Hellespont swim to the far bank. A thing to brag about fifty years down the line, though not likely to mark me as deeply and permanent as Bear's claw stripes. Things went fine until halfway across, and then the river took hold and carried me downstream. I've never been the best of swimmers. I fought west, but the river pulled me its way, southward. By the time I struggled to shore, I was far below the town and had washed up again on the eastern bank. I slogged out of the water and had to flounder along muddy flats and ledges back to the thatch bar. The tender drew me a warm cloudy beer, and I sat and drank it and dried off in the sun until the mud cracked in geometric shapes on my forearms and shins and could be shucked off with a scrub of palms.

The next day, money arrived. The great facilitator.

TWO WEEKS LATER I rode down the main street of the raw capital town of the new Nation, Tahlequah. In hopes of finding Claire immediately,

I stared at every woman walking or riding. I passed a mercantile, and a young man coming out the door stopped and looked at me long and hard. I kept going and noted out of the corner of my eye that he was sloping along the storefronts in my wake. He had a pistol holstered at his hip like a gunfighter, and he bore watching.

When I got to the hotel he was still coming. I positioned my horse so that when I dismounted, she was between him and me. When I had both feet on the ground, I put a hand on the grip of the pistol at my waist.

The man walked right up across the mare from me so that we were eye to eye across the bow of the saddle.

He said, I know you.

Well, I didn't know him. He was a short full-blood, his skin burned by the prairie wind to the color of oiled leather, wearing a dusty overlong black suit coat over jean pants and a white shirt all rusty around the collarless neck. Big brown clodhopper work boots. He looked like a farmer dressed up to come to town.

I said, You have the advantage of me, sir.

—We passed some time together. Up Deep Creek.

—Deep Creek?

—You cooked good porridge.

—Oats?

—Also, we were together down by the river. A flat place. Killing ground.

—Wasseton, I said.

He stepped around the mare's head and faced me top to bottom. He had his right coattail pulled back behind his holster. Wasseton was all grown up.

What do you do in such a case? I put out a hand to shake.

He looked at it and then, for lack of better idea, he shook back. Taking his calloused hand was like gripping a cow horn.

After you shake with a man ready to draw his pistol on you, what do you say?

Wasseton looked downward.

—You could have saved him, he said.

—It wasn't up to me, I said. You might recollect that there was an army of soldiers and Tennessee mercenaries calling the shots that summer and fall.

—You could have done something.

—We saved all we could save.

Wasseton looked off down the street, thinking. But I knew enough about gunplay not to look where he was looking or even at his face. I watched his pistol fist.

He said, I been wanting to kill you a long time.

If I was him, I'd have wanted to kill me too. So there weren't any hard feelings on my part.

—Factor this into your judgment, I said. None of us, not me nor Bear nor any of us, chopped up any soldiers. Your people put us all in danger. We made the only deal we had left. You'd put us in a corner.

—It wasn't right, what you did.

—What would you have had us do different?

—What you did wasn't right.

He was still looking away.

—Look at me, I said.

And he did. Eye to eye.

—I'll agree with you, I said. What happened was wrong. It was all wrong from the start. But what else was there? I'm not saying that as an excuse. I'm wanting to see if there was an option that escaped us.

—I don't know.

—Me neither. And not from lack of thinking about it.

Wasseton looked off down the street again, deciding what to do.

I said, If there's a bar in this town, why don't you close your coattail over your pistol and we'll go sit and have a drink together and not kill each other today.

He was a sensible young man, always had been. He took me up on my offer and told me to call him Washington. Times had changed.

I was the one buying, so of course we drank the best they had, which was at least from Tennessee, second only to Scotland, and not by coincidence but by direct lineage. We talked for three or four drinks about our mountain homeland, how it had been and how it had changed since Washington last saw it. And then, at a certain point of whiskey camaraderie, we contested to name all the colors the mountains and their foliage are able to take on. Any tinge there is between white and black. We competed to find exceptions but could not score points against each other. We didn't even bother talking about green. Without question, every shade of it would be accounted for by our homeland. We went straight to red, but found that all degrees from the faintest pink to old blood were expressed by the leaves or flowers of some plant or another or by the autumn sunset sky. We went on down the colors, even all the purples, including puce. And the yellows including cadmium, which I had to describe to Washington, and he immediately named both a flower and an autumn leaf as examples of it. Blues were a little harder, but we managed to cover all the shades from robin's egg to the indigo of ironweed to the unnameable color of the tallest peaks just before full dark in late summer. We drank another whiskey to celebrate our stalemate.

Washington said he had never gotten used to this edge of the prairie and found the great flat emptiness to the west like a suckhole in a river, like the Leech Place, pulling you toward destruction, whereas the uprisen and folded mountains of his youth held you protected down in them like being cupped in the Savior's hands.

—So they've saved you? I said.

—A little bit. Most of the time. You're enough to make a man backslide.

—Come on home, I said. Sometime before long, just throw a leg over a horse and ride on back. We'll make a place for you.

Out on the street, we shook hands and began to part. And then I said, I'm out here looking for Claire Featherstone.

—On out of town a ways. Big brick house. Hard to miss.

And it was hard to miss. Its shape was etched in my memory. Cranshaw. A massive plug of brick and a row of white columns across the gallery.

I knocked at the door. Presented a card to the same woman, now a little greyer and stouter, who had passed my card back to me several years before. She showed me into a parlor, where I sat for a long while listening to the pendulum of a big clock knock down the passage of time at each end of its arc.

Claire came sweeping in. She had changed some, become a full woman.

—Why are you here? she said. Said it pretty much in midstride, barely through the door.

I had ridden a thousand miles and had been fool enough to expect our first meeting to be a rush together, teeth clashing in an urgent first kiss as in olden days.

I shook my head, turned my palms up. Gestures of confusion and defeat.

—I wanted to see you again, I said.

—You might have written saying you were coming.

—It was a sort of spur-of-the-moment trip.

—How long have you been on the road?

—I left Charleston in the spring.

She summed the intervening months in her head and said, You could have written. But she said it softer.

—I wasn't sure I'd make it. I came the long way.

We sat. Tea was called for. We had a moment. Reminiscences, et cetera. The glories of youth. Time's winged chariot. All very polite. No sunburned buttocks or late-night river couplings allowed.

Then another black woman, younger and darker than the one who'd answered the door, came into the parlor carrying a wailing baby bundled in little white blankets. All you could see was a face like a barn owl's, just as round and flat and pale and fierce. Like all babies. If they had the physical means, they'd kill you without conscience to fulfill their slightest immediate desire. Same as house cats, which if they weighed two hundred pounds would not accede to our existence for a single day.

The woman presented the baby to Claire. She took it in her arms and turned halfway from me and made an adjustment in the upper portions of her clothing.

How could one have the courage to take a thing so predatory to one's breast? God knew something fundamental about the nature of his own creation when he failed to give babies teeth and claws.

Claire turned back over her shoulder to me and said, Featherstone is out riding. He rides for hours every day in every weather. He won't be back until dark. He will be sad to have missed you.

—Well, tell him I'm sad to have missed him too. My aim has never been quite as true as I wish it to be.

We were polite to the point of disgust. I began saying the things you say in preparation to leave. Claire leaned and kissed me on the cheek. The barn owl rested fiercely in a crooked arm between us. I gave a little head nod of a bow and left without another word, for I wanted to think I still had some pride left. I didn't say, Write me, or anything of the kind. I figured that chaste kiss was my last communication with Claire.

I went out to the yard and Featherstone came riding up. He was slimmer than previous, not quite an old man but getting there. And just as vain in regard to dress. He wore the latest style of riding attire and a little round pair of smoked glasses. No hat. His hair was still full to the temples, though cut short and entirely silver as new-honed steel. He didn't seem the least surprised to see me standing in his front yard. He dismounted and dropped his reins and walked straight to me.

I put out a hand to shake, but he reached with wide arms and grabbed me in a bear hug.

—I've missed the hell out of you, he said after he let me go.

He insisted we take a walk. He had something he wanted to tell me. He did not think I would believe it.

We walked silently a long way toward the bleak western horizon. Nothing worth describing. The sort of place they have plenty of out there.

I finally pulled up and said, Tell me what you have to say, and we'll see whether I believe it or not.

His story was this: He was currently living a second life after dying a death that did not meet his approval. It happened a few years before, during the bad times after the Removal. On the same night, young Ridge and Boudinot had been gutted by Ross men in their front yards, with their wives and children watching from the upper windows. Old Major Ridge was shot dead by an ambush party while taking one of his boy slaves into town to be doctored. For months afterward, the survivors among the Ridge bunch fought the Ross bunch in a bloody feud. Featherstone sometimes rode out at night, fighting on the side of the Ridges. It was like a return to the glorious days of his youth—pony clubs, pistol flash, and hoofbeat. Risk and blood. Moonlight and magic. But on a chill drizzly night when he felt he was about to take a cold, he decided to stay home. He felt every year of his advancing age in the aching joints of his traitorous body. After a dinner of roasted hen and baked sweet potatoes and collard greens, he went to his study and began reading, once again, some witty lines from *Don Juan*. An amber inch of smoky Islay whisky quivered in a heavy glass on a side table. He slouched in his wing chair with his tall-booted feet on a stool and the fire logs burning low, their split faces checked and grey, beginning to hiss instead of crackle. And then he had a strange pain in one side of his head. The Byron fluttered into his lap. He fell asleep, and in his sleep he died the death of a saint, not even waking briefly enough to mark his own passing. The kind of death God awards to a bare few of his most beloved. Painless and unforeknowledged.

Yet enormously disappointing. All his life he had wanted to die riding against enemies at a gallop with pistols flashing and a plume of back-flung gunsmoke marking his passage out of the world.

I didn't approve of an easy death for him either, and I said so. Especially not a death of inexplicable mercy when he deserved at least a fair share of the worst that could be laid on him by God or man. There wasn't even a slight degree of justice in the death he described. For the rest of us, the punishment begins somewhat previous to passing, in the pain and suffering and fear that comes before. And in the hope for living too, for that is also a part of the punishment. Why should Featherstone, especially, get off clean?

—My feelings exactly, he said. Which is why I believe I was brought back. So that next time I can go harder. I arose the next morning at dawn with a blinding headache and a slight lack of firm grip in my right hand and a discernible droop to the eyelid on that side. All famous tokens of death. But I also arose with a great determination to set some things right during my second life. And the first thing I turned my attention to was Claire. I'd not previously treated her entirely as I should have. As a wife, so to say.

—Great God, I said.

—And I want to square things with you too, he said.

—If you keeled over right now, the single shred of justice would be the fact that the only two significant scars your hide would carry into the grave are from Bite's teeth and my pistol ball.

—Now, see, that's where you're wrong, Featherstone said. You're making a young man's mistake. You need to let your anger fall away. It won't get you where you want to be. It's poison. But it will rise from you like smoke from a fire if you let it go. And anger is not a becoming feature as you grow older.

He reached out to me and touched me on the shoulder. He said again, Let it go. Stay here with us awhile.

All I could do was shrug off his hand and say, A little too much marital bliss for a bachelor to stand. I mounted up and rode away.

I RODE WEST. The way to the Nightland. But also, in the mythology of my mother's people, the direction of new beginnings, where when you've fouled your life past all understanding, there's still hope. The direction of last-chance salvation. When the sunset was in my face I made camp.

I slept on the open ground and watched the enormous sky off and on between brief bouts of sleep. It was a dark night, without any moon at all and utterly cloudless. The air was dry and the stars were sharp points in the dark and there seemed to be a great many more of them than I ever remembered seeing before. And then it came to my attention that it was a night of meteor showers. Spouts and shoots of light, both thin and broad, arced overhead. So I got my scope from its leather case and stretched out its articulations and lay on my back in my sleeping robe peering into the universe. For hours I looked through the eyepiece, as if down into a well. And the longer I looked, the deeper down I thought I saw. The shape of Creation appeared like a funnel, a maelstrom, a maw. Vertiginous. Made to swallow us down its narrowing throat.

Then I heard a slight rustle in the long grass, and a young grey wolf went walking by on slender legs just past the end of my ground cloth, and it gave me one glance down its long snout as it passed, a moment's locking of eyes, and then it was gone without ever changing its gait or in any other way passing judgment or even opinion concerning my unexpected presence.

When I awoke just before dawn, heavy dew had risen all around me, and the outermost layer of my sleeping robe was wet. When the sun had just risen in its dimmest form, I crawled out and stood and shook my sleeping robe, snapping it sharply. Drops of water globed around me, rainbow colors in the morning light. I mounted up and headed east. I rode back into America and across Tennessee to home.

When I rested at the last mountain gap, it was autumn, drizzle and fog so thick I could hardly see past my horse's ears. Otherwise it would have been a long view down a familiar broken landscape. I could have traced the drainages of numerous creeks, all of them twining together to make the river by Wayah. The cool damp air smelled of wet growing leaves and rotted dead leaves. A redtail hawk sat in a Fraser fir. It stared my way and shook water out of its feathers. It spread its wings and its tail, and it bowed toward me—or lunged, perhaps. I thought there was recognition in the look it gave me, and I put up an arm straight into the air as a salute, for I guessed the hawk to be a representative of the mountains themselves, an ambassador charged with greeting me upon my return.

4

BACK AT THE FARM, I FOUND THAT IN MY LONG ABSENCE THE HOUSE had been conquered by my increased tribe of long-headed, blue-speckled bird dogs. I climbed the front steps, and two of them sleeping in a wedge of sunlight on the porch growled at me without bothering to lift their heads. The feathering of fur growing from their forelegs and from the leathers of their ears had twisted into knots and collected burrs and beggar lice. Inside, another pair of dogs occupied the brown leather sofa in the parlor, and it was scarred to the pale quick from their razorous toenails, as were the dark-stained heart-pine floorboards. Silver-blue dog hair drifted in airy mouse-sized clumps across the floors and congregated in corners and wreathed the legs of furniture, settling in a pale haze over tabletops and lamp globes and Turkish rugs. Upstairs, more dogs lolled on the bedsteads. All through the house, the lower panes of the windows were opaque with overlapping nose prints.

The dogs were of the mind that someone has to be in charge, and if no one else was willing to step up with conviction and claim the job, they'd jump right in and be the boss themselves. The help had become scared of the pack and avoided conflict with its members. Mothers refrained from letting their babies roam free after dusk. They had taken to leaving the front door standing open at all hours and in all weathers, and the dogs became accustomed to going and coming as suited their moods. The bird dogs had gradually forgotten every bit of English they ever knew, and when it was spoken to them they ignored it, as if it meant no more than the sound of the river flowing. They had long since ceased to fetch. The word *down* meant nothing to them. Previously, at its softest utterance, they would dive for the floor with their chins between their paws and their tails thumping in anticipation of the next request. Now they glared a blank rebellious glare toward all the world of man.

I reinstituted the old regime. I went to the woodpile and took up a stick of pine kindling, and with it in one hand and a pistol in the other, I routed the dogs from the house. They milled about in the yard and finally retreated under the porch. I announced to all the farm's inhabitants that I would bivouac by the river for the night and would light a fire and cook my own supper and breakfast from the food in my saddlebags. But by dinnertime of the next day, I expected the house to be cleaned and biscuits to be baking in the oven.

In the following days, I reintroduced the bird dogs to human language. When they failed to heed—or, worse, growled at me—I grabbed them two-handed by the loose skin at the scruffs of their necks and shook them hard like their mamas had done when they were pups. One young male dared to wheel and bite me on the forearm, and I bit back hard. When the dogs conceded I was sovereign over them, I rewarded them with quail livers and sections of hog bowel. I walked about the newly reclaimed house and wondered how it would be occupied in some unimaginable future when the blue dogs and I would all be underground.

I REOCCUPIED MY house and grounds, claimed my place in the world. Though with a great paralyzing sadness, for I now believed Claire was truly gone and Waverley had died in my absence. All I could do about any of it was put a bench under the dogwood tree by Waverley's grave and go there in the afternoons to read. That's the way it is at some point in life. An inevitable consequence of living. A lot of things begin falling away.

I believe that was the last year Bear and I used the winterhouse, and only for a few nostalgic days during the most blue and howling blizzards. Bear was becoming fragile as a champagne flute, and his chestnut color had faded gradually to sepia. But he had not lost a hair on his head and there were still quite a few threads of black mixed in with the silver, and he still gathered some of it into a queue in the back and let the rest fall to his shoulders. He talked a great deal about several new opinions he had developed in my absence, one of which was that we come to value the fall of the year more and more as we age and decline. It is easy in youth to become emotional at the overwhelming symbolic autumnalness of withered peaches and reddened honey-locust pods. Later in life, though, the season becomes more actual to us, not sentimental, just sadly true. Therefore, autumn was now Bear's favorite season by far, replacing early summer in his affections. He ached with newfound pleasure all through autumn's many stages, the slow day-by-day coloring of fragile dogwood and sumac and redbud in late summer, then maple and poplar, and the sudden netherward jolt of the first frost and the overnight withering of the weeds, and finally the heroic fortitude of oak, its most persistent dead leaves gripping the branches all through the bitterest winter until finally cast to earth by the push of new growth in spring. And above all, the waxing and waning of the several moons—End of Fruit, Nut, Harvest, Hunting—commanded Bear's deepest interest. The different ways they rise and fall in the sky and change from one to the next, from milky and enormous in late summer to tiny as a fingertip and etched hard as burning phosphorus against the wee stars in cold early winter.

And, big or small, whatever the season, the moons had begun to streak across the graphite bowl of sky at a harder pace in the later years. Alarming, really, how all the wheels of the world—the days and nights, the thirteen moons, the four seasons, and the great singular round of the year itself—begin spinning faster and faster the closer we get to the

Nightland. We're called to it and it pulls us. And the weaker we become, the harder and faster it pulls.

As proof of the acceleration of time, Bear told how when he was a boy he had a pet heron that settled in to village life and ate shell corn out of his hand and would not even fly away south for winter but walked about in the snow by the riverbank, leaving forked prints where it stepped, and its color looking in accord with the blue light of a cloudy snow day. It stood nearly as tall as a man and so towered over Bear and followed him about his daily rounds, and when Bear fished with his bow and arrow the heron fished with his stabbing grey beak. The point of the story was, time back then was different. Days went on and on and did not flash by as now.

I told endless doomed travel tales. The lay of the western land, strange animals and people, bad weather, the big Mississippi, and Claire. Bear, though, didn't have a lot to say about love that winter, except that he had pretty much forsaken carnal desire. He just loved Sara without expectation. As a result, everything was better between them. Sara developed a degree of respect for him, even some affection. She treated him something like a just-met father newly returned home after a long life in a distant land. Bear said they had shaped a new ground on which they might stand together in a new light. The biting red-headed baby had grown into a boy, and Bear treated him as a grandchild. Bear said that everything was amicable with Sara so long as he was able to forget the many blissful nights they had lain together.

However, Sara's new attitude did not in any way influence the other women of her clan. They all still held Bear in jolly contempt. The eldest of them, the humped and increasingly tiny widow of Hanging Maw, a centenarian at the very least, still lived on, though she diminished visibly every year and had come more and more to resemble a rough-barked oak stump, sawn off about waist-high. Grandmother Maw still hoed weeds from corn rows in high summer, but she kept having to cut her hoe handle shorter and shorter each year as she settled closer to the ground. Bear said she hardly acknowledged him as they passed in the course of their daily rounds, other than to growl a phlegmy warning at him: Back off.

MY BUSINESS WITH the Government—and, in particular, the War Department—went on and on, becoming more and more ridiculous. After several years of argument, they finally sort of surrendered to one of my more outrageous assaults and sent down a deputy or a secretary or some such officer to conduct a census of Cherokee to qualify us for possible payment of money related to transportation and sustenance for removal to the new Nation, which, of course, we hadn't done. They didn't intend to pay the whole amount I claimed we were owed, but just the six percent annual interest on the magically persistent number of $53.33 each. Funny how something as insubstantial as four numerals and a decimal point can take on a life of its own. It doesn't sound like much, but it went back quite a few years and promised to go on many more years into the future, given the pace of business in Washington and the fact that we had no intention of ever removing to the new Nation. Of course, since the payout was calculated per capita, the magnitude of any reckoning depended on how many times you summed that $53.33 before applying the six percent. So it's fair to say that we all had an intense interest in running our census of Indians as high as we could make it go—consistent with accuracy, of course.

Identity, though, is a difficult matter to tease out, especially in a time of flux. How to tell a spaniel from a retriever when all dogs have become middle-sized and brown? Should we go by some arbitrary blood quantum wherein half makes an Indian and forty-nine percent makes something else? Certainly forty-nine percent does not a whiteman make, at least not by the laws then prevailing in our state and most others. Or do we go by the old ways, the clans and the mothers, blood degree be damned? Or by what language someone dreams in or prays in or curses in? Or whether they cook bean bread and still tell the tales of Spearfinger and Uktena by the winter fire and go to water when they're sick? And what if they did all those things but were blond and square-headed as Norsemen? Or do we just hold a dry oak leaf to their cheeks and cull by whether they are darker or lighter?

And, on a personal level, do adoptees count?

So it really boiled down to these essential questions: Who is an Indian and who is not? And how do you get the former category to number as high as possible?

In regard to both questions, I found an ally in the deputy secretary who came down from Washington. He was named John Mullay, and he fetched up at Wayah highly tubercular and downward bound. The long journey had not helped his health. His eyes lay black in his head and his skin was colorless as side meat and dewed with death sweat. His other problem was that he belonged to the Democratic Party. In Washington, it was looking like the Whigs had them a sure winner in Zachary Taylor, and come November they were going to put out the Democrats. Mullay held his job purely by patronage, and if the presidency changed parties, his job would go to a Whig right after the inauguration, no doubt about it. The seam I found to work was this: I had met Zachary Taylor on one of my early trips to Washington, when he was young and I was younger, and we had discovered ourselves to be possibly related through our fathers' families. One of those kinds of relations where everybody studies on it and kind of agrees to be third cousins by way of somebody's granny's second husband. But nevertheless, we had acknowledged each other as kin, which is all that mattered. I didn't make any specific promises to Mullay, but I also didn't keep it a secret that if the election went as expected, I would soon be in a position to help him keep his job. Under circumstances and for considerations I did not need to specify.

But I don't want to make this seem all bloodless and mercenary. I grew to like Mullay quite a bit and was drawn to him in a sort of protective way. He had come down south hoping that the elevation and mountain air might work some healing miracle on his bad lungs, for he was already at the stage of despair where you spit furtively in your handkerchief and try to fold it real fast to hide the red smear from your companions and yourself. And I believed I might do some good against his disease. Jollity seemed called for. And fresh air and the open road. Nothing like a trip through the mountains in autumn.

To conduct our census, I insisted, we must beat the bushes ourselves. Anything less would be a dereliction. We rode great distances together. According to the expense accounts, three hundred and sixty-five miles. Just the two of us a-saddle, riding everything from carriage paths to pig tracks. I showed him a grand time, and the weather abetted me. The Harvest Moon waxed and waned as we made our journey. That particular autumn was dry and brilliant as you could ever hope for. Day after day of blue skies and yellow poplars and red maples. We went from cove to cove looking for Indians to count, and at night we stayed at the various inns and drank the best of their French wine and went to our rooms early and read novels by candle flame. During the next day's ride, we recounted the salient plot points from our reading in great detail. We rolled into farmsteads, both of us half lit from the flask of Scotch we passed back and forth, and when people came out onto the porch I'd say, Hey. They'd wave and say, Hey, Will. Then they'd go back inside. And then I'd say to Mullay, Those are Indians, no doubt about it. And Mullay would record them in his ledger without alighting from his saddle.

The final two days of our journey were marked by a plague of green and yellow and orange parrots, clouds of them. They were big as ravens, and they arrived in a great racket of conversation among themselves and began tearing apart the last of the apples to get at the seeds. In three days, they had stripped the trees bare of fruit and then they flew on elsewhere. Mullay was as amazed and delighted as a child by our jungle full of parrots.

When we were finished traveling, we had turned up a sight more qualified Cherokee than anybody would have guessed possible. A staggering number, actually. This despite the fact that not one of the contentious members of the Long Hair community would even talk to Mullay, much less give him their names and particulars, for they suspected that he was really collecting information in preparation for a second Removal.

All in all, it was a first-class job of highly ardent and imaginative census taking, and when Mullay went back to Washington—a much healthier-looking man, I should add, ruddy-cheeked and plumped up and with a newfound grin on his face—I kept adding to the roll by mail, turning up qualified Indians left and right. And though some have claimed that our census was conducted much in the way that small towns will sometimes vote half the graveyard in a tight election, we had our standards, which were strict but comprehensive. We agreed to acknowledge that identity is both who you say you are and who the world says you are, a topic Mullay and I discussed daily on the trail. By the definition we arrived at, I, for example, was marked down as a member. Some called foul. But I would stand pistol in hand on the field of honor to defend my place on the roll.

Later—in the second and last year of the presidency of my vague kinsman Zachary Taylor—Mullay returned south, still miraculously holding his job. He came down to put a touch-up on our census, which had evoked the adjectives *mythic* and *vaporous* in two different newspapers.

Mullay had sadly declined in health. This trip, he could not ride as we went about our travels, and I sat with him on the carriage seat. His face was blue as skim milk in the shadow of the canvas top. On the few occasions when he tried to walk, he depended on a pair of canes. And all the time we were together, the roll of names got longer. The day he headed back to Washington, he stuck out his hand to shake in farewell, but I grabbed him around the shoulders and hugged him, for I knew we would never meet again in this world.

Upon Mullay's return, a figure was settled upon—many multiples of $53.33 at six percent—which meant that those on the roll were owed, collectively, a staggering figure. A check was drawn in my name for disbursement. But even that was not the end to it, for the annual interest on all those $53.33 shares would continue to build with never an end in sight as long as we or our heirs kept refusing to move to the Territories.

Mullay died shortly thereafter. News of his passing sent me into a state of gloom that lasted longer than I could strictly justify.

—

I WOULD LIKE to avoid the topic entirely, but here it is. I held upward of four dozen Negroes at the height of my enterprises. If I'm being more than a little bit honest, I'd have to say that it is awfully easy, when you get so old you can't do anything else, to look back on some of the actions of your full manhood and feel a distant and nearly painless regret. As an emotion, it has about the color of dust in the wind. Now that it's too late to do anything about it, you suddenly entertain the notion that you might have been slightly and altogether inadvertently in the wrong. It is a sweet and melancholy feeling, and an easy path toward self-forgiveness, but false. Maybe it is an inevitable part of becoming old, like arthritis and weak eyesight. We all get it, if we live long enough.

Bear was not exempt from self-congratulatory regret. In his last years, he often thought back on his vast killing of animals. He said he didn't regret one animal he killed out of hunger, but it was the hunting for trade he wished he hadn't done. In the young days of the world, there had been prayers to the animals, the dwellers in the wilderness, begging their pardon for the necessity of killing them for food and spilling their blood, bear and deer especially. They hold a great deal of blood, an embarrassment of it, like killing a man. It spills out all over the place. So there were rules for dealing with it. You fed the river with the blood of bear and deer that pooled in the fallen leaves. When you spilled it, you prayed and fed the river, and you were square with the world. But that was back when the women farmed and the men hunted, and together they made a living that neither could accomplish alone, a fact acknowledged in the very marriage ceremony, which included an element of trade, an equal exchange between woman and man of corn for meat skins. But then, not long ago, all of a sudden there was money to be made from killing, to the extent that deerskin was currency and the buck a more common denomination than a dollar and of equal value. You'd see men leading long strings of packhorses with twenty badly cured skins stacked high and stiff across the back of each one. Lots of bucks.

In the face of so much money, men did as they always do; they lost their manners. The prayers went away, and then before long the bear and deer went away too. And Bear always said it like that: the deer went away. Or the deer left. He never said the exact truth, which was that people killed every valuable animal they could hunt down for cash money or in trade for tin pots or gingham cloth at the post, and never acknowledged that the elk and bison didn't just wander off somewhere else and disappear from this world entirely but were every one hunted down. In a note of unintended irony, the place where the last one in each section of country was killed usually became memorialized in the name of a creek or a cove or a ridge. Or at least with a rotting patchy hide tacked to a barn wall.

Bear described walking up to a badly wounded buck sprawled on the ground too weak to move, one hind leg broken by a ball and twisted beneath it and another ball in its belly, blood blackening the leaves around it. An entire branch of antler sheared off near the skull by another missed ball. Bear remembered the look in the buck's eye as it watched him coming to cut its throat and sell its skin for a dollar.

—There's not a prayer for that, he would say.

Bear was always in a wistful mood telling that story. I heard it a dozen times. But back in the trade-hunting days he would not have been wistful. He would have wanted that dollar, would have wanted a great high stack of them.

As for me, I didn't want to plow my own fields or split my own rails or milk my own cows, so I ended up owning men and women and their children. And if there are any prayers for that, I wish somebody would teach them to me.

Bear was as honest a man as I ever knew, with others and with himself. And still he indulged that self-exonerating version of the past. So it is one of the things I list among his lessons that I'm not now much inclined to ask anyone's sympathy or understanding, nor am I inclined to ask forgiveness from anyone, including myself.

—

IN FAIRNESS, I should mention that Bear was also a slaveholder. It was a short and singular experience. In one of those years between the Removal and his death, Bear came into possession of a man named Cudjo, his exact match in age and infirmity, a genuine old African brought over on one of the last of the ships. I never understood how the deal worked, except that it was a notably poor trade involving some old debt concerning ginseng and three or four horses and also carried some element of personal grudge with his trading adversary.

Though Bear understood slavery perfectly, he found the institution remarkably uninteresting, at least on his end of it. Immediately upon taking possession, he told Cudjo he was welcome to hang around if he cared to, but he was not to call Bear his master and he was not to expect much of anything from Bear other than what anyone in the community could expect—which was that if there was food in the pot you were welcome to eat a bowlful. A single bowlful, by the way. Those were the local rules of etiquette. And if that didn't suit Cudjo, he'd better move on.

In short order, though, the two old men grew enormously fond of each other. Cudjo was a genius of language, and even the daunting proliferating verb tenses of Cherokee took him no time to learn. As soon as they could talk to each other, they found consonance in their boyhoods. Cudjo told a youthful story involving himself and a lion that made a great impression on Bear. Blood and honor and courage and weaponry. They showed off old scars, claw marks from a better time. And they quickly reached an agreement recognizing each other as equal hunters and warriors, representatives of an antique style never to come round again in this world.

Very soon they began making a little joke between themselves at the expense of others. In front of some ignorant third party—particularly if the party was white—Cudjo would refer to Bear as Master. Bear would look at the ground and shake his head and then waggle one bulbous-jointed forefinger and say that being Cudjo's master was a job you couldn't pay him a pile of silver money to take on. Nor gold money neither. A man can make the mistake of becoming slave to his own possessions. Cudjo was too much responsibility to shoulder. And so, therefore, no thank you to masterhood.

Then Cudjo would say, Nevertheless, old Bear's my master now. He holds paper on me.

Then they'd both laugh like a pair of jays.

Bear would threaten to sell Cudjo straight to some brutal bullwhip cotton farm in Mississippi—except, sadly, Cudjo was so old as to be totally worthless. So why bother trying? And then Bear would walk away.

In more serious moods, or drunk, they proclaimed that they were brothers and would lift their shirts together and turn their backs in unison to show their old claw scars, shining in five parabolic silver lines against the darker skin.

For the short time of their relationship, they lived together as equals in the townhouse, and on cool nights of that year's spring and fall they slept on the same narrow platform closest to the fire, though they both set a boundary at sharing a quilt and so kept separate bedclothes.

Cudjo died shortly before Christmas. He just fell out one frosty morn, walking down the road. Bear saw to it that Cudjo was buried in the same manner as if he had been born in the mountains and had been a member of a clan. Bear took on the job of heaping stones atop the grave himself, though as an old man from the previous distant century, he had every right to beg off from the job.

Bear didn't deliver much of a eulogy after the stones were heaped up. He just said, You never know when somebody will pull you to them. And then we all walked back down the creek to home.

Those were the years when I was full of industry. No more pining for Claire, at least not much. She was just gone. I had the several mercantiles, all scattered through what had been the Nation's eastern boundary and about a day's ride from one another. And there was also the law practice, requiring my frequent attendance at the court days of a half dozen different counties all the way down into the foothills. And the businesses in Wayah. In other words, I spent a great portion of my life a-saddle.

Nothing got by me back then. I had feelers out in every direction. At one point, the legislature came up with some freakish bit of minor law-making designed to encourage silk production. Our state, after all, has aplenty of mulberry trees, and its leaves are all a silkworm will deign to eat. The bill offered all kinds of subsidies and legal benefits such as easy incorporation, which was then neither common nor much encouraged by state law. Elsewhere, in the lowland counties, the silk incentives went largely ignored. But I took one look at the state's offer and saw immediately what an easy cow it would be to milk. And the way I found to work the new law to our advantage didn't have an awful lot to do with visioning the Indians picking apart cocoons and winding silk thread onto bobbins and selling it at market in Charleston or Philadelphia.

For appearance's sake, I did go so far as to put in an order for a package of silkworm eggs and applied for a government check to pay for them. And then I set about incorporating the Indians. Turned them all into shareholders in the Cherokee Company. And their business was not just silk but encompassed all their joint interests, or at least the ones I found interesting. Most particularly, the corporation interested itself in the ownership of all that enormous boundary of land Bear and I had been buying and buying for years and holding together with spit and promises and, now and then, kited checks. We set the corporation up with limits so that each shareholder could own property individually but could not sell to anyone but another shareholder. However they thought of themselves—as a people, a community, or a tribe—was their business. As far as the state was concerned, they were now a legal corporation.

Before I'd even finished drawing up all the paperwork, the little black worm eggs had hatched into black threadlike worms and then they fattened on mulberry leaves and shed their skins and turned pale. But then, before a single one of them had spun even an inch of thread for a cocoon, they all curled up and died. And that was the end of the mountain silk trade, which was fine with me. Bear said any enterprise that depended for its success on little wiggling grubs was bad for the soul. The one exception being, of course, the making of yellow-jacket soup.

The worms died. But the Cherokee Company lived on.

Some of my detractors claimed my whole purpose in such dealings as the silk trade was just self-interest, to make it easier to sell the Indians all my cheap, steep mountain land. Others said I was following old Bear's wish to re-create a homeland for them and undo all the Federal Government's efforts to move them out and make way for progress. They said Bear was an upsurger, perhaps a revolutionary, and had long ago sworn never to make peace with the white men and had cast a spell on me and set me on my present misled course, and thus together we had accomplished what Tecumseh and Osceola and many others could not—to fight for a homeland and hold out against the Government. Others among my critics said I was making a wilderness kingdom for myself to lord over like some biblical patriarch, and in darkened voices they said that whether my rule would be benign or despotic was still to be determined.

IT WAS ONLY natural at some point that I would stand for election. My first office was the state senate. It just meant a couple of months out of life every two years to travel down to the capital and have a brief convivial drunken time of lawmaking. The state's needs were fairly limited back then. From my first term, I mainly remember that the rotunda of the capitol was a space that sweetened every voice. Under its dome, a crow would have sounded musical. Most Monday nights during the session, between dinner and the drinking hours, some of the members of the house and senate gathered there to sing the old sentimental songs. One night, a young house member, a rich dandy from down at the coast with a splendid affected voice, sang one of the sad songs from the *Winterreise*. Then later, over pints at the Sir Walter Tavern, he translated that particular song and summarized the others to me. The songs were chapters in a story about a wanderer grieving for his failure at love, and in one song he writes the name of his beloved on the ice of a frozen creek. I was proud to announce to the table that I had performed the same futile gesture years ago and had agonized for much of a year over thoughts of the creek melting, the water that had shaped the six letters flowing away from me, passing from one watercourse to another all the way to the Mississippi and then down to the salt Gulf to mix with the oceans of the world. That's the way you think when you're that age. At least some do.

5

IT OCCURS TO ME THAT I MIGHT BE GIVING THE IMPRESSION THAT those years of my life after Claire were lived monkish. That I still waited for her, celibate as some pining heroine in a novel. That path never entered my mind, partly because I believed it futile, Featherstone being capable of living as long as Granny Squirrel. Year after year, I did not know whether Claire loved or hated me or, worse, did not think of me at all. Had Claire been fully mine since I won her as a boy, I would have lived a life of utter fidelity. No doubt in my mind whatsoever. Even the way it turned out, it is fair to say that I was, in a way, forever faithful to her. First point in evidence, I never married. And, two, I have never had a woman for very long. Neither point entirely of my own choice. Nor have I ever denied a woman. So I'll pause here to make a few brief comments in regard to love's ravaging histories during my middle years.

For many years I entertained the belief that I would meet someone, a woman who would be my woman in a deeper way even than Claire. A true wife. *The* woman. And I was not content to wait for fate to throw such a woman in my path. I would fling myself in hers. In Washington, I discovered again how the steep inclines of the galleries to the Senate chamber provided opportunities for meeting ladies of a certain kind.

Which is to say, high-minded and of a desirable class and nevertheless somewhat desperate for male companionship; otherwise, why would they inflict Senate speeches on themselves? And if I happened to be in a position to ask them to join me at an embassy party or a reception at the White House, all the better. None of them made a perfect fit, but many were good company for a while. I remember one fairly plain woman, twentyish, sitting with me on the lawn of the White House for an Independence Day picnic, her pale summer dress falling all around her like cake icing in the remnants of light from a long summer day. Fireworks spewed across the sky and lit her upturned face and she was suddenly beautiful. The spectators made spontaneous sounds of *ooh* and *ahh*. Toward the end of the show, balls of fire the size of moons fell to earth and killed two or three of the spectators, and we were both appalled and drawn closer to each other. The brevity of life, and so on. We were somewhat intimate on the ride back to her hotel in the shelter of my carriage. I remember her string of pearls broke, pearls spilling onto the seat and rolling across the carriage floor.

And there were certain other women scattered all along my usual routes of travel. One lovely woman lived in a little two-store town shoved right up against the base of a great humped mountain a day's ride north of the nearest railhead from Wayah. I loved her dearly. For several years, I made the long detour to see her on the way to and from political business in the Nation and Washington City. She was a schoolteacher and a spinster, and much taller than men commonly like their women to have grown. All she ever told me of her age was that she was on the down side of thirty. She had beautiful soft hair the color of a dove's breast and green eyes and creamy long legs that turned under into unfortunately long narrow feet, but she had a behind with curves to break your heart. At least, they broke mine. There were times I would ride a hundred miles out of the way for a night with her. She had spent the previous ten years tending her father, who had been blinded when she was a girl by the kick of a horse he was blanketing out in a paddock in an ice storm. So when I visited, it was fairly easy for us to carry on however we liked as long as we kept it real quiet. For a while, it was a close call whether she was the one woman or not. And I still don't know. I never had the chance to finish finding out. Her father died suddenly of a stroke, and soon afterward she began dying of consumption, and it was a lingering death with all the translucent beauty of the disease. And at the last all the brilliant blood.

At the opposite end of some scale to which I do not entirely subscribe were all the heart-gladdening whores at Welch's place. I lump them into one capacious category along with the Senate ladies. I would not have discriminated against them and would have taken any of them as a wife if my heart had told me to. But in its mysterious way, it didn't. One pretty aging whore among them, though, has stayed in my memory all the way to now because the first time I was with her she grabbed my ready member in her fist and said, Wherever I go after I die, I hope I never see another one of these bastards again for all eternity. That didn't portend well for the remainder of the evening. But she went to work and rode me as if her passion knew no bounds. Four times that night, according to my old ledger.

At one point well after the onset of middle age, I courted the very pretty young daughter of a fine family from the county seat. Her grandfather had been one of the town's founders just after the Revolution. When a treaty moved the boundary line between America and the old Nation a notch westward, he rushed in to grab the best newly available land and had thus become important. The pretty girl was half my age and fairly stern-tempered, but she was attracted to the romanticism of the Indians and the good she thought she might do among them. She and a grievous widow aunt came visiting Wayah to tour the area and see all my enterprises—the post, the smithy, the mill, the craft shops, the school and the church, the farm with its slaves and paid Indian workers, the wagon roads we had built. The day had about it the air of talking to bankers about taking out a loan of considerable scope. We rode three-across in the second seat of my best carriage, the grievous aunt sitting blackly in between. The aunt was about my age, give or take a few years, and I found that fact gloomy.

Everywhere we went, people came to the carriage and asked favors, complained about their neighbors, detailed conflicts entirely unrelated to me. They all expected me to adjudicate. The pretty girl said hardly anything. She looked off into the distance. About three in the afternoon after a long day of touring, the aunt said, So, Will, you're king here? I said, No, ma'am. No kings here. Not these days.

That pretty girl and I went far enough in the direction of apparent matrimony that the principal newspaper in the capital ran a piece of gossip stating that the rumored nuptials of the senator, a man of fairly full years, and the beautiful young Miss Amor should give hope to old bachelors everywhere.

Then, very suddenly, she married a young army lieutenant. In considerable haste, I should add. The timing such that later the arrival of their first child might fall within an agreed-upon span—a sort of social grace period—wherein the birth would have to be accepted as at least possibly horribly premature. All I got out of it was a tearstained letter.

And all along the way were brief mountain resort passions. Summer flings. Over the years the women I attracted were transformed from bored nearly grown daughters still accompanying their parents into youngish spinster aunts. And then into faded widows and pale unhappy wives and the occasional desperate nanny.

In the last category I was once forced by overwhelming desire to make my way, long past midnight, onto the servants' floor up under the eaves of the Warm Springs Hotel for an assignation with the beautiful, sad-eyed keeper of three miserable outsized blank-faced children, the get of a plantation owner from near Cheraw. I was powerfully drawn to her for the loveliness of her thin mouth and because, when I first saw her on the lawn near the river, she was carrying a copy of *Werther* even though she had no opportunity to read it, her attention being occupied with keeping the idiotic and bovine children from falling into the water and being carried away into Tennessee.

I flirted outrageously.

Then two nights later, thinking about how love will draw you to strange places, I paced cautiously down the narrow hallway under the eaves. It was black but for the brief globe of light my outheld candle threw onto the oiled floorboards and up the yellow walls. Door by door, I traced the diminishing painted numbers. At twenty-three, I pecked a knuckle, and she opened her door into a room scarcely as long as the bed and only wide enough to allow three feet of open floor for dressing. The bed was a two-tiered bunk like a railway berth with dingy linen curtains ringed to slide on rods.

There was a roommate. When I climbed onto the top bunk and flopped onto the thin mattress beside my nanny, a giggle rose from below.

—I don't think I can do this, I whispered. Come down to my room.

But she would not. No matter how I pled.

It was a declaration of identity. If I wanted her, I had to accept her for who she was, with all the lack of privacy her world afforded. I buckled down and did the best I could, as silently as I could. She gripped me hard in her arms and legs like I was all the life left offered to her, gripped me with more strength than I could have imagined in those slender limbs. The next day, my torso ached. At the breakfast table, I secretly probed my rib cage but found no positive evidence of fissures.

I made that dark and blissful pilgrimage many times throughout a wet stormy August. And then without warning she and her employers were gone on the long journey back down into the hotlands. I stood on the gallery and watched them roll away in a carriage, followed by a wagon heaped with their trunks and bags. She would not look my way. The children roiled mindlessly about her on the rear seat.

For all the months of autumn and on into winter, I wrote her fervid letters and imagined rescuing her from her life and marrying her. Even now, I do not doubt that with the least encouragement I would have done it. Committed marriage.

I sent her packages of books, perfume, silk scarves, silver bracelets. Shameless expressions of desire. By Christmas, however, when she had failed to write back even once, I finally conceded defeat.

I kept a wooden box of mementos, my museum of failed love. A pearl from a broken strand. A handkerchief spotted with blood. A dollar bill of antique currency. A letter, its blue ink smeared in three places across cream paper. An octavo edition of *Werther.*

I NEEDED HELP. My life was in disarray. I had been trying to do everything, run everything. Keep all the books for the tannery and wagonwright and shoemaking shop, the smithy and all the stores scattered across four counties. On top of my political duties in the senate.

And, I admit, certain elements of the business had been left unattended. For example, my ledgers often served double duty as personal journals. And sometimes attention to the latter superseded the former. I loved those blank books. Their physical characteristics. The texture of their paper, the regularity of the black parallel lines across their pages. I had been buying those elegant leather-bound volumes from a bookmaker in Washington for many years. They were sized perfectly to fit my saddlebags, since I mostly lived mounted and moving. I was a fairly meticulous record keeper, though indiscriminate. On any specimen page you might find a great variety of mismatched entries, any kind of thing that had struck my mind on the day in question. A hand-drawn table of debts owed and debts collected. Amounts taken in and paid out in various of the businesses. Land sales and purchases. Lists of creditors and debtors. And then all mixed in would be observations on the appearance of the moon or the way fog had risen from a cove of the mountains, or wry observations concerning the behavior or the attire of other lawyers in court. And then, in code, a notation on what woman I had briefly fallen in love with at some roadhouse.

Tallent studied page after page. I could see in his face he thought it all a mess.

He said, If you want to expand my duties even further, I can fix this, but some things have to change.

—How so? I said.

—This sort of thing, he said, flipping to a page and studying it and then reading aloud:

My birthday. 40 years old. Celebrated without a cake. Total eclipse of the Ripe Corn Moon. Rode 18 m. to Welch's, partially in the dark. F-k-d H.D. 2 t.

—Yes? I said. A problem?

—I mean, who do you think would find that last notation impenetrable? Or at all useful?

So I gave Tallent a free hand to put things in order.

He said, Thank you, and expressed the heartfelt opinion that a proper accounting of business dealings should mainly concern itself largely with money and expressly not include a record of moon phases and poontang.

—That would be a fair enough start, I said. So I take it that I should keep two journals rather than just the one.

BEAR DIED IN the Planting Moon, during the waxing of it. Nothing dramatic precipitated his passing. No clash with Nature or sudden revelatory conflict against his fellowman. He was just old and worn out. We piled quilts and pelts around him in the townhouse and kept the fire built high, for he was chilled the entire time.

Bear had always been very good with people about to die. He held their hands, looked them in the face, and did not lie to them. He'd say, You're in bad shape. Awful bad shape. Not doing a bit good, are you? And it comforted them. They looked at him like he was the only one who knew even a little what they were going through. I, on the other hand, was useless at those times. I stood with my hands in my pockets and had almost nothing to say for fear that I would make some faint acknowledgment of the shadow of death glooming the room. Like we all might otherwise be exempt from it if none of us said any one of its horrible names.

During those final days, Bear didn't say much, but he often held his hands up to the firelight and studied them, their fronts and their backs, turning them, spreading the fingers and clenching knotty fists. At the time, I wondered what he was thinking. Did he wish to grab something? A knife handle or rifle grip or a soft breast? Maybe a gesture expressing one last wish of possession. Something to hold.

I don't wonder at all these days. I know he was looking at the swollen knuckle joints, the veins thick as night crawlers under the creped skin of his handbacks, fingernails broad and luminous as the insides of mussel shells, the polished skin of his palms marked deep with intersecting lines like the rivers and roads and boundaries of a map to an unknown territory. Bear was thinking that, taken all together, his hands looked exactly like the hands of his father.

Now, I hold my hands up to the electric bulb and think those same things. The bright new light, unknown to all past history, is not flattering. Not flattering at all. It glares grim. The pupils of one's eyes clench in the face of it. The future will not favor the old. We need shadows. Candlelight, moonbeams, embers.

Oddly, in the days after Bear's death, the hard-hearted women of Sara's family mourned him as a great man and beloved husband. They all wept bitterly and with no irony whatsoever. Even old Grandmother Maw said over and over, tears running down the deep channels of her face, that Bear was about the best man she had ever known in her entire long life. Excepting, of course, the incomparable Hanging Maw, who had lived in a different world before white men had become so overwhelmingly dominant, and in that younger world it might have been somewhat easier to achieve eminence. All the women of the several generations cried and cried, and I believe to this day that every tear was genuine.

It has been stated more than once in print that Bear's body was buried in a secret location. Not true. The grave simply no longer exists. Bear had chosen a shelf of land down by the river as his gravesite. I helped stack smooth stones over the blanket-wrapped body. The grave stood for only a few years, and then spring floods broke it apart and scoured the shelf of land bare. The stones were all scattered and his bones washed away. So now he is gone entirely from the physical world he loved so powerfully.

I'll go no further with this topic. Grief is not a thing that can be convincingly shared with an audience. Our worst pain is confined within our own skin. I'll only say this in conclusion. A time of earth died with Bear, and I hope he found peace and Wild Hemp in the Nightland.

NOT LONG AFTER Bear died, the U.S. Government became suddenly urgent and imperative in its ongoing attempts to convince our remnant of the Cherokee to remove west and join their brethren on the bleak Indian Territories and be done with us for good, and the time seemed opportune. I was not at all sure things could be held together without Bear, but I determined to give it a go, for I was all the chief we had now.

A representative named Hindman was sent down to travel from community to community, any place with a townhouse, and hold meetings to convince the people to sell out and leave. Hindman, of course, couldn't understand yea or nay in the language, nor did he trust me one inch to translate, so he required a neutral linkster. I don't even pretend to remember how I arranged it or what foolishness I committed to make it so, but the Government was persuaded to hire Tallent as adjudicator of languages between Hindman and the people and myself. Never mind that Tallent had been an employee and friend for many years, and that despite his long residence among the Indians, several among their many verb tenses remained an impenetrable mystery to him. To be fair, the language divides time into confusingly fine fractions and conditions and qualifications. In the official paperwork, Tallent was listed as a prominent mixed-blood freeholder, though every drop of blood in him, to my knowledge, was Scot, and he even knew what plaid his clan had worn into battle.

To begin our journey with Hindman, we met after morning coffee on the main street of the raw new town to the west of Valley River. It was the first day of a bitter December, and us setting out to slog crusty trails all day and some nights pitching camp in blowing snow or freezing rain. I shook hands with Hindman from horseback, neither of us wanting to be the first to dismount in honor of the other. He was a

Philadelphia lawyer, and he looked it, and that's all I need to say by way of description. We made mild observations about the conditions of the roads and the weather. The hooves of our mounts sucked in and out of the mud as they shifted around. Hindman made a great show of laying down his orders to Tallent not to add or take away anything in his translations, one way or the other. And Tallent swore that he wouldn't. He put his hand to his heart.

I'm afraid I might have muttered some phrase along the lines of *Great God* or *Shit fire* in a somewhat louder voice than intended.

So right from the start of the trip, things did not go well, nor had I expected them to. Long before we first caught sight of each other and traveled together and made offers in the wilderness to kill each other, Hindman and I had nurtured a blood hate just from our correspondence. We had been dueling with lawyer letters for better than a year. Of course that was a major part of the trouble, our being two lawyers. Lawyers have got to fight somebody. It's their nature. And I claim no personal exemption.

We rode out of town, following the river up the valley, heading for the first council meeting at the Long Hair community. Riding past fallow fields with nothing but dull green clumps of cresses growing in old furrows to offer any color besides the brown and grey of dirt and fodderstooks. The trees on the mountains to either side were stripped down to the bones of their trunks and limbs. Valley River, needless to say, was a landscape fraught with memory for me, and I was both rhapsodic and morose.

I rode sort of sulking, saying nothing, spaced to the rear of our little column. Hindman chattered on, talking to Tallent about the remoteness of the place and the backwardness of its thinly scattered people until he made it clear that he feared he had fetched up at the world's nethermost quarter. When we were about halfway to the Valley River settlement and had not yet crossed into my land, Cranshaw came into sight through the trees, not a ruin but in steep decline, as if it were beginning to strike the eye as a blur—all the edges of the bricks, the white paint of window sashes fading away.

Hindman paused in his nattering and turned and raised his voice to the grating pitch of most Yankees and asked me if I was sad that I didn't own all the land within our sight in addition to the boundary we would cross a few hours hence in our journey.

I didn't say a word back to him. I sat inside myself and waited.

He suspected I was a larcenist, and land was at the heart of his suspicion. He'd gotten a few people in Washington believing the same. It was clear he would like nothing better than to come up with charges against me that would stick. Me behind bars was his most arousing dream. Poor man, to lack more stirring imagination. But if I was poaching on the Indians, he certainly couldn't figure how, and it frustrated him. So why let him interrupt my memories? Out in the river, breaking its black flow, I could see a big flat rock where Claire and I had once waded waist-deep and sat face-to-face cross-legged in the humid aftermath of a July thunderstorm eating red pepper jelly on water crackers with a good white Italian wine from Featherstone's cellar. The wine's maker I fail to recollect, though if I quit chasing after it maybe it will come back to me. But I do remember that we touched each other fairly personally and discussed the weaknesses of Byron's rhyming in certain stanzas of *Don Juan*.

But Hindman had little patience for my silence. A few slogs of horse hoof in road mud, and he couldn't help but start yapping again. He said, I understand that people in this part of the world have gotten used to talking about your holdings in square miles instead of acres. And even so, the total number is staggering.

—It's all the same, whether you measure in miles or acres or by the square rod. Arpents would be my preference.

—Arpents? he said.

I rode on and waited. I sang an old song inside my head.

In a minute he said once again, Arpents?

—It's a unit of measure, I said. French in origin.

—French, he said. There was a critical tone to his voice.

—Is it just the amount you object to? I said. The fact that I own a certain broad swath of country?

—It's the methods used to obtain it.

—Paid for out of my own pocket, most of it. And the rest owned by Bear's people.

—That old troublemaker, he said. You and your chief have kept yourselves busy for years obstructing the good of the country and accumulating vast tracts of this mountainous land. And building your little empire atop a flimsy web of debt. It's my understanding a great many people hold paper against you.

—No law forbidding that. I respect it enormously. Any country would fall to scobs and flinders without paper. That's all a nation is. Paper. Otherwise it's all just land in general left to its own devices.

We went on arguing at each other that way for several miles. And things became more personal the farther we went along.

At some point, loud enough that he couldn't help but make it out, I might have responded to one of Hindman's opinions by saying that he could kiss my ass.

Hindman pulled up crossways in the road. He said, I understand you may think you have cause to resent my presence here, but if we are to travel together through this backward wilderness we might at least be civil to each other.

I looked around. Took my time about it. In the near distance, I saw cultivated fields, cabins with smoke rising from mud-and-stick chimneys. Cows and sheep and goats. A man walking by the river with a broadaxe balanced on his shoulder. It seemed like settled farmland to me. Green and plotted and platted. But the view from Philadelphia somehow made it into a raw wilderness as screaming as any Smith or Winthrop encountered in the early days of Virginia or Massachusetts.

—Wilderness? I said.

—In that it is little but a nursery of savage habits and operates retrograde to civilization, which is much impeded by your holding such immense tracts of it.

I'd had all I could take and could no longer sit within myself. A flaw of character without doubt. I said that I guessed he must like things much better up in the civilized parts of the country, where they can take their mudsill factory workers—some of them still salty from the boat ride over and jabbering a language of no use here whatsoever, people as ignorant as if they had just emerged stunned and blinking from the twelfth century—and proceed to work them to death in factories as dim and violent as the mines of Bolivia. And the children too, almost down to the cradle. As soon as they can walk and take orders, they're put to the wheel. And that's the mighty and benevolent and praiseworthy force of free labor and capital, which is about all civilization boils down to for people like him. And opinions such as his are not even paper but just words falling from his mouth like horse manure. And with less value, for you can't even fertilize your garden with them.

Hindman said, I'll not suffer to be told what this country is or is not by little more than a thief.

I rode slowly right up to Hindman, keeping on coming way past any normal talking distance, closing until I was so near to him that our stirrup irons clashed against each other and the cook kettle hanging behind my saddle rubbed soot on the near haunch of his pale grey gelding.

We locked eyes with each other. Neither of us would give way, and the horses were confused and danced where they stood and snorted smoke from their nostrils into the cold air. There was a great deal of sawing at the reins on both our parts to try to keep them in place and not give way. The horses slowly wheeled together in the road, flank to flank, as if spoked to some hub only horses recognize and grant allegiance.

The whole time, Hindman and I did not let up glaring. He was all red-faced and smirking. It was the sort of situation that so often turns to gunplay.

Tallent had been hanging back but suddenly came riding closer. He said, How about us all just slowing down here.

But even as Tallent was talking, I was reaching under my coat with my right hand to draw something out, a quick motion. And Hindman was already flinching to take a bullet.

But what I pulled out was a leather cigar case and I offered it out to Hindman and said, Smoke? My voice all mild and companionable.

Hindman took a moment's pause during which he remembered to breathe.

He said, Hardly, you son of a bitch.

Duelists have paced off their brief distances and leveled pistols at each other's hearts for a great deal less outrage to honor than Hindman's comment.

But as a former duelist, one who knows the gravity of bloodshed, I shouldered the responsibility of circumspection. I looked around to Tallent and said, There's civility for you. That's the way they do up where he's from. But you can't hold it against them. They're bred to it and don't know any better. I wouldn't walk across the road to piss on such a man if he was lit afire.

I reined my horse aside and just barely touched him with the spurs. With little transition he leaped forward and went from a dead stop to a gallop. Hindman sat fuming and watching me disappear up the road at a high rate of speed, clots of mud flying back from the hooves of my mount.

Tallent figured his job charged him with staying alongside Hindman, so he did. And all the way over the ridge to the settlement, Hindman pumped him for useful information against me. They rode at the slow rate of conspirators. By the time they crossed the ridge to the townhouse it was coming on dark, and I had been there for more than two hours. And I had not been idle for any of that time.

The people had become all agitated. The Long Hairs were a stubborn and contrary bunch all on their own without my help. Not even hard-shell Welsh Baptist missionaries had been able to civilize them very much. Their head man was named John Owl, and he was all dressed out in turban and whiteman britches and coat, and it must have been clear from Owl's very posture that we were thick as thieves. So Hindman didn't have a chance from the start.

When the meeting began, the townhouse was full of people and all hot and smoky with a great fire built up high with hickory logs, and it was all the light there was, but that was aplenty. The place smelled like bear grease and woodsmoke. Hindman got up and stood near the fire and talked, circling about so that he could look at the people ringing the room on the wall benches. He talked slowly, in a careful booming courtroom voice, pausing at artful intervals to let Tallent catch up with him. And Tallent did his best to link Hindman's words into Cherokee. It was a meticulously accurate job of translation, with no slant or opinion added in my favor, so I worried that Tallent might be taking his silly hand-to-heart oath seriously.

Hindman made a fine lengthy argument, laying out all the many points in favor of everybody picking up and moving west and forsaking hearth and home and everything that's yours and familiar in favor of a life you can't even imagine. He said how the new Nation was underlain by fertile dark soil so loose you could harrow it with a currycomb. And none of these inconvenient mountains to contend with, just pleasant hills. He went on and said the Nation had extra-good weather, unlike this place that is a steaming jungle in summer and mud and slush in winter, as now on this particular day of the moon. A nice dry climate out there, but not too dry. And the main thing offered by moving west was to be with their own people, not surrounded by those who wish them ill as here. And the hunting out there was still good and not all killed out. And also schools and churches and courts and that sort of thing. Order prevailed out west. They had their own lawmen on the new Nation. And every head of a household would get from the Government $53.33 in expenses for the journey. What land they gave up here would be made up for, many times over, at the other end. That was the rule of America. Effort would find its just compensation.

He went on and on, but the people were not saying a word or making any expression on their faces. And everybody kept looking to where John Owl and I sat whispering to each other all through the talk. Hindman concluded by saying a great many respectful things about his confidence in the people and their head man, praising their wisdom and Owl's strong leadership.

Then he said it was only fair that I have a turn to talk before they came to a decision. Saying it in a tone of voice like it was only his generosity that was allowing me to have the floor at all. He went and stood near the door, and Tallent sidled over and stood beside him to tell him what I might say. *Traitorous* was the word in my head as I watched them murmuring back and forth.

I hadn't planned a thing in the way of argument. Bad luck to do so. And it was the same way in court. If I wrote it all out, I'd get nervous. Just talking in the spur of the moment was better. And I remembered to use Bear's lesson about how to use light and quiet.

I didn't even rise from the shadowed bench where I sat. I leaned forward into the firelight with my forearms resting on my thightops and my fingertips all touching in a shape like a cage of bones. Feeling in my face and hands the warmth from the fire, and knowing those were all the parts of me visible to the people arrayed in the shadows around the room. I couldn't see much of them at all, but I pretended I could. I looked into the bright fire and the darkness and talked in a low voice so everyone had to pay attention to hear.

In good plain Cherokee I said, Now, I reckon people can make up their own minds without another windy speech. All I've ever wanted was for our people to have as free a choice about where's home as anybody else in this world. Live where you want to live. Stay or go.

I leaned back into the dark as signal that I was done. My hands and face went black.

Then it was Owl's turn. And he had a different sense of show. He rose and stood near the fire and put on a face of deep study. Brooding deep and painfully. He paced about and let everybody look at him struggle with his thoughts a long time before he said his say.

Finally, with great effort, he said this. I don't know any place but here. Neither do you. Any man wants to go somewhere else, walk through that door and keep walking. Don't look back.

There was considerable stir and mutter from the crowd. But nobody got up and walked out.

After a minute, Owl said to Hindman, Looks like we'll stay. Said it in English.

The people attending the council were all too polite to stare at Hindman in order to gauge his reaction. But I looked straight at him, and he was flaring mad.

He came stalking my way and loomed over me. Tallent followed right at his heels.

Hindman said, I won't ever let you ride out ahead of me again. And I want a vote. Every one of these fools needs to be forced individually to own the damned idiot choice he's making.

Word for word, Tallent rendered that speech exquisitely into Cherokee for the room at large, getting every noun and verb perfect. Nothing added and nothing taken away. And then suddenly everybody was looking at Hindman.

But Hindman was looking at Tallent. You ass, he said. That was private conversation.

I was looking at Tallent too. But I was grinning ear to ear.

I turned to Owl and said, Hellfire, vote 'em if they care to vote.

All the nights following, things went roughly the same. Settlement to settlement, anyplace with a meetinghouse. I won and Hindman lost. He gradually became downcast. You could see he was not used to losing. Especially to some wilderness lawyer who couldn't be agent to anybody but penniless Indians.

Journeys all eventually reach a conclusion, the bad and the sublime both. The day we rode to the final battle in Wayah was chillier than anything before. We went up and over a high ridge, and there was blowing ice on the wind and old grey snow crusted deep in the trail. Hindman and I spoke little to each other, and Tallent seemed relieved by the silence. We all rode shrouded in blankets. The day was coming up on the briefest of the year, and we had set out late and had made bad time, having to break trail through snow. The long and short of it was, we had to sleep the night on the cold mountaintop. We made fire and strung canvas in the dark. Supper was a mush of bacon grease and corn grits. Tallent spooned it out vaporous into our tin bowls. And then we crawled under all the coats and blankets and saddle pads we had among us and went to sleep under a depressingly starless sky.

I woke up the next morning with the fire dead and the tarpaulin glazed over with frost and the horses shivering with nuggets of ice hanging in their manes and tails. Hindman was up right beside me, spooned close. We two enemies lay like wedded mates in a bride bed until Tallent struck a good blaze and got coffee seething, and then we rolled out of the covers with our hair standing in points and sat cross-legged, grim as death, on our blankets, and supped from the steaming tin mugs that Tallent carried to us. Nobody looked at anybody else. Nothing rougher-looking than middle-aged men at dawn.

From that point our business was over quickly. The Wayah council went just like the others. After the entire Snow Moon of travel together, all the people Hindman had convinced to go west amounted to ten griping malcontents and a half dozen deer hunters hoping for richer game lands, a new place where the elk and buffalo hadn't all been killed out when their granddaddies were young. That was it. Fewer than two dozen converts after all his hard preaching. Tallent and I rode home, touched with the belief that Bear would have favored our actions that month.

6

I HAVE LITTLE TO SAY ABOUT MY ROLE IN THE WAR. AS A SUBJECT, the entire period bores me senseless. My tolerance for stupidity is at low ebb, especially when the stupidity's my own. Of course at the time, right after Sumter, I was wildly enthusiastic for armed conflict in the way only politicians can be. And of course I misjudged the degree of rancor between North and South and reckoned in '62 that the Union splitting in twain would be no more bloody than when the Methodists did it in '44.

On the floor of the senate in the days after the bombardment, I promised that we mountaineers and Indians would fight the final epic battles of the War at our guarded passes and mountain fastnesses. I somewhat shouted out that proclamation, as I recall.

Foolish, yes. But eloquent.

As the war years passed, however, I became more and more sad when I thought about cranking out that old rhetoric, for it came to pass that I was prescient in knowing that I would indeed fight the War's last losing battle. Neither bloody nor grand, however, but doomed. An anticlimactic end-time resistance in the clouds.

I celebrated the start of the War by raising new facial hair, a drooping mustache and the dashing little triangular tuft of whisker that some cavalrymen grew beneath their lower lips, called an Imperial in honor of a recent feckless French emperor. Mine, though, grew in mixed with grey, for I was no longer young.

There are enough old men claiming to be colonels around the South these days to make you think the Confederate Army had only one rank other than general. Every little crossroad town has two or three of them sitting on a bench, whittling and spitting and swapping pocketknives. Some county seats have as high as a dozen. But I was indeed a genuine colonel, though nobody would ever have called me a soldier. I had no training or experience and, prior to '62, had never served a day in uniform or fired a musket very often, not even for purposes of hunting. My venison tenderloins and bear haunches were provided for me by the Indians as trade. However, I was not completely lacking in expertise with weaponry. I've discussed my proficiency with dueling pistols. And also I could—and still can, if called upon to do so—handle a shotgun with astonishing accuracy and enthusiasm. I am a somewhat legendary wing shot against quail and pheasant, not so much for the sport as for the braising or roasting that follows. The only real suggestion of military training I ever displayed was an ability to open a champagne bottle in the style of Napoleon, with one dramatic spewing stroke of a saber blade.

But in those days, anyone volunteering to finance a legion out of his own pocket was welcome to name his own rank and all of those below him. So I became an immediate colonel, and I needed officers beneath me. Since Tallent was my head bookkeeper and chief assistant and old friend, he suddenly became a major. For lieutenants, we recruited the best of the boys working in the various enterprises. In truth, we were a legion of lawyers and bookkeepers and shop clerks. About all the difference the War made in their duties toward me was that on rare occasions, when we couldn't avoid it, Yankees shot at us.

And we were a legion, not a regiment, mind you. I have always been quick to correct anyone who got it wrong. Legion, I say, a full by-God legion.

I first called us the Drowning Bear Zouaves, for I wanted to lead the most extravagantly exotic bunch of soldiers in the whole Army. It ought to have been enough that we were mostly Indians, with just a smattering of Highlanders. And that a few among us even went armed with spears. But for some reason I wanted us dressed out in the ridiculous Zouave costume to boot. All I can say is, it was a different time, different fashions, and I was not alone in my momentary enthusiasm for baggy gauze pantaloons and tasseled fezzes. There were a number of Zouave regiments, though only in those first months of conflict when much of the country, both halves, acted as foolishly as drunks in the moment before a bar fight. Luckily, several among us, Tallent included, didn't care to wear outfits that they thought made them look like harem girls, and they went so far as to threaten insurrection if I ordered them to do so.

Remember, I was already into the middle years. The time of life when several of your parts start hurting that never did before, and I'm not just referring to various joints and knuckles. Of course, old is relative. I'd trade everything I have right now to be in that youthful shape again. But I believe the only reason I spent those four years living rough and bivouacking in the woods and riding horseback from place to place in heat and cold, rain and shine, was to keep Bear's people from being scattered into regiments where I could not dictate their treatment and where I could not work to keep them out of the fighting, to keep them from coming to any harm I could stand in the way of.

Inconveniently, though, many of the Indians were ripe for battle and could not be argued out of enlisting. They saw the War as a rare opportunity to collect on old debts against the Government, felonies and misdemeanors stretching back to General Rutherford's fire-and-blood trek through the mountains in the previous century and, beyond that, all the way to when murderous Spaniards wore metal hats with crests like a cock's comb.

All I could do was ensure that we spent as much of our time as possible staying out of the Yankees' way. My idea of how to conduct war was to lead my legion off into the mountains and wrap ourselves in the deepest wilderness, where we could not even ride our horses but had to walk them by their reins, scrambling up rocky paths and black-dirt game trails. Guarding the passes for the end-time battles.

The summer of '63 we spent in profound isolation high on a mountain. I dispatched letters to Richmond declaring that we were immersed in the job of digging out saltpeter for gunpowder from a great overhanging rock cliff that Bear had discovered as a young boy in the previous century. No one could deny our new nation needed gunpowder. What we dug, though, was pitiful. You could not have powdered an artillery piece for one battle with what we took out that summer.

But we saw not a soul other than ourselves for all that time, and we had a fine dry camp sheltered by the high ledge, which the Indians called a cave. Many among us spent a great deal of time hunting, and we ate pretty well on mostly wild hogs and a deer or turkey now and then, and we stayed up late, smoking and watching the fire and reading, for I always had a satchel of books with me—Arthur tales, *The Odyssey*, *The Aeneid*. I would read aloud to the Indians, translating on the fly, and they enjoyed those old tales immensely and would repay the favor with tales of their own, stories of little magic moon-eyed people that secretly share the world with us, and monsters that live in water or in the sky or under the ground, also the visible real animals and their intelligences only slightly different from ours. I had heard nearly all the stories a thousand times from Bear in the winterhouse, but I still loved them and believed you could always be enriched by them every time they came around. The days and nights went like that, on and on. A little work, some hunting, a great deal of lounging by the fire and telling tales and cooking. We ran out of liquor pretty soon, and it was the kind of place and time where that did not matter at all. I liked being settled for those months at the cave and was peaceful and content because, as a younger man, I had often gone years without sleeping in the same bed for more than a few nights in a row. All in all, that summer was about as pleasant as war can be. Or life in general, without any further qualification. In that cool green elevated world, it was rather hard to tell that it was fighting season in Virginia.

Not long after that happy interlude, though, I began to feel that something had gone a little off with my nerves. People began to think of me as prone to occasional disorder. And I guess I was. I know I was turbulent in my thoughts, my mind beginning to darken. Anger shadowed me during those war years. I fastened onto ideas and could not let go. I developed, for example, deep and persistent notions on the rendering of soldiers' clothing proof against moisture, thereby promoting cleanliness and reducing chills of the body, thus preventing the spread of infectious diseases. I made a pest of myself writing letters to Davis and Lee on the matter. In demonstration of my proposals, I often wore an entire suit of clothes treated with a concoction of beeswax and a thick piney herbal mash so that I rode bone dry in a squall, but my clothes hung stiff on my frame and I crackled when I walked and smelled at all times like an old moldered tent pitched in the forest. Imagine an entire army marching in such attire. And yet, I must add, more of our men died of disease than from Yankee steel and shot. So draw your own conclusions as to my delusion.

I'll admit I sometimes let anger take me toward improvidence. In one action we could not avoid, the son of a great warrior from back in the days of the Red Stick Wars was killed by the Yankees. It was a stupid skirmish I should never have let happen. We were assigned to guard a bridge. No one had attempted to cross it for days, so we got up a ball game. And then damned if the Yankees didn't come along right in the middle of play, taking us at a disadvantage. We ended up winning the skirmish, but there were several casualties, including the great warrior's son. In the final moments of fighting, the Indians took revenge by scalping Yankees both living and dead. Two days later, my younger officers were appalled when a journalist came around sniffing after a sensational story. Tallent and his lieutenants despaired at what might appear in every Yankee paper, in screaming great type at the head of the front page. REBEL INDIANS SCALP SAINTED UNION DEAD. SAVAGE CONFEDERATES MUTILATE BODIES OF SACRED FALLEN MILLWORKERS.

Tallent and the boys came to me as a group to discuss what to do. I insisted on talking to the journalist myself, being the only one among us with relevant experience dealing with their kind. The writer was a little plump-faced man in a baggy brown suit. Bulging coat pockets, ink-stained fingertips. It took all of a minute for me to realize he was too sharp to mislead for long. All I remember saying to him was, Here's your lead: Yankees scalped! They had it coming.

Because of those instances and a dozen more, my behavior did not sit well with the powerful in Richmond. I was eventually thought unsound of mind by most of those above me. I was court-martialed a time or two on charges of little merit, which came to nothing more than a great deal of correspondence and residual bitterness.

Needless to say, beset all around as I was, I valued any loyalty and affection I could get. So I took great joy at the eventual outcome after five of the Cherokee were captured in a skirmish and taken out of the state and held prisoner for weeks. The Yankee officers offered them a deal of great ridiculousness that displayed nothing but contempt for them and their native ignorance. They were told they would be set free and given an impossible five thousand gold dollars if they returned with the scalp of their murderous scalping colonel. The captive men made a show of conferring and talking among themselves very solemnly and deliberatively in their language. And then they took the deal, promising to return with my raw scalp by the Ripe Corn Moon. They crossed the high peaks at a jog trot, laughing all the way. And five days later we were sitting around my campfire in a hilarious mood due to the deep gullibility of the northerners, who thought money was the world's only driving wheel. I remember our celebration involved a certain amount of whiskey and tale-telling and me cooking a boar loin over hickory coals with juniper berries and a Tuscan wine for flavoring. It was, all in all, a rather fine night of warfare.

We had our last engagement with the Yankees several weeks past Appomattox, and the majority of historians certify we took the last fatality of the War, which is why I say my early wild pronouncements about the final battles being fought in our mountains were, in a greatly diminished way, absolutely true.

The Yankees had come over the ridge from Tennessee and occupied a little town set down in a river valley amid high mountains. It was the town where many of my earliest courtroom battles as a green lawyer took place, so it meant something to me to come back leading what was left of my legion.

We got onto the ridges above town where we could watch the Yankees through a glass, and I'm afraid I grew more and more agitated and intemperate as the day went on. I swore to kill them all or be killed by them rather than let them swagger about our town. But I didn't have much force to back my anger. By various powers of attrition, we were drawn down to a group that would hardly have made a regiment, much less a legion—but nevertheless notorious and feared, mainly due to that colorful scalping incident. About all we had left for strategy was to pick at the Yankees with little fights along their flanks. We lost one man, and several others took wounds. After a few days of that sort of thing, I scattered the Indians along the ridges and told them to light fires after dark all across the mountains surrounding the town. They were to whoop and sing and dance so as to appear numerous. Some of them had skin drums, and a couple of Scots Highlanders had pipes and fiddles. Come nightfall, they poured war music into the valley all the way to first light.

I waited until about dinnertime, and then I sent a tall hook-beaked Indian, one of the last full-bloods, into town. I coached him to deliver a curt phonetic message: Now! Colonel Will says this. We are all around you. Surrender, please. Or else die with your bloody scalps decorating our pommels.

Sadly, the Yankees did not surrender. They informed us instead, in a lengthy written message, of Lee's agreement at Appomattox Courthouse a month earlier. I had not heard of Lee's surrender, but I studied on the way things were for no more than a few seconds and then said to my officers, Well, gentlemen, if Lee's gone on home, I reckon we're done too. Four fucking years down a hole.

I first sent some men, Indians and Highlanders both, riding hard west toward Wayah with nearly all our horses, which the Federals surely would have taken for their own use, horses having become scarce since nearly as many had been killed in battle as men.

My surrender was a show, and the whole town turned out to watch. I came strolling down from the mountains accompanied by Tallent and my personal guards, the tallest Indians among us, all well better than six foot, even before you got to their hats and turbans. I had changed from my normal dress clothes into breechcloth, greasy buckskin leggings, and moccasins laced with woven strands of horsetail dyed red and blue and strung through eyelets cut from the quill ends of bird feathers. From the waist up, I went naked, nothing but beads and feathers tied in my hair, a leather thong around my neck with one curved black bear claw as pendant. And I had not been barbered for some time. We had been living rough. So my hair was longish and I had a growth of grey beard. I'd painted myself up all striped with ochre and lampblack in the old manner. A long rifle slung over my shoulder on a lanyard of plaited leather. After four years of woods living, I was lank; all the bones in my chest showed through the skin. Me—an attorney, a colonel, a chief, and a senator. An acquaintance of presidents. Coming into town like some icon of the olden days erupting into the baffled present.

And then, when we began negotiating surrender, the lawyer in me came blooming forth. I became quite rational despite my wild attire. I said that the Indians left with me were none of them soldiers but men in my private employ—bodyguards, as it were. And I insisted that as such, they were exempt from having to lay down their guns as Lee's ill-conceived surrender agreement required.

I think even I was surprised to prevail with that shabby argument. The Yankees scribbled on the paper to amend their surrender contract with a little marginal addendum, and I insisted that we all initial the change. Much dipping of nibs and blotting. But then when it came time for me to sign on the bottom line, I don't know what came over me. I became agitated and claimed again that there were hundreds more Indians on the ridges, cavalry too, and I was their chief and colonel. At my sign they would descend and scalp every man of them, and nothing but my whim kept it from being so. True, I said, men have survived scalping. But it's not an attractive way to end up. Your whole head heals to a red puckered scar. Ladies—at least the great majority of them—dislike the look of it quite a bit.

The Yankee colonel looked confused. He was smoking a little stub of cheroot that stunk like rabbit tobacco, and he examined the glowing tip of it for a long time, and then he cut his eyes to Major Tallent. Tallent gave one little vibratory head shake to the Yankee and then touched me very gently on my bare painted shoulder, dipped the steel pen nib in the inkpot, put the shaft between my fingers, and thumbed the dire paper an inch my way. I signed in the most formal and florid of my several styles of handwriting.

And then I looked at the Yankee colonel and said, If not for these Indians, I wouldn't have had a thing to do with this goddamn war.

Then, accompanied by my guard and trusty Tallent, I walked out without another word. All of us fully armed. Noble old Lee could have used a better lawyer.

·

DESPITE MY SMALL victory against the Yankees, Pyrrhic indeed, I now believe that leading the Indians into the War was the greatest of my failures, or at least prominent among many. The War was no business of the Indians. They ought to have stayed home. For that matter, we all should have stayed home. And this belated realization was darkly underlined when, within a matter of days, we were hit with a smallpox epidemic. It was widely believed that two of our returning warriors brought the disease into the community after a Yankee officer took them apart from the others and showed them a little glass bowl in which a strange red fish with sad bulging eyes swam slow circles in water cloudy from its own shit. Its entire remaining life was held within a circumference you could almost have compassed with your fingers and thumbs. A nasty world of unimaginable limitations. Find therein what symbolism you will. For me, bowl and fish represented the Yankee vision of life.

Immediately upon returning home, the two men who'd been exposed to the Yankees and doomed to witness the red fish fell desperately sick and broke out in blisters and died. And soon they were joined by more than a tenth of our people.

It was a dark time, the worst in my memory. The sickness came in waves, half a moon apart. The heralds were mouth sores, headaches, and vomiting, in that order. Then the eruptions. Pale skin of forearms rising up like plowed ground. Faces so swollen in welts people couldn't see out from under their eyelids. In the worst cases, the rash spread from head to toe, pustules overlapping one another in plates all down the body.

There wasn't anything to do about it. Nothing in the way of doctoring was available other than herbs. Some took a decoction made from milkweed. The leaves or roots, I forget which. It tasted terrible and was thought to be helpful only on the slim logic that the milk of the mature plant resembles pus. Some others swore by poke root on even shakier grounds. In the outer world, there had been various forms of inoculation against the disease, at least as far back as when old insane Cotton Mather was taught the trick by his slave Onesimus. But none of us had done it, there being a substantial risk of death in the process. Looking back, maybe I should have insisted upon it. But then, neither had Lincoln been inoculated, for he had come down with a mild case just the year before.

Whether you lived in Wayah or New York City, once you got it you either died or you scabbed over and got well. The survivors felt lucky to be scarred deep for life. White pockmarks sprayed across their faces, down breasts and backs. Scars more extensive than Bear's or Cudjo's silver claw marks, though considerably less interesting to tell about in old age.

I went from cabin to cabin visiting the sick, more useless than a preacher or an herb doctor. Dying people retching and insensible, sometimes two or three to a cabin. Young and old alike. All prostrate and pustuled and unable even to hobble into the river and immerse themselves in the cool brown water of late spring in hopes of life. Not life everlasting, but just a little bit more of it. And me with nothing to offer whatsoever on either the physical or spiritual front.

The healthy among us lived every day in numb fear of the first little blister rising on the roof of the mouth. During the waking hours, we went about constantly rubbing our tongues against our palates.

After three waves of sickness, the disease tapered off. Among the very last to go, Tallent.

He lay sick in his house. Fevered. His bedding damp and soured with sweat all the way through the sheets into the ticking. The rash red on his cheeks and arms. Sores overlapping and leaking. A vomit bucket handy. He came in and out of sense.

I sat in a chair by the bed and held his hand and wiped his face with a cool cloth. The sweaty hair at his temples was nearly as grey as mine. I said, Little brother, you're not doing a bit well, are you? Very poor indeed. Bad, bad.

I buried Tallent on a rise near a grove of chestnut trees. A good view down to the river. Those days, there were a lot of burials. We got to where there were no words left for the eulogies. We just shoveled dirt and walked home, thinking whatever we felt toward the dead inside ourselves. I won't go into it any further, other than to say that year by year the world darkens down and things are always going away.

7

After the war, nothing was ever the same. All of the South was a mess. The flow of money dried up. No money anywhere. Yankees trying to run everything and determined to beat us down in the peace at least as bad as in the fighting. No place left in politics for those of us who had been the big men less than a decade earlier, mainly because our conquerors had banned many of us from holding office at any level. I can't even imagine what songs Yankee carpetbaggers and scalawags sang under the sweetening dome of our old capitol. Not Schubert, I'd bet.

On the national level, the Government was corrupt right up to and including the old gutless white heads on the Supreme Court. But it was fair enough for the victors to take over entirely. We former big men should have been a lot better. We had failed utterly as leaders and deserved whatever beating we were required to take. And neither was the South the only target of the Yankees. Just look at what they did out west. Immediately after they finished with us, they aimed their armies toward the setting sun and fought Sioux and Cheyenne and Apache—too many peoples to list. For the next few decades, Yankees won and everybody else lost. It's hard to hold politicians with big armies back from fighting somebody.

But not all was devastation. The countryside was still beautiful, no matter what moon of the year it was. As soon as the vines overtook them, Sherman's many burnt-out white-columned plantation houses became as picturesque as Wordsworth's ruined abbey. So during that period of my life, the road offered a great comfort, for it was still open and free. Fine to be out roaming on a good horse, observing the change of seasons, the progressive bloom and wilt of flowers, and the phases of the moon all through the pale spring and aching deep green summer and into the melancholy yellow fall. Watching the seasons seemed particularly pressing now that the stack behind me rose higher than the ones ahead, even at my most optimistic reckoning of life span. Where better to be than on the road to test day by day the assertion that the hardest thing in life is to remain constantly attendant, especially since it gets harder to do the farther along you go?

For all those reasons—or excuses—I did not wish to be home much. Aside from cultivating what my friends ironically referred to as my rich inner life, part of my reasoning for living mostly in transit was that if I kept moving I was a more difficult target to hit by those looking to collect debts or serve papers or ask favors.

Needless to say, for long stretches of time, I did not take care of my duties with great mindfulness. I left the majority of work to my current generation of young clerks, under the direction of Conley, one of the legion's lieutenants. Conley, though, was no Tallent. The business that he and the boys could not handle without my presence was immense. When I returned home, the accumulated paperwork waiting for me was stacked waist-deep around my desk, shoulder-high against the walls. When I opened a desk drawer, the stuffed papers rose up to meet me. They spilled from chair seats like white water over river rocks and filled a vast number of old wooden claret crates until there was only a winding trail for passage from the doorway into the depths of my study. But I'm not blaming my boys for everything. Or even for anything. Right here I should digress to say that many of them went on to distinguished careers in law and business, and several served terms in the state legislature and the Congress, and that's as close to a father's pride as I'm allowed.

The problem was me. I failed to keep up with correspondence. Many checks went unwritten, and a few went uncashed, lost in the piles that accumulated around me. All those pale stacks of paper loomed like malignant spirits, grown taller and more powerful every time I drew up courage to go home and address myself to them. They haunted my place—the increasingly olden Jeffersonian octagon—so fiercely that I wanted to strike a match to it all and ride away with a pretty yellow light spewing upward at my back. Every day that I was in residence, I had to face a string of people expecting things from me—money and decisions, neither of which I enjoyed doling out.

During this time, I made a pointless trip up through the Cumberland Gap and beyond. I returned road-weary midafternoon on a beautiful late-summer day, intending to make a quick turnaround and go back out jaunting until at least the onset of November, maybe follow the New River up into Virginia. The grass in the front yard stood knee-deep, and the grey-painted porch boards were speckled with black mildew. Inside, the furniture was shrouded in white sheets. The facets of the cut-glass chandeliers hung dull with dust from their armatures by their little twists of corroded wire. Everything smelled of damp and must and old bitter ashes spilling from the fireplace.

Conley came hustling around, all concerned.

—Will, he said. We didn't know you were coming.

—Evidently.

—You mostly send word. We'd have had the furniture uncovered and the grass cut.

—I intended it to be cut regularly whether I'm away or not.

—Grows so fast, the help can't hardly keep on top of it.

—It's two shitting feet high.

—Been a real wet summer. Rain, rain, rain.

There was a sound of footsteps overhead in my bedroom. A door closed, and then the descending squeak of step treads. I walked into the foyer and looked down the hall. A nut-colored pretty girl came slipping downstairs, all sleepy-headed and rumpled. She smiled sort of ruefully our way and went on down the hall and out the back door.

Conley said, Excuse me for a minute.

He went running after her. I stood where I was and waited with unexpected patience.

When Conley returned, I said, How'd that come out for you?

He said, Sorry.

I said, Some of you need to scythe the yard and pull the covers off the furniture and sweep the floors and open the windows. And for God's sake, get somebody to change the sheets on my bed.

While everybody got busy, I took a bottle of claret and a book from the shelves and went up to the bench under the dogwood tree by Waverley and read until nearly dark.

The next morning, Conley awaited me when I came downstairs. He sat at the dining table with a notebook. Before I could even pour coffee, he began going down his list of things I needed to attend to. All my affairs fallen into indescribable disarray.

First, there was a fistful of notes long overdue for payment. Lawsuits pending. A pressing matter. The Beaver Creek land, the slopes on both sides up to the ridge, would cover the debt. A buyer had made an offer.

—Hold or sell? Conley asked.

—Hold.

Second, there was an epistolary feud needing to be calmed, for it had heated up nearly to the point of gunplay. The story was this: Since learning to write in English, Big Dirt and Dreadful Water had been engaged in an epic poison-pen tournament based on the reopening of an old grievance concerning the parsing of an elk carcass on a hunting trip back almost into the last century, when they were both young. The issue was whose musket ball struck the killing blow. Honor was at stake. They had traded many letters full of insults and allegations, even though their wives were great friends and relatives, both being members of the Bird Clan.

—Talk to the wives, I said.

But Conley already had. The little round women were no help whatsoever in calming the dispute, for they viewed the two men as irrelevant for all purposes beyond providing a sure source of amusement. Conley handed me the full sheaf of back-and-forth correspondence. I riffled through the pages, reading a phrase here and there. Literacy, a blessing or a curse? In the end, I pitched the letters into the fire and said, Tell Big Dirt and Dreadful Water that every path through the world but peace leads to eight kinds of loneliness.

—That's it?

—Yes. It's excellent advice. I wish I'd always followed it. Present it to them with conviction.

Number three. The church and school, having been built more than twenty-five years previous and virtually identical in design and materials except for the steeple, were falling apart at exactly the same rate. Should the failing shake roofs be replaced or just patched?

Answer: Patched.

And also, Conley said, the paint on the clapboards was peeling off both buildings in flakes as big as a man's hand. Repaint or let go au naturel?

Answer: The latter.

Four. I had been in charge of building and maintaining roads in that section of country for decades. Which one should the crew work on next?

—The worst one.

—That would be the wagon road north, Conley said. It keeps washing out in hard rains. Two different times recently, wagons with their oxen and drivers had tumbled into the ravine. It would be a very big job. Did I want to direct the road crew in the needed repairs or should he?

Answer: Change the designation from wagon road to bridle path. Alert the press.

On and on.

Conley reached the second dozen on his list, or somewhere thereabouts. The season having come round to the end of another summer, in anticipation of cold weather, our new preacher wanted to know how deep snow had to lie before he could call off services. And the schoolteacher wanted to know the same.

—We've not even reached the equinox.

Conley shrugged. They've been asking, he said.

I paid both men's salaries and provided room and board entirely out of my own pocket. My answer was, Two shitting feet high at the very least.

DUTIES AND RESPONSIBILITIES. I'd sit at my desk for hours drinking coffee and trying to reduce the stooks of paper that needed attending. Work all day until my buttocks clenched in spasms from inactivity. Look up from the desktop and refocus my eyes out into the room, and the piles had not diminished in the least. And when I went out among the people, some of them called me Will and some called me Colonel or Senator, and a few called me Chief, but only with a certain tilt of irony to their voices.

When they needed me, though, people still considered me the ultimate arbiter. I was the law. The high sheriff. Squire over white and Indian alike on my vast diminishing holdings and the adjoining remote unowned mountain land far from the nearest county seat. So people knocked on my door at all hours of the night to report crimes, and in those disrupted first years following the War there were a great many more than before, especially murders.

For example: come late spring, a bedraggled little circus had stopped in a nearby settlement of ten or fifteen families, a few brown cabins hunkered beside a stout stream. A patched tent was erected atop the ball field. And then that evening, a spectacular lamplit one-night show with a juggler and a slack-rope walker and a daringly clad girl who swung upside down on a trapeze with her hair hanging long in a point toward the ground. The main attraction was an old dim-eyed elephant with not too many years left in her but enough strength to sit on her hind legs on a big three-legged stool and use her trunk to hoist her trainer up to ride astraddle her neck and march two laps around the ring and sit back down and blow. On command, while making a sound like tooting a bugle, she could squirt water from her trunk out into the crowd and flap her big veined ears, stained and tattered along the edges as a blacksmith's leather apron. It was an evening of wonders the show folk put on.

The morning after they cleared out, it was discovered that one of the musicians—a banjo picker and Ethiopian delineator, an artist of the burnt cork—had been killed, his head knocked open. He had been thrown into the millrace and his body had lodged face up against a board that was slid partway down into a slot in the race to regulate the flow of water to the wheel. All the blacking was washed away from his face, and underwater it looked up at you hopefully and strangely pale, the whitest thing in all the visible landscape. The top of his head was broken open in a bloodless mess the color and texture of caul fat.

No one would move him until I could come to investigate. And so for the better part of a day, all of the boys and most of the men had made the same precarious journey that I did upon arrival—walking spraddle-legged along the cross braces of the race to stare down through the rushing water onto the upturned countenance. The dark suit of fancy clothes and the longish black hair and even the cheeks of his face fluttered with the flowing water as if driven by a high wind.

When I acted like a lawman and asked questions, everybody talked about the amazing show, happy to tell me all about its many unexpected delights, especially that elephant. But nobody knew anything at all about the killing other than to repeat vague mutterings concerning somebody's wife, though whose wife they could not or would not specify. And furthermore, who knew what old grudges and passions had prevailed among the departed animal trainers and painted clowns and contortionists and jugglers?

I had the dead man pulled out of the water and buried in the churchyard. I paid out of my own pocket for a simple stone marker and wrote an epitaph myself, which read:

SHOWMAN

D. 1867

I CAME FROM FAR AWAY EXPECTING PROFIT,

BUT INSTEAD SUFFERED A GREAT LOSS.

At least we got a new addition to our word hoard out of the death. Previously, of course, there had been no reason to have a term for elephant. But long after her departure, the people kept marveling at her many features. It was all the talk. Those amazing ears. The people settled eventually on a name for her: *kamama utana*. Big butterfly.

UPON MY RETURN HOME, I found that against my best advice Big Dirt and Dreadful Water had continued their poison correspondence. And finally, when words became insufficient, Dreadful Water had cut Big Dirt a long slashing wound down his chest, bone-deep. Big Dirt was home trying to heal. And when I went to see Dreadful Water, he was more morose than remorseful.

—Me and Big Dirt were such friends back in the old times, he said. Damn him.

These were old grey-headed men fighting about something they could hardly remember. And the little stout wives had suddenly sided devoutly with their husbands and were now enemies too.

I went from one to the other of the four parties saying exactly the same thing to them all: Stop this stupid shit you're intent on doing to one another. When people get to the age you are, anybody that shares even a few of your memories is a treasure beyond price. Love them and forgive their foolishness and hope they'll forgive yours.

I bore up under such responsibilities through three seasons, right up to the start of the next summer. And then I'd had all I could take. I fled, hitting the road once again, aiming for Warm Springs.

8

THE WARM SPRINGS HOTEL WAS A WONDROUS REFUGE DOWN IN ITS remote river gorge, four days from the nearest railhead. A summer resort, mostly. For the better part of two decades—before and after the War—I was frequently a resident in all quarters of the year, including the depths of winter when the hotel was nearly empty and cold drafts blew through the dark ballroom and the lawn was blanketed in snow, marred by a narrow path down which only the bravest guests ventured to immerse themselves in the steaming water of the pools.

Even in the lowest of low seasons there was money to be made at late-night card games and unattached women to court. Wealthy young widows and their spinster-cousin travel companions. The sad and needy wives of wealthy old men who napped through the afternoon by the broad lobby fireplace with their hands crossed over their uprisen bellies and then, after a big pork dinner, retired immediately to bed. And of course the lovely governesses, smart and brittle and filled with resentment.

The healthful waters of the several springs rose from the ground heavy with minerals from down in the earth's core. Thick-textured and buoyant. You could probably pitch a baby into any one of the pools and it would bob right back to the surface. And the water was nice and warm, a little better than a hundred degrees except after a hard rain, when it inexplicably became hotter. It carried a faint sulfurous odor, but only enough to seem medicinal.

The water was said to be both diuretic and laxative, and the guests were encouraged to drink freely. So the help went up and down the halls day and night carrying china chamberpots, the contents sloshing under domed lids. Some among the guests contended for bragging rights as to quantity of water imbibed. I remember, before the War, one stout and somewhat elderly woman, attired in maroon to advertise her availability as a widow beyond the bounds of the last degree of mourning, powder caked in the creases of her face, claimed to drink as high as two gallons a day to no apparent detriment—but with no diminution of the neuralgic pain in her right hip, which burned as fierce as ever. Others among us credited the waters with relief from rheumatism, migraine headaches, psoriasis, and certain cancers.

But the finest use I could find for the hot water was a good long chin-deep soak in the middle of the night. Watching the wheel of the sky turn overhead. Orion in winter swinging his blade below his belt. The Seven Sisters, once distinct but becoming a singular and blurry patch against the dark as my eyesight waned. Jupiter and Saturn and Mars scattered about among the stars, depending on the year. The moons arcing overhead in whatever slivers or orbs they were scheduled to show at that particular time on that particular night. Lovely, the way the sky works. The constellations and planets and moons. Enough recurrence to assure us of the probable continuation of the universe, but not so repetitive as to become boring during the limited span we have to watch it all spin around.

We went to Warm Springs in search of magical waters, fresh mountain air, amusements, adventures, relief from pain. It offered unlimited leisure for as long as you could afford to stay, which for most was the entire summer. The hotel accommodated upward of three hundred guests, and it would be full all through the hot months, when wealthy plantation folk from the steamy lowlands came up for relief from the relentless and wasting heat and also to wrench their sick bowels back to health in the midst of what they called wilderness.

Many of us while in residence at the Springs swore allegiance to various strict diets. The harshest among us claimed to live on just the extreme essences, pure spring water and fresh air. I was not immune to the fashions of the Springs. One summer before the War, I forbade myself the consumption of animal food for nearly an entire summer. I lived on salad greens and sliced tomatoes and red wine. But at some point I reckoned I could not face a life without sausage biscuits. My first meal of meat was chicken thighs soaked in vinegar and hot peppers and cooked to a char over hickory coals. I sat at one of the communal tables in the dining hall and had to hold myself from planting my face in the plate like a dog at its dinner.

On foggy evenings in midsummer when it was cool enough for a fire to be lit in the big hearth, the delight of the flatlanders knew no bounds. A wood fire feeling good in midsummer; who could imagine such a wonder? Anyone who ever stayed there remembered at least two hard facts: the ballroom was two hundred and thirty-three feet long and the gallery was faced with thirty-five fat Doric columns.

I loved that gallery, which a few among us called the veranda and a lesser few the piazza. It stretched the full length of the building. A long row of green rocking chairs—three to a column—looked across the lawn to the river and the ridge of the western mountains. Scattered across the lawn were big old oaks and poplars with their trunks whitewashed from the ground to the height a painter could reach with dripping upstretched brush.

One summer evening before the War, rocking with the men on the gallery and looking out at the view with just enough light to see the smoke from our cigars and the faintest distant jag of ridgeline above the black river, one of the cigar smokers and Scotch drinkers, a man who featured himself a seasoned traveler, opined that anyone with genuine taste would find Warm Springs as superior to Saratoga as a mountain stream to a tidal gut.

For close to twenty years, any time I was in residence, no matter the season, the help knew to bring my coffee and an ounce of Calvados out to the rockers at sunrise. Hardly any of the guests stirred before breakfast began to be served in the dining hall, so I had the place to myself to rock and read and watch the fog lift off the river. Of course, I could have sat and rocked and watched virtually the same view from my own porch, but at home I would have been a stationary target.

I TRAVELED THE FINAL LEG of the journey to the Springs, riding from midday into night. The ferry at the crossing above Alexander was unaccountably delayed, but at least the roads were dry and the moon was coming on toward full, though its blue wash of light filtering onto the roadway through the fully leafed trees revealed barely more than I could have seen without it. The river was broad most of the way, the light falling on it like rubbed pewter, and the road in many places was hardly elevated above water level.

I did not make it to the Springs until nearly midnight, and the hotel's day had wound down to a close. Out front, a groom remained awake to take my horse. A few night owls still smoked and sipped in the rockers on the gallery. I went inside and asked at the desk that the trunk of clothes and personal effects I kept in storage might be sent to the room. I collected forwarded mail and scanned the lobby. The lamps were dimmed down to flames no brighter than candles. Dinner was of course long over, and the doors to the dark dining hall were closed. A table of cardplayers gambled on. A couple in their early thirties, acting rapt with each other and apparently unmarried, began singing one of the new songs. They came together and danced a few steps, unselfconsciously and pressed very close, and then the woman pulled away, laughing. She held out her hand and the man kissed the back and then the fingertips. And then he turned it over and kissed the cup of her gloved palm and then, above the button, her bare veined wrist. She looked at her wrist as if she had never seen it before, and then she wheeled with a becoming flare of skirt and walked across the lobby to the steps that led to the sleeping rooms. Her dancing partner and I both watched her go. The Gypsy palm reader still sat behind her little table, the hand of a grey-headed man in his sixties smoothed out flat in hers. She traced curves of lifeline and heartline very slowly with her forefinger, a calculated thrill running through every nerve of her customer and in itself worth the dollar her reading cost. As I walked to the bar, the Gypsy cut her eyes to me and went back to work. In passing, I heard a few of the words she said: *tribulation followed by final peace.*

The fate of us all, I thought. The easiest of predictions. None of us escape it.

At the bar in the corner, three older men sat humped over their nightcaps. They had spaced out along the bar stools incommunicative, maintaining the etiquette of men urinating together. I sat in the seat that best corresponded with the prevailing isolation.

I ordered a ham sandwich and what I intended to be a lone Tanqueray with lime and sugar. And a light. The bartender moved a lamp from the other end of the bar and set it in front of me. I twisted up the wick and began sorting mail. Nothing particularly personal, only desperate business correspondence from several lawyers either saying why I urgently needed to pay their clients or why their clients couldn't pay me. And several periodicals, among them the latest *Appleton's Journal* and a *Cornhill Magazine* many months in arrears of its cover date. While I ate the sandwich, I scanned an article in *Appleton's* on the state of recent fiction. Its judgment was harsh, on the grounds that we live in a happy, beautiful, virile age. And yet our stories are unnecessarily glum. We do not want sighs or tears. We are all seeking happiness, whether through money or position. It is our privilege to resent any attempts to force unhappy thoughts on us. We rightly object to being made sad by our reading matter.

I decided those sentiments were occasion for a few more drinks.

And then the younger man who had kissed the woman's wrist sat down on a stool beside me, his elbow and hip brushing mine as he took his seat. He still hummed the last bars of their song, which had about its melody and lyric the drama of desire and youth.

—Nice hotel, he said, after he had hummed to the end of the chorus.

—Yes, nice, I said.

—Nice guests, too.

—Nice.

He introduced himself, and I shook his hand and gave my name.

—Not the noted colonel? he said.

I said, That war's over.

—Well, damn, he said. Nice to meet you.

He put out his hand again and I shook it again.

The other lonely drinkers were drawn to his excess enthusiasm. They circled around, drinks in hand. Soon we were a group, old pals. Our conversation touched upon all the chief occupations at the Springs: eating, bathing, riding, drinking to excess, dancing, playing cards, walking to certain nearby rocky prominences to take in vistas, flirting to a dangerous degree, and gossiping without cessation.

One of the relentless topics of talk recently had been the Woman in Black, a widow who dressed in the first degree of mourning, though some said knowingly that the required year and a day had long since elapsed. She had apparently come to the Springs to regain her health but seemed indifferent whether she gained it or lost it entirely. Her mind ran only in doleful channels. She took meals in her room rather than in the dining hall and, of course, never appeared in the ballroom. From morning to late afternoon, she was given to solitary walks along the river road. She was seldom seen by other guests except during her gloomy passages through the lobby on the way to the sleeping rooms, her hem dragging dusty or muddy depending on the weather. One of the drinkers said his wife held the opinion that for the Woman in Black, all clocks had stopped at the moment of her husband's death, never to start again.

I speculated that she would surely die of heartbreak.

One of the older men snorted back a laugh. And all the others—men even more middle-aged than myself, with well-earned bellies rising plump under bright-colored expensive waistcoats, and also the young romantic—ganged up against me and agreed ruefully that no woman had ever died of grief. Not a one of their gender in all the history of the world. Men die of heartbreak. Women die of old age. That's why we always precede them in death. Just study the language of obituaries for proof.

I raised a toast to heartbreak.

And after a reluctant pause, they all raised their glasses with me.

At that down note, the other men drained the bottoms of their glasses and called it a night. The bartender made exaggerated motions of wiping up and closing down. I ordered a last double and carried the glass with me out the door and onto the gallery. The moon stood above the far ridges, a ring of light around it in the hazed milky sky. The night was damp and cool, and the fog was beginning to gather in the lowgrounds. I put my riding coat back on and stuffed the mail into one of the deep pockets.

I crossed the river on the wooden bridge and walked in the dark along the river road and turned onto the steep path up the mountain leading to the jump-off, an overlook, a vista popular among the younger guests for a flirtatious scramble in groups up the rocky trail to watch sunset. And then scramble down in the twilight and quickly change from walking attire to evening dress for dancing, any occasion for a wardrobe change being always welcome among the young.

I climbed the steep trail, meticulous in my effort to keep gin level to gravity and not to the pitched ground. Huffing and blowing, I attained the well-worn rock ledge, a projection of mountain into space, a sharp angle aimed off to a far western prospect. I tipped the glass to my mouth and swallowed it all down. Drew back and threw the empty glass at the moon.

Failure, of course. Proven by the festive sound of breaking glass faint against the rocks below.

Then, off to my right, a polite clearing of throat. A woman's throat. I supposed I had interrupted a tryst.

—Excuse me, I said.

I looked along the ledge, expecting a couple. Bodies pulling a discreet distance away from each other.

Instead, silhouetted, sitting with feet dangling over the edge of the jump-off, a lone black figure.

—Again, I said, Excuse me for interrupting.

BACK AT THE HOTEL, I climbed the stairs from the lobby to the Palm Court, a small private upper lounge around which, on three levels, the better sleeping rooms were arrayed. Two men sat in red-painted rattan chairs. They wore expensive-looking suits, one grey and the other black. They both had on collars and ties of the most current fashion. The one in grey was young and big-chested. He sat thumbing a magazine. Despite being indoors, he kept his hat on, but tilted far to the back as if in grudging concession to the requirements of etiquette. A pale stripe of untanned forehead shone yellow in the uplight from the lamp flame. The one in black was considerably older and thin and bald. He bent forward in his chair, holding his hatbrim delicately two-handed, watching with fascination as his fingers rotated it slowly by small degrees around its circle.

They both looked up from their studies and remarked my passage through the court. I nodded and said, Gentlemen, and went on to my room.

I had barely taken off my riding coat when there was a knock. I released the latch and found the two men standing shoulder to shoulder in the passway. They shoved in and closed the door behind them.

—I should ask what this is all about, I said. But what's the point?

I went and stood against the far wall by the window with my arms crossed.

The older man threw his hat on the bedspread and sat down beside it. He did not look at me, and he seemed very tired.

The young one stood inside the door and glared across the room at me.

—This is all about money, he said. That's all there is separating us from a full appreciation of one another.

—Who are we talking about? I said.

—Williams. Whose else money you holding?

I thought down the long list of names. Maybe Sloan or Slagle. Most of my other creditors would be civilized enough to have the sheriff serve papers. A few were such earnest Christians that they might just send a Baptist preacher to set my mind right.

—I suppose this is where I take a beating, I said.

The young man clenched his hammy fists and looked at the bulging knuckles.

—Hitting people, he said. Not my line of work.

—I have every intention to pay Williams back, I said. Or Slagle, or whoever we're talking about. If that matters.

The little old man leaned forward from his seat on the bed and began working his hat around and around again. He seemed not at all interested in the conversation.

—Then pay, the young one said. That's the simple thing. It's been a year since your note came due. Be a sport. Give us the money. It being light, we'll tote it to the carriage ourselves and call this matter done.

He named an amount that would widely cause an intake of breath.

—There's no money right now, I said.

—And yet you're here, the younger man said. I asked for rates at the desk. This place ain't free.

I turned up my palms.

The younger man looked at the man on the bed and said, There's days I don't think they can print paper money fast enough to make me keep doing this job much longer.

The little man did not look up or even cease rotating his hat.

—Look, I said. Everything I've got is in land. A great deal of land. Not immediately solvent. There's money coming from the Government to pay off all my notes. But it takes time.

—Time, that's exactly the problem. Everything would be fine without it. But we're here to impress upon you the tedious exigencies. Our boss is tired of waiting and wants his money. Business is all this is.

—There's more to it than that, I said. Williams and I are friends. Going back long before the War.

—Well, sure you're friends. As long as the money rolls in.

—I had a hand in making him plenty of money when I was in the senate. Road construction money, railroad money, that sort of thing.

—But not lately you haven't made him any money. And it's the regular flow that's of the most particular interest. Look, here's the way it works. When Williams wants something from you, you're friends. Gratitude and loyalty rule the day. When you need something from Williams, business is business. Study your contracts down to the last word. I ought not have to tell you this.

I said, No, you ought not.

—So, the money?

—I haven't got the money. I could show you the papers, the correspondence with Washington. I could have copies of them drawn up. It all goes back quite a way. To $53.33 at six percent. For more than three decades.

—That's all you've got to offer? Papers and fifty-some dollars?

—Papers that will soon lead to a great deal of money.

—If I hired you to build me a house, would you show up years later and unroll a floor plan and expect payment?

—It's something you could show to Williams. It's all coming to a head soon.

—After thirty years?

—Any day now.

The younger man looked toward the older man on the bed, who appeared to have nodded off briefly. His chin was tilted down and his hat was still between his hands. It was at least one in the morning, and he looked exhausted. Grey whiskers were beginning to sprout across his upper lip and the wattled skin under his jawbone. He roused awake and looked around.

The younger man said to him, We stay any longer, he'll try to kite a check on us.

The older man didn't make a sign to show his thoughts one way or the other.

The younger man looked back at me and said, Just fuck you and all your sorry lot. Shitting debtors. My bane in life.

He walked out the door and tried to slam it behind him, but it banged the heel of his shoe, so he walked off and left it standing ajar.

The little older man rose and looked in the mirror over the dressing table. He rubbed his hands down his face to compose it. He touched the pale bags under his eyes with two fingertips as if to press them back into youthful tautness. He put his hat on his head and adjusted the angle of the brim with great precision. When he was satisfied at its cock, he stepped up to me and for the first time looked me in the eye. He made a little movement, no more extensive than a shiver. A straight razor with a tortoiseshell handle appeared in his hand. With one gesture, he flipped the flickering blue blade open one-fingered by the crook end of it and reached out underhanded and slit me a long thin wound through my trousers.

It went from a few inches above my knee up the inner side of my right thigh all the way to the nub of my groin.

By the time I bent and grabbed myself two-handed, the razor was folded back into its handle and had disappeared into a coat pocket.

—I noticed you dressed on the left, the little man said. You can thank me for my attention to detail any time you care to.

Blood ran between my fingers and wet the front of my rent trousers and dribbled down my shins and wet my socks and shoe tops.

HALF AN HOUR LATER, I sat spraddle-legged on the edge of the bed with the Gypsy palm reader kneeling between my feet. I wore only the bedspread gathered around my middle for modesty. The Gypsy dabbed at my thigh with cotton-wool soaked in peroxide. White foam rose up along the length of the wound.

—This is not greatly worse than shaving nicks I've had, she said. It's long, but it ain't much more than broke the skin.

—That's not how I bled.

—Well, I guess it's a powerful place to be cut, she said. But looks like you'll have to live awhile further.

She leaned and kissed the inside of my knee. A little generous rough cat's-tongue lick in addition.

The Gypsy getup—green headcloth, red skirt, yellow waist sash, and cream peasant blouse—lay in a bright puddle just inside the door. She wore only my white terry bathrobe gapped open above the waist to show a long shadow between her breasts. Her brown hair was wet and combed in one swoop straight back all the way from her hairline to her shoulders. Across her crown you could still see the parallel tracks of the comb teeth, all the way to white scalp.

Looking up at me, with the red lipstick and dark makeup washed away, she looked like what she was, a moderately pretty woman from Valdosta with a crease or two beginning to deepen around the corners of her mouth and eyes.

—You lay back and be still and I'll go easy on you, she said.

I WOKE UP at the first edge of grey dawn and opened my eyes to the Gypsy supplementing her income from my wallet. She turned and found me awake and fanned the few bills like a hand of cards. She made a show of holding them to the window, studying their marks. In her most oracular voice she said, In recompense for a great deal of pleasure, you will suffer a minor financial loss. Then she plucked out a twenty and put the tens and fives and ones back in their places.

Twenty dollars, I thought. An acre of good farmland. Ten acres of steep mountainside.

—And now the palm, she said. Complimentary.

She sat on the edge of the bed and scratched a match head and lit the candle. Held my hand tilted to the light. She looked confused. Nothing seemed to factor. She traced her fingertip down the old wide burn scar from Featherstone's spit crank. A white stripe running diagonal from the base of my forefinger to the hand heel.

—This confounds everything, she said. It cuts across heartline and lifeline both. It's the fate you've got, for whatever that's worth.

She kissed me on the brow and blew out the yellow teardrop of flame and went out the door.

I fell back into hovering half sleep and then emerged into full consciousness some brief time afterward, singed and weary and defeated by the night's long tiresome events. The light was rising to full dawn outside the window. I dressed and walked through the empty lobby and across the dewy lawn. Soggy shoes and socks. The river was uncommunicative no matter how much I stared at its face, but I waited on a bench by its side until the dining room opened, and then I went in for coffee and one soft-boiled egg, woefully undercooked and quivering mucus in the cup of its little crystal pedestal.

9

THAT AFTERNOON I WENT OUT DRIVING HUNG OVER THROUGH the countryside, following the river road in a slender racing cart I kept stored in a shed behind the Springs. The spokes of the two wheels were painted yellow, and the upholstery of the seat was red and tucked and rolled, and all the members of the frame were lacquered glossy black. I carried a little flat silver flask in one hip pocket and a little flat Remington vest pistol in the other. In case the razor man reappeared.

A low day. I drove aimlessly at high speed along the road that followed every bend of the river.

At some point after I had turned around and headed back to the Springs, the left wheel started working itself off the axle, wobbling and canting a considerable degree off plumb. I pulled up and sat, wondering how one went about fitting the hub back secure without tools.

One of these tall slouching proud mountain men came walking down the road. He hardly deigned to look at me and would have kept on walking had I not called out and requested that he fix my wheel.

Perhaps my tone was inappropriate.

The man said, Step out into the road a minute for me.

As soon as my second foot touched the dirt, the man hit me three times in the face. The last two blows were particularly well aimed, as they were struck while I was falling. The horse backed a step against the traces and then stopped. I lay in the road and watched the man walk away.

I raised up onto my elbows and called out, Sir. I meant of course to pay.

But the man kept walking and did not even turn to look over his shoulder before he rounded the next bend in the road. I rose upright and tried to spit and clear my mouth, but instead of the manly gob I intended to produce, my lips spluttered and sprayed blood as from an atomizer down the front of my fashionably pale driving coat.

WE MET ON my way back into the Springs with the wheel wobbling and my mouth swollen and scabbing in two places. A spot of blood rising through the fabric on my upper thigh where the razor cut had opened back up. A dark figure walked ahead of me, shaded by a black parasol scalloped like a bat's wing with its decoration of crepe. All the heavy layers of women's mourning attire pulled downward by gravity from bonnet to hem, all black. Upon passing, I removed my own slouch-brimmed hat and gave a nod of greeting. The widow looked up, her face vague behind the veil. So I did not immediately recognize Claire.

But she did me. She lowered the parasol and lifted her veil with a hand gloved in black kid. She said, Will?

Then the leaf-filtered afternoon sun fell on her face. The shock of recognition. Much awkward surprise on both our parts.

I must have looked to her as if I were wearing a mask bearing only a few points of correspondence to the face she had known and maybe loved all those years ago. But Claire was still immediately the same to me, a recognition deep past the point of heartbreak.

Mourning suited Claire, her pale face against the black. I sat on the cart seat and remembered swearing to her years and years before, up on the Lizard Bald, that whatever separations life might throw at us in the unimaginable future, whenever we met I would hold her close to me. No matter what. All my young heart urgent behind my oath.

Of course, I had broken my promise out on the new Nation. And now again an embrace eluded me. How to hold the Woman in Black?

Instead, I climbed down from my seat and stood in the road facing her and said, Are you well?

An idiotic question. Claire's face was white as cotton. She was not well, not at all.

But if we did not exactly dash into each other's arms, we were at least warm in our meeting. Sad smiles on both sides. Claire would not climb up and ride back to the Springs with me, so I fell in beside her when she turned and continued walking downriver. I led my horse and festive cart behind us by a long swag of reins. Claire's muddy black skirt trained in the road.

In the years since I had seen her, Claire had lost a lot. The owl-faced baby had grown halfway up and then died of a fever and congestion of the lungs, blood flowing from both ends. And Featherstone had finally passed to the Nightland. His second death was surely only a little more satisfactory to him than the first, for he did not go nightward in a blaze of pony-club gunfire. He was thrown from the back of a young stallion. Bucked off headfirst into a fence post. Old bones shattered to powder all down his frame. After a brief period of unconsciousness, he came awake and wiped a smear of blood from his brow and directed that he be carried into the parlor and seated in his wing chair of death. He called for a tumbler of Scotch and a wet cloth. He drank and wiped his brow and fell asleep. He died by the fireside exactly like the first time, except this one was final.

So Claire had come back home. Where else to go, alone in the world as she was. But not entirely lost, for she was wealthy from selling out all of Featherstone's holdings.

—He was awfully old, I said.

Exactly the wrong thing. For which I have a talent.

Claire made a puffing sound. Somewhere between angry huff and stifled laugh.

I yammered cringefully onward, not the least cool and contained within myself but saying exactly what I was feeling, that Featherstone was the biggest son of a bitch I ever knew. And yet now, finding that he had passed to the Nightland, I had to admit I loved him in some regretful way. What a bastard. And yet the world withered a little without him in it. Part of me still wished I'd put a ball through his heart way back then instead of just his thigh.

Claire put her hand on my arm and said, I miss him pretty bad too.

Then she said, Not long ago, I saw you in a dream and you were about the age when you fought that stupid duel. A young man.

She sounded disappointed in me for succumbing to the passage of time, as if its marks on me were a personal failure. But I had been assured by many women her age and much younger that I remained remarkably and attractively youthful. Concessions to this odious middle passage of life were few. My hair, though increasingly grey, persisted across most of its former territory. And I had not grown an entire belly but only displayed a slight virile thickness through the barrel. But of course there's no arguing against the dreamworld. Its requirements are strict.

She said, I'd guess you're carrying a flask?

—Tanqueray and lime. There's some left.

She reached out a hand.

I took the flask out of my pocket and unstoppered it and wiped its threaded mouth carefully with a clean handkerchief.

—Ever the gentleman, Claire said.

She took a pull and then wiped with her own handkerchief, cambric trimmed in black. Twisting around the rim in parody before she handed it back.

—Looks like a rough day for you, she said.

I touched my beaten face. Looked at my pocket watch and did the arithmetic.

—Rough seventeen hours, I said.

—There's a great deal of gossip about you here, she said. Senator, colonel, white chief. But beset all about by creditors and ill-wishers and lawsuits.

—They have time to talk about me? I thought you occupied all their attention. The Woman in Black. Tragic and melancholy.

Claire reached her black hand back out, and I put the silver flask in its curve. She turned it up and finished it and handed it back.

—But, good God, Will, a Warm Springs Gypsy? How the mighty have fallen. I would have preferred a more extraordinary melodrama.

—Me too. But just so you'll know, I'm planning on changing everything about my life real soon.

—Well, that will be fun to watch.

I turned my palms up. I live to serve, I said.

She was quiet for a while. The broad river was smooth and brown, and at some point in our walk we passed a big flat rock in the middle of the water on which someone had planted a Rebel flag. The handsewn artifact drooped in sun-bleached folds from a pole only head-high. It was meant to signify something about identity and defeat, though what I could not say. Too many possibilities.

Claire said, Featherstone greatly regretted being too old to fight Yankees, but he was thrilled when Stand Watie and his Cherokee cavalry captured that Union ship. He reckoned it a first in military history.

—What river was that boat on?

—I don't know the name of it.

—Must have been pretty narrow.

—Was it bad for you?

—What?

—The War.

—When we weren't needing to scalp people, it was mostly fine. A long camping trip. But all in all, the second stupidest thing I ever did.

—Second?

—Right behind letting you ride away in the wagon that day.

Claire said, You don't know how long I hurt.

—I hurt now.

—For the record, this is not a contest and I was not talking about you and we'll not allude to that day anymore.

I had sense enough to reach out and touch her, a hand on the black shoulder, a joint of bones I knew the shape of in my strongest memory. I told Claire about my dreams of her in the winterhouse with Bear. Dreams that still came to me at least twice yearly. Her fleeing from me, slipping through my arms like smoke when I tried to hold her.

I said, From the time I was thirteen, it was you or no one.

—You ask too much.

—That's my gift.

When we were three or four river bends from the Springs, Claire said, You drive on. Let's deny them further topics of discussion for today.

But before I could turn, she reached out and tapped two fingers to the hollow below my bottom lip.

—Perhaps you should grow an Imperial.

—I had one. But I cut it off after the surrender.

OFFICIALLY, THE BATHING HOUSES closed an hour before dinner, but it was always possible—for a handsome gratuity—to obtain a key from an attendant. Three in the morning, Claire and I in the water neck-deep. Moonlight falling pearly all around us. The air was so cool and damp that steam rose thick from the surface of the spring and made the summer moon and stars look large and vague. I could hardly see her, though she was barely more than an arm's reach away. The river flowed all but silent behind us, its sound like a deep exhalation. The lamps of the gallery had long since been puffed out by the white-coated attendants. Only a single yellow insomniac window remained lighted all down the long face of the hotel. The thirty-five columns pale in the moonlight. The lawn already silver with dew and the whitewashed tree trunks ghostly all the way down to the riverbank.

Despite my fervent suggestion to the contrary, Claire had insisted we wear bathing costumes. We moved around in the heavy water like two loads of dark laundry.

—My God, I said. We've seen every square inch of each other. Whence arises this sudden modesty?

—Sudden? she said. That was a very long time ago. Another world. We've long passed the statute of limitations on those memories.

—Not for me. They're equivalent to capital murder. Unforgivable. I could mention certain particulars.

—As a person, there are elements of you that just won't do.

—*O wad some Power the giftie gie us / To see oursels as ithers see us!*

—Yes, that's just the sort of thing you need more of.

—I'm working on it. Day by day.

We swirled about each other in the sulfur-smelling water. Claire's hair curled at her temples and at the back of her neck exactly as it had at sixteen. At sixteen, I had thought Claire was the prettiest thing I had ever seen. And also at seventeen, eighteen, twenty-three, thirty. But now, these many years later, she was only some of the person I remembered. I had never guessed she could ever look like this. She had been awfully pretty, but now she was beautiful. Rich beyond my imagination to conjure. She seemed full and complete. Though the rational, unenraptured part of me figured that no one, man or woman, gets to be full and complete ever. We all go about burdened with the reality that we are the broken-off ends of true people. It is the severe vengeance Creation takes on us for living.

Notwithstanding, she looked awfully good in the steam and moonlight.

I lifted a dripping hand out of the water and touched her damp hair. It was all gathered up in the fashion of the day. Bunched and rolled and crimped.

—I wish you'd do your hair the way you used to, I said.

—I don't remember.

—A thick braid down your neck. And when you took the braid apart and raked your fingers through your hair, it fell long and waved and wild across your shoulders and down your back.

—You recall so exactly?

—I'll revise. When you undid the braid, your hair was waved at the ends and ruched at the nape.

I swam close and reached behind her to pull out the various pins and barrettes that held it in place, but she pulled away from me. Water swirled. Steam rose to the Green Corn Moon.

—This is not easy for me, she said. How to grow old?

—Going to water is a start, I said. It's supposed to do you good.

SCATTERED ABOUT MY ROOM, a great deal of widow's lingerie. Sheer and fragile as the shed skins of snakes. Claire held an item to the lamplight and it was luminous and of no color at all, like the stripe in the ribbon of lamp flame between the blue base and the waved yellow top. So slight I could not tell what part of the body it was shaped to fit. She dropped it to the floor, and it fell slowly as if nearly weightless.

Claire did not pretend that she did not drink, as many women do, by taking only patent formulas, proper and medicinal but strong with alcohol and laudanum. She mostly drank London gin, clear and straight. She had taken quite a bit of it through the evening, and sometime around four in the morning she went to the open window and leaned out and retched briefly into the darkness. Then to the washbasin, where she poured tooth powder from its perforated tin very liberally over her wetted finger and scrubbed out her mouth.

—There, she said.

She smiled, but her eyes were wet and a little red in the lamplight.

We tried kissing, and contrary to my expectations, we were more awkward at it than we had been at sixteen. A skill diminished by time. Back then, the awkwardness had arisen out of our rush to melt into each other. Though *melt* is not necessarily the right word. We collided with some hope that all the pieces shattered in the collision might form a pleasant pattern afterward. Now it was the avoidance of collision that was our trouble, the insistence on pulling back into the limits of our individual persons, so carefully delineated all these years.

After the kissing went badly, we tried just holding each other. And that was a little better but still awkward, a bumping of the soft and hard parts of the body. I said aloud that at least we were both lean enough that the points of our hips still clashed against each other as they once had done. After all, how often in midlife do you get to repeat any element of the distant past whatsoever? And by the way, we both being in the range of a half century old, any assertion of occupying a midpoint in life was a highly optimistic note to strike.

I became aware that I was talking too much.

—How come I'm still in love with you? I said.

—One of the mysteries.

THREE NIGHTS LATER, I stood at the far end of the ballroom. Lights dim. The band played all the current waltzes and a few of the popular songs of the day. Dancers moved across the floor in shapes like water, if water were considerably less graceful than it is. I waited and waited. And then through the wide French doors down the two-hundred-thirty-three-foot length of the ballroom, Claire entered. All the heads turned. She wore a shining silk dress of midsummer green, close at the waist, full below. Her hair was drawn up in an approximation of the current fashion but much looser, stray locks falling around her face and shoulders. A thin band of black crepe no wider than my finger around her upper arm. I went to her and gave her my hand, and we danced.

Oddly, hardly anyone was scandalized. After that first waltz, a few muted gloved hands met in applause directed our way. I credit the free and generous spirit of the Springs. Something in the water.

WE WERE CLOSE TOGETHER all the way from high summer to the equinox. The progression of wildflowers, blooming and fading in the ditches, and the phases of the moons were all the calendar I needed. By day, we spun along the river road and on country lanes in my colorful cart. After dinner we climbed to watch sunsets at the jump-off. Waltzes late into the night. Much wine and other spirits. In the foggy hours after midnight, tangled abed in one room or another.

One evening we waded out into the river to the broad rock with the Rebel flag. Wobbling barefoot over mossy riverbed cobbles, Claire with her skirts held knee-high, me with cuffs rolled over pale shanks and a half bottle of champagne sloshing in my hand. As twilight fell in the gorge, I lit a fire no bigger than the lid to a bucket. Striking a blaze from a nest of sticks and tinder collected in a hollow of the rock and feeding it with driftwood lying about. We watched the fire burn and I told Claire about Granny Squirrel's potion made from just such a river nest. Me fasting and drinking the tea brewed from it in an effort either to forget her or bring her back.

—Granny Squirrel's spells rarely failed, she said. So maybe that one just took a long time.

—Maybe. I've always tried to maintain the attitude that being happy interferes with our perceptions of the world.

—Did she ever die? Claire said.

—Possibly. During blueberry season one year, she never came home from picking. We looked and looked and all we found was her basket, half full. Nobody knows what happened. She might have just moved on.

—How old would she have been?

—Couple of hundred. Maybe more.

SUMMER WAS SUDDENLY DONE, wheeled away too quickly. Overnight, abandoned cornfields bloomed with head-high purple ironweed, burning and blinding and visionary. Autumn never the best of times for me.

Letters arrived daily from Conley and others. Debts and responsibilities. Things falling apart. Every morning, carriages rolled away taking summer people back to the lowlands. We had reached the sad time of year when the ballroom was used only on Friday and Saturday nights and the two upper floors of bedrooms were dark and empty. Dogwoods and sumac already burning red and poplars fading to yellow. Time to go.

Claire and I had not talked at all about a future. We never had before. When we were young, we worked under the assumption that all the life there was or would ever be was right in our hands at the moment, so why bother speculating about a future entirely lacking reality? But the future had waited in ambuscade and now pressed down on us with all its weight.

LATE ONE NIGHT, along about the equinox, I asked her to marry me. We were sunk to our chins in the steaming spring, and a light rain fell around us without even the force to pock the water. I interlocked fingers with her and pulled her to me and said what I had to say about loving her for so long, yearning and despairing. And about the power of second chances. While I talked, Claire's eyes teared up, which I took as a good sign.

But when I was done she shook her head. Not yet, she said.

—If not now, when?

—I need some time to think about it.

—Time, I said. That's exactly the problem.

THE NEXT DAY, Claire put back on her mourning. All the dismal black layers. Green summer was passed and gone. Time again for heart grief. She came to my room dark and weighted down. I held her in the doorway, the Woman in Black. Hugging a bleak stiff figure. I looked her in the eye and argued all the muddled and desperate wisdom of my middle years against her gloom. We are not made strong enough to stand up against endless grief. And yet pain is the constant drone of life. So if we are to have any happiness at all, it is only in the passing instant. This past season together had been an exception to the general miserable conditions of existence. As had those two summers back in the old world. Surely it is a sin to reject the few gifts we are given. Be happy in the flash of time granted to us or hurt forever. Those are the harsh and contradictory rules Creation has laid down for the game we're forced to play.

CLAIRE ABOVE ME, white bedcovers crisp and bunched in folds at her hips. Through the window, a thin final curvature of End of Fruit Moon falls down a milky sky to the black jittery ridge. The upcoming new moon will mark the beginning of the new year. An odd time to start, with the dying of summer, the fall of leaves. Claire moves in private abstraction. I am not absolutely necessary to whatever pleasure she's finding. Her veil on, and nothing else. On the floor a dark pool of mourning clothes. The netting a blank scrim over her face. Only when she leans a certain way to the left and turns her head and catches the backlight from the candle stub burning over her shoulder on the washstand do I see any features at all beneath. A fierce determined silhouette. The only signet of passion her full and slightly parted lips.

I raise a hand to lift the veil where it swags below her chin, but she stops me, presses the hand back down to the one place where we connect. Moth wings hiss in the candle flame. She finishes, pressing down hard, and only then lifts the veil with a sweep of wrist and forearm, a motion I remember from our youth. She falls onto me.

I doze off with her in my arms and awake to the sound of ankle boots being buttoned. I reach to her where she sits on the edge of the bed and try to make her stay, but she will not. She stands and studies her grim attire in the mirror, bends and smooths a hand over rumpled crepe.

—I have to go tomorrow.

—Go?

She draws the veil back down, leans, and kisses the corner of my mouth, the veil between our lips grainy and resistive.

—Go where?

No answer.

—Where? I said.

—Away.

—This will break us both, I said.

OVER HER PROTESTS, I insisted on taking her to the railhead. No dawdling allowed for enjoying the brilliant autumn weather. And little conversation. We did the four-day journey in two. Spinning along the river road from dawn into dark, skipping the usual pleasant night at the inn in Alexander and driving on to the Eagle Hotel long after dinner with the horse exhausted and steaming in the cool night. I hired another for the next day's travel, which began before dawn. We fell out of the mountains like a dropped stone and reached the railhead at midnight. An eastbound train waited at the station. Its lamps were lit and steam huffed rhythmically from the engine. Ready to roll. Porters transferred bags in a hurry. Claire kissed me a sort of smeared glancing blow and was gone up the two steps into her car. I sat on the carriage seat with the reins loose in my hands and watched the taillight until it disappeared around the first bend in the rails. All the autumn stars were sprayed across the sky, and the dew was rising in the grass.

FOUR DAYS LATER, autumn sun already set, I walked out to the gallery of the Springs with a glass of whiskey. There sat the razor man, smoking a cheroot and rocking very slightly in a rocker. The exact black suit of clothes from summer. I looked around for the stout boy, but he was nowhere to be seen.

—Have a seat, the razor man said. He palmed the arm of the chair next to him and set it bobbing. I sat one chair down from it and took the Remington out of my vest pocket. It was not much of a weapon. If you stuck out your forefinger and cocked up your thumb to imitate a pistol, the Remington would be considerably smaller. But at six feet of range, it could put a little precise hole through your head from one ear to the other. I set it in my lap and sipped my drink.

—Pretty little gun, the man said. You ought to have bought it in chrome. Then it would look like a piece of jewelry. A brooch.

I was too old to start finding deep personal symbolism in the pistol I carried.

—It's been my experience in all departments of life that the pretty ones will kill a man faster than the others, I said.

—How's your thigh? he said.

—Thigh?

He drew on his cheroot and looked upward and puffed out an irritable plosive cloud of smoke.

He said, So I take it that thanks for my generosity is still forthcoming. Oh, well, they say charity is its own reward.

—We could do this all night long, I said. What do you want?

—Me? Not a damn thing. As far as I'm concerned, you can do what you want. You're of no interest to me whatsoever.

—And yet you're here.

That got a smile out of him.

—It's the same old business, he said. Money. That's all there is. The driving wheel of everything.

—Who? I said. Williams?

—Not just Williams now. I'm representative for a sort of consortium.

—They've ganged up against me?

—Yes indeed. A gang wanting their money that you owe them. And failing cash repayment, they want your land. All of it.

—All my land? That's complicated to define. There's my land in my name. And the people's land in their names. And their land still in my name from back when they couldn't own property, and that's a lot.

—This is not the least bit complicated. They want everything with your name on it.

I did rough calculations. Not enough room left over for people to live on. Cornfields overlapping one another, cabins standing cheek to jowl, fishermen jostling each other on the riverbanks, and the dead woods thick with frustrated hunters.

—The inhabitants? I said. The people. What of them?

—That's what the Indian Territory is for. The West.

—No, I said.

—No? the razor man said. No is what you have the freedom to say when you're in charge. You're not exactly calling the shots here.

—So what do we do? Duel or what?

He laughed and turned aside and spit a fleck of tobacco from his tongue.

—Duel? he said. I don't do that ancient shit. I kill people if they need killing.

—If they don't kill you first.

He took off his hat and showed his balding pate and turned his bagged and wrinkled eyes toward me.

—Kill me first? he said. Good God. I'm a thousand years old. Get in line if you want to take your turn with your tiny pistol. If my job was to kill you, you'd have been dead three months ago.

He sucked a lungful of smoke and I took a drink. We both looked off toward the river. Neither of us said another word, and it seemed a competition not to be the first to speak.

I finally scored the point.

—Here's the only thing pertaining, he finally said. In the spirit of your old friendship, Williams just sends a word of advice. You need to go home and attend to business and not let love rule your life.

—That's it?

—Go home, he said. All kinds of shit's waiting to fall on you when you get there.

10

WHAT FOLLOWED WAS A PERIOD OF LIFE SO EMPTY THERE WASN'T even anything to dream about. All that I had was gone.

Someone should write a sad ballad with that line as title. In a minor key. Fiddles droning, old women keening grim lyrics containing the words *broke, ruined, busted,* and *failed.*

As Bear had said, I was a man with payments. I did not want to default. I was no willing welsher. At the heart of the problem was the flow of money backing up my cascades of paper. After the War, government checks were not reliably forthcoming. Neither the long-delayed final payout nor even the annual interest on the $53.33. Nor could my many debtors pay me back what they owed. All kinds of loans remained outstanding. Everything from pure objective business deals to a handshake loan I'd made with an old friend to pay for his twin boys to go to Harvard. Now he wouldn't even talk to me. A few of my other debtors at least wrote back with excuses. This was the Reconstruction, they all pointed out, one of the most ironically named government policies ever, since its goal seemed to be plowing us all into the ground rather than building anything back up. Money was tight, et cetera, et cetera. As if that was news to me. I'd sit at my desk and read the letters and wonder what rates the razor man charged and if he might offer a volume discount.

There might have been some angle to work, a three-bumper shot I might have made in my youth. But I could not even imagine it now. Some days the weight pressed so hard I lay in bed until sunset, sipping claret and reading novels from before the War: *Carwin*, *Pym*, and the like.

Before long, lawsuits began flying. Court dates loomed. All kinds of opportunities for loss presented themselves.

Money, though, was not at the head of the list for me. The worst loss was to see the land go. Our holdings were not one big square country. We had our core territory, which was fairly regular in its borders. But nearly half the total was scattered about in pieces, some of them two days' ride away. Bear's vision had been far-flung, and some of our original purchases at the land auction had defined the outer boundary of his imaginary homeland. It was left to me to fill in the empty spaces of our map as time went on. But for all kinds of reasons, that hadn't happened.

So those broken tracts were the first to go. And it hurt me awfully deep when I signed the papers on the river land that included the Drowning Place where Bear had fought his namesake battle. A man wanted the land to grow corn on the flats by the river and to log the steep mountainsides of oak and chestnut, and he was willing to pay cash money.

ABOUT THIS TIME, I began to lack the strength of spirit to manipulate visiting journalists to my ends. But they kept coming nevertheless. So I delegated Conley. A poor choice, it turned out. His first and only adversary among the tribe of journalists was a writer from *Lippincott's Magazine*, and Conley failed utterly in the contest. Needless to say, the main thing about failing against journalists is that your defeat fetches up in cold print for all to read unto eternity, same as the Celts against the Romans at Telamon.

Conley spent two days giving the usual tour of the community. The grey and off-plumb schoolhouse and church. Various oddities among our citizens to represent local color. A weary ball game with neither bloodshed nor gambling. A few remnant basket weavers and potters doing their work under a drooping shed roof.

And then, after some months, Conley was sent a fresh copy of *Lippincott's* in which the article appeared. As if he might be proud of his contribution.

He didn't even try to hide the story from me. I still read widely, and he realized he couldn't get a lot past me. He came to the house and handed me the issue in question all fearfully, as if he expected me to fall into a rage as I read.

The story started out pleasantly enough, pretty much like they had for decades. The southern mountains are a land of forgetting. Railroads and telegraphs, work and hurry, are left behind at the first pass. An entire paragraph on the beauteous landscape largely untouched by man.

So far, so nice.

But then the article turned to a catalog of varied local rumor and misinformed shit-ass opinion in regard to me. I was portrayed as a deep mystery, existing only to be solved by the writer. Local folks had been scrounged up to say all kinds of things about me, and since the tales had been collected at considerable effort on the writer's part, they were thus presented reverently as entirely possible facts. And the various possibilities were arranged in descending order.

Number one. The Indians living in the colonel's vast boundary of land were a Christian people existing in peace and prosperity for many decades. He had been their benevolent sachem, their white chief, who had accumulated for their benefit a territory nearly as large as some minor European countries. Specific examples of such tiny nations were not forthcoming, though perhaps a little embittered borderland principality fitted into a seam between France and one of her several neighbors was intended. But sadly, our vast and hard-won homeland was shrinking day by day under the current unfavorable economic conditions of the South. Leaving us all in jeopardy.

Number two. For decades, the Indians had been little more than slaves, abused and bled white by the melancholy colonel, who ruled over them and a vast lawless wilderness as autocratically as a pharaoh, claiming for his personal property every penny of congressional appropriation since the Removal, which amounted to a squandered fortune. And now the whole kingdom was falling apart due to a combination of poor stewardship and outright malfeasance.

Three. The Indians were godless heathens, living in a state of primitive licentiousness and unbridled passion, and the colonel had not only condoned such a retrograde state but immersed himself in their manner of free love and pagan rites with great enthusiasm for such a long time that a great many half-breed children and full-grown adults milled about his grand estate with noses embarrassingly like his own. He herded the people toward Christian ways only to the extent that it looked favorable to outlanders. As long as his people kissed the Bible and said something convictional about Jesus loving them when visitors came calling, the colonel was happy. Otherwise, it was fine with him if they went right on praying to the souls of animals to beg forgiveness for killing them or believed whatever they wanted about witches and herb doctors and spirit healers. An unidentified white woman in the area was quoted as saying that the colonel hadn't moved the people further toward Christian conduct because it might cut down on all the relations he had with their women. Another unidentified source said, There's enough of them running around saying he's their daddy that just the boys of them would make a pair of baseball teams.

Finally, the Indians were nothing but a sad remainder of primitive humanity, debased and starving, living in total isolation and disarray, and the colonel was a madman chained to the floor of his own house.

And that was but the first couple of pages. Illustrated with a fine etching of high jagged peaks and deep jagged gorges and tiny human figures dressed in the current fashion standing by a boiling river and looking upward toward impossible summits in rapt attention. From that point on, it just got worse and worse.

When I finished reading, I sat in my chair by the fire and closed the magazine and set it on the side table. Conley was already trying to figure what other kind of job he might do henceforth. Plowman, scrivener.

You could look in his face and see that he believed his future sent back miserable tidings.

I said, Everybody with an inkpot and steel pen and an hour to kill gets to take a shot. About all you can do in defense is present them a moving target.

I made a little faking motion with my head and shoulders, an old ballplayer's move.

—Yes sir, Conley said.

Then I riffled the magazine back to the starting page of the story and studied it further, looking particularly at the author's credit.

—Rebecca? I said. That's a fetching name.

Conley shrugged.

—Pretty? I said.

—I didn't take note, Conley said.

I just looked critically at him.

—She was pretty, he said.

—Awfully, awfully pretty, I said, and smart as can be? Snapping grey eyes and little curls of pale hair escaping around her temples from underneath the brim of whatever kind of stylish yet unusual hat she was wearing?

—Something like that.

—And about all you said while she was here, no matter what question she asked, was Yes, ma'am?

—If she'd requested me to deny my Savior, that's the answer I'd have given.

—And that business about me chained to the floor?

—I just acknowledged that it is a current rumor.

—That's what they're saying?

—You've not been seen out in the world much these days. People get to talking.

Conley paused a long time, and then he said, But damn, she was plenty pretty.

—Well, I said. That's all right. Pour us a drink and we'll commiserate about women and their hard hearts.

—

THE WORST PART was the walk up to the precipice. But after I had been pushed off the lip of the cliff and was falling in midair, everything relaxed.

The Government sent down a man. F. A. Dony, Special Agent, Bureau of Indian Affairs. He escorted me to the nearest court town. Just the two of us on a three-day jaunt.

The final night of the journey, we camped by a river. Had a fire going and dinner done. Lounging on our blankets, yellow light flickering halfway up the tree trunks, woodsmoke, all that sort of thing. Dony had been sitting a long while writing in a tight hand on big loose correspondence sheets.

—Read me the opening of what you just wrote, I said.

—It's private correspondence back to my supervisor at the Indian Office. Government business. A sort of report.

—Last time I paid attention, the Government dealt with Indians through the War Department, and what they wanted was to send all of us west.

—Times change.

—Read me just the first two lines of what you've written. We're men out traveling together in the wilderness. Show some collegiality.

—You may not like it.

—Name me something I do like these days.

—All right. The opening lines are these:

I have just completed a journey through the wilderness to the nearest court, including a memorable bivouac atop the Soco Mountain, with no other company than the notorious Colonel Cooper. Contrary to expectation, he has been a charming companion and a trusted guide, so long as one is willing to bide one's time and patiently indulge his idiosyncrasies.

—As is necessary with every person I've ever known, I said. Every damn one of them. So, all in all, a very good and fair beginning, ignoring the fact that we are still on our journey rather than at its end. Not out of the woods yet. But let's call it poetic license and go on. Your writing fascinates me.

—Second paragraph.

I arrived here expecting to find a thief, an enemy. I found instead a man embattled, beset on all sides. He is being sued by everyone he knows and also by a good number of strangers. Creditors from a dozen counties in four states are trying to seize the land he owns to settle their claims. And the Indians occupying the land in question, the people he has lived among for nearly half a century, are also suing him, their former White Chief, on the grounds that a significant portion of the land had been bought on their behalf. But much of the paperwork memorializing that intent has never been legally filed. So they have been left with little choice. If they do not get in on the suing, they may be left out entirely. But there are few hard feelings in either direction. In fact, coincident with their lawsuit, the Indians have issued a proclamation making all his descendants members of the tribe for all time. Though from what I can tell, that is an empty symbolic gesture since he never married and has no legitimate heirs.

Against all prudence, the Senator seems intent on testifying against himself in court. Yesterday while riding tack and tack up a rugged mountain trail, I asked him why he insisted on following this self-destructive course. He answered that when he was a boy, cast out by his own people, these Indians took him in and had ever since been his only family and this land his only home. And if a man lacks something to fight for, he is truly bankrupt.

None of which negates the fact that these people are in a precarious situation, liable to be evicted if the Senator's enemies prevail in court. At issue is a vast territory. But deeds have gone unrecorded for decades, loans in many directions have been defaulted on and then covered by three-party checks and old promissory notes reassigned so many times that the paper is limp and greasy and feather-edged from handling and the signatures are unreadable palimpsests. Collateral sometimes involves mules and futures on shell corn and next year's peach crop. By such manner of business, the ownership of a wide swath of mountain topography has become all tangled in the courts. The Senator's many opponents are trying to seize his land and evict the Indians from it and then parcel it off and sell it.

Dony stopped and said, That's as far as I've gotten.

—Real good, I said. Not a major point of disagreement between us. No denying that I put the people in a position where they had to sue me to keep my enemies from taking all the land I've accumulated for a half century all the way back to Bear's original four hundred acres. We were buying land after the Removal at such a furious rate and with such complete consonance between ourselves that it didn't seem to matter much whose name was on which paper. We knew what we meant to do. Make a homeland with boundaries as big around as we could draw them. Though not as big as Bear's mind could encompass. So one way of looking at it is that we were doomed to failure from the start.

—That's all fine, Dony said. But that was a long time ago, and you're about to have to stand up in court and account.

—Yes, that. But we're days away from testimony, and the future will be what it will be. And you have several more pages in your hand.

—They're not part of the report. More in the way of a personal journal.

—Well, that's an explanation, but not an excuse. Let's hear them.

—Private, Dony said.

—Great God, I said. Back in the dim past I published poems that were blood straight from the vein. Every line was pain, and yet I laid them out for the public view. Read on.

—This has to do with last night, Dony said, and his voice changed slightly when he addressed himself to the page.

The campsite the Senator selected was his favorite, he claimed, situated in a flat place at what he called the gap of the mountain. There was a stone ring filled with old charcoal, and a long view back toward the western summits. We settled the horses and collected wood and struck a fire in the pit and sat cross-legged on our bedding admiring the view. The Senator did not even begin cooking our supper until after dark, and I was, by then, faint with hunger. We had eaten only biscuits and tea since dawn, and the meal he cooked took hours to complete for he prepared an elaborate stew from a pair of unidentifiable midsized game birds with chopped bacon and onions and an entire bottle of red wine and a great fuss about the thickening of the sauce and the roasting of potatoes. The key to the dish, he said, was a long slow meeting between birds and fire and wine.

Very long, as it turned out. So, we had plenty of time as the night wore on to brew a full black pot of coffee, which proved necessary to keep me awake until our dinner was ready.

During the cooking and the coffee interlude, Cooper talked about literature of the present moment and politics of an antique time. He still held grudges against Jackson and mourned the untimely death of Crockett. His primary interest in that era—which seemed to him recent and to me dead history—was to find the exact point where America veered wrong. When it came to literature, though, his was a generous spirit. Everything he read, new and old, seemed to enjoy his full approbation, which I took to be the sure sign of a lonely man, indiscriminately happy for the company of a fellow human voice.

It felt like midnight when the Senator declared the stew done and opened another bottle of wine and served our dinners into tin bowls. For a time neither of us spoke, but only concentrated on the result of his long cookery, which was splendid. I ate, I'm afraid, without regard to manners. Hungry and tired from the trail, sitting inside a warm yellow circle of light in the middle of a chilly black wilderness—the meal seemed the best I had ever eaten. And the wine—the same excellent burgundy he had poured so profligately into the cooking pot—was perfect, and I said so. He did not even offer a thank-you but instead criticized his browning of the onions and his selection of the wonderful accompanying wine, which he said lacked the necessary sad autumnal quality, but it needed to be drunk for otherwise his enemies would take it from him and swill it with pork rinds and pinto beans. His opinion of the meal was that he could have done a lot better all around. The dish fell mournfully short of his mental image of the perfect stew composed from game birds and wine. But it was the best he could do, given the materials at hand and the time available.

I begged to differ as to the quality of the meal and asked what in this brief life does not fall under the same disclaimer as to time and materials.

Afterward, we drank more coffee and looked at the fire, and he talked about the puzzling methods by which the native peoples of the Andes form constellations by looking at the shapes of the black parts of the sky rather than the individual stars. And also the indigenous ghosts of this very mountain region, one of which was noted for her ability to skewer a man on her long sharp forefinger. After a drowsy period, he aroused briefly and said, Hark! Do you hear wolves?

Then he fell suddenly asleep. As for me, the many cups of coffee buzzed in my head. I lay awake until near dawn, watching the sky pass through the limbs of trees, and gave names of my own devising to the passing shapes. The Great Miasma. Sixteen Random Points in the Dark. The Greater and Lesser Guinea Fowls.

Come morning, I was awakened by the sound of clanging pots. The Senator was busy brewing coffee, frying eggs and bacon. My headache was blistering.

When Dony was finished, I said, Not a bad start. We'll work on it some more tomorrow.

DONY AND I eventually made it to court, and it was a sorry show. Boring, really. In the past, my interest in court had been artificially enhanced by the fact that I got paid when I showed up to lawyer. So, this appearance being gratis, I won't go into detail.

I had been left with no honorable choice but tell the truth against myself. It was painful at the time, like one of Granny Squirrel's formulas where you raked yourself all over longways—including the tongue and the privates—with a seven-barbed scratcher made with the sharp bones of seven animals, and then again crossways with another scratcher made from the barbs of seven plants, scraping deep until the blood ran.

In retrospect, though, I believe we should all have to testify against ourselves at some latter point in life. Lay out our flaws with a clerk writing it all down for the permanent record. It is a bracing and chastening experience, and I rather got into the spirit of the thing during my time on the stand.

The upshot was that Dony stepped in at the final moment before my utter annihilation and offered all the Federal money they had withheld from me all these years to pay off most of the core of our land, a fraction of what Bear wanted but enough to live on. Better than nothing, but not a gift. Not a cent more than what we were owed down the long years of principal and interest. But at least the people would have an ongoing place to live.

For me, it was more like an execution halted halfway through. I was stripped of everything but my house and just a few acres to live on. Little but taters and beans ever after was their vision for me. At least in the negotiations, I stuck firm on including in my holdings the long slope of pasture up to the dogwood tree where Waverley rests.

And that was about it. Dony went back to Washington. I went back to my diminished home. To some extent, it felt like I had never been in this world at all. Which was all right with me as long as the people could go on with their lives about the same as always, if that's what they wanted to do. Bean bread most of the time, deer meat when they can get it. Booger Dances on winter nights, Green Corn Dances in summer. A fellow named Swimmer taking over working the spells and formulas where Granny Squirrel left off. The thirteen moons rising and falling through the long round of the year.

PART FIVE

...

bone moon

IT'S A BAD IDEA TO LIVE TOO LONG. FEW CARRY IT OFF WELL. BUT nevertheless, here I am. In retreat but still in play, so to speak. Dying mid-stride would have suited me better than living on and on into withered old age. I've never required the death that Featherstone hoped for: drawing blood to the last breath, pistol fire lighting his path to the Nightland. I just wanted to keep busy, moving forward through the world, not letting it bog me down, resisting the netherward pull as Bear did, all the way to the end.

These days, Bear's old question—If you're to die tomorrow, do you spend the time praising Creation or cursing God?—seems much less theoretical than it did back in the winterhouse.

In the old days within Granny Squirrel's recollection, before the arrival of the Spaniards and their metal hats, living long was different. Little changed during your span of time, birth to death. Individual people, of course, came and went, but that's the unfortunate transitory nature of people. The physical world surrounding you, though, remained about the same from start to finish. Short of utter apocalypse, the landscape was what it was throughout one's brief life. Animals all the same. No unexpected pigs or elephants erupting confusingly into the world. Food was food. Clothes remained clothes. Meaningless innovations in hat styles had not yet occurred. All that you had learned in childhood remained largely in effect lifelong. When you got old and approached death, it was not an unrecognizable world you left, for we had not yet learned how to break it apart. Back then, about all that changed during your time on earth was that a few big trees had fallen and many new trees had grown in their places. Trunk diameter, really, was all that was in question. Whether you measured the span with your thumb and forefinger or your outstretched arms.

All of which may or may not reduce your sadness at leaving the world. Does overwhelming change, the annihilation of all you know, create an intensity of memory that would not have existed otherwise? When all you know is lost and gone forever, does it become sweeter in the mind? Does it make you want to let go or hold on even tighter?

All I can say is that we are mistaken to gouge such a deep rift in history that the things old men and old women know have become so useless as to be not worth passing on to grandchildren.

A STRICT SENSE of justice would call it only fair for me to live in poverty and not in my comfortable house with lovely May to watch over me. But when did fairness ever rule our lives? It is best not to study too much on who gets what they deserve. It can lead to an overly complicated interpretation of God's personal attributes.

Fair or not, I gained a second fortune, smaller than the first but comfortable. And I did it the easy way. Some years after I lost everything, the railroad began pushing into the mountains. Tunnels were dynamited through sheer rock, deep gorges spanned with high trestles. The usual tedious business of construction—made epic, however, by the highest mountains and steepest grades east of the Rockies. And I'm sure that amid all that work we must have had our own John Henry, worthy of a tragic spike-driver blues. And also our version of that perfect song about pines and the head caught in the driving wheel and the body on the line, the narrator pleading to know where his woman slept last night. You don't cut train tracks through such country as ours without a lot of blood on the rails. How else to explain the recent stories of a headless engineer roaming the Swannanoa grade at night, swinging a lantern and looking for what he lost? A spirit haunted by the railroad and haunting it at the same time.

I had invested a little money in the railroad company in the dim past before the War, sometime right after I went out with Calhoun scouting a route for a possible line across the mountains. I'd forgotten that old investment, and it was missed in the bankruptcy. But I do remember what a pleasant trip that was. Paid for by railroad money, so we went first class. No trailside bivouacs for Senator Calhoun, only the best of inns. He was an interesting companion, wise and frightful and crazy. I learned a lot from him. And if pressed I could tell you the weather every day of the journey and particular songs a fiddler played at an inn one night down on the Saluda River. But that would be beside the point. The point is that suddenly some old paper stuffed in a desk drawer was like the beggar Jack meets in the tales. With a bowl that will brim with food on command. Fill Bowl Fill. The money came rolling in again, enough to live on quite comfortably and even to send me on a fashionable grand tour of Europe. Now, though, I have train tracks running between my front porch and the river. No headless engineers on this stretch of track, but plenty of other ghosts.

THE TELEPHONE CALLS keep coming, almost weekly. I walk down the hall and take up the black earpiece on its braided cord and listen to the hiss and crackle of static on the wire like the sizzle of distant gunfire. A voice that might be no more than a spirit says its one syllable over and over. Possibly my name.

—Will? Will?

No louder than a breath of air.

—Present, I say. Right here still.

And then I say, Claire? Claire?

Is she even alive? Odds are against us on that. Nearly everybody I know is dead.

—Please speak louder, I say. Please speak.

Nothing but a sound like ham frying.

Claire's telephone calls are flesh wounds of memory, painful but inconclusive.

After each call, I climb the hill to the bench under the dogwood tree and visit Waverley for a while. With little effort, I call up images of Claire's face at twelve, seventeen, twenty-three, thirty, fifty-two. Perhaps my memories are accurate, and perhaps they are purely an act of creation. I have nothing to test them against one way or the other, for I don't believe Claire ever had her picture taken. And I know Bear never did.

I've heard that Crazy Horse, a noted recent Sioux, successfully avoided the diminishing stare of the lens. A wise move on his part. Crockett would approve. Wander off the stage of history and leave only a moving target. A mystery.

When I was young, photography was barely a glimmer in the eye. And even much later, living remote as we did, we had little opportunity for portraits. I have a memory, though, and a physical artifact supporting it, that I cannot explain. I remember very clearly, years before the Removal when I was still just an orphan boy, that a circuit-riding photographer passed through in a covered wagon trailing a reek of chemicals. He was a kind of showman with a great deal of long dark hair slicked back from his brow and extravagant sideburns and mustaches. He and his little Chinaman assistant had become woefully lost in a journey intended to be from Charleston to Washington City. They stopped at the post for directions and to ask if they might ply their trade out in the yard for a day or two to make some traveling money. They had a stuffed pony under the arched canvas lid of the big wagon. The showman told me that in cities the pony never failed to attract the young children and their mothers. I mentioned that we had a right smart of live ponies in the vicinity, but he persisted in his belief that the dead pony had special power to draw customers. The assistant dragged it out from the wagon's clutter and stood it up in the yard, and it looked old enough to have come from the time of the Phoenicians. It had dull glass eyes as black and blank as gobs of axle grease, and its red hair was rubbed down to the dry hide in patches around its withers and muzzle and knees. The photographers were only there two rainy days. They came inside at night and drank coffee in the post, and the showman fell asleep and the assistant and I talked about books long into the night. Even though I invited them to sleep inside or at least on the porch, they retreated under the wagon bed together and moved on before dawn of the third day without even cooking breakfast. I know for a fact that Claire did not come to have herself memorialized with the pony, for she was off in Valley River and there were no customers other than myself. I paid a dollar for a portrait. One buck. I remember this all as clear as day.

And I have the proof. Open the hinged case and see even now, resting in faded blue velvet, a dim silvered picture of a boy from an olden time. His face is hopeful and earnest and he's looking straight forward, right into the camera. His arm is hooked over the neck of a threadbare dead pony standing stiff and slightly off plumb and staring black-eyed and aslant into infinity. The boy hugs the pony to him. He's not smiling, but the expression on his face says Yes to whatever might come along.

The problem is chronology. The history of photography. Numbers won't exactly sum. If my memory is correct and that's me in the picture, daguerreotypes did not yet exist. If that's not me, who is that very familiar boy eager to press forward into the world?

Was there some slick-haired showman and his genius assistant several years ahead of Daguerre and the rest of the world with their invention, trying to make a buck with a camera and a dead pony in the hinterlands, imaging Indians and countryfolk? I doubt it. But who is to say?

I've got that picture, and it looks an awful lot like me.

ALL IN ALL, I'm glad I don't have such a specific remembrance of Claire at that age. What if her photograph had been made in bad light that left unflattering shadows, squinted eyes, a tight-lipped mouth like an axe cut? Her beauty all diminished by mechanics and chemistry? I'd just as soon have nothing to contradict my memory, which, regarding her, is a clear stone with a thousand facets. When I forget one, I can always make up a replacement.

And the same for Bear. No pictures, I'm certain. You couldn't have beat him with a stick and gotten him to submit to the dead Cyclops eye of the camera. His younger brother, though, was photographed in his later years. In profile. And there is enough similarity between them to serve as adequate memorial. Steep cheekbones and hooked nose, thick hair cut square to the shoulders. I don't require any more than that. My memory works fine without further prompt.

I am glad to think that Claire and Bear succeeded in avoiding the camera. I see their achievement as an enviable resistance against the modern age. When everything is immediately available and infinitely reproducible, nothing is valuable. How can it be? How many times might beauty or heartbreak or love be replicated and still have meaning? It is like running the soul under a die press. Reproduction breeds worthlessness. Claire and Bear remain singularities.

I believe fervently in what I have just said. But of course right this instant I would pay an enormous sum of money for a little daguerreotype of either of them, the filigreed case crusted with powdery corrosion, face blurred and no bigger than the tip of my littlest finger.

I do have a copy of the one photograph ever taken of Featherstone. From the later years. He is indistinguishable from the Old Possum. Exploding white hair, little marsupial eyes looking out cold and fierce onto the world.

As for myself, I sat for photographers any number of times, from middle age to antiquity, and the results were widely reproduced in newspapers and periodicals. Captions underneath identifying me as white chief, senator, colonel, all that sort of thing and more. Pictures from the period when my successes were widely honored, and also the period where I was sued from all directions. In my opinion, those portraits vary in small degrees from looking like memorials of coffined cholera fatalities to the images in Wild West newspapers of dead outlaws killed in gunfights.

FROM MY FRONT PORCH, I can look beyond the shining rail lines and across the river and up to the big blue mountains sitting against the sky like embodied truths, like perfect beings without fear or desire. This day they are just a scant shade darker than heaven. Workers have rigged cables thick as a man's arm from one high blue ridge to the next across the great span of a deep green cove hollowed out by a bold stream once clear as glass and now the color of shit. A steam engine turns wheels, and the sagged cables tighten, and the biggest tree trunks—old giant poplars and hemlocks and chestnuts and oaks, some of them twelve feet through, remnants of a younger, better world—come rising slowly out of the cove depths. They fly through the air.

But at such distance, even with my glasses, I cannot see the cables, so the backlit cylinders of the old dead trees rise into the sky like an ascension, stately and full of grace. Up in those coves toward the highest ridges is where Charley and his people fled and were caught. The mountain fastnesses. The old flyers end up at a siding near the river to be loaded on railcars.

Every day the passenger train rolls by, between ten forty-eight and ten fifty-five in the morning. After breakfast, I wait on the porch. I sit tipped back in a straight chair reading Lucretius for the second time this year. I consult my watch. The twelve-gauge Parker rests propped against the rail of the porch, which at this late date has settled and pitches at a slight angle to the horizontal, declining from the front door to the steps that descend into the yard. As a concession to age, I've fitted the stock of the Parker with a rubber pad inside a sleeve of leather laced tight to the stock. Altogether, it is an aesthetic that pleases me. Dark oiled leather, worn walnut, steel with the bluing rubbed away from much handling. The grip fits my hand at the exact angle of the diagonal silver brand across my palm.

I have gotten the railway I once wanted so badly.

And what has it brought? The ravages of tourists and logging.

And what has it taken away? Everything else.

Every afternoon the log train rolls east, the trees so freshly cut I can smell them like incense on the air as they pass. I can tell whether they are mostly oaks and chestnuts or hemlocks and poplars, and thereby I know what pieces of the mountain have most lately been taken down. The black and hideous locomotives spew coal smoke and throw off cinders and shake the ground. They are ruinous noisy machines that hold no reference to anything in the green world or to the past in general.

I cannot bring myself to shoot the dead trees, so I shoot tourists instead. The distance from which I can hear them coming varies. Windless mornings like this with the fog still hanging on the river give the longest warning. I check my watch. Ten-thirty. I wait and read.

The thing I've always admired about the ancients is their ability to clarify the obvious, like the first mapmakers entering an undiscovered country. Lucretius holds the reasonable and obvious opinion that without space nothing could happen because there wouldn't be room for movement amid all the clutter. Everything would jam up against everything else and squeeze to a stop. Case in point, the attic of my house. It is crowded with all the artifacts of my life. Wooden crates of old notebooks and business papers, volumes of yellow-paged literary journals, a crate of clouded Murano champagne glasses from one of which Davy Crockett once drank Moët's. Also a small wooden box in which my young self kept its tiny art objects. A perfect obsidian bird point with flaked edges as sharp as broken glass, a few little faceted stone crosses that Nature—or the artisans of some old original people from before Noah's flood—salted in the earth for us to find and be struck with wonder, a prehistoric clay pipe bowl fashioned in the shape of a man and woman rutting each other in such a convoluted manner that all you see is asses and elbows and nether parts. And a thin wristlet of Claire's hair which she plaited for me to remember her by, back in another world. I wore it against my skin until it threatened to fall apart. And also at some deep stratum is there a tattered map, a rusty key, a moth-eaten wool coat with maybe some slight fragrance of lavender left in it if you breathe deep enough?

Now, when I climb the steep stairs to the dark attic, I cannot find the map or key or coat. I can't even make my way five feet through the congestion of the things I have accumulated in a near century of living. All matter and no space left for me to move forward.

And according to Lucretius, time works similarly. Without it everything would happen all at once. A beautiful and horrible explosion of simultaneous events, an instant of awful frenzy and then, ever after, black nothing. So of course time is necessary. But nevertheless damn painful, for it transforms all the pieces of your life—joy and sorrow, youth and age, love and hate, terror and bliss—from fire into smoke, rising up the air and dissipating on a breeze.

We all, when we're young, think we'll live forever. Then at some point you settle for living a great long while. But after that final distinction is achieved, survival becomes at best uncomfortable. Everyone and everything you love goes away. And yet it is your fortune to remain. You find yourself exiled in a transformed world peopled by strangers. Lost in places you've known as intimately as the back of your hand. Eternal rivercourses and ridgelines become your only friends. That is the point when living any farther either becomes ridiculous and amusing or else you fall away and follow all Creation through the gates of death to the Nightland.

You're left with nothing but your moods and your memory. Pitiful and powerful tools.

I COCK MY HEAD to aim an ear toward the first low-pitched rumble from upriver. I put the book down and take up the Parker.

At this moment on the train, Pullman porters in white jackets walk the aisles much the way they do before reaching long tunnels cored through the mountains. For the tunnels, the porters lift the yellow flames of candles to touch the charred wicks of kerosene lanterns swinging from the ceilings, and they warn passengers not to be alarmed by the sudden onset of darkness. As they approach my house, the porters go through the passenger cars lowering windows on the side exposed to my front porch, and they tell the tourists that the sound of a discharging firearm should not cause concern.

It is a deal I have struck. I promise to use loads no greater than birdshot, and the railroad administrators and the local sheriff promise to ignore me.

I rise and stand and carry the Parker to the porch rail. When the locomotive approaches, the engineer blows the whistle and waves. The armatures to the drive wheels pump relentlessly. I put the padded cup of the gun butt to my shoulder and aim rather generally. I trip one trigger. The kick steps me back. I brace myself and fire the second barrel.

The forlorn echoes are nearly lost in the clamor of the train. And if the birdshot even carries as far as the tracks, it rattles off the car windows like the first hard pellets of rain at the front edge of a thunderstorm. It is partly my railroad, and fine birdshot is harmless against metal and glass. The whistle blows two short friendly notes, and the locomotive turns the curve and drags its train behind. In the end, just a fading rumble coming from down the river and black smoke settling over everything before the mountains form up again, shorn and damaged and eternal.

AUTHOR'S NOTE

. . .

I WOULD LIKE TO REMIND THOSE READERS FAMILIAR WITH THE SOUTHern Appalachians that *Thirteen Moons* is a work of fiction. The geography and human history inside these covers have been filtered through my imagination. The village of Wayah, for example, will not be found on a map. Nor should my Valley River be confused with the Valley Town communities that existed on the Cherokee Nation. All historical figures and locations are used fictionally, and sometimes I've changed their names and sometimes I have not. Will Cooper is not William Holland Thomas, though they do share some DNA. The capture and execution of Tsali is still a matter of considerable disagreement both in regard to fact and interpretation, but however it actually happened, it was most certainly different from Charley's story here. In other words, anyone seeking historical or geographical fact should look elsewhere. I would suggest these books as a start:

Duncan, Barbara R. *Living Stories of the Cherokee*. Chapel Hill: University of North Carolina Press, 1998.

Duncan, Barbara R., and Brett Riggs. *Cherokee Heritage Trails Guidebook*. Chapel Hill: University of North Carolina Press, 2003.

Ehle, John. *Trail of Tears*. New York: Anchor Books, 1988.

Finger, John R. *The Eastern Band of Cherokees, 1819–1900*. Knoxville: University of Tennessee Press, 1984.

Godbold, E. Stanley, Jr., and Mattie U. Russell. *Confederate Colonel and Cherokee Chief: The Life of William Holland Thomas*. Knoxville: University of Tennessee Press, 1990.

McCarthy, William Bernard, ed. *Jack in Two Worlds: Contemporary North American Tales and Their Tellers*. Chapel Hill: University of North Carolina Press, 1994.

Perdue, Theda. *Cherokee Women, 1700–1835*. Lincoln: University of Nebraska Press, 1998.

Speck, Frank G., and Leonard Broom, in collaboration with Will West Long. *Cherokee Dance and Drama*. Norman: University of Oklahoma Press, 1951.

For help along the way, I would like to thank Barbara Duncan, education director of the Museum of the Cherokee Indian; George Frizzell, head of special collections at Western Carolina University's Hunter Library; and Wanda Stalcup, director of the Cherokee County Historical Museum. I hope none of them will be too bothered by the liberties and detours I've taken with the facts they aimed me so directly toward. I would also like to express appreciation for the libraries of Appalachian State University, Duke University, Florida Atlantic University, the University of North Carolina at Chapel Hill, and Western Carolina University.

PHOTO: © PHIL BRAY/MIRAMAX FILMS

CHARLES FRAZIER was born in Asheville, North Carolina. *Cold Mountain,* his first novel, was an international bestseller and won the National Book Award in 1997, as well as the Sue Kaufman Prize for First Fiction from the American Academy of Arts and Letters.